PAOLA SANTIAGO
AND THE
FOREST OF NIGHTMARES

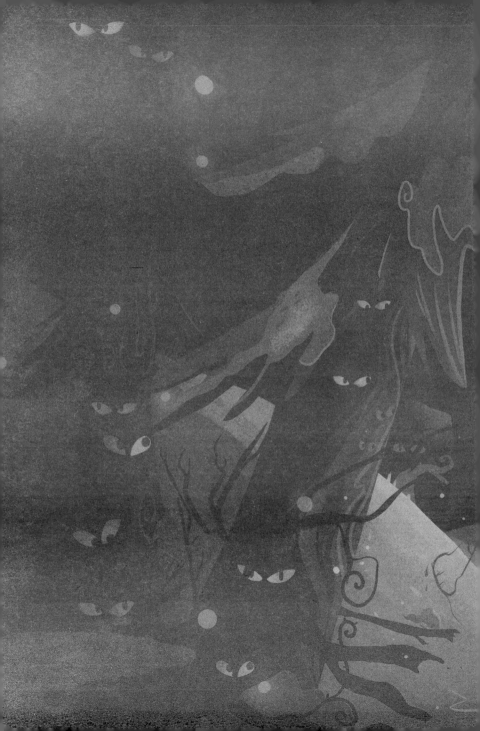

PAOLA SANTIAGO
AND THE
FOREST OF NIGHTMARES

TEHLOR KAY MEJIA

RICK RIORDAN PRESENTS

Disney • HYPERION   LOS ANGELES NEW YORK

First Hardcover Edition, August 2021
First Paperback Edition, August 2022
10 9 8 7 6 5 4 3 2 1
FAC-025438-22168
Printed in the United States of America

This book is set in Janet Antiqua Std/Monotype
Designed by Jamie Alloy

Library of Congress Cataloging-in-Publication Control Number
for Hardcover Edition: 2020034434
ISBN 978-1-368-05160-6

Visit www.DisneyBooks.com
Follow @ReadRiordan

SUSTAINABLE
FORESTRY
INITIATIVE
Certified Chain of Custody
Promoting Sustainable Forestry
www.sfiprogram.org
SFI-01054
The SFI label applies to the text stock

For every kid stuck measuring their worth in percentages and fractions. You are the person you believe you are. You are the hero you dream of being.

CONTENTS

ONE

There's *Almost* Nothing Worse
Than Meat-Medley Pizza

If it hadn't been for the dream she'd had about her estranged father the night before, maybe Pao's bonding time with her mom's new boyfriend wouldn't have been quite so awful.

But her luck never worked like that.

Six months ago, Paola Santiago had walked out of a collapsing magical rift after defeating the legendary ghost-turned-god, La Llorona, and freeing the spirit of the Weeping Woman's last remaining lost child.

Pao had tamed a chupacabra.

She had even earned the respect of the girl who had tortured her in sixth grade.

And yet, she still didn't have the power to turn this guy into dust? Ideally right now, across the sticky table of this pizza place?

Maybe if she glared at him a little harder . . .

Pizza Pete's was full tonight, with chattering families, screaming kids, and illuminated arcade machines trying to trick dads into digging deeper for quarters. GHOST HUNTER 3!, one of the games, flashed in acid-green letters.

No way that's *realistic*, Pao thought, narrowly avoiding a scoff. Like a series of zeroes and ones blinking on a screen could ever get close to the real thing. Binary code was incredibly versatile, of course, but Pao had learned firsthand that there were some things that math and science couldn't fully capture.

Pao's mom looked at her like she had heard the almost scoff. Pao stared back insolently, tempting fate.

Ever since winter break had started three days ago, Pao had been prohibited from scoffing. Also scowling, smirking, stomping, and swearing (even using mild words like *stupid* or *jerk*). The message was clear: There was no room for sullen Pao when *Aaron* was around.

To be fair, though, it didn't seem like there was much room for *any* version of Pao. So why couldn't she mope to her heart's (dis)content?

Because moms were unfair, that's why.

In the arcade, three boys a little older than Pao were hurtling full speed toward *Ghost Hunter 3*. "I hear it's, like, actually scary!" one of them squeaked.

"Yeah, Sully said the guys that made it went to *real* haunted houses and, like, *slept* in them and *saw* things."

"So cool! They're, like, *actual* experts!"

I'm so sure, Pao thought, returning to her scathing inner monologue. Like a bunch of white guys with phone cameras in a tourist trap knew anything about real ghost hunting.

But the truth—and Pao's terrible secret—was that she would have given anything to be fighting real ghosts or monsters right now. She would have been thrilled to see a terrible hairy Mano Pachona, or a full-grown slavering chupacabra. Anything to prove that last summer had been real. That she had actually been through something.

That she wasn't just a freak who no longer belonged in her own life.

Across the table, Aaron shifted uncomfortably in his seat, grinning goofily when he caught Pao looking at him. No one had spoken a word in nine minutes and forty-three seconds. So much for bonding.

Her mom was looking desperate now, and for a second, Pao almost felt sorry for her.

But only for a second.

After Pao's disappearing act last summer, things had improved between her and her mom. For a while. But Pao had quickly realized that accepting her mom's differences, as she had done while trapped in the endless throat of a magical void, was actually a lot easier than getting along with her in real life.

Especially now that her mom was dating Aaron.

Pao tried to ignore him, thinking of her dream the night before instead. Even a nightmare was better than this guy. She'd been walking through a dense pine forest, a weird green light filtering through the trees. The road she'd walked was long and straight, and at the end of it was a silhouette she'd somehow known was her dad.

It made sense, Pao thought, that she hadn't seen his face. She hadn't seen her dad in real life since she was four years old. Her mom never even talked about him. But in the dream, Pao had run toward him anyway, like he was coming home from a long absence and she couldn't wait to throw her arms around him.

Of course, she hadn't made it that far. Just before she'd gotten close enough, the ground had opened at her feet. A massive crack in the earth took Pao with it as it gave way, leaving her father shouting from the cliff above.

After waking from a nightmare like that, shaking and sweating, was it any wonder Pao didn't want to spend the evening fake-smiling over greasy food with a total imposter?

Across from her, Mom and Aaron chewed in silence, exchanging an awkward look between them.

Pao could have made it easier for her mom, she knew, but right now that was the last thing she wanted to do.

Why would she want to help someone who hadn't even noticed that her daughter was suffering the aftereffects of one of her notorious nightmares? The kind she had experienced ever since she was little and had led her to enter a magical rift to fight a legendary ghost.

Her mom was supposed to be *highly* attuned to this stuff. She always had been before . . . but tonight she'd just told Pao to get a handle on her hair and wear a clean shirt. Like it mattered how Pao looked for this totally inappropriate ordeal.

Mom had met Aaron, a firefighter, at the bar where she worked and within *six weeks* had decided that he was meet-the-kid material. But impulsive choices were kind of the norm for Maria Santiago. Even Bruto the chupacabra puppy had given them an *isn't this too soon?* look as they'd left the apartment tonight.

For about a month, Mom and Aaron had lied about him coming over to "fix the TV" or "drop off a book" or "look for a stray neighborhood dog" (Pao's personal favorite excuse). Last week her mom had finally come clean, and now they all had to play nice.

At first, Pao had been offended by the lying—she was almost

thirteen, she could handle the truth!—but an hour into forced bonding, she found herself wishing Aaron really *was* just the guy "redoing the shower grout."

The boys in the arcade were fully enthralled by *Ghost Hunter 3* at this point. The screen showed one of those cheesy paranormal-activity videos, all shaky camera and blown-out colors and vague, pixelated shapes.

Pao remembered a time when it would have been her and her two best friends, Emma and Dante, crowded around the machine. Dante would have been effortlessly good, Emma hilariously bad, and Pao in the back, refusing to play, mocking people for believing in ghosts.

But she'd barely spoken to Emma in two months. And Pao and Dante were pretending things were normal between them . . . but then why had she told her mom that he was too busy to tag along tonight when he really wasn't?

Not even science held her in the same thrall these days. Her microscope lay unused on the dusty top shelf of her closet. And she hadn't bothered entering the fall science fair at school.

Everything had changed. And Pao didn't know how to change it back.

"Ooh, that game looks scary!" Aaron said, snapping Pao out of her moody thoughts. "I'm not sure I could play it. Probably give me nightmares."

This time, Pao really, really couldn't help it. The scoff took over. It used her body as an unwilling host, like rabies in the brain of a raccoon, and a *pfft* sound escaped her lips. All Pao could do was hope no one heard it. But of course, her mom had laser-focused on her the moment Aaron had said *nightmares*.

And in terms of death glares, La Llorona had nothing on Pao's mom.

She smiled at Pao, a kind of snarly smile, all her teeth showing. A *don't screw this up or I'll take away that phone you just got* kind of smile. "Paola, why don't you tell Aaron what you're working on in school?"

"Invisibility," Pao said after a beat, pulling a pepperoni off her pizza and rolling it up into a greasy little tube. Her mom hated when she did that but wouldn't dare say anything in front of "company."

"Sounds pretty advanced for seventh grade!" Aaron said earnestly. His blond hair fell into his eyes, and he pushed it back. His face was that healthy-looking kind of tan that white people get when they go skiing or something. Pao wanted to wipe pepperoni grease on it.

"It's more of a social experiment than a scientific one," Pao clarified, watching her mother's eyes narrow even more. "You know, camouflage, deflection, that sort of thing. Luckily, I'm getting plenty of practice at home."

Pao had always distrusted people who smiled all the time, and Aaron's ski-catalog grin never faltered. She matched it with something akin to a grimace, knowing she'd pay for the comment later but not caring.

"Well, middle school is a tough time," he said, leaning down to look her in the eye. "I'm sure things will get better. Hey, only a year and a half until high school, right!"

"Yeah," Pao said. "Because high school is historically easy on freaks."

"Mija, you're not a freak," her mom said, waving a hand.

"You're just advanced for your age—the other kids are probably jealous."

Pao definitely would have rolled her eyes if her mom hadn't snapped her head to look across the room right at that moment.

"Oh! Isn't that Emma?" She waved, not noticing that her only child was ready to sink into the floor. "Emma! ¡Mija! Over here!"

It was noisy, and Emma was sitting at a crowded table with at least five kids from school. Pao kept her eyes on her plate and hoped that Emma didn't hear her name being called.

"Who are those kids she's hanging out with?" Mom asked, craning her neck. "They sure have . . . interesting hair!"

Emma's new friends dyed their hair in bright colors and wore jean jackets with patches and pins all over them. They kept up with current events and sometimes participated in protests. Across Pizza Pete's, they all laughed loudly at something, and Pao glanced up reflexively, just for a second. Emma didn't look their way.

"The Rainbow Rogues," Pao muttered, trying not to sound sarcastic.

It didn't matter anyway. Her mom was back to talking to Aaron, and Pao was back to being invisible.

Her eyes drifted over to where Emma's blondish-brown hair (complete with a new purple streak) was just visible over the tall back of her seat.

In September, when Emma had decided to come out to her parents, Pao had been with her—via speaker phone—for moral support. Emma had been nervous, but after all the worry and wondering, her parents had been nothing but supportive. Mrs. Lockwood had even bought a LOVE IS LOVE sticker for their SUV.

Emma had confessed her secret to Pao just a week after they'd returned from the rift, and together they'd plotted the best way to tell her parents. After Emma did it, Pao was so proud of her best friend she'd thought her heart might burst. The next day, they'd eaten every flavor of frozen yogurt in one giant cup to celebrate.

Pao had known this meant Emma could finally stop hiding. At last she'd get to be her whole, shiny self for the world to see. Pao had even convinced her to go to the first yearly meeting of the aforementioned Rainbow Rogues, Silver Springs Middle School's LGBTQIA+ club.

They'd both been surprised by how many openly queer kids went to their school, and Emma had walked out bubbling with excitement and plans to go back.

But the more time they'd spent with the Rogues, the more out of place Pao had felt. ·

There were plenty of kids in the club who weren't ready to decide how they identified yet, and even kids who just called themselves "allies," so it wasn't her lack of specified queerness that made Pao feel left out.

It just seemed like most of the kids who were comfortable enough to be out at school were, for lack of a better phrase, rich and white. Their parents drove them to and from the meetings in their fancy cars and sent them to school with organic lunches. They bought their kids unlimited poster board and, like, the *nice* markers in every color whenever they wanted to make protest signs.

Pao, with her bus pass and her subsidized lunch, couldn't have the Rogues over to her small apartment or chip in for supplies. They never made her feel bad about those things, of course, but the way they were *overly* nice about them somehow made Pao feel even worse.

And then there was Emma, who was *so* focused on making sure Pao had a good time that sometimes Pao felt she was holding her back. There was no reason for Emma to be the odd one out. She fit in perfectly, and Pao wanted that for her.

So the next time Emma asked Pao to join in—they were protesting a new Starbucks going in across from a locally owned coffee shop—Pao had made up an excuse. After she did it enough times, Emma had stopped asking.

Pao knew it was normal, people growing apart. But that didn't make it any less sad.

She pushed her plate away, her appetite suddenly gone. "I have homework. Can we go home now?"

Aaron had just taken another slice of "meat medley." The worst pizza variety ever. Sausage, ham, *and* pepperoni? What was it trying to prove?

Her mom opened her mouth, undoubtedly to chastise Pao for being rude, but before she could form the words, Pao's drinking glass exploded in front of her, soaking her space-cat shirt in all thirteen types of soda she'd combined from the fountain. It left them a whole different kind of speechless than before, which Pao couldn't help but enjoy just a little.

There were glass shards on her lap and all over Aaron's slice of meat medley. Next to the glass, a quarter was spinning like a top. It must have come from one of the kids playing in the arcade.

After taking a second to recover from her shock (and to make sure Emma and her cool friends hadn't seen), Pao glanced at her mother, who looked murderous.

"Come on!" Pao said. "You can't possibly think this is my fault!

It was a freak accident! Look!" She held up the quarter, which had just stopped spinning and fallen onto its side.

Tails, Pao noticed, then shook herself before she went down a probability and statistics hole.

Her mom, thankfully, had turned her withering glare onto the kids shrieking in front of *Ghost Hunter 3*. "Honestly, where are their parents?" she asked, looking at Aaron to check his reaction. When he nodded, she continued. "Throwing quarters around, breaking glasses? So irresponsible."

Pao bit her tongue. Her mom had left her unsupervised (or in the care of their elderly neighbor, Señora Mata) for the greater part of her childhood. Now that Aaron was around, she was suddenly Suburban Susie of the PTA?

Not that she was judging her mom for how she'd raised Pao. It was hard to juggle a kid and a more-than-full-time job on your own. But why did her mom have to pretend to be someone else just to impress this guy?

Wasn't that, like, the opposite of what she always told Pao to do?

As the two adults chattered about bad parenting, Pao tried to soak up the soda on her shirt with two paper napkins, only to end up leaving little bits of wet pulp all over it. She was almost too lost in thought to notice.

"I'm going to the bathroom," Pao said, standing up abruptly.

No one stopped her.

At least this nightmare is nearly over, she thought.

By now, she should have known better than to think things like that.

TWO

The Bad Kind of Boy-Girl Weirdness

In the ladies' room *(gendered bathrooms, how archaic)*, Pao skulked against the wall waiting for a frazzled woman to herd three sauce-smeared little kids into the largest stall. The other stall was out of order.

Maybe if Pao stayed in here long enough, her mom and Aaron would forget about her. She could live here, in the Pizza Pete's bathroom. Get all fifteen top scores on *Ghost Hunter 3* at night when no one was around.

She took an environmentally irresponsible amount of paper towels from the dispenser and began to daub her shirt again. It was already tie-dyed, so maybe the weird splotches would just blend right in? Old Mom never would have noticed. New Mom probably had opinions about children with stained shirts.

The woman finally emerged from the stall, looking much worse for wear as she took out sanitary wipes and cleaned the squirming kids from head to toe.

Pao knew her mom was probably getting impatient, but she just wanted some time alone. To steel herself for the last few minutes with Aaron. And to get rid of the feeling inside her that something weird was about to go down.

"Sorry," the mom said when one of the kids blew a raspberry at Pao.

"It's fine." Pao smiled. A more genuine one than she'd managed for Aaron.

"Never have kids if you prefer going to the bathroom alone," the mom said, but she tucked in the little boy's shirt and smoothed down the baby's hair, kissing the oldest one on the cheek before ushering them back outside.

Moms have it rough, Pao thought. And given that she'd seen (in the crazed eyes of La Llorona) arguably the *worst* one in history, Pao was reminded that she should be more patient with her own.

That is, if she could get her away from Aaron long enough to try.

Now walk out of here with a smile, Pao told herself. She would try harder with her mom, even after this awful bonding experience. She would not, even if it would be really funny, crack a joke about how sometimes, in chemistry, a bond between three elements was so unstable it caused an explosion, or a deadly poison. . . .

Seriously, she wouldn't.

Despite Pao's resolution, the long walk home with her mother was uncomfortably silent.

Aaron had ridden his bike back to wherever he lived after the world's most awkward good-bye. Pao knew her mom hadn't forgotten her subpar performance at the pizza place. She was probably brewing a lecture like a strong cup of tea.

The Riverside Palace loomed ahead. The moment they walked through the apartment door, their tense silence would blow up into something too big to control. Pao stopped her mom under the broken streetlamp and looked up at her.

"If it's another snarky comment, Paola, I just don't know if I can—"

Pao cut her off by hugging her tight. They were almost the same height now, and Pao's forehead rested against her mom's cheek.

"I'm sorry, Mom," she said, humiliated to feel tears pricking her eyes. "It just feels like everything's different since I got . . . lost." To Maria, Pao's life-changing ghost hunt last summer had been a simple case of getting lost in the wilderness around the Gila River while looking for her friend. Señora Mata, Dante's grandma, was the one who'd advised Pao not to tell her mom the whole truth.

Pao stepped out of the hug and noticed that the lines around her mom's eyes looked softer than before.

Pao sighed, stretching for something genuine she could say to her mom in this moment. "I just . . . don't want things to change so fast," she said finally. And despite its lack of ghosts or void beasts, that really *was* the truth.

"Mi amor." Her mom sighed and pushed the too-long bangs off Pao's forehead. "We can't stop the world from changing. But this?" She gestured between the two of them. "This is forever. No matter what else is different, this will always be the same."

Pao nodded, not trusting her voice, not knowing if she could even trust the sentiment, but vowing to try. Yes, her adventure last summer had been amazing, and maybe she was having a hard time fitting back in to this life, but it was the only life she had. She would have to make the best of it. She remembered what she'd learned in the throat of the rift about forgiveness.

"I love you, Mom," Pao said.

"I love you, too, mija."

They walked the rest of the way home with their arms around each other's shoulders, tripping and laughing through the parking lot. At the base of the stairs, they ran into Dante, who was just getting home.

"Hey, Dante!" said her mom. "We missed you at pizza tonight!"

Dante's eyes darted to Pao's, and she raised her eyebrows in the universal signal for *please lie to this adult.*

"Uh, yeah, Ms. Santiago. Sorry. Soccer practice, you know."

Pao looked at her shoes, avoiding his eyes.

"Well, I'll give you two a minute, hmm?"

"Uh, I have a lot of . . . homework," Pao said, but her mom had already slipped through the door of apartment C and closed it behind her.

"You know I hate to miss a pizza party," Dante said, not quite meeting her eyes and not sounding sorry to have missed it at all.

Pao felt her face heating up. "Just sparing you," she said. "Bonding time with Mom's new *boyfriend.*" She said the word like it was something gross before she remembered who she was standing in front of.

Not that they'd ever used words like that, which were too embarrassing even to utter.

Cheek-kissing and hand-holding were one thing when your life was on the line, but in the hallways of middle school, physical displays of affection were something infinitely different. And Pao wasn't at all sure she hadn't liked things better before, when they were just friends.

But she couldn't say that to Dante.

"I didn't know your mom got a boyfriend," he said, his gaze falling to the ground.

"Yeah, sorry. She just kind of . . . dropped it on me. I figured dinner would be awkward enough without turning it into some kind of—" Pao stopped herself before she could say *double date*, but Dante's face turned red like he had heard it anyway.

Pao knew she should talk to him. Tell him about Aaron the Awful and her dream about her dad. The old Pao-and-Dante would have discussed it all. But things weren't the same between them these days.

As if to illustrate the point, the now Pao-and-Dante shuffled their feet, looking anywhere but at each other. Did he know things were different, too? Pao wondered. He had to.

When they'd started school again, Pao had been sure their friendship was unshakable. It had survived for years, after all, and gotten them through their confusing, terrifying, out-of-this-world shared experience. Pao was convinced they'd always fit into each other's lives as effortlessly as they had in the cactus field.

It was just seventh grade. There was no way it could be harder to navigate than a magical rift filled with supernatural monsters and a bloodthirsty all-powerful ghost, Pao figured.

She'd figured wrong. It wasn't just hard—it was impossible.

One day, shortly after her mom had started letting her out of the house again, Pao had asked Dante if she could come over to his place after school like she had a thousand times before. Dante had turned red and said, "Not today," in a totally uncharacteristic way. Pao had let it slide. Maybe he was feeling weird about things being different, too, she figured. Eventually they'd talk about it. **They always did.**

But then she couldn't help bringing up that she wanted to ask his abuela about being a Niña de la Luz (a shocking confession Señora Mata made after Pao and Dante had returned victorious from the rift). He'd shut her down swiftly, saying the last thing his abuela needed was a million questions about something that had happened to her a long time ago.

He'd left Pao out front, totally bewildered, and slammed the door.

They didn't talk for three days after that. A new record.

And even when they'd started walking to school together again, the tension was still there. Dante rolled his eyes and glanced around furtively whenever Pao mentioned the Niños, or the rift, or anything about last summer. It was like he wanted to just forget about it. Like he was embarrassed about the whole thing. Embarrassed about being with *her*.

He hadn't invited her inside since, and the few times she had seen him coming home with his abuela, he'd rushed his grandmother through the door to avoid Pao.

So tonight, in front of apartment C, aware of just how long this awkward pause had been, Pao asked, "How was soccer?" in a falsely bright voice instead of telling him what was really going on, because she couldn't stand to put any more distance between them.

Unfortunately, she said it at the same time Señora Mata opened the door.

"Alberto?" she asked, her voice a little shaky. "Where have you been? I thought you were coming home with the milk hours ago!"

Alberto? Pao wondered. Dante whispered something to his abuela and sent her inside, closing the door behind her. Who was Alberto? And hadn't Dante just said he was coming home from soccer practice?

"Pao, I gotta go," Dante said, his face flushing just as it had when she'd asked to come inside a few months ago. That sent the gears in Pao's brain whirring and spinning—a welcome distraction from all the moping she'd been doing lately.

"Dante," Pao said as he looked sullenly at the ground, "are you okay? Is she . . . ?"

"She's fine," he snapped. "We're both fine. I'm just busy, and I don't have time to examine all of Bruto's paranormal features with you or whatever, okay?"

Pao suddenly went from being curious to feeling like she was about to cry. She'd known that she and Dante weren't on the same page right now, but he'd never insulted her before. Not in a serious way, at least.

"Sorry," he said when she didn't reply. But he didn't really sound sorry. "I just have a lot going on, okay?"

"Yeah," Pao said, getting angry now that the near-tears feeling had passed. "Fine. Me too. I'm gonna go home and do something horribly embarrassing like take pictures of Bruto's toenails. Don't worry, I won't tell your cool friends about it."

"Pao . . ." Dante said, rubbing a hand over his face. "It isn't like that."

But it was. Pao had known it for a long time. And if he didn't want her help, she wasn't going to keep trying to be his friend. Or his . . . girl-you-kissed-once-on-the-cheek-and-sometimes-held-hands-with-when-you-were-scared, either.

"Good night, Dante," she said in as dignified a way as she could muster, and went inside before he could reply.

There was only so much becoming a better person she could be expected to accomplish in one night.

THREE

Enough Monochrome to Make Anyone Want to Puke

Pao's resolve to better herself lasted almost twelve hours.

Nine of which she spent dreaming again.

In one of the dreams, she was surrounded by pine trees with eyes that glowed green like the monsters that had come out of the rift last summer. Those eyes followed Pao as she walked down the path that had taken her to her father before.

Only this time, he wasn't where he was supposed to be.

Instead, Dante's abuela was there, pacing back and forth like she was looking for something she'd dropped in the road. "Alberto?" she asked, shuffling along in her house shoes. "Alberto, ¿dónde estás? What are you doing all the way out here? Did you chase that cat again? You know he always comes back. . . ."

"Señora Mata?" Pao asked tentatively, approaching her slowly. "Can I help you find something?"

"Maria!" Señora Mata said, looking up sharply at Pao. "I told you not to go running around with that Beto. He'll get you into trouble! And now you're coming home so late. . . ."

Beto, Pao thought. Where had she heard that name before?

"Señora?" Pao said, brushing aside the half-formed memory. "It's me, Paola, from next door. . . ."

"Oh, you can't fool me, Maria," said Señora Mata. "I know you don't want me to mother you, but somebody has to."

Maria? Pao thought, at a loss for what to say next. Did she mean Pao's mom? But the two of them hadn't met until Pao was four, when she and her mom had moved into the Riverside Palace . . . right?

"Okay, señora," Pao said, aware that the old woman was still waiting for an answer. "I'll stay away from Beto. You're right."

Señora Mata smiled, but her eyes appeared vacant, looking through Pao instead of at her. "Bueno, bueno," she said. But even as she spoke, the smile melted off her face, replaced with a gradually dawning look of horror.

"Are you okay?" Pao asked, glancing around for the source of Señora Mata's fear. The wind whipped the evergreens into a frenzy. Their green eyes darted this way and that, and Pao heard the trees chattering to one another, though their words were indecipherable in the hiss of brushing needles.

"He calls," Señora Mata said, her voice hoarse. Her eyes were focused on Pao's face now, their dreaminess gone. "Paola, he calls to you."

"*Who* calls?" Pao asked, her heart in her throat, even though she knew this was just a dream. "What's going on?"

"You must go," Señora Mata said. "Or he will topple the world to find you."

"Okay," Pao said. "I'll go, but who—"

"Bueno, Maria," said Señora Mata, straightening up again. The wind in the trees died down, and the eyes stopped their frantic darting. "Por favor, come over for cooking lessons next week. You know you'll never get married si no puedes cocinar."

Pao's heart was still pounding out of her chest, but Señora Mata's eyes were vacant again as she drew her crocheted shawl around herself and went trundling off into the dense trees.

"Alberto?" she called. "Alberto, we need to get home before it's dark! Leave that gatita tontita alone!"

And then she was gone.

Pao was alone on the road, the trees calm, and ahead of her was a silhouette. Her father's.

Come to me, Paola. . . . His voice seemed to echo from the trees all around. *Come to me.*

"How?" Pao asked, inching her foot toward him, waiting for the crack in the earth to form between them again.

Instead, glowing green figures sprouted from the ground and unfolded like paper dolls. They encircled Pao and started rotating around her in some kind of weird ghostly dance. The glare they created hurt her eyes.

"Dad, help!" Pao screamed, no longer able to see his outline. "Help me!"

The figures spun faster still until the forest—and the road at her feet—disappeared, and there was nothing left but green light.

Pao awoke, sweating again, even though it was December.

The green shapes from her dream had followed her.

She jumped out of bed, swatting at them, a scream lodged in her throat.

But they were already fading. Soon their round little paper-doll heads were the only things left, floating around Pao. She watched them disappear one by one.

Had they ever really been there at all? Pao wondered, sinking back onto her bed. She had probably just been experiencing a hypnopompic hallucination, she told herself, remembering the term from her days of child sleep testing, her heart rate slowing as she retreated back into the comfortable world of science.

Even on her best days, Pao wasn't a morning person, and this morning was far from her best. The image of her father was still so close, like she could reach out and touch him. And Señora Mata? She'd said *Alberto* again in Pao's dream, just like she'd said outside the apartment last night. But Pao's dad was César.

Before the events of last summer, Pao might have drawn the logical conclusion that she'd been thinking of her father more often lately because her mom had a new boyfriend. And her subconscious had conjured Señora Mata because of Pao's interaction with Dante last night.

But these days, Pao knew that her dreams weren't always just dreams. In fact, it was Señora Mata who had called Pao "the Dreamer" last summer. Ondina—La Llorona's youngest ghostly daughter—had accessed Pao's consciousness through her dreams to draw her into her mother's supernatural realm.

But Ondina was gone now. Her spirit had been freed, and La Llorona and her glass palace had been destroyed. The rift was closed for good, and (aside from Bruto) there were no more monsters in Silver Springs.

Then again . . .

Pao remembered the trees from her dream. Pine. There were no pine trees in this part of Arizona. Could these new dreams be coming from a different rift? And did they actually have something to do with her dad?

Or maybe you're just reading way too much into this because you're bored with your life and mad about your new rent-a-dad, said the practical part of Pao's brain. She groaned. It was only seven thirty a.m., way too early to be this conflicted. After the night she'd had, Pao had expected to sleep in until at least ten.

She rolled over with a huff, pulling her faded purple comforter over her head and closing her eyes against the winter sunlight coming in through her window. At the foot of her bed, Bruto whined once at her theatrics, then resumed his hell-beast snoring.

If only she could get a little more sleep . . .

That's when the giggling started in the kitchen, followed by the unignorable grinding of the blender.

Pao flung herself out of bed with a loud *ugh*, startling her chupacabra puppy. She stomped into the hallway with him trotting at her heels, the ridges on his back standing up straight in alarm. She was sure she was doing every single thing on her mom's list of forbidden behaviors at once.

In the hallway mirror, she saw that pieces of her too-long bangs were sticking up at odd angles. She also noticed a massive backpack casting its shadow across the floor of her mom's bedroom. So Aaron was here. He hadn't spent the night, had he? No, Maria wouldn't go that far. Not without talking to Pao first, at least. She hoped.

"Morning, Paola!" her mom said when Pao entered the kitchen. Her voice was bright and happy. "Look who just dropped by!"

Aaron was standing beside her, giving Pao that grin again.

Pao's first impulse was to yell at them for being so loud, but she didn't want to get in trouble. Instead, she stood sleepily in the kitchen doorway, knowing the evidence of her nightmare was all over her face. She didn't try to hide it like she had so many times before. Now her mom would ask what was wrong, try to get her to take some weird tincture . . .

Maybe she would even send Aaron away for the day.

And then, if Pao did it carefully enough, she could ask Maria about César. . . . Instead, it was Aaron who spoke, leaning over her mom's shoulder, fingers intertwined with hers beside the blender. "We were just making smoothies—can we whip up one for you?"

Her mom didn't wait for an answer, just smiled even brighter and said, "After that, Aaron wants to go for a hike! I told him you wouldn't be up until close to noon, but since you're here, why don't you get dressed and join us!"

Smoothies? A hike? Who was this woman and what had she done with the moody, tarot-card-reading mom Pao was used to? The one who slept until her bar shift started in the afternoon and said people who engaged in the "outdoor industrial complex" led "mundane, internal lives."

The one who cared if Pao had a nightmare and was always eager to tell her what it meant.

But she's happy, said another voice in her head as Aaron and her mom waited for a response. *And you said you would try. . . .*

"I'll pass," Pao said as politely as she could with all those thoughts swirling around her brain. "Not much of a . . . *hiker.*"

Mom recovered quickly. "That's fine, mija. You're on vacation. Why don't you see if one of your friends wants to go to a movie?" She reached into her purse hanging on the hook by the fridge and fished a ten-dollar bill from her wallet.

She had never given Pao money voluntarily before. Not once in her entire life. And *rarely* if Pao asked, which she almost never did.

As Pao took the cash (deciding not to mention that there

wasn't a single person she wanted to see a movie with right now), she felt like she was reaching into another dimension. One where the curtains were open to let the sunlight in, and there was no incense choking her with its smoke, and some jolly blond man was offering her a smoothie.

It wasn't the worst place to be, but it wasn't home. And with Aaron here, it was difficult not to think of the shadowy face of her dad from her dream. She couldn't help but wonder why she was being forced to get acquainted with this stranger when she'd never been allowed to know her actual father.

It was difficult, despite her promise, not to blame her mom for all of it.

"Sure," Pao said, but her own voice sounded far away to her ears, and she couldn't quite catch her breath. She went back to her room and sat on the edge of her bed, her head in her hands. Bruto whined from the doorway, his big green eyes concerned.

Pao stayed there until she heard the faucet run and the giggling move to the front room. Then it was shoes, keys, and the door. The quiet after they left, which she'd thought she'd wanted, just made her feel worse.

She wished she could go upstairs, tell Dante about her dream, and ask him if his abuela was all right. But Dante wasn't talking to her. She thought longingly about sitting down with her mom, getting answers to all the questions about César that Pao had never been brave enough to ask.

But her mom had gone on a *hike* with *Aaron*. She obviously didn't care if Pao was having nightmares, or about anything else she was going through.

Her dreams, Dante's abuela, her mom's new bizarro personality . . . All these puzzles were too big for Pao to solve by herself. So she did what she often did when she felt overwhelmed and out of control—she looked for a problem she *could* solve.

Unfortunately for her mom, the only one coming to mind was that big blue backpack, the one that the dimpled dental model had left behind in the bedroom.

"Come on, Bruto," Pao said, manic energy coursing through her. "Let's go find out what Aaron's hiding."

Bruto, to his credit, remained where he was, lying in her doorway, looking up at her balefully. If he could've talked, he definitely would have said, *This isn't a good idea. We should do something else, like go for a walk or play fetch.* His big puppy-dog eyes tried their best to remind her that just last night she'd promised to be good.

But sometimes a certain feeling welled up in Pao. The same unignorable urge that had caused her to rebel after Ms. Jenkins had canceled their third-grade class trip to the planetarium. Or had made her intentionally add too much baking soda to the science-class volcano, knowing it would make a gigantic mess.

Then there was the time the landlord, Mr. Shaw, had raised the rent, and Pao had convinced Dante to help her cover the driver's seat of his very expensive car in honey. . . .

This same instinct had caused Pao to set off on an incredibly dangerous adventure last summer, when the police wouldn't help them search for Emma.

That was the thing about Pao—maybe the *main* thing about her. When something was wrong, she couldn't sit still.

So that's why, with Bruto now trotting reluctantly after her, Pao went into her mom's totally off-limits bedroom, praying that real-life hikes took as long as they seemed to in movies.

• • •

There's something a little liminal about a grown-up's room, Pao thought as she tiptoed across her mom's carpet.

Every object in here screamed at her to leave. Told her that whatever she found, it wouldn't be worth the trouble it would cause.

But then there was Aaron's backpack. Too big for a day hike. It had at least twelve pockets, any of which could be hiding damning information. Pao didn't know which to choose first.

The reckless thrill running through her made her feel like herself for the first time in a long time. Maybe that's why she dug right in. She decided to start with the small pocket in the front. Bruto whined as she unzipped it.

She ignored him.

Gum wrappers, hotel key cards, and a weird amount of unused toothpicks still in their cellophane wrappers. A little odd, but nothing resembling a deal breaker. Pao moved on.

The side pockets were empty save for a few interesting desert rocks. *Probably picked up on his* hikes, Pao thought. The middle zipper pocket held receipts, two spare phone chargers, and an empty wallet.

Maybe Aaron's secret was that he was the most boring person in the world.

Although that's hardly a secret, Pao thought.

The main section had a drawstring closure, and Pao pulled it open slowly. Bruto turned his back on her and flopped down in the threshold with a disgusted snort. She'd make it up to him later with Starbursts—she always saved the yellow ones for him. He didn't have to know that giving up the worst flavor in the pack wasn't much of a sacrifice.

Inside the backpack, she found a pile of neatly folded clothes.

Like, a lot of them. Apparently, the few times Pao had seen him hadn't been flukes. He really *did* only wear blue in varying shades. Annoying, but again, being boring wasn't a crime.

The real question was . . . why so many clothes?

Pao told herself there could be lots of reasons, but deep down in the pit of her stomach she knew there was only one. She might not have entered the school science fair this year, but her powers of deduction were still unrivaled.

Aaron had been living in a hotel (hence the keycards), and now that a pizza bonding night hadn't resulted in death or dismemberment, he was moving in. And Pao and her mom hadn't had even one conversation about it.

The reckless, electric thrill that had brought Pao into this room morphed into something like that out-of-control science-class volcano. Her hands were shaking as the feeling spread through her.

Pao had come in here to find incriminating facts about Aaron so her home life could go back to normal. Another woman's phone number on a lipstick-stained napkin, evidence that he'd voted for a Republican, something her mom would never forgive. Pao had never expected *this*.

Last night, Pao had opened up to her mom. Told her she didn't want things to change too fast. She'd trusted her mom to understand. But she hadn't. The very next morning, there had been smoothies and hikes and backpacks full of blue clothes, and it made Pao want to scream.

And throw things.

She wanted to, at the very least, leave a mark on this room she wasn't supposed to be in.

So she did.

Pao grabbed the comforter off her mom's bed and tossed it on the floor. She swept a pile of folded laundry off the top of the dresser into a heap beside it.

Chest heaving, eyes prickling in a way she was determined to ignore, Pao approached her mom's night table—the most private place in the house. She opened the top drawer first. It was where her mom kept her tarot cards bound up in scarves and ribbons.

Pao's tears spilled over.

She scattered the cards across the room, throwing them by the handful until the drawer was empty. But the tears kept coming. The big, helpless feeling Pao had been fighting ever since she returned from the rift had overtaken her, and stopping seemed impossible.

Aaron was moving in. Emma was living her own separate life. It was only a matter of time before Dante would acknowledge the weirdness between them, and then he'd be gone, too.

There was no room for Pao anywhere. Not after everything she'd been through, not with everyone pretending it had never happened.

The second drawer contained journals and notebooks, the most secret of her mom's possessions. Even on days when she had felt extremely bored, lonely, or curious, Pao had never dared to read them. Today, with shaking hands, she pulled a few out and opened the covers to see her mom's familiar handwriting on every page.

Pao was so tired of being the adult when she was still constantly treated like a kid. Tired of always having to remind her mom when it was time to pay the bills or blow out the candles before they burned down the house. Sick of never being listened to when she knew—knew without a doubt—that moving in with your boyfriend a month and a half after meeting him was just plain stupid.

With the Niños last summer, Pao had found out what it felt like to be appreciated for who you were. To be on your own and accountable without having to fade into the background and act like it was someone else's idea.

Pao could have handled her old life with her mom, and Emma, and Dante, and there's no question she would have chosen it over hunting monsters and ghosts with the Niños. But this wasn't her old life. And whatever this life was, she didn't want it.

She didn't want to read her mom's private thoughts, either. She didn't want to know how Maria felt or who she was when she wasn't playing the part of Pao's mom. Right now, Pao just wanted to be angry at her forever.

The first journal hit the ground with a satisfying thud, its cover splayed, pages folding and falling out of the binding. The second one landed half in and half out of an open dresser drawer. The third hit the wall behind her mom's bed and slid down to land with all the lost socks and hair ties.

Pao took out the final notebook, planning to aim it at the vanity mirror above the dresser, but something stopped her cold.

Beneath the journal, stuck to the bottom of the now-empty drawer, was a Post-it Note.

César Santiago, it read, and below it was a PO box address.

In Pine Glade, Oregon.

Pao wasn't proud of it, but she waited until she knew Dante would be at soccer practice before she snuck upstairs to speak to Señora Mata.

She'd wanted to do it a hundred times since they'd returned

from their adventures, but she hadn't been ready to openly disregard Dante's wishes. To put any more strain on their already-awkward relationship.

Now she was.

Pao's dreams were telling her something was wrong. She felt, all the time, like she was being watched. Like something was about to happen . . .

Unfortunately, she was running very low on adults she could trust. And not just adults, she realized, thinking of Dante and Emma, but people in general.

Pao knocked twice, looking around furtively to make sure Dante wasn't coming home early.

The coast was clear.

Señora Mata opened the door, looking a little disheveled, her eyes staring somewhere over Pao's left shoulder.

"Hi, Señora Mata," Pao said. "Can I come in?"

"Maria!" said Dante's abuela, smiling widely though her gaze still didn't quite meet Pao's. "Finally here for that cooking lesson, hmm? ¡Adelante!"

FOUR

The World's Least Compatible Lunch Ingredients

By now, Pao really should have been used to her dreams coming to life. But Señora Mata's behavior was freaking her out even more than the green shapes she'd seen floating around in her room first thing this morning.

Knowing it probably wasn't the best idea, and that Dante would be furious if he found out, she had decided to play along with Señora Mata. At least until she could figure out what was going on, and how to help.

"Thanks so much for the lessons," Pao said, following Señora Mata into the kitchen. "You were . . . so right about cooking being the best way to find a man."

If Señora Mata thought it odd that Pao was mentioning a conversation they'd had in a dream, she didn't mention it. *But that doesn't necessarily prove anything,* said the more scientific part of Pao's brain. More data was definitely required.

She would just have to collect it as quickly as possible, because with the state her apartment was in right now, she didn't know who would be angrier when they returned to the Riverside Palace—Dante or her mom.

"And I'm through with Beto," Pao said to Señora Mata, leaning on the counter and trying to channel her mother—if her mother was, in fact, the same Maria—as much as possible. "You were right about him, too. Bad news."

Pao was trying to remind the old woman of the dream, to get her talking. If Carmela had really known Pao's mom when she was young, maybe she'd known Pao's dad, too. And maybe whatever she knew could help Pao make sense of her dreams, and the way she'd been feeling lately. Like whatever had happened last summer wasn't over—that it was now a part of Pao, whether anyone wanted to acknowledge it or not.

At the mention of Beto, Señora Mata looked up from the counter, on which she had arranged chocolate chips, sour cream, a ball of masa, and a jar of whole bay leaves.

Pao's worry spiked. Señora Mata was the best cook she knew. Unless she was trying out a *really* unusual recipe, something was obviously very wrong.

"That boy is trouble," Señora Mata said. "Bad trouble. You stay clear of him, mijita."

"Yes, ma'am," Pao said, taking a deep breath. "I met someone new, anyway. . . ." She hesitated as Señora Mata took a cookie sheet out of the cupboard above her. "César Santiago? He's much better."

With a crash that startled Pao half out of her skin, Señora Mata dropped the cookie sheet. Her eyes were too wide now, and they seemed to meet Pao's for the first time since she'd walked through the apartment door.

"The names," she said. "Paola, you must understand. The two names are one."

"What about them?" Pao asked, her heart racing like it had in her dream. "What names? Señora, are you all right?"

"He calls," Señora Mata moaned, clutching her ears as though blocking out the sound. "He will not stop. He knows it, and he will not rest until he has done it." She stumbled toward Pao, her hands outstretched, until her palms were on each of Pao's cheeks. "He knows the answer, Paola. . . ."

"The answer to what?" Pao was really scared now. She wanted to get help, but Señora Mata was holding on to her face too tightly. "How can I help you, señora?"

"The answer . . ." Señora Mata said, her voice weaker now. "You must find it first."

"I don't know what you're talking about," Pao said. "The answer to what's wrong with you? Can finding him help?"

Señora Mata relaxed a little, looking up at the ceiling as if in disbelief. "Of course," she said. "Yes. Of course. It's time, Maria. My boy is waiting for me. . . ."

And then she collapsed on the ground.

Pao screamed and knelt down next to Señora Mata, trying to rouse her, but she wouldn't stir. "Wake up!" Pao said. "Come on, señora, wake up! I'm so sorry. I shouldn't be here, and I shouldn't have upset you. . . . I'm sorry."

Leaning close to Señora Mata's face, Pao held a hand in front of her mouth to make sure the woman was still breathing. The warm puff of air against Pao's palm brought tears of relief to her eyes.

This situation reminded Pao of how her adventure had started last summer—Señora Mata's trance, the way she'd collapsed on the floor. The eerie wave of green mist that had forced Pao and Dante to leave her behind. By the time they'd returned home, Señora Mata had been her usual impish self again.

Pao tried to find some comfort in that, even as she wondered if this was another paranormal problem. Even that would have been preferable to the alternative: that the old lady was sick. Maybe that's why Dante hadn't wanted Pao to come over. . . .

Was it Alzheimer's? Pao didn't know much about the disease beyond what she'd seen when her mom watched *Grey's Anatomy*. She feared she may have worsened the señora's symptoms by upsetting her. As she got a pillow from the couch to put under Carmela's head, Pao felt racked with guilt.

"Stay here, señora." Pao lay the old woman's head down as gently as possible and dug her new phone out of her pocket. But once she had it in her hand, she hesitated.

Of course, most people would have called 911 immediately. But Pao knew 911 would bring police, and the residents of the Riverside Palace were especially vulnerable to law enforcement. It was hard not to remember Sal, her younger friend from Los Niños de la Luz, who had been taken by ICE, along with his parents, from the apartment below.

Or for that matter, Señora Mata's own warnings about involving the authorities in their lives. Pao suddenly wondered, what did Señora Mata's ID say? Was she a legal US citizen? Would the alleged hundred years she'd spent as an immortal monster hunter affect the information on her papers?

What would the police (or the hospital, for that matter) do with a woman who was, technically, almost two hundred years old?

Pao's heart was hammering out of her chest. She was so frustrated with the state of the world, not to mention terrified about the condition Señora Mata was in. How were you supposed to get care for the people you loved when the "care" dispatched was equally likely to kill them or ruin their lives?

And how long did Pao have to find out?

She wished her mom were here, despite everything. But she couldn't call her when she'd just trashed her bedroom. And Dante would lose his mind if he got here before Pao had a plan. So she opened her phone and selected a contact she hadn't used in a long time, praying to the gods or the santos or whoever was listening that she'd get an answer.

"Pao?" Emma's voice on the other end was suspicious, and there was laughing in the background, like Pao was interrupting something cool and fun. "Did you call me on purpose?"

"Yeah," Pao said, her voice sounding shaky even to herself. "Hi. Um, I'm with Dante's grandma and . . . something's wrong. I . . . don't know what to do?"

Before Emma could answer, two things happened in quick succession. First, the door opened, revealing Dante, and second, the green paper dolls from Pao's dream popped up around Señora Mata, bathing the tiny room in green light.

"Pao?" Emma said through the phone speaker that Pao was now holding away from her head. "Pao, are you still there?"

"WHAT HAPPENED TO HER?" Dante roared, seconds later.

"I—" Pao said, frozen in the green glow. "I don't . . . I didn't mean . . ."

"Pao?" Emma said, her voice tinny through the phone. "What's happening now? What do you guys need?"

"WHAT ARE YOU DOING HERE, PAO?" Dante yelled, crossing the room in two steps to kneel beside his grandma. The moment he crossed their circle, the green figures disappeared.

That's one problem down, Pao thought.

"We need . . ." she finally choked out to Emma. "We need to

get her to the hospital, but we can't call 911. We can't bring the police, Emma. What do we do?"

"Pao?" Emma said. "I need you to listen carefully, okay? I learned all about this in the Rainbow Rogues' De-escalation-Not-Policing-for-Community-Justice lunchtime webinar."

"What?" Pao asked, panicked as Dante started shouting at his abuela to wake up. "What is that? What do we do?"

"We need to call a private ambulance," Emma said. "They're not affiliated with the hospital or the police, okay?"

"We can't pay for a private ambulance!" Pao said, picturing the ten dollars in her pocket and knowing there was no way Dante had any more.

"I'll call for it, okay?" Emma asked instead. "Are you at Dante's place? I'll use my dad's credit card—this definitely counts as an emergency, and it's exactly the kind of thing I should be using my privilege for anyway!"

Pao almost smirked at that—this girl had definitely taken the Rogues' mission to heart—but the situation was too serious for humor. She reminded Emma of the street address, shouting to be heard over Dante's repeated pleas for his abuela to wake up.

"I'll text when they're on their way, okay?" Emma said. "It's going to be all right, Pao."

"Thanks, Emma," Pao said, really meaning it.

"I'll meet you guys at the hospital," Emma said. "I mean, unless . . ."

"No, yeah," Pao said. "Of course, meet us."

"Okay," Emma said, and Pao could hear her smiling. "Okay, I will."

They hung up, leaving Pao with a borderline-hysterical Dante and a still-unconscious Señora Mata.

"Emma's calling an ambulance," Pao said, and Dante fell silent. "It's a private one. No cops. She's gonna pay for it with her dad's card."

"What are you doing here?" Dante asked again, still looking down at his abuela. "And what were those green things I just saw? Pao, I told you she was—"

"You didn't tell me anything!" Pao interrupted, her temper flaring. "You didn't tell me she was forgetting things, or that anything was wrong at all! You just shut me out, Dante. Why didn't you let me help? Aren't I supposed to be your—" There it was again, the word she couldn't bring herself to say. "Friend?" she finished feebly.

"Yeah, because you're always so helpful, Pao?" Dante said, laughing in a strangled sort of way. "Because this isn't, like, entirely your fault to begin with, right?"

Pao felt it then—something culminating between them. Something bigger than their relationship's lack of definition. Something he'd been hanging on to for so long it was crystalizing, like carbon atoms in the earth's crust forming diamonds.

"What do you mean?" she asked, her own voice sounding far away. "How could this possibly be my—"

"She was *fine* before that green mist stuff, and the candle flames changing colors, and that creepy voice!" Dante said, like the words were exploding from a place in his heart where he'd kept them locked up all these months. "She was fine until you were 'the *Dreamer*' and we had to go off on some quest, and now she doesn't remember stuff, and she's sick and she might be dying, and it's all because of *you*!"

Pao took a step backward to take him in—the tears gathered at the corners of his eyes, his face flushed with anger. *This* was what he'd been trying to tell her all the times he'd brushed her off this year.

Dante, her best friend and maybe more, hated the part of her that still wanted to talk about Bruto and the Niños and the monsters and the void. He wanted to forget it all because he was losing his abuela and he blamed Pao for it. For everything.

She'd thought it was just the paranormal stuff he wanted to forget. She'd never imagined he wanted to forget *her*, too.

"I didn't . . ." Pao began, trailing off, because what could she possibly say? That it wasn't her fault? That as the Dreamer she hadn't brought the mist and the monsters and the danger to their doorstep? That she hadn't actively, in a room right below where they were standing now, wished for more of all those things to happen?

"Abuela," Dante was saying again. "Abuela, wake up, please."

Pao couldn't even say she was sorry. She couldn't say anything until the ambulance Emma had called pulled up, looking like any other ambulance. An EMT knocked on the door, and without any more fanfare or conversation or chances to explain, they were all headed to the hospital.

The EMT asked questions as they went, and Pao answered them as best she could. Dante sat beside his grandma, silently holding her hand, letting Pao do the talking despite everything he'd said about not needing her.

When the EMT asked what Señora Mata's symptoms had been before she lost consciousness, Pao hesitated. She had so far avoided telling Dante how long she'd been at his apartment or why, but it seemed she couldn't put it off any longer.

"She was acting strange," Pao said. "She thought I was my mom back when she was a teenager. She talked about a boy my mom used to date and how he was trouble. She was . . ." Pao steeled herself for Dante's wrath. "She was going to give me a cooking lesson, but she was picking really weird ingredients and stuff."

"And then what happened?" the man asked.

"She . . . seemed to realize where . . . or . . . *when* she was," Pao said haltingly, wondering how to explain this without talking about her dreams, or the green shapes, or the real reason she'd been in apartment K. "After that, she got upset. She was talking nonsensically, like she was afraid. That's when she fell, and I couldn't wake her up."

This answer seemed to satisfy the EMT, who hooked up Señora Mata to an oxygen mask and several monitors, which Pao guessed were for blood pressure and heart rate.

But Pao couldn't help but notice that after her brief interview, the driver turned on the ambulance's siren and significantly increased their speed.

She wanted to say something to Dante, to apologize, but he never met her eyes and Pao didn't trust her voice, so she stayed quiet. It allowed her, at last, to reflect on the events of the morning and what they might mean.

Was Señora Mata confused, her words the result of a natural disease? Or were they connected to Pao's dreams of her father and everything supernatural that had happened to her last summer?

Dante's abuela had told Pao this mysterious *he* would never stop searching until he found her. That he would bring down the world before he let her slip away. That he was looking for an answer, and Pao needed to find it first.

In that moment, Pao just *knew* Señora Mata had been talking about her dad. Somehow, he'd become aware of Pao's trip into the rift last summer. And he had the answers she'd been searching for ever since.

If she could find her father *and* get the answers she needed to cure Señora Mata at the same time, how could Pao do anything else but try?

The Post-it Note with her father's PO box address on it was burning a hole in her pocket. Her plan was already half-formed by the time they reached the hospital. She would go to Pine Glade—a place that sounded like a furniture polish more than a town, but that was beside the point. She would find her father, learn how to save Señora Mata, and get the answers she needed about the Niños. She would figure out a way to keep them all safe, for good.

Pao looked at Dante, who hadn't glanced up at her once since the ambulance took off, with a sinking feeling in her stomach. The feeling told her that, this time, she would have to do it alone.

FIVE

Worse News Than a Haunted Bingo Bonnet

The Silver Springs hospital was on what Pao not-so-affectionately referred to as the "golf course side of town."

Which was really typical, she thought as the ambulance pulled into the bay and they prepared to unload Señora Mata.

Pao trailed along behind the EMT and paramedics, feeling increasingly out of place as they got Señora Mata admitted and handed Dante a clipboard with an inch-thick stack of paperwork.

"Are you both family?" asked a nurse (STACEY, Pao read on her name tag in a daze) as she started wheeling Señora Mata's gurney toward the ICU.

"Um," Pao said in her smallest voice, turning to Dante.

Without looking back, he said, "I am," and walked through the door behind Stacey, leaving Pao alone in the hall.

She paced up and down, trying to stay out of everyone's way, torn between guilt and frustration. She wanted to sit down in a corner and cry. She wanted to barge in there and make Dante talk to her.

Luckily, she didn't have time to do either before Emma arrived.

"Pao!" Emma ran toward her, her sandy-blond ponytail bouncing and purple streak bright under the fluorescent lights.

She wore skinny jeans and a long-sleeved white T-shirt with rainbow sleeves. There was paint under her fingernails.

When she reached Pao, they hugged as if it hadn't been months since their worlds had drifted out of each other's orbits. Pao was so relieved to see her, it was like an actual weight had lifted off her shoulders.

"Are you okay?" Emma asked, real concern in her big blue eyes. "Where's Dante and Señora Mata?"

"In there," Pao said, pointing to the double doors of the ICU. A lump in her throat made it hard to talk.

"Oh, you didn't have to wait for me!" Emma said, her cheeks turning pink. "Should we go in and see what we can do to help?"

Pao wanted to say yes. To say anything. But instead, the lump in her throat grew, and she found she couldn't hide how she felt from Emma. Not that she'd ever really been able to.

"He . . ." Pao attempted, her eyes welling up. "He doesn't want me in there. He says . . ." Tears spilled out of Pao's eyes for the second time that day, and Emma stepped forward to embrace her again. "He says it's my fault," Pao said into her best friend's shoulder. "That she's sick because of me, because of . . ." She lowered her voice, stepping back to look around for eavesdroppers. "Because of what happened last summer."

Emma's jaw clenched, and her eyes looked sad. "In that case, it's *my* fault, isn't it? I'm the one who got taken. . . ." She shook herself a little. "What happened to Señora Mata, anyway? She just collapsed?"

Pao pulled Emma aside, into a little waiting alcove with faded red chairs and a table with a few out-of-date magazines on it. "Promise you'll keep this a secret?" she asked.

They had posed that question to each other so many times before. But that was back when they'd had no other girl friends to confide in. Now, when Emma's answer really mattered, Pao waited for her to scoff at the childish request and make some cool comeback like *Radical honesty is the only way to fight oppression* or something.

"Promise," Emma said instead, and stuck out her pinkie.

The gesture was so familiar it almost made Pao cry again, but she linked her pinkie with Emma's anyway, and they twisted their hands around in their secret-keeping handshake. They'd invented it in the fourth grade, when Pao had revealed that Lily M. had a crush on Dalton Jenkins, even though she'd promised not to, because she just *had* to tell someone.

As they finished up the handshake now (with an elbow bump and a round of breathless giggling), Pao wished their secrets were as simple as other people's fourth-grade crushes. But it hadn't been that way for a long time.

At least, not since last summer.

And so, Pao told Emma everything. About her dreams of her dad, the problems between her and Dante, Señora Mata's strange behavior, and her mom's awful boyfriend with his backpack full of blue clothes. The destruction in her mom's room. Her dad's PO box. And finally, the scene in Dante's kitchen when it had all come together and Pao's harebrained theory about what it all meant.

By the end, Emma's eyes were as round as quarters. "So the green things from your dream were really there?" she asked, as if she were confirming it for herself, not like she didn't believe Pao. "And you think your dad will know how to wake her up?"

Pao nodded fervently. "I mean, there are too many clues for it to be coincidence," she said. "The dreams, the address . . . And Señora Mata seemed the most lucid when I said my dad's name. She knew him when they were younger, I think. Just another thing my mom lied about . . ."

Emma chewed her lip, the familiar furrow between her eyebrows revealing that she was thinking hard. "But Oregon is really far away, Pao," she said. "And don't you think your mom's gonna be furious when she finds out you trashed her room? She'll probably ground you for the rest of middle school."

All true, Pao thought, collapsing into a chair and burying her face in her hands. "I know," she said, the words muffled by her palms. "But I have to try, don't I?"

"Okay, let's think this through," Emma said, sitting beside Pao. "Maybe we hang out here for a bit, make sure Señora Mata's *really* out because of magic dream stuff and not because of, like, an actual human thing?"

Pao looked at her blankly, trying to pull herself back from the crazed planning stage her brain had already entered.

"You know, humans?" Emma asked, a mischievous smirk playing around her mouth. "We get things like the flu, broken toes, the desire to wear Native headdresses to Coachella, and other unfortunate maladies?"

"I don't think a broken toe did this to Dante's abuela," Pao deadpanned. "Or a headdress, either. Wait, unless it was haunted! Do you think maybe the good-luck bonnet she wears to bingo—"

"Let's just . . ." Emma said, gently but firmly, taking Pao by the elbow and steering her back into the hallway. "Let's go in there and see how she's doing. If it's not a normal illness or a . . . haunted bingo bonnet, we'll go from there, okay?"

Pao knew, no matter how much she dreaded confronting Dante, she had no choice but to follow.

In the hospital room, two doctors stood over Señora Mata—a very tall balding man, and a very short man with a ponytail—both talking rapidly in low voices.

They look exactly like Pinky and the Brain, Pao thought, these two laboratory mice from a cartoon she'd watched on fuzzy cable when she was little. Brain was a little evil genius, and Pinky was his dopey, much taller counterpart.

The thought made Pao laugh inwardly . . . until she caught sight of Dante.

He sat in a chair against the wall, the paperwork in his lap, looking bleary-eyed and despondent.

Pao had been vacillating between anger and guilt since they'd gotten into the ambulance, but in this room, guilt took over with full force. He and his abuela both looked so small and helpless. And they were alone, Pao realized, with whatever the consequences of this were going to be. The hospital bills, the rehab . . . She stopped herself before she could consider anything worse.

She would fix this, if it was possibly within her power to do so. Even if she couldn't promise it to Dante right now, she would promise it to herself.

Emma approached Dante and put a hand on his shoulder. "You okay?" she asked as Pao skulked against the door feeling awful and restless and ready to bolt before he could yell at her anymore.

"Excuse me, it's family only in here," Pinky said.

"We're her grandkids," Emma said smoothly, staring down the doctor like her father had donated this wing of the hospital. Which, technically, he probably could have. "We're his cousins."

Pao nodded her agreement, not trusting her voice as the doctor looked back and forth between the three of them.

"My mom married a reeeeally white guy," Emma said by way of explanation, adding this adorable shrug that Pao knew no authority figure could resist.

"Well, I certainly wasn't . . ."

"No one was saying that you . . ."

"How's she doing?" Emma cut through the doctors' hemming and hawing and sent them back to Señora Mata's bedside. "My dad is out of town, but he'll be calling soon for an update, so I want details."

Pao watched her work, a little in awe of how effortlessly she bossed them around. Pao was great at lying to parents, or crafting plans to get them into or out of places they shouldn't be, but Emma had this way of walking into any room with a calm authority. Like anyone inside would be lucky to hear what she had to say.

Maybe that was because everyone had always treated Emma that way, Pao thought, remembering what had happened at the police station after Emma had gone missing. The cops had immediately pegged Pao and Dante as criminals, even though they were just two scared kids.

Emma would never have been treated that way.

In fact, at this very moment, the doctors were giving her an official-sounding report while Dante watched, looking totally bewildered.

"She's obviously unconscious, but her vitals are stable," said the Brain. "She doesn't seem to need assistance with her heart or lungs."

There was a hesitancy in his voice, Pao thought, one that indicated a medical mystery.

"But?" Pao asked, drawing their attention to her as she stood in the doorway.

Emma looked at her, too, but Dante kept his gaze fixed on the paperwork in his lap.

"We're having trouble getting a reading on her brain activity," the doctor admitted. "It's like she's here"—he gestured kind of pathetically at Señora Mata's form in the bed—"but *not* here. We need to run more tests. It's probably just that our machines aren't picking up the signal correctly. . . ."

The look on his face told Pao he didn't really believe that. They were just as baffled by Señora Mata's condition as Dante was.

She wondered what they'd say if she told them that Señora Mata had recalled a conversation they'd had in *Pao's* dream. And that just before they'd brought the old woman in here, she'd been surrounded by otherworldly figures made of green light.

From across the room, Pao caught Emma's eye. It wasn't a haunted bingo bonnet, but it definitely didn't seem to be a normal human malady, either. Emma nodded infinitesimally at Pao and then turned back to the doctors.

"Now, I'm sure, as professionals in your field, you're both aware of the statistics facing feminine-presenting Latinx people in a health care setting, correct?"

Pinky and the Brain just stared at her.

"Namely, the research that indicates Latinas receive the poorest quality health care in the nation after Black women? That they're less likely to be believed, advocated for, or treated properly during their first hospital visit than their white counterparts, and that care sharply declines in subsequent visits?"

Still no answer, not that the lack of response slowed Emma in the slightest.

"Señora Mata is a human being, vital to her community and beloved by her family. We expect you to treat her as such continuously throughout her stay here unless you want my dad to sue you both for discrimination and neglect. Got it?"

"Of course your grandmother will be given the best care we can provide," said Pinky smoothly, while the Brain nodded vigorously.

"Good," Emma said. "Now, Pao, why don't you take Dante to get a pen for all that paperwork, while the good doctors and I talk strategy."

Pinky and the Brain looked like they might prefer that hypothetical discrimination suit to being trapped in a room with Emma for another minute, but Pao knew her friend's plotting face better than anyone, so she took Dante's elbow and steered him toward the door.

"I don't want to leave her," he said when they reached the threshold. "What if . . . ?"

"Emma has it *so* handled," Pao said as convincingly as she could. "We'll get snacks and a pen, and we'll be right back, okay?"

Dante nodded at this and finally followed Pao into the hallway.

She was going to give him more background, but before she got a chance, Dante turned to face her in the same alcove where Pao had filled in Emma.

"You know something," he said, his tone accusatory even through his mask of exhaustion and grief. "Something you haven't told the doctors, or me. What is it?"

Pao hesitated. She knew she had to come clean, but there was every chance that once he heard what she had to say, he would never talk to her again.

"I . . ." Pao began, and then two things happened in quick succession.

One, her phone rang, her mom's face flashing on the screen.

And two, several people screamed from the hallway around the corner.

It wasn't hard to decide which one to handle. Pao would choose random screaming people over her mom's wrath any day. The problem was Dante, who was staring at Pao, still waiting for an answer.

"I'll tell you everything," she promised. "But we should probably figure out what's going on with . . . that, first."

Luckily—okay, extremely *unluckily*—for Pao, the situation didn't wait for them to find it. Before she could even finish her sentence, *it* was barreling down the hallway right toward them.

SIX

Supernatural Cleanup in the ICU

At first, it looked like a rogue old lady patient galloping down the hall. She was really moving, Pao thought, and instead of chasing her, the nurses seemed to be running *from* her—and that's what all the screaming was about.

But it wasn't just the old woman. There was a man beside her, too—younger and dressed in a suit and trench coat instead of a hospital gown. *He* wasn't running, exactly—he was lurching in their direction, Pao realized. In fact, they both were. And that wasn't the only strange thing about these runaways.

While the nurses had normal, solid bodies—evidenced by one of them bumping into Pao as she ran past in terror—the patients were mostly translucent. Through them, if the fluorescent lights hit just right, Pao could see the blinking lights of the coffee maker at the nurses' station as they passed it.

Pao looked at Dante, sure he would immediately comprehend what was happening and what needed to be done, but his eyes were fixed on the two very out-of-place spectral figures, his features frozen in horror.

"We have to help!" Pao said, grabbing his shoulder and trying to shake him out of his trance.

Dante nodded once, and when he finally looked her in the eye, something passed between them. Some kind of unspoken truce.

Though she hated to admit it, the adrenaline coursing through Pao's veins felt good. The fact that she and Dante were the only two people in this hallway who understood what had to be done also felt good.

The muffled, anxious feeling that Pao had been carrying around with her since her return from the rift was gone for the first time, and she was flying, Dante beside her, both of them knowing exactly . . .

Pao looked at Dante's empty hands with concern. "You have the chancla, right?"

Dante grew exasperated. "You know I don't!" he said. "Abuela took it from me when we got back! She said I was too young to have such a powerful weapon."

With a horrible sinking feeling, Pao remembered.

"Wait," she said. "I think she was wearing her slippers when we got in the ambulance! Do you—"

Dante was already heading for the door.

"I'll keep them distracted," Pao said, jerking her head toward the fantasmas. "But hurry, okay? I can't hold them off for long without the club."

Dante nodded and ducked inside. Pao closed the door behind him and stepped forward, silently wishing him luck. They'd be toast without his weapon.

Pao was handy with the knife she now always carried wrapped in a bandanna in her sock, but there was nothing like an Arma del Alma if you wanted to defeat a creature of the void, and Dante (well, Señora Mata, really) possessed one of the only two Pao had ever seen.

The last time she'd fought void creatures outside of La Llorona's palace, Pao had been wielding a magical flashlight that could repel them, but it had eventually shattered. Her adversaries then had been ahogados—the ghosts of kids who had been abducted by La Llorona and used in a sinister experiment to resurrect her own children, whom she had drowned with her own two hands.

Pao had freed the ahogados when she defeated La Llorona. She'd released their trapped spirits and allowed them to move on to the place where souls go to rest. But the void was vast, as large as her own world, if not larger. Just because she'd dispatched one ghost overlord didn't mean there weren't more around.

And these fantasmas were all the proof Pao needed. The two figures' eyes burned green in their wasted faces, their jaws hanging slack like zombies from that movie Pao wasn't officially allowed to watch yet. By the way they mindlessly staggered forward, Pao could tell they were soldiers. Someone had sent them here, just like La Llorona had sent the ahogados.

There was a new general in town. But who could it be?

Did they have something to do with Pao's dad? Or whatever was wrong with Señora Mata?

She had no time to find out. The fantasmas had rounded the corner at the nurses' station and were trashing everything in their path as, side by side, they moved toward Pao.

"Come on, Dante," she said under her breath. "Hurry up."

Pao was itching to run down the hallway, confront the fantasmas, and fight them with nothing but her knife and her wits, but she knew the smarter course of action would be to wait for backup.

Unfortunately, she didn't get the chance to be smart.

The old woman ghost, just twenty yards away, stuck her nose in the air and, like a hound catching the scent of a wild animal, locked her venomous eyes on Pao. A feral snarl erupted from the specter's throat.

"Oh crud," Pao said, her mom's edict about mild swearing holding even here. The man ghost reacted to the sound, and both of them abandoned their destruction of property to head straight for her. Pao beat on the door behind her, even as she reached into her sock for the knife. "We've got trouble out here!" she yelled.

There were only two living, breathing people left in the hallway—the nurse who answered the phones and a custodian with a bucket and mop.

The nurse made for Pao like she was going to rescue her, but Pao waved her away. "Run!" she told the woman. "I've got this!"

"I can't just leave you, you're a—"

But before she could say more, another snarl echoed through the trashed hallway, and Pao saw the nurse's determination waver.

"I know what I'm doing," Pao said. "Just go."

And whether it was Pao's confidence or the woman's coward-ice, the nurse finally scampered off.

The custodian, on the other hand, didn't seem nervous at all. He was just a little taller than Pao, though she was sure he was at least her mom's age. He wore a black bandanna tied around his head, and his skin was a little darker than Pao's—the first nonwhite person she'd seen since she'd walked through the doors of the hospital, in fact.

For some reason, that made her feel a little calmer.

Instead of running away, he unscrewed the mop head and stepped into the center of the corridor holding the handle like a staff. "If you're gonna pull that knife, you better do it, little girl," he said. "They're not slowing down."

He was right. The door behind Pao remained stubbornly closed, and as much as she wanted to, there was no time to check on Dante, Emma, and Señora Mata.

Only to protect them.

Pao drew the knife, unwrapping it from her bandanna with steady hands, freeing it just as the first fantasma reached her. Pao lunged, blade-first, feeling a little guilty about stabbing a grandma, half expecting her to offer cookies or a lecture for not calling more often.

But of course, she didn't. This fantasma wasn't a real grandma any more than the ahogados had been Pao's middle school classmates.

The knife connected with the ghost's shoulder, and with another snarl, the woman leaped backward, missing a chunk of her arm but still alive—well, sentient anyway—and very angry.

Pao used the space between them to set her stance, and then she struck again, this time taking a piece of the grandma's leg. That slowed the fantasma down.

Pao had almost forgotten the way it felt when a knife bit into fantasma flesh. It was nothing like shattering them with Dante's Arma del Alma, but it was still one of the strangest sensations Pao had ever experienced, like cutting into frozen slime that was somehow both gel and solid at the same time.

It made her whole arm feel numb, but there was no time to

stop. Just as she created some space between herself and the first ghost, the custodian shouted, "Watch out behind you!"

Pao whirled to face the second fantasma, trying to back away enough to see them both, not wanting either of them out of her sight while they were still growling and swiping and killing indiscriminately.

The man ghost was much quicker than the old woman, who Pao now saw had engaged the custodian behind the nurses' station. Pao focused her attention on the male fantasma now. In his long brown trench coat with a suit underneath, he looked like a banker from fifty years ago.

But his expression said he'd much rather rip Pao to pieces than offer her a high interest rate on a new checking account, and she didn't intend to give him the satisfaction.

"Eat metal!" she said, feeling very cool as she stepped forward and jabbed her knife right into the man's face, taking a chunk of his cheekbone with her.

Unfortunately, her strike had left her exposed, and before she could regroup, the fantasma had both his ghostly arms around her.

"No!" Pao screamed as the shock of his cold grip went right through her, freezing her to the bone. "Help! Dante! Um . . . Janitor Guy!" Pao's arms were pinned uselessly against her sides. She tried to kick the fantasma as he lifted her feet off the ground, but her sneaker toes just bounced off his ghostly shins.

Still, no one came to help. And his grip was only getting tighter.

"I'm sorry I called you Janitor Guy!" Pao called out, her face so tightly pressed into the ghost man's musty trench coat that she could only see the wall beside her. "I didn't mean to offend. . . . I just don't know your . . . name. . . . Ow!"

The ghost's grip had become nearly unbearable. What was he going to do, squish her to death? He didn't seem to have a weapon, so it probably wasn't out of the question.

Obviously, sheer physical prowess wasn't going to get her out of this, so Pao turned her energy inward, commanding her brain to come up with a solution.

Dragging Pao's toes along the ground, the fantasma headed toward the exit.

"Think!" Pao yelled aloud, knowing she must sound crazy, but no one was around to hear her, and she was totally blanking on ideas. Ahogados and void beasts always had just one objective—to drag their victim into the rift. Except with Ondina it had been different. Ondina had wanted Pao to come willingly.

But the rift is closed, Pao thought, picturing the giant mouth shutting as she'd escaped by the skin of her teeth last summer. There was nowhere for these fantasmas to drag her to. Yet, as soon as they'd seen Pao, they had *definitely* stopped searching and instead focused their energy on attacking.

Why?

"What do you want?" she asked her abductor in desperation. "Where are you taking me?"

The fantasma didn't answer, of course. He was almost at the stairwell, and Pao was running out of options.

She kicked out again, more in frustration than anything else, and this time her foot got tangled in the ugly trench coat. The fantasma stumbled as the material tightened around his legs, and his grip loosened for a moment.

It was enough. Pao wiggled out of his grasp and hit the ground running, her breath short from being squeezed too tightly. Otherwise, she was mercifully intact.

She had to get to Dante. They needed his Arma del Alma to vaporize these things, and they needed to do it fast. The random appearance of fantasmas wasn't the only problem awaiting them now. Other people had seen the ghosts. This place was about to become a crime scene *and* a news bonanza.

"Dante!" she screamed. She was nearly at the door of Señora Mata's room, when dancing green lights appeared at her feet. "No!" she cried for the second time. "Not again!"

The paper dolls unfolded and formed a circle, just like they had in her dream and in Dante's kitchen. Pao tried to pass through them, or to cut them with the knife, but they wouldn't budge. They held her in place as they began to spin.

Outside the circle, the two fantasmas abandoned their fight with the custodian and headed right toward her as if the green glow was guiding them in for a landing. But before they could reach her, the door to room 201 flew open and Dante skidded into view, a blue corduroy slipper in his hand. Pao watched with fascination as it magically transformed into a club that glistened under the fluorescent ceiling lights. Seeing that never got old.

"Stay inside, Emma!" he shouted over his shoulder before leaping toward Pao.

The fantasmas got to her first.

Pao nearly screamed when the old woman materialized right in front of her, walking through the green circle like it was no denser than smoke. The fantasma's jaw was still hanging loose, her eyes burning with green light.

With two clawlike hands, she latched onto Pao's throat and bent close—too close. She smelled like mothballs and mildew and something much more sinister all at once.

"*Come to me, Paola,*" she said, her mouth never moving, like the voice was being projected from somewhere else. The horrible hissing, grinding sound made Pao want to cover her ears. "*Come to me and I will tell you. . . .*"

But before Pao could find out what the fantasma wanted to tell her, its head exploded in a shower of glittering dust.

SEVEN

Sometimes Honesty Is Actually *Not* the Best Policy

The green figures once again dissipated the moment Dante stepped through them to get to Pao.

Around them, the hallway was utterly destroyed. Paperwork from the nurses' station was strewn all over the floor, and the machines that had been beeping and whirring productively just minutes before were now nothing more than rubble.

One of the fluorescent lights overhead had been smashed, and it flickered and sparked ominously where it was still attached to its casing.

"Are you okay?" Dante asked Pao, giving her a once-over for obvious injuries.

"I'm fine," she said, though she wasn't really. She was still thinking about what the fantasma had said. The way its words had echoed the ones her father had uttered in her dreams.

She shook herself, locking eyes with Dante. "Is your abuela okay? And Emma? What happened in there?"

Dante shook his head. "The doctors are hiding in the bath-room off Abuela's room. She's still unconscious, and Emma's in there watching her. I told her to stay put."

As if on cue, Pao heard footsteps running toward them.

"Are you guys okay?" Emma asked, skidding to a stop beside them. "That was incredible! I was watching through a crack in the door. What *were* those things? And how did . . . ?" She trailed off when she saw the looks on their faces. "Right," she said. "Questions for another time."

"I told you to stay—" Dante began.

Emma cut him off. "She's fine. The doctors are still in there—I mean, they're hiding, which is a little questionable, ethically, given the danger to their patient, but—"

"I hate to bust up this reunion," the custodian said, walking up behind them, "but I suggest you kids get out of here pronto. All those Karens who were working the floor have definitely called the cops by now."

Pao knew he was right, but there was too much left undone. "We can't leave without—" she began, but Emma was two steps ahead of her.

"I'll stay here," she said. "I'll watch Señora Mata and keep you guys updated every step of the way." She held up her smartphone. "I'll just pretend I was hiding inside her room the whole time and I didn't see where you went, okay?"

"No *way*," Dante said, the club shrinking back into a chancla now that the threat had been eliminated. "I'm not going anywhere until I know she's safe."

"Dante," Pao said, wishing they had more time, "I don't think she's gonna be safe *unless* I go."

"What are you talking about?" Dante asked, looking between Emma and Pao with a positively mutinous expression on his face. "She's sick, okay? She's got . . . Alzheimer's or dementia or whatever. The doctors will treat her and—"

"Dante," Emma said gently. "You heard the doctors. They don't know what's wrong with her. And they said after a few days of no brain activity it'll get harder and harder to wake her up. . . ."

He whirled on Pao. "And *you* know?" he asked, half-desperate, half-furious. "You know what's wrong?"

"I don't," Pao said, shaking her head. "But I think I know who will."

Her phone rang then. Her mom again, of course. Pao could practically feel her getting angrier and angrier the longer Pao went without answering.

"I've been having dreams again," she said to Dante, silencing the call and getting right to the point. "Dreams about my dad. Your abuela knew him, and last night she was in my dream, too. She told me he's looking for an answer, and he knows how to get it, and we need to get it before he does. She said that's how we can save her."

"Pao, you haven't seen your dad since you were four!" Dante said. "What could he possibly have to do with this? And where would we even find him?"

"Oregon," Pao said simply. "That's where he is. And that's where I have to go."

"This is insane," Dante said, backing away from both of them. "You're both nuts. We can't do this again. I have to stay with her!"

"Yo, this isn't really any of my business," said the custodian, still standing behind them. "But if you stick around here, they'll have you in juvie before sundown."

Pao, Emma, and Dante all turned to look at him.

"Right, sorry, I'm out," he said. "Good luck with your abuela, kid. And listen to her, eh?" He pointed at Pao. "She's kind of a badass."

He jogged to the exit stairwell before any of them could react.

"Okay, he's random, but he's right," Emma said, using her authoritative voice again. "Your only legal guardian is in some kind of mysterious coma, Dante, and it looks a lot like you two just trashed an entire hospital wing for fun. Best case? You end up in some group-care nightmare until she wakes up. Worst case, it's jail. You're better off leaving this to me and helping Pao."

Dante looked like he was being physically ripped in half.

"I'll take care of her, Dante," Emma said. "And I'll text you every hour if you want. It'll be cool. I'll be your guys' Max Gibson!"

Dante and Pao stared at her blankly.

"Max Gibson? *Batman Beyond*?" Emma said, rolling her eyes affectionately. "She's, like, the nerd who stays home and looks things up, keeps everyone's cover stories intact and stuff." Emma paused, looking pained. "Although on the show she's dark-skinned, and you guys know I would never culturally appropriate, even for a metaphor, so—"

Out the broken window at the end of the hallway, Pao could hear sirens. Like, a lot of them. "We have to go," she said. "It's now or never."

Dante closed his eyes and clenched both fists. "Fine," he said. "Like I have a choice. Like I *ever* get a choice."

"Will you feed Bruto for me?" Pao asked Emma. "And play with him every once in a while? He likes walks and yellow Starbursts, and he'll protect you if any more fantasmas show up and—"

The sirens were getting louder.

"I'll take care of him," Emma said. "I'll take care of *all* of them. You guys just go, okay? Before it's too late."

"Thank you," Pao said, hugging Emma briefly and fiercely. "Thank you."

"What are best friends for?" Emma asked, with a little smile.

"Ready?" Pao said to Dante, who just scowled.

It would have to do.

With one last look at Emma, Pao bolted for the stairs the custodian had taken, Dante close behind her. She knew where they needed to go, she just didn't know how they were going to get there with cops and firefighters descending on them like cicadas in the end times.

They only had to go down one flight to get to the first floor, but Pao didn't want to go anywhere near the lobby, because that was where the responders would congregate.

She motioned to the left instead, down a dark hallway that looked unoccupied. The monitors were all silent here, the nurses' station empty.

That's a small-town hospital for you, Pao thought, spotting the exit door at the end, thankfully free of staff or police. She didn't dare look at Dante as they pushed through it and stepped out into a courtyard on M Street, around the corner from the main entrance.

"We need to get away from here," Pao said, more to herself than Dante.

"Obviously," he retorted anyway.

He doesn't mean to be a jerk, Pao told herself. *He's just in pain.*

"Any other brilliant observations? Or should we get this over with and turn ourselves in?"

He doesn't mean to be a jerk. He's just in pain, she repeated. *He doesn't mean to be a jerk. He's just in pain.* After three or four more repetitions she stopped wanting to kick him in the shins. Would she step on a toe, though? Maybe.

They stuck to the side streets, ducking behind a house or a

bush whenever a car drove by. Pao didn't know if the nurses had described her and Dante, or if Pinky and the Brain had come out of the bathroom yet, but it was safest to assume she and Dante could be recognized.

And if they were, there was every chance that whoever did the recognizing would call the police. The "Karens" (as the custodian had called them) definitely didn't need an extra reason to report two suspicious brown kids in their neighborhood.

Which was why Pao and Dante needed to get out of town as soon as possible.

Two-story houses gave way to one-stories, then condos, then apartment complexes. Even in December, the sun was blazing overhead. They'd been running, hiding from drivers, and checking over their shoulders for more fantasmas for almost an hour when they finally hit the trailer park outside of town.

Her mom had called three more times, and Pao ignored the fourth call now, not even bothering to check her twenty-seven unread texts. Pao already knew what they would say.

She turned off her phone, feeling a pang of guilt for worrying her mom. But that disappeared immediately when she remembered Aaron and his backpack full of stupid blue clothes.

Who cared what her mom thought? Maria wanted to move some guy in, become a totally different person at the drop of a hat? What did she care if Pao was gone?

Right now, Pao had only one goal in mind: Get to the cactus field by the Gila River.

Dante hadn't said anything for a long time, but Pao expected she'd hear from him when he realized where she was taking them.

It doesn't matter, she told herself. Emma had said it—the

longer Señora Mata stayed unconscious, the less likely she was to wake up. Pao had to get the answer the señora had told her about before it was too late.

Pao couldn't help it if her estranged father was the one who had it, right? And who could blame her if she wanted to get some of her own questions answered, too?

Because whatever was going on—the appearance of her father in her dreams, and everything that had happened afterward—it was proof. There *was* something strange about Pao. Something she'd been in the dark about her whole life.

The events of last summer hadn't been a fluke. There was a *reason* she'd been drawn into that rift, and why she wasn't ready to move on from what had happened to her. She could only hope her father would know what that reason was.

The sun was sinking, Arizona serving up one of those sunsets they plastered all over travel brochures to make people forget about the heat. Pao and Dante were past even the last of the mobile homes now, with nothing in front of them but open desert and the promise of the Gila.

Pao slowed to a fast walk, her legs burning from all the running they'd done, and chanced a glance at Dante. His surly expression hadn't faded one iota, and his eyes were still looking determinedly at anything but her face.

She understood why he was angry, and that he was scared and confused, too. But did that give him the right to be this mean to her? Things had been off between them ever since school started, and now this. Would their relationship ever get back to the way it used to be?

Was that even what Pao wanted?

As if he could hear her thoughts, Dante finally looked at her, something like disbelief slowly changing his face.

"Pao?" he asked at last.

"Yes?" she replied.

"Why does it look like we're headed straight for . . ."

The appearance of the cactus field's boundary finished his sentence. Dante whirled around to face her.

"What are we doing here?" he asked, his cheeks flushing again. "I thought we were going to Oregon."

"We are," Pao said, repeating her mantra over and over to keep herself from escalating this into an argument. *He doesn't mean to be a jerk. He's just in pain. He doesn't mean to be a jerk. He's just in pain.*

"Really?" he asked scathingly. "Because this looks an awful lot like we're going to the Niños' camp by way of a stupid unnavigable maze when my abuela is in the hospital *waiting for us to fix her brain before it stops working forever.*"

The mantra fell off the record player of Pao's brain with a loud, angry screech.

"Sorry," Pao said. "Did you have some perfect, easy way to get us to Oregon that you conveniently forgot to tell me?"

The flush was creeping down Dante's neck now. "You're the one who always has the answers, Pao. I'm just your pathetic sidekick, right? The guy with everything to lose who's always getting dragged into things he never asked to be a part of."

"I didn't ask for any of this, either!" Pao shrieked, remembering when they'd fought like this before, during their first trip into the cactus field. It felt like a million years ago. That Dante and Pao had been best friends, bulletproof. They'd made up in minutes because they'd both just been scared.

This wasn't about being scared. And Pao didn't think they were best friends anymore. She didn't know what they were now.

"Really?" Dante asked, his voice dripping with sarcasm. "So you haven't been *waiting* for something like this to happen ever since we got home? Trying to drag it all back up every day so you can feel special again?" The old Dante would have teared up here, but this one had nothing but cold fury in every muscle of his face.

"Dante," Pao said, taking a step back. "That's not—"

"I bet you're *glad* she got sick," he said viciously. "You'd watch anyone or anything suffer as long as it meant you got to play the ghost-hunting hero again."

"I didn't—" Pao tried again, but Dante was still going.

"You should have just stayed," he said. "If coming back here was all you wanted, you shouldn't have come home in the first place. We'd all have been better off."

Pao felt like he'd kicked her in the stomach. He certainly looked like he wanted to. She was almost afraid of him in this moment, his face flushed with anger, painted red by the setting sun.

"I'm sorry," she said, her voice small.

Dante didn't answer, and Pao realized she didn't even know who she was apologizing to. Thinking back on the past few months, she'd lost track of what had made them special, made them work so well together.

She'd thought it was boy-girl weirdness, their attempt to turn friendship into something more, that had changed everything. Instead, it had been Dante, sitting right above her in his room, weaving a story in which Pao was the villain and he was the victim.

And now? She barely knew the angry boy in front of her.

Pao had pulled away, too, she knew. She hadn't been the friend she should've been. She vowed that she would be that friend now, no matter how angry Dante was, no matter what he said. They would do this together, and by the end, they would remember why they mattered to each other.

They had to.

"Look . . ." Pao said now, knowing she would have to keep this plan to herself for the time being. He was in no space to hear how much she wanted to repair their friendship. "No one's gonna let us on a bus or a train unaccompanied tonight, and one thousand eighty-seven miles is a long way to walk, so . . ."

"So, what?" Dante asked, his voice flat, his gaze far away.

"So," Pao said, keeping her voice as even as she could, "I figured we know some kids who don't let things like Greyhound age restrictions get in their way. And they happen to owe us a favor."

Dante just glared at her shoes.

"We spend one night with the Niños to throw my mom and the cops off the scent, we ask Marisa to help us get out of town, and we don't look back until we've figured out how to save your abuela, okay?"

When Dante met her eyes, Pao thought she could almost see him in there, the boy she'd known since pre-K. "This is still about helping her, right?" he said, like he was testing the waters. "Not about your obsession with all things paranormal?"

"It's about getting to Oregon as fast as possible," Pao promised. "It's not my fault my only friends are immortal monster hunters, okay? If I knew any regular people, I swear I'd ask them for help instead."

"One night," he said.

"One night," Pao echoed, and they crossed the barrier at last.

EIGHT

Knock, Knock, Nobody's Home

The first time they'd traversed this cactus field, Pao had been carrying her magical flashlight—the same one that had repelled the ahogados. It had acted as a kind of compass, guiding them through the magically twisted landscape and pointing the way toward the powerful rift the field was supposed to protect. The flashlight had been a gift from her father for her fifth Christmas— the one and only time she'd heard from him after he left.

This time, Pao had nothing but a vague hope that having once been to the Niños' camp she could find it again, the way Naomi, Marisa, and Franco always could.

Dante kept pace with her, his eyes sweeping up ahead rather than scowling down at his shoes. *He'll come around*, Pao told herself, once she got to the bottom of everything. They would find their way back to each other, even if they'd never been so far apart before. . . .

They kept walking in silence, but they'd only gone a short distance when Pao noticed that the landscape was already changing.

Before, it had taken them hours to follow the flashlight through the maze of the cactus field. They'd crossed miles and miles of the same light-colored sand and passed the same stubby cacti until Pao had thought she was losing her mind.

Now they were definitely going in the right direction. If they weren't, this field would have just spit them right back out where they'd started. But that rock was new, Pao was sure, and the cacti were already getting taller and spindlier, and the sky . . .

Pao's stomach sank. An eternal dusk characterized this place, but they'd gone from sunset to twilight, and now the sky was deepening toward night. Something was definitely wrong.

The problem became clearer when the massive cacti that formed the entryway to the Niños' camp came into view.

"Where is everyone?" Dante asked, his tone accusatory again, as if Pao had done this on purpose. He walked up behind her but stayed a few feet away as they surveyed the site together.

Dante was right. No one was here.

"No, no, no," Pao said, walking up to the firepit, its ashes long cold. "Where's the cookfire? Where are the tents?"

There was nothing left of what had made this place a home. Only a few pieces of broken furniture and some other discarded items. Pao felt a sob catch in her throat.

"Well, what now?" Dante asked.

"Just . . ." Pao said, turning away from him, holding up a hand. "Just give me a second, please."

To Pao, this wasn't just the thwarted first step of a plan. Dante hadn't been dreaming of this camp for months while his best friends pulled away, while his mom was too busy having her "shower retiled" to notice something was up.

A whisper in the back of Pao's mind had always told her that there was a place for her. That if things got too unbearable at home, if she really, truly didn't fit in, there was somewhere else she could go. . . .

She had staked everything on it. Her sanity, her friendship with Dante, Señora Mata's life. And it was all gone.

"You realize this is the first place the police will look for us, right?" Dante said as Pao went quietly to pieces, trying not to cry. "After what happened last summer?"

She wanted to snap at him, but she didn't, because he was right. What had been a sanctuary, a barrier between her and the people undoubtedly looking for them by now, and a gateway to her father had now become a liability.

"What's the plan here, Pao?" Dante asked, clearly not noticing, or caring, how upset she was.

"I don't know," Pao said, more to herself than him. "They were supposed to be here."

"Based on what, exactly?"

The old Pao would have had some kind of retort. Even the new Pao was supposed to be trying to repair things with Dante. But she was too tired to do either of those things right now. Night had fallen in earnest, the stars were twinkling above them. In the distance, Pao thought she could hear sirens again.

"Hello?" Dante said, his voice cutting.

"I'm sorry!" Pao said. "Obviously this is a major setback! And I'm worried about being found and I'm worried about your abuela, and, yes, sue me, I'm also worried about our *friends* who are supposed to *live* here and whether they're okay! Not that you'd be the least bit curious about that, I guess."

Dante rolled his eyes, and the gesture held none of the affection it once had. "They're a bunch of immortal monster hunters with magic weapons," he said, and even out here, he lowered his voice. Like someone was just waiting around the nearest cactus to call him a freak. "I think they'll be fine without our help."

"But look at this place," Pao said. "What if something really awful happened?"

"Something really awful like their grandmother and sole legal guardian being in some freaky coma?" Dante asked, back to shouting again. "Don't start pretending like you care how your friends are doing now, Pao."

"What are you talking about?" Pao asked, the cold, tired numbness back, all the fire extinguished.

"You dropped Emma," Dante said. "Right when she needed you the most. And I've been terrified all year, trying to deal with what's going on. But did you notice? No. It was always *the Niños* this and *the void* that. You never once asked how I was doing."

From being cold, Pao was suddenly boiling over. "You never told me anything!" she said incredulously. "I was going through stuff, too, okay? But if you had asked for my help with your abuela, you *know* I would have been there for you!"

Dante opened his mouth to reply, but Pao kept going.

"And I didn't *drop* Emma," she said. "I saved her life, and then I helped her come out to her parents. I even convinced her to join the Rainbow Rogues!"

"Yeah," Dante said. "And then, once she wasn't one of your experiments anymore, you left her high and dry until you needed something again. Face it, Pao, you're too obsessed with yourself and all this"—he gestured around at the deserted camp—"to be a good friend to anyone."

This time, she didn't bother explaining herself. Dante had made up his mind. She just stood there, staring at her shoes, willing the tears prickling her eyes not to well up.

"We don't have much time," she finally said when the awful silence couldn't stretch one second more. "If you want to go back, fine. If you want to go ahead without me, do it. As for me, I'm going to find a way to save your abuela."

Dante scoffed. "I'm not leaving this up to you," he said. "*I'm* going to save my abuela. As long as that's still your plan, I'm here."

The implication of his words was louder than the words themselves. He was only here because they had a common goal. If he didn't need her to save Señora Mata, he'd be long gone.

Pao was too sad and tired to unpack it all, so she just nodded in what she hoped was a grateful way. Despite everything he had said to her, she wasn't ready to leave Dante behind.

"The bus station is closed by now," Pao said, "and we'll look super suspicious sneaking back into town at night. I say we get a couple hours' rest here and then walk into Rock Creek at first light. See if we can catch a bus from there." The neighboring town was seven miles away, but hopefully no one there would recognize them.

Dante tersely nodded once, and Pao took the fact that he ignored the gaping holes in her plan as a good sign.

"You can sleep first," Pao offered, an olive branch. "I'll keep a lookout."

"Wake me up in an hour," Dante said. "I'll take over. Don't fall asleep."

"Okay," Pao said in a small voice, settling in against the quartz blocks that had once surrounded the Niños' massive campfire. She couldn't help but wonder what had happened to Marisa when the flames were doused. It was hard not to remember the grisly scene from her dream last summer, when Marisa, grieving for

Franco, had swallowed a red-hot coal in a ritual that made her the leader of Los Niños de la Luz.

Where was Marisa now?

Within minutes, Dante was snoring. Pao huddled against the chill, feeling her eyelids droop, willing herself not to fall asleep. . . .

Just an hour, she told herself, forcing her eyes open, not daring to blink until they stung and watered.

Just an hour . . .

Pao was back in the forest for the third night in a row. The glowing eyes in the trees watched her, casting a green light on the path. But this time, she wasn't alone.

Dante walked beside her, but like her father had been, he was a silhouette. From every angle he was nothing but shadow.

"Dante?" she said. There was no answer. He just walked inexorably forward, faster than Pao could keep up with, like he was absolutely sure of his destination.

"Dante, wait!"

He didn't. And soon, Pao was by herself, with nothing but the trees and their eyes for company.

"Dad?" Pao called when she'd been walking for what felt like miles with no sign of anyone. The forest around her transformed, becoming the place where she'd seen her father the other night, but still he didn't appear. "Dad, where are you? I have to talk to you!"

Nothing happened.

"Señora Mata?" Pao tried. "Are you in here?"

The wind stirred in the trees, and the light changed as if a shadow had passed in front of the sun. Goose bumps chased themselves up Pao's arms as the atmosphere became more sinister.

She broke into a run, turning left when the path forked, toward where the green glow was brighter. Through the trees, down what she assumed was the other fork, Pao thought she saw Dante, but when she called out, he didn't turn.

She was about to push through the trees and grab him, shake him, demand that he speak to her, when she saw it: a man's silhouette. Her father again. But this time he was lying on the ground.

"Dad!" She ran to him, Dante's shadow forgotten, ignoring the increased stirring in the trees, the big staring eyes growing more agitated the closer she got to her father. "I'm here! What can I do?"

A green force field surrounded him like a bubble—like the one that had literally pushed her and Dante out of the Riverside Palace last year. She pounded on it while her father lay facedown inside.

"Help me!" Pao shouted. "Someone, please!"

No one came. Around her, the paper dolls sprouted up and unfolded again, bright green against the deeper color of the foliage behind them. They began to spin.

Beyond the harsh glow they created, Pao could just make out her father finally stirring.

Paola, he said, his voice in the rustling of every tree branch. *Time is running out. Come to me, before it's too late.*

"I'm coming!" Pao said. "I'm on my way!" She wanted to ask him questions—she needed to—but the spinning sped up, and her father disappeared, and so did everything else, until the glow was the only thing Pao could see.

An enormous green spotlight, projecting her silhouette into the sky.

NINE

The Return of Everyone's Least Favorite Niña

When Pao woke, bleary-eyed, the harsh contrast of her shadow in the green light still burned into her vision, the sky was dark. And someone was yelling at her.

"I should have known it was you! Everything's quiet for months, but then you come around, and suddenly it's weird green light and dancing ghost things. . . ."

Pao looked up from the bottom of the firepit, where she was curled up among the ashes. Naomi was peering down over the border of quartz blocks, looking like she wanted to shake Pao. Or hug her. Or both.

Pao had fallen asleep after promising not to. She sat up and glanced guiltily over to where Dante lay, his back against the firepit. He was snoring. Pao blew out a breath of relief. The last thing she needed while trying to explain everything to Naomi was Dante and his Pao-is-the-source-of-all-suffering-in-the-world routine.

"The Niños are okay?" Pao asked, standing up and brushing off the ashes as best she could. She must have sleepwalked in her dream, which was new. No matter how terrifying the landscape, she'd always stayed put before.

"We're fine," Naomi said tersely, using the plural even though she appeared to be alone.

Pao decided not to mention it.

"So, are you gonna tell me what those green things are?" Naomi asked. "Do I need to be worried?"

Pao sighed, slumping against the blocks. "I don't know," she said. "I don't know what they are. They started out just in my dreams, but then . . ." Pao trailed off, not sure how much to tell Naomi. "They don't seem to do anything bad on their own," she said finally. "I was hoping you guys might know what they were."

Naomi shook her head. "Never seen anything like them," she said. "They do have that void feel to them, though, don't they?" She appraised Pao with an eyebrow arched. "What *have* you been up to the past few months, little tourist?"

"Don't," Pao mumbled. "I'm not a tourist. Not anymore."

"Then what are you doing here?" Naomi asked.

Pao glanced at Dante again, making sure he was still asleep. He stirred a little, but within seconds he stilled, his eyes closed, all the anger melted off his face.

"Hello?" Naomi asked, waving a hand in front of Pao. "Are you gonna talk, or did you just come here to gaze at your little boyfriend against a different backdrop?"

Pao felt her face flush. "He's not . . . I wasn't . . . Ugh!"

Naomi looked amused in her detached way, as if Pao were a puppy chasing her tail.

"What are *you* doing out here all alone, anyway?" Pao asked, trying to change the subject from the messy dynamic between her and Dante. "Where is everyone?"

She didn't think Naomi would let her get away with it. The amusement was suddenly gone from her face, her eyes distant.

"Gone," she said, a strange edge to her tone. "Moved on once they realized there were no more monsters. I guess there are other rifts to protect. . . ."

She looked bitter, upset, and Pao knew there was more to the story than she was letting on.

Whatever the source of the expression, Naomi shook it off quickly. "Anyway, back to you. Why are you bothering me in the middle of the night?"

Pao wasn't sure how to answer. She was still reeling from the absence of the other Niños. She'd been counting on the whole crew being here. Los Niños de la Luz. Naomi and Franco and Sal, but Marisa, especially.

Marisa would have helped her for sure. Naomi was a loose cannon. She wasn't a leader. She did what she wanted, not necessarily what was right. Pao wasn't sure the state of Dante's abuela and her own need to find her long-lost papá were going to pull at Naomi's heartstrings.

"I need to get to Oregon," Pao said when the quiet had stretched on too long. "Two fantasmas attacked us in the hospital, and Dante's abuela—who apparently used to be a Niña—is unconscious and losing her memory. I've been dreaming of a forest. . . ." Pao paused, worried again about giving too much away. "Between the dreams and what Señora Mata said before she went under, it seems like the answers are there."

"Oregon?" Naomi said, her eyebrow shooting up. "How do you know that's where the forest is?"

Pao shrugged. "Just a hunch, I guess."

"Oh, she has *hunches* now," Naomi said to the sky. "Look out, world, you're not ready for Paola the super-tourist!"

"Whatever." Pao rolled her eyes. "Can you help us get there or not?"

Naomi appraised her. "I suppose you're not going to tell me any more?"

"I suppose you're not going to tell *me* any more?"

"I suppose you're going to keep answering my questions with questions until we both die of old age?"

"Aren't you immortal?"

"Isn't it past your bedtime?"

Dante stirred again, cutting their banter short. Pao's eyes darted toward him, resting until she was satisfied with his level of unconsciousness.

"Trouble in paradise?" Naomi asked, her smirk back in place.

Pao shook her head. "He doesn't want to be here. He's . . ."

"Threatened by your connection, right?" Naomi interjected, her eyes back on the horizon. "He just wants to retreat into something easy and safe. That's so typical of her. . . ." Suddenly she seemed to remember Pao was there. "I mean *him*. Whatever."

"Why do I get the feeling we're not talking about me anymore?" Pao asked.

Naomi sighed, looking tired. There were dark circles under her eyes, and her white hair looked listless even as it glowed under the light of the moon. There was something about her stare, too—it had a mania that hinted she'd been alone too long.

"Why didn't you go with them?" Pao asked.

Naomi scoffed. "And leave all this?" As she said it, an old shopping cart with half its wheels fell over, hitting the quartz bricks of the firepit with a metallic crash.

When Pao was sure the sound hadn't woken Dante, she looked back at Naomi, her own eyebrow raised this time.

"I hate it up north," Naomi said, pulling at the frayed cuffs of her jeans. "I *like* the desert. This is our home. It's where we work. All that greenery? Actual seasons? No thanks."

Pao had learned a little something about silence since her last venture into this cactus field. Sometimes it was the quickest and most efficient way to get what you wanted.

"Fine." Naomi relented when the quiet had become unbearable. "Maybe a *small* part of me was sick of listening to Marisa defer to Franco for every little thing. Like, she's just throwing her power away. Everything she wanted and sacrificed for . . . she's just gonna hand it over to some puffed-up jerk with a savior complex? And I'm supposed to support it?"

Though she was still doing her silence-as-a-tactic thing, Pao thought privately that Naomi had a point. Pao had been there when Franco returned to the camp, and she'd watched Marisa immediately attach herself to his arm. Marisa's intimidating timeless-leader-of-Los-Niños persona had instantly slipped away as she'd settled back into his shadow.

Marisa had told Pao that she and Franco would share leadership duties. But it didn't sound like that was how it had gone.

Naomi, stewing in Pao's silence, exploded before Pao could ruminate further on what had happened here.

"I mean, it's his fault the rift got out of control in the first place!" Naomi said, getting up to pace back and forth, running her hands agitatedly through her bone-white curls. "We were here to watch the opening, protect the town. Underestimating a fantasma—even a leyenda!—just because it's a crying woman? He walked right into her trap and almost let everything get destroyed!"

"What's a leyenda?" Pao asked, but Naomi didn't seem to hear her.

"But let's not hold him accountable for being the worst leader we ever had," Naomi continued, dust flying up in the wake of her combat boots. "No, let's invite him back in! Let's let him take the lead on the most important mission in the Niños' history! Let's spend all night *giggling* with him by the fire and leave behind our . . ." She trailed off, remembering Pao was there. "Anyway, I hear non-desert humidity's a silent killer, so I stayed home."

But Pao wasn't listening anymore. She'd been so wrapped up in Naomi's story that she hadn't seen the pieces falling together until this moment.

"Wait . . ." Pao said. "They went north? For the biggest mission in Niños' history?"

Naomi stopped pacing and looked at Pao like they were in a spy movie and she'd just caught her leaking secret information.

"You know something, don't you?" Pao asked, getting to her feet and walking toward Naomi. "About why there were fantasmas chasing us at the hospital, and why I'm seeing a spooky forest in my dreams."

"I don't know why *you're* seeing anything," Naomi said. "You're a tourist who, yes, helped us out of a serious jam, but it makes no sense for *you* to know all that while *I'm* in the dark about everything."

Pao was angry now. "This isn't about you, Naomi! People's lives are at stake!" She took a deep breath, gathering herself before fixing the other girl with her most no-nonsense stare. "So I'm asking, where did the other Niños go? And what do you know about what's happening?"

Naomi met Pao's gaze with an even fiercer one of her own. Then, suddenly, she seemed to deflate. "I don't know why I'm protecting them anyway," she said. "Marisa told me not to tell anyone, but I know she's just following *his* orders. What am I afraid of, you messing it up?" She sat on the firepit wall with a tired chuckle. "Like I haven't considered sabotaging the whole thing myself, just to show her what a complete loser—"

Pao cleared her throat pointedly.

"Fine, yes," Naomi relented. "I'll tell you what I know. But I'm doing it because I *hope* you'll ruin everything. Not because I trust you. Just so we're clear."

"Whatever," Pao said. "I don't care about your motives. I just want to save Señora Mata and stop more fantasmas from attacking sick people." *And, if there's time, also find out why my dad abandoned me and who I really am,* Pao added silently.

"Yes, they're going north," Naomi said, like she was already bored by the conversation. "Franco had all this equipment, ways to track magic activity that he never showed us how to use. He can locate any rift in the world with it." She said this part with her teeth mostly clenched, like she was irritated about how impressive it sounded.

Meanwhile, Pao was getting starry-eyed about this equipment. As skeptical as she was about Franco, how cool would it be to use equipment that *tracked and measured* something everyone thought was made up?

"Anyway," Naomi said again, bringing Pao back to earth from her first space-out in ages. "Lately his readings have been going crazy. At first he thought the machines were malfunctioning, they were so high. He pinpointed the energy to a single location. Apparently there's magic collecting in one place—a place a thousand miles from the nearest rift."

"Did it start happening after we closed the void?" Pao asked.

Naomi shook her head. "That's the thing," she said. "It was weeks after. No one knows why. It's just gathering at this single point like a storm."

There was no doubt about it, Pao thought. Naomi wanted to be out there. She was, like, *longing* to be chasing this magic anomaly with her friends and fighting whatever fantasmas came along as a result.

"And this gathering point?" Pao said. "It's in Oregon, isn't it. The southern part?"

Naomi looked at Pao, straight into her eyes, like she was trying to x-ray the contents of her brain. "Yeah," she finally said. "It is. Although I can't for the life of me figure out *how* you know that."

"Me neither," said Pao, her brain already going a mile a minute. "But here we are."

This magical anomaly was centered near her dad. Pao just knew it.

She remembered how he had looked in her dream, lying there helpless, the green force field surrounding him.

Now fantasmas were chasing her in real life, and weird green things were stalking her dreams, like she was some kind of target for the creatures of the void. Had she put her father in danger, too? Was that what the nightmares had been trying to tell her?

Naomi leaned back against the blocks and looked up at the stars—so much easier to see now that there was no bonfire. After a beat, she asked, "You're gonna go after them, aren't you?"

Pao nodded. "And you're gonna stay here?"

"Where else could I go?" Naomi asked, that sad chuckle escaping her lips again. "I've been fourteen for, like, eight years. I can't drive; I can't get a job. I've basically just been freelancing around here for meals while I figure out my next move."

"Freelancing?"

"Sure, you know, ghost-hunter-for-hire-type stuff. There's plenty of work. Now that the rift is closed and there's no monsters to keep them in check, the little household spirits are running rampant. I get rid of fantasmas, collect whatever reward I can, and keep moving on."

"Sounds lonely," Pao said.

Naomi shrugged.

"You can come with me and Dante if you want," Pao said. "We could use the help."

"Pass," Naomi said witheringly.

"Yeah, I get it," Pao said. "Who wants to go through the trouble of discovering a magic anomaly and fighting new monsters when you can help kindergarteners with the duendes in their walls."

"Watch it, small fry," Naomi said.

"No, I mean it," Pao insisted, using the same super-earnest expression that had always gotten her mom off her back when she was plotting something a little shifty. "Franco's got all these lofty ideas and aspirations about saving the world? Let him have them. Someone has to be on the ground, helping the real people. Isn't that what the Niños are really about?"

Naomi didn't immediately retort, which Pao took as a good sign.

"And Marisa," she continued, noting the crease that appeared between Naomi's eyebrows at the mention. "She's always been a little too high and mighty, if you ask me. If she wants to run off with Franco, get cozy on their long trip north, fall in love or whatever, who cares, right? They deserve each other."

The crease disappeared. "Leave Marisa out of this—she's being brainwashed."

Pao raised both hands. "Totally," she said. "Franco seems to have that effect on people. But not on us. That's why we're here and she's out there, huddled in a tent with him, telling secrets and forging bonds, and—"

"When are you leaving again?" Naomi asked, glowering.

"Sorry," Pao said. "I'm just impressed. You went with your gut and didn't let yourself get sucked into that miasma of charm and chiseled jaw and piercing eyes and—"

"I know a guy in Rock Creek," Naomi said flatly. "He might be able to get you as far north as Central California. For now, catch some shut-eye. I'll keep watch the rest of the night and take you there when the sun's up, make sure no ghosts or police mess with you on the way. That's as much help as I can offer."

Pao smiled with all her teeth, hoping it looked natural. "Thank you," she said. "And hey, maybe when we're done saving Dante's abuela and getting an up-close and personal look at the magic anomaly, I can come back. Hang out and help you with"—she gestured around at the "camp," which honestly looked more like a trash heap where a feral cat lived—"all this. I really do admire your sacrifice, you know."

Naomi grunted noncommittally, but Pao saw her scan the camp with new eyes.

Pao, smirking, lay down on an abandoned sofa cushion.

Sure, Naomi thought she was taking them as far as Rock Creek, but if Pao had laid the groundwork right, the older girl would be along for much more than the first seven miles.

This time, when Pao drifted off to sleep, no ghosts followed her.

Little did she know what the next day would bring.

TEN

Close Encounters and Chorizo Burritos

Pao opened her eyes to the sight of Dante, his hair wild, springing to his feet with his club drawn. He'd apparently just discovered someone in their midst.

Naomi lounged against the firepit laughing her head off. "Stand down, hero boy," she said. "You really expect to hit anything swinging wide like that?" She stood up and jabbed beneath his too-extended arm. Dante pulled the club in, his eyebrows knitting together in a scowl to rival any of Naomi's.

Pao wanted to tease him, too, remembering their fighting lessons last summer, the way Naomi had gone mercilessly for Dante's weak points until he was angry and reckless. But she didn't. The last thing she wanted was for him to explode again.

Even if he didn't like her very much right now, they still had to work together.

Dante turned to Pao, and she was ready with a smile that said, *Let's bury the hatchet before a fantasma buries one in us.*

"What's going on?" he asked. "What's she doing here?"

"I'm right in front of you," Naomi said, the playfulness gone from her tone. "And I live here, so if you want my help, don't be a jerk."

"I don't," Dante said, whirling on Naomi. "We have this under control. Thanks anyway."

Pao thought *under control* was a bit of an overstatement, but she decided to keep her opinion to herself.

"Naomi showed up while you were asleep," Pao explained in her gentlest tone. "The other Niños are gone, but after I told her we're trying to save your abuela, she agreed to help us find a ride north."

If Naomi was surprised that Pao didn't give Dante all the details about Franco and the Niños and the anomaly, she didn't show it.

"Why are you so interested in helping?" Dante asked Naomi. "You know we're not doing any more suicidal favors for you, right? Because we're not."

"I haven't asked you to do anything," said Naomi, bristling, and Pao watched her plan begin to unravel as their egos circled each other, hackles up.

"Not yet," Dante said. "But face it, help without strings attached isn't exactly the Niños' style."

Pao hadn't expected this tension between the two of them. Last summer, Dante had wanted nothing more than to be a Niño de la Luz, and his unbridled admiration for Naomi had annoyed Pao endlessly.

But, Pao recalled now, that had been before the pair had gone off on a mission together. One that ended in Dante being abducted by ahogados.

Naomi glared daggers at Dante. "I'm not part of Los Niños de la Luz anymore," she said. "And even when I was, you didn't know anything about me."

"You let me be taken," Dante said in a low voice, and as much as Pao wanted to interrupt, to stop this interaction from wrecking her plan, she couldn't. She had never heard Dante talk about what happened. He'd resisted every time Pao had tried to bring it up.

"We were outnumbered," Naomi said. "I did the best I could."

"You didn't need me," Dante continued, as if she hadn't answered. "Just the club. As soon as I'd done what you needed—driven the ahogados toward camp—you turned your back."

He took a step toward her, and for a terrible moment, Pao thought he might hit her. Instead, he dropped his voice even lower and said, "I believed in you—your 'community' or whatever—but it was all conditional, and it almost got me killed. I won't let that happen again."

Pao privately felt that *any* help was the kind they needed right now, but he had said *we* and she needed him on her side, so she stayed quiet. Best to keep the boat still for now.

"We had an objective," Naomi said, shrugging. "We were trying to stay alive."

"No matter the cost," Dante said, and finally he unfolded his arms.

"Look, I'm gonna do a lap, make sure everything's secure *in case* I'm leaving." Naomi's eyes darted to Pao, who tried to form a facial expression that simultaneously meant *Don't worry, the plan is still on* and *Don't tell him anything more* and also *Please don't change your mind about helping us just because my friend is kind of a jerk now.*

From Naomi's eye roll, Pao guessed she'd only succeeded halfway.

When Pao and Dante were alone, she turned to him, still

feeling the sting of everything he'd said last night, the ache in her chest that sat right in the place where their friendship once had.

But they didn't have time to talk it through. The Niños were moving north. Pao's mom had probably mobilized the whole town looking for her by now. Señora Mata was barely holding on. . . .

And, somewhere, Pao's dad might be in danger, as magic gathered all around him. She had to reach him in time to get the answer she needed to help Señora Mata. Not to mention some answers of her own.

"What does she want from us?" Dante asked the moment Naomi was out of earshot. "I don't buy this new *I quit the Niños and just want to help* thing. Especially not from her."

"I may have tried to convince her that going north to find the other Niños was in her best interest?" Pao said in a wannabe-lighthearted voice, knowing that Dante wouldn't like it no matter what tone she used. "She hasn't agreed, but she did get annoyed enough to offer a ride from her friend just to get rid of me, so that's something."

Dante was looking at her with disbelief. "You actually *want* her to come with us, don't you?" he asked. "On some return-the-lost-Niña mission. You told me this was about helping my abuela, Pao. Not about playing hero again because you're mad that your mom got a boyfriend."

Today, Pao's mantra about Dante hurting her because he was hurt didn't seem to be working. She felt the place behind her eyes get hot, a sure sign she was about to cry.

Dante seemed to struggle with something for several silent seconds before he finally said, "I'm sorry, okay? That was a low blow. I'm just worried, and I don't want to get derailed by being pawns for these guys again."

It was the most Dante thing he'd said in a long time, and Pao fought the urge to spring forward and hug him. She didn't question where all his resentment from last night had gone, or what had made him apologize. She was just glad he was acting like her friend again.

"I get it," she said. "I'm worried, too. And it's not about the Niños, okay? I promise. They're tracking a magical anomaly thing up north with some instruments of Franco's. Naomi is a means to an end. And the end is saving your abuela and stopping whatever's happening here for good."

Dante just looked at her like he was seeing her for the first time. The silence was unnerving.

"I mean, we're two thirteen-year-old kids, who have *definitely* been reported missing by now, trying to travel over a thousand miles," Pao said as logically as she could. "I was hoping Marisa and Franco would be here and one of them would have a magic door we could step through and pop out right where we needed to be. But they're not, and that door probably doesn't exist, and it would definitely be easier to get to Oregon with Naomi's help than on our own."

He was quiet for another long minute, and then he smiled, a forced thing that didn't quite reach his eyes. But it was something. "Okay," Dante said, stuffing the now chancla-shaped weapon back in his pocket. "I trust you."

Pao's heart soared.

The walk into Rock Creek was long and quiet.

Naomi and Dante wouldn't meet each other's eyes. Pao walked between them like a buffer, but she couldn't figure out what to say. She had planned to use this time to convince Naomi to come north with them, but she didn't know how to do that and keep Dante on board at the same time.

Unfortunately, the two-hour-twenty-minute walk was over before she could get a handle on her warring loyalties.

"The garage doesn't open for another hour," Naomi said. "We'll have to lie low until then."

"I'm starving," Pao blurted before she could help herself, and out of the corner of her eye she saw Dante nod before he used that strange half smile on her again.

"Breakfast burritos it is," Naomi said, and she steered them left onto a long dusty road heading into town.

Seated in a sticky vinyl booth with a tall strawberry-banana agua fresca in front of her, Pao came back to life a little.

They'd bought three pairs of big cheap sunglasses from the dollar rack with Pao's money, which Naomi said made them look more conspicuous, not less. But they made Pao feel better. The glasses, combined with Naomi's eye-catching silver hair, made it so no one would look at Pao and Dante for too long.

While they waited for their food, Pao turned on her phone for the first time since last night. She knew she'd have to make her call quick to prevent her mom from tracking her, but an update from Emma about Señora Mata might make this first part of the trip go more smoothly.

The phone rang twice before Emma picked up. "Sorry, Mom!" she said on the other end. "It's Alex asking about the posters for the rally. I have to tell them I can't make it!"

Pao waited until she heard a door close on Emma's end. "You there, Emma?"

"Yep! But if anyone asks, you're a Rainbow Rogue named Alex

who loves metalworking and dumpster diving and abhors the gender binary."

"That's me all right," Pao said, cracking a smile for what felt like the first time all day. "What's up on your end?"

"I'm keeping it together," Emma said in a half whisper. "Your mom called, like, five times this morning, but I think I convinced her that I'm hiding you in my room."

"How'd you manage that?" Pao asked.

" 'Nooo, Ms. Santiago,' " Emma said, and Pao could just picture her eyes going big and round for her innocent act. " 'I haven't seen Pao once since earl—I mean yesterday! I'm sure she's fine *wherever* she is, but it's definitely not here *at all*!' "

Pao was laughing in earnest now. "That was so bad," she said.

"That's the point," Emma said, laughing, too.

Pao had to admit she'd missed Emma's ability to make her smile no matter how dire the circumstances.

"So you don't think she suspects I've left town?" Pao asked, ignoring Dante's eyes on her.

"Nah. My guess is she just thinks you're mad at her and you need to cool down for a few days."

"Good," Pao said. "How's Señora Mata?"

"I'm on my way to the hospital now," Emma said. "I stayed pretty late yesterday. They had to move her to another floor because of the damage the ghosts caused, but there's been no change in her, for better or worse."

"Okay, thanks," Pao said. "What did they say about the fantasma attack? Are there tabloid reporters filming for alien activity yet?"

Emma paused for a long time. "Um, actually . . . they're calling them drug addicts from the other side of town. They claimed they broke in looking for pills."

Pao rolled her eyes. "Of *course* they did. These people see literal ghosts and change the story to blame poor people within twenty minutes. Unbelievable."

"Disgraceful," Emma said. "I mean, nonwhite people are accused of drug offenses at a staggeringly high—"

"Emma?" Pao said, sensing another Rainbow Rogues' lunchtime webinar coming on. "I gotta go before my mom sics her Find My iPhone on me. Text me when you see Señora Mata, okay? I'll check in again as soon as I can."

"You got it!" Emma said. "Happy to be your guy in the chair!"

"I don't know what that means," Pao said.

"Byeeee!"

The line went dead.

"She's on her way to see your grandma," Pao said to Dante, bracing herself for a cutting comment. "Said she was moved to another room but she hasn't gotten any worse."

They both knew that was just a nice way of saying she hadn't gotten better, but Dante's face remained strangely blank.

"Thanks," he said, and that was all.

Pao's phone rang, and she realized she hadn't turned it off. She pressed the power button hard, relieved when the little apple glowed briefly on the screen and then disappeared.

Not enough time to trace her, and she was sure this taquería didn't have Wi-Fi anyway.

"So, who's your friend?" Pao asked Naomi to break the awkward silence. "The one giving us a ride."

"The one I'm going to *ask* to give you a ride," Naomi corrected.

"No guarantees. His name's Johnny. He works in his dad's garage and makes regular trips up to Fresno for . . . car stuff."

Pao glanced at Dante, wondering if he'd have a problem with this, and sure enough, his jaw tightened and his eyes closed for a brief moment. But he didn't say a word.

"He owes me a favor," Naomi continued, oblivious to Dante's discomfort. "A few months back, there was a particularly nasty fantasma in his parents' well, and I got rid of her for them. He said if I ever needed anything to just ask."

"Cool," Pao said, trying to sound casual, like mechanics often owed her favors as well. "How'd you get rid of the fantasma?"

Naomi waved off the question, as if it had been easy. "Most of the ones tied to a specific place are just trying to wrap something up. They're attached to an object, or bitter about a wrong that was done to them in that location. It's just about tracking down that source, cutting the cord that's tethering them to the world of the living, and setting them free."

Pao thought about this as their food arrived at last—three of those massive chorizo-and-egg burritos that only hole-in-the-wall taquerías did right. She inhaled hers in record time, as much out of urgency to leave as of hunger.

Still, Dante finished first.

"I'm gonna go wash up," Pao said when it became clear she couldn't just lick off the red-tinted grease on her fingers. "Then we head out?"

"Garage opens in twenty," Naomi said, "but he'll be there by now. Probably better to get him before there are customers anyway."

"Be right back," Pao said, and she slipped into the yellow-tiled bathroom.

She'd been washing her hands for a few seconds, closing her eyes as the warm water and her full stomach reminded her she'd barely slept in two days, when the stall behind her opened and a breathtakingly beautiful woman exited.

Pao did a double take. She was sure that the stall had been open and empty before, but again, lack of sleep. She must not have been paying close attention.

And yet she felt that weird prickle on the back of her neck.

The woman smiled a little sheepishly, then stepped up to the sink beside Pao.

Her skin was a light, luminous brown, her eyes huge and so dark they drew your gaze whether they were turned on you or not. Her black hair hung in perfect waves nearly to her elbows. It was movie-star hair, Pao thought. The kind that always made Emma say it must be extensions before Pao went on her tirade about beauty standards again.

For once, the memory didn't make her sad.

"I love the food here," the woman said in a lightly accented voice. It was like honey, or the smell of the dark liquor Pao had seen her mom pour over ice at her job. "Whenever I'm passing through, this is the first place I stop."

Pao smiled, still rinsing her hands, even though they were no longer soapy. Why was she doing that? she asked herself, but she didn't stop. "I just had a burrito," she said. "Chorizo. It's my first time here, but it was excellent."

"So messy, though," the woman said, laughing a lilting laugh and holding up her perfectly immaculate hands as if making some sort of point. The sleeves of her bright-red dress went down to her wrists, but they were perfectly dry.

"Totally," Pao agreed, not altogether sure anymore what she

was agreeing to. "Where are you headed?" This question seemed very important, and she dried her hands slowly and carefully while waiting for an answer.

"North," the woman said a little wistfully. "Always north."

"We're heading north, too," Pao said eagerly. "My friends and I. We're just filling up first."

The woman's eyes sparkled. "What a happy coincidence."

Pao nodded so hard her head felt a little swimmy afterward. She was supposed to be somewhere, wasn't she? It seemed important, but she couldn't remember.

"Maybe I could trouble you for some help," the woman said, leaning a little closer to Pao, who had made no move to dispose of her paper towel. "You see, I'm going north to help my sick amá, but my husband, well . . ." She pursed her lips like she wanted to say more but couldn't.

"What?" Pao asked, leaning forward herself.

"He doesn't get along with Amá," she said, her sadness like dark molasses in a glass jar. "We argued. He . . . went home without me. To the south. Now I must spend the last of my money on a bus ticket instead of buying her the medicine she desperately needs. Unless . . ."

That was a travesty, Pao thought, furious at the man's heartlessness. She had to help. She *would* help. Only . . .

"I don't have a car," Pao said mournfully. "My friend, she's . . . We're going to ask someone to give us a ride as a favor. I wish I could help."

Even when the woman's face fell, she still looked beautiful. "I truly believe you would." She touched Pao's cheek like a mother might, her hand cold and impossibly soft.

Then she bared her teeth and lunged.

Pao jumped backward just in time, flattening herself against the cold tile of the bathroom wall as the woman's gorgeous features turned feral, her long red nails swiping dangerously close to Pao's eyeballs.

"What is this?" Pao asked, holding up her hands to ward off the woman's attacks.

A snarl escaped the woman's lips. She stepped forward, closing the distance between herself and Pao in a single step, her eyes wide like a predator about to overtake her prey.

Pao's mind was still hazy and muddled, a paper towel balled in her fist. She needed to do something, she knew—draw a weapon, push past the woman, run, at the very least.

But before Pao could pull her knife, the woman was upon her, fingernails glinting in the fluorescent light of the bathroom, and Pao was too confused, too confined to stop her. *I'm going to be slashed to ribbons right here in this bathroom with my friends right outside, and—*

The woman's razor-sharp talons stopped a centimeter from Pao's face. Her expression was conflicted, flickering between human and monster. Pao watched, frozen, hardly daring to hope.

After an endless moment, the woman's mouth moved grotesquely, like she was one of those ventriloquist puppets come to life. *"Come to me, Paola,"* she said, her eyes turning from brown to glowing green as if a switch had been flipped.

Pao didn't get a chance to ask what she meant, or react at all, really. The green eyes flicked back to brown, and the woman—now human again—brushed her dress casually, fluffing her hair and reaching across Pao (who flinched) to take a paper towel for her hands.

"Thank you, sweet child. Travel safely."

"I will," Pao said slowly, shaking her head to clear it. She was sure something had just happened—something terrifying. Her racing heart was proof.

But all she remembered was washing her hands.

The bathroom door closed like someone had just exited. But hadn't the place been empty before? Pao was alone now, looking at her hands, feeling like her head was full of cotton balls. She'd washed her hands for so long, her fingertips were wrinkled. Why had she done that?

"What, did you fall in?" Dante asked, cracking half a smile. Clearly the food had improved his mood, Pao thought, but she couldn't smile back. She still had the distinct feeling she was forgetting something. Something important.

"Sauce on my shirt," Pao said vaguely, not knowing how to explain the rest.

He shrugged and turned away, but Naomi's eyes lingered a little longer on Pao's, like she knew something was up.

"You good, pipsqueak?" Naomi asked as Dante made his way to the front to buy hot dog gummies for the road.

"Yeah," Pao said. "There was someone in the bathroom . . . a woman. But I can't remember. . . ."

"Very specific," Naomi said, raising an eyebrow, waiting for more.

Pao didn't elaborate.

On the way out the door, on top of a glass case filled with phone cards, photos of the store from the fifties, and dusty boxes of papaya chicle, there was a small altar. In the center was a portrait in a white lace frame.

The subject was a strikingly beautiful woman, her dark eyes drawing Pao's even through the glass. QUERIDA ELENITA was embroidered in blue across the top of the frame, along with a birth date and a death date some fifteen years ago.

"You coming?" Dante called from the door, which was standing open, letting in the brisk morning air.

"Yeah," Pao said again, pulling her eyes away from the portrait at last.

She had never spent any time in Rock Creek, she thought as she stepped out into the bright sunlight. She certainly didn't know an Elenita. . . .

So then why did the woman in the frame look so familiar?

ELEVEN

Transporting Minors Across State Lines and Other Ways to Impress Girls

Juan & Sons Auto Repair was one of those tiny cluttered shops that looked like it had gotten messy in the seventies and no one had moved a thing since.

Not even the weird cymbal-banging windup monkey on the top shelf growing cobwebs from its ears. Pao stared at it for a beat too long—its eyes were following her, she was sure of it.

Either that, or she was still jumpy from . . . whatever that had been at the taquería.

Naomi took point, warning them under her breath not to speak unless she gave them express permission. Pao hid a smile. It was almost like old times, Naomi being embarrassed by them.

Pao slid her eyes over to Dante to see if he remembered, too, but he wasn't looking at her. She tried not to feel too disappointed.

The garage was empty except for an old red car that was super shiny, every edge rounded. Pao didn't know the first thing about cars, but Dante seemed impressed.

"Karmann Ghia?" he asked, circling it.

A lanky guy slid out from under the car, sneakers first, a red bandanna over his nose and mouth and a greasy wrench in his hand. He was lying on one of those wheeled boards they let you play with in elementary school gym class when the teacher has run out of other tortures for the day.

"That's right," the guy said, pulling off his bandanna and wiping his sweaty brow with it.

"Sixty-four?" Dante guessed.

Pao was shocked. What did Dante know about cars? He had lived his whole life in an apartment with a little old lady who rode the bus.

"Sixty-*five*," the guy answered with grudging respect in his tone. "Good guess, though. They're practically identical in every way. Not sure even I could tell the difference."

Dante grinned at the compliment. "She's pretty cherry."

"Yeah, the guy who owns it is a collector. He brings 'em here for tune-ups, because he likes to tell us we did it wrong." He smiled, a lopsided thing, and stuck out his hand. "I'm Johnny."

"Dante."

Johnny tied the bandanna around his forehead, holding back long curtains of glossy black hair. His face was halfway between a boy's and a man's, with a few proud hairs clinging to his upper lip. His smile was bright against his deep-brown skin. He wore blue jeans and a white T-shirt with a leather vest over it. "What can I do for you, hermanito?"

"Uh . . ." Dante said, but Naomi stepped around the car and into view.

"Hey, Johnny," she said, and immediately the man-boy's face flushed red, his hands jamming into his pockets.

"Naomi," he said, trying and failing to hitch his cool back into place. "What's up? Haven't seen you around in a . . ." He got stuck between *while* and *minute*, and what came out sounded like *whimmit*.

Naomi chuckled and shook her head before stepping forward to bump fists with Johnny—who promptly dropped his wrench. When he stooped to pick it up, Pao saw that his vest was engraved with a vulture skull on the back.

"Sorry," he mumbled, his flush creeping down to his neck. "What brings you to Rock Creek?"

"I need a favor," she said, just like that, and Johnny started nodding like a bobblehead.

"Yeah, anything!"

"These friends of mine need to make a trip north. Far as you can get them."

Pao was pretty sure the vulture skull on Johnny's vest made him part of a local motorcycle gang, but she didn't dare say anything. Any ride was better than none.

"I got a transport going to Fresno on Thursday," he said eagerly. "I'll have a brother with me, but I'm sure I can get them on board after what you did for my folks."

Pao started to panic. Thursday? It was only Monday. If they had to hang around Rock Creek for another three days, they'd get caught for sure. Emma could only hold off Pao's mom with her faux bad acting for so long.

If they lingered here, they'd end up back home, where Pao's mom would keep her locked up forever after two disappearances in one year. Señora Mata might not recover. And Pao would never find out what this magic anomaly had to do with her dad, or why he had left, or if there was something special about her, anything at all.

"We can't wait until Thursday," Pao said firmly, and Johnny's eyes darted to her for the first time. Pao knew the look well—she was too young to be of interest to him.

He was already shrugging that *nothing I can do* shrug when Naomi chimed in.

"Yeah, sorry, that's not gonna work," she said. "They need out of here today."

"Today?" Johnny gulped, his protruding Adam's apple bobbing up and down almost comically. "I don't know if I can make today happen, Naomi. Not even for you. The . . . car parts won't even be ready for another two days."

Pao's eyes darted between them. From the shifty look in Johnny's eyes and the understanding in Naomi's, she was pretty sure they weren't talking about actual car parts. Or, if they were, the parts hadn't been obtained legally.

Any ride is better than no ride, Pao repeated firmly to herself, physically biting her tongue to keep from commenting on the transaction occurring in front of her. She'd just have to hope the ride didn't end with the cops pulling them over.

Pao hadn't historically had the best luck with police. And she doubted anyone in this group had fared any better.

"Well, maybe," Naomi said with a gleam in her eye, "you make an unscheduled road trip?" She looked at the shiny red car pointedly.

For a change, Dante cracked a smile that didn't look forced—probably at the prospect of cruising north in this thing.

"This car?" Johnny asked, his eyes bugging out now. "Naomi, they will seriously kill me! Everyone. My pops, the hermanos, the guy who owns this car, *everyone.*"

"Or," Naomi said, her warmer-than-usual demeanor cooling considerably, "maybe the next time a fantasma's haunting your home and you're unprotected, *that* will kill you instead." She straightened her shoulders and jerked her head toward the exit. "Come on, guys. We'll find you another ride."

Pao had her doubts about walking out in the open only a few miles from where her mom was *definitely* looking for her by now, but she knew better than to argue with Naomi when she got that steely look on her face. Pao, along with Dante, pivoted to follow her out, not knowing what they'd possibly do now. Wild thoughts of stowing away in the cargo area of a Greyhound bus swirled around in her head until—

"Wait!"

Johnny caught up with them just before they exited the garage.

Naomi stopped, but she didn't turn around. She just waited.

"He won't be back to pick up the car until tomorrow," he said breathlessly, digging the keys out of his pocket and simultaneously sending a shower of candy wrappers and receipts fluttering to the cement floor.

Naomi turned just a little.

"Maybe I take her for a test drive?" Johnny offered.

"I'm listening," Naomi said.

"Maybe I get a flat tire and get stranded with no cell service until tomorrow?"

"That would be a shame," Naomi said slowly, spinning around the rest of the way to face Johnny, who had that dopey puppy-dog smile on his face again.

"Yeah," he said, looking a little hypnotized. "Listen, as long as your friends aren't, like, fugitives or runaways or anything, it should be no problem getting them to Fresno."

"Oh, they're probably both by now," Naomi said offhandedly. "Or, if not yet, they will be in a few hours."

Johnny smiled uncertainly, like he thought Naomi might be joking.

She didn't smile back.

Within thirty minutes, Johnny was in the driver's seat of the Ghia, Dante beside him in the passenger seat, and Pao stretched out lengthwise in the back. In an effort to keep the shaky new peace between them, Pao had allowed Dante to take shotgun.

Well, it was also because she had absolutely nothing to talk to Johnny of Juan & Sons Auto Repair about for the eight hours and thirty minutes he estimated it would take them to get to Fresno, and she was sure he didn't want to get stuck talking to her, either.

Instead, Pao figured she'd spend the trip trying to figure out what the heck they were going to do once they got to the end of the Johnny's stolen-car express line. By her calculations (done on her phone, which she briefly turned on to use the map), the town where her dad's PO box was located was another eight hours north of Fresno.

There was no way Johnny was going to take them the whole way, no matter how big a crush he had on Naomi. They'd be in an unfamiliar city, alone and at odds, with only one night to figure out how to get back on the road north.

Pao had never even been to California. There were beaches there, right? That was pretty much all she knew.

Maybe Dante would win over Johnny with his random-but-convenient knowledge of cars by the time they got there, and he'd be willing to help them find somewhere to crash. Or buy them bus tickets? Usually Pao liked things to be a little more locked down, but she had the next six hundred miles to come up with a plan.

Well, she'd done more with less time, that was for sure.

As Johnny started the engine, Naomi leaned down to the window to say good-bye. Pao met her eyes reluctantly.

She'd been hoping Naomi would change her mind, realize that she belonged with the Niños, and come along. Pao's pointed comments about Marisa falling even more "in like" with Franco were supposed to have galvanized her.

Unfortunately, it hadn't worked like that.

"Be safe, kid," Naomi said, her brown eyes standing out more than usual against her silver hair. "You'll be okay." She went for a sort of side-five-slash-handshake, and when Pao reached out awkwardly to join in, Naomi slid a twenty-dollar bill into her palm, a move so smooth it reminded Pao of a magician who had performed at Ryan James's sixth birthday party.

That clown had been creepy, but Naomi was as cool as ever.

"It's not much," Naomi said, "but it's what I've got."

"Thanks," Pao said, her mind racing. She wanted to step out and beg Naomi to come with them, but she knew nothing so blatantly vulnerable would ever work on a girl who'd left her entire biological family, and after that her chosen family, just because the vibe hadn't felt right.

Pao's mom would have said something like *She's such a Sagittarius,* but Pao didn't know when Naomi's birthday was, so she couldn't blame it on astrology.

Instead, Pao slid the money into her pocket and said, "Hey, if

I see Marisa on my way north, I'll tell her you say hi. Anything else you want me to pass along? To her or Franco? Or I guess both of them, since they're sort of joined at the hip now, right?"

A pang of something (annoyance? jealousy? real pain?) crossed Naomi's face, but it disappeared so fast, Pao was almost sure she'd imagined it.

"I said what I needed to before she left," Naomi replied. "She didn't want to hear it."

"Man," Pao said, "I guess we've both changed. I keep secrets now, and you . . . give up? Who woulda thought."

"I did not—" Naomi began, but Pao tapped the back of Johnny's seat.

"We better get a move on," she said as Dante turned the dial on the radio, trying to find a station that wasn't half static or a radio evangelist. (*Radiovangelist?* Pao wondered. What *were* those guys called?)

"Sure thing, pipsqueak!" Johnny said, and Pao bristled.

Any ride is better than no ride, any ride is better than no ride.

"Later, Naomi," he said, looking up at her through his dark eyelashes. "Maybe when I get back we can—"

"Just get them there safe," she said, smirking affectionately. "And call me if you run into any more fantasmas, yeah?"

"Sure thing," Johnny said.

Naomi gave Dante a terse nod, which he barely returned, and then the car was in gear, backing out of the garage and into the street. Pao watched out the rear window as Naomi got smaller and smaller, evidence that the first *two* plans she'd come up with had failed spectacularly. She was wondering what that meant for the rest of the journey, when suddenly . . .

Naomi stopped getting smaller.

In fact, she was getting bigger now, waving her arms to stop Johnny. He slammed on the brakes as she approached Dante's window, panting.

"Get in the back, hero boy," she said, shooting a half grin back at Pao.

"What?" Dante asked, clearly offended.

"I'm coming with you. Let me in."

Despite Dante's grumbling, Pao's heart was growing like the Grinch's. She'd only seen the movie once, at Emma's, but Pao remembered the image so clearly. The tiny shriveled heart expanding until it burst out of its frame.

Her plan had worked! She wasn't useless, and Naomi was coming with them, and everything was going right again. Okay, it was only one thing, but still . . .

Dante squeezed himself into the back seat beside Pao, staying as close to the window as he could and not looking at her directly, but also not saying anything mean, which she figured was a start.

Naomi settled in the front and changed the radio station.

Johnny said something cheesy about being happy to have her aboard.

Naomi ignored him, turning around to look at Pao. "I don't give up," she said. "That much hasn't changed."

Pao grinned. "Glad to hear it."

Naomi smiled back, showing her canines. "I want my twenty dollars back."

TWELVE

Are We There Yet?

Riding in the Karmann Ghia was deeply cool for the first, like, thirty miles.

After that, Pao started to notice how much the car rattled at high speeds. Pao knew a little about mechanics from the summer she was ten, when, after realizing she'd never get her hands on a real rocket engine, she started talking to a downstairs neighbor who was always working on his pickup in the parking lot.

Cars, rockets . . . it was all combustion, and she'd figured some knowledge was always better than none.

She hoped this rattle was from misaligned tires, or just minor body damage that was causing friction at high speeds. The alternatives—improper fuel octane or ignition timing, an overheating engine—were much more likely to derail this little trip before it truly got under way.

Pao tried to focus on anything other than the rattling and the fact that sometimes Johnny laughed nervously as he cajoled the car from one gear to the next. Or how little room there was in the back, and how difficult it was, with Dante lost in thought beside her, to avoid even an unintentional elbow bump.

Had they really been holding hands just a few months ago?

Pao couldn't help but compare the way they were now to the way they'd been last summer. Sure, they'd bickered then, and bantered, and flat-out disagreed sometimes. But she'd never *really* wondered whether he was on her side.

Not until lately.

Regardless, he wasn't talking, and it was too loud in the car to chat with Naomi—Johnny insisted on keeping the windows rolled down because he didn't want the car to "smell like people" when he gave it back to the owner. So Pao spent her time staring out the window.

The trouble was, there wasn't much to look at besides the flat landscape of Arizona turning into the flat landscape of eastern California. The most interesting thing Pao saw in the first fifty miles was a hitchhiker.

But the hitchhiker *was* pretty interesting. Pao had to give him that.

He was middle-aged and tall, with broad shoulders. He looked a little like the silhouette of Pao's dad from her dream. That was the only reason she noticed him. Well, that and the fact that his pants and sweater were both bright red.

Pao got the strangest feeling as they approached the exit ramp where he was standing, his thumb out in the universal sign for *I need a ride*. He wasn't the first person she'd seen wearing all red today. But she couldn't remember who that first person had been. . . .

They pulled even with the man, the car's engine chugging strangely. Johnny jiggled the gear shift helplessly as they lost speed, allowing Pao to make eye contact with the hitchhiker. He was staring right at her.

After the red outfit, the first thing she noticed was his hair—long and dark, shot through with silver. He had it pulled back in a ponytail to expose high cheekbones and the deepest, most beautiful brown eyes Pao had ever seen.

She was a little mesmerized. This man was everything she had imagined as a child when she'd dreamed of her father. A tall, handsome, distinguished-looking man who would never tire of her questions, who would share her experiments . . .

When the hitchhiker smiled at her, Pao forgot the purpose of her mission. Señora Mata. The magic anomaly. Even her real father, and her multiple reasons for wanting to go north. All she could think about was picking him up.

"We should stop," she said quietly. And then louder, "We should stop!"

The engine caught, Johnny whooping in victory as the car shot forward, leaving the man in its dust.

"What were you saying, Pao?" Johnny asked as they reached highway speed once again.

Pao's brain felt fuzzy. She didn't know what Johnny was talking about. "What?" she asked, shaking her head like there was water in her ears.

"You were saying something," Johnny persisted. "When I was trying to get the car in gear. Did you want to stop for a snack break or something?"

Pao's cheeks heated up in embarrassment—and not just because Johnny insisted on talking to her like she was about eight. Pao didn't know if or why she'd said whatever Johnny thought she said, but she felt everyone's eyes on her, expecting an answer.

"Yeah, uh, just because the car was acting up. Good job making it . . . work again." Pao smiled feebly.

Johnny shrugged, apparently satisfied with (or at least bored by) her weak explanation. Dante's eyes, however, stayed on her a little longer.

It was Pao's turn to avoid eye contact now. She looked back out the window.

Two miles later, she saw a cross posted beside the road, with roses piled underneath it. QUERIDO ALÁN, it said in blue script. They were moving too fast for her to read the birth and death dates.

Goose bumps erupted along Pao's arms, and she didn't know why. Was it because they'd been so close to engine failure on this same stretch of road? The fact that it could have been their names on the cross?

Or maybe she was just understandably wary of dead people after her brush with the fantasmas at the hospital.

Either way, she decided to stop looking out the window for now.

Eavesdropping, unfortunately, didn't prove much more interesting. Dante was as silent as ever, his jaw tightening more and more the farther they got past the California border, like there was something in Fresno he was absolutely dreading.

Which made no sense, Pao thought, frustrated. From what she knew about Dante (which was a lot, she liked to think), he'd never been to California, either.

Knowing it was a risk but feeling strange and off-balance after her brief memory lapse earlier, Pao took out her phone and turned it on.

Immediately, three notification windows popped up. Another

twelve missed calls from her mom, and a couple of texts from Emma.

Pao dismissed the missed-call alerts and went straight to the texts.

Status update, the first one read. *Señora Mata's situation hasn't changed. They're chalking up the weird readings from the brain activity machine to a malfunction or rare complication. At my insistence, they've called in some fancy specialist from Seattle and are borrowing a different brain scanning machine from a hospital out of state. Both will take a few days to get here, but HURRY!*

Twelve minutes later, she'd sent another:

Status update two: Hospitals are dead boring. Almost makes you wish a ghost would show up. She'd added a winking emoji, followed by a ghost sticking out its tongue.

Pao laughed a little, drawing Dante's eyes.

"Your abuela's okay," Pao said, quietly enough to be heard only by Dante but loudly enough to carry over the engine and freeway noise. "Emma got the doctors to call in a specialist to stall for time."

"Great," Dante said, and Pao couldn't tell if he was being sarcastic or sincere.

As if he'd heard the thought, he turned to her, his eyes open wide, his mouth sitting funny on his face, like he hadn't decided whether or not to tell her something.

Pao waited, hating the fact that she was holding her breath.

Finally, he said, "Thanks for checking on her," and looked back out the window.

Pao let out her breath, feeling her whole body deflate along with her lungs.

Her phone buzzed. Another message from Emma, sent just now.

How's the quest? Dante over his grumpy mood yet? She added a GIF from the movie *Inside Out*—the angry red guy with his head on fire.

Pao smiled, but it faded almost immediately. *Not sure,* she replied. *Things are weird between us. We got a ride to a sort of halfway point. The driver is annoying and the music sucks, but it could be worse.*

Emma sent a sad-face emoji. *You guys will make up,* she said. *You always do.*

It's different this time, Pao sent back. *He's different. I don't know what to do.*

I thought it was good? Emma asked. *You guys seemed so cozy when we got back from everything this summer. I just figured you were an *item* now.*

Pao cringed at the word *item*. Probably not a good sign. *Not at all,* she typed quickly, hitting Send and immediately beginning another message. A long one. *I thought so, too, kind of, at first anyway. But he's been distant and weird all year. We were probably better as friends? I don't know if I'm even ready for anything else. Maybe I'm just scared.*

She had never admitted that to anyone before. Something about the lull of the car noise, the impersonal background of the text thread, and the fact that it was Emma on the other end made it easier to be honest.

Feeling reckless, and a little brave, she hit Send again.

This time, the three dots that meant Emma was typing appeared, disappeared, and appeared again twice. Pao was about to revise her opinion about how easy being honest was when the message finally came through.

You were all alone, she wrote. *I had no idea. I'm sorry.*

It was Pao's turn to type and delete and type again.

It wasn't your fault, she answered finally. *I just never wanted to get in the way of you being happy.*

I'm happy with you, Emma wrote back immediately, and this time, Pao's smile lingered. She double tapped the message until the little heart appeared and hit it.

I gotta get offline, Pao wrote reluctantly. *Mom's probably gonna call again any second. Check in soon?*

You got this, Emma replied. *I'll be here whenever you need me.*

As long as I'm an eighth-grader named Alex who likes eating out of the trash.

Emma sent three laugh/cry emojis, and Pao reluctantly turned off the phone again. With Dante still gazing stonily out the window, Pao couldn't help but wish it was her *other* best friend in this car with her, even if said best friend didn't have a magical ghost-smashing club.

THIRTEEN
Enough Spit to Vaporize a Demon Dog

Three hours into the trip, the only change was that the little mountains had become kind of medium-size mountains.

Pao was hungry and tired, and she had to pee. Were they ever going to stop?

She was about to ask when a blessed blue sign appeared:

REST AREA—2 MILES

Pao would just have to hope they had a vending machine or something, because they couldn't risk going into a town for food. Not when they were barely out of Arizona and Pao's mom had undoubtedly alerted the authorities by now.

The rest area consisted of two bathroom buildings (*gendered again, ugh*, Pao thought), a bright-red awning over some picnic tables, and a little grassy area where dogs could do their business. Pao found herself missing Bruto terribly. Even picking up his monster-size demon-dog turds would have been worth it just to have him along.

The surrounding area was flat for miles, hills standing sentry in the distance. Johnny parked the car, looking around shiftily (*probably for cops*, Pao thought, doing the same thing herself).

Apparently satisfied, he pocketed the keys and climbed out, folding down the front seat and allowing Pao to escape and finally, mercifully, stretch her legs.

"Ten minutes," he said, his voice a little tense. "I want to be back on the road as soon as possible."

Pao couldn't argue with that. She made a beeline for the bathroom, trying not to notice Dante moodily wandering off past the dog section instead of partaking in any of the rest area's amenities.

In the little building—which was mostly a glorified outhouse— she took her time washing her hands, not eager to get back in the little red torture chamber for another five hours. But she knew they were sitting ducks if they weren't in motion.

When Pao got back to the car, Johnny and Naomi hadn't returned yet, and Dante was nowhere to be seen, either. There was a prickling feeling on the back of her neck—they were exposed here, vulnerable, and she was worried about Dante.

Chill, she told herself. *Just because he's avoiding you doesn't mean something's* wrong *wrong.*

Her stomach growled. Forcing herself to stop scanning the parking lot for her friend, Pao dug in her pocket for her last three dollars (left over from the sunglasses in Rock Creek) and went off in search of a vending machine.

At first, she didn't see one. But then, about fifty yards from the rest area proper, she spotted it, near the fence that bordered the highway. Pao thought it strange that it would be so far from the rest of the amenities, but her stomach told her to make for it anyway.

Up close, she saw that the vending machine was purple, the

lighting inside it bright green. The candies and drinks all had Spanish names Pao didn't recognize. Things like dulce de muerte and golpe de veneno.

Pao squinted inside, hoping to get a clue as to what kind of snacks these packages contained. She'd finally settled on something called botana de protección when she realized the keypad was strange as well. Where the selection numbers should have been, there were just symbols.

Some of them Pao recognized from her mom's tarot cards and books, but many were totally foreign to her. She put a dollar into the money slot and, as directed by the display, pressed the button in the very center, where the five would have been.

This symbol, Pao knew. It was the mal de ojo—a circular eye that her mom claimed protected you from jealousy or evil energy. The vending unit started whirring and blinking like a slot machine, but nothing fell from the shelves. Instead, all around Pao, the green paper-doll ghosts from her dream began to rise from the ground, encircling her, beginning the mad dance she was growing all too familiar with.

"Oh no, here we go again," Pao moaned, pulling her bandanna-bound knife out of her sock, unwrapping it, and holding it at the ready. She couldn't see beyond the ring of spinning green shapes to know whether wide-eyed tourists were pointing their phone cameras at her yet, but it was only a matter of time.

"What do you want?" Pao shouted, jabbing with the knife, unsure if it would be of any use against these things—which seemed, as ever, to be made of light.

She didn't get the chance to find out. As she lunged, the circle moved with her, keeping her right at its center point. "What the—" Pao shouted, thrusting again and again, moving forward, then back.

The glowing dolls stayed just out of reach, and the speed of their spinning increased.

"Dante! Naomi!" Pao shouted, racking her brain for commonalities between the various times the green spirits had appeared. They didn't seem to be picky about whether she was asleep or awake anymore, that's for sure.

"What do you want?" she shouted again in pure frustration.

The green guys didn't answer this time, either, not that Pao had expected them to. They just spun faster, no longer discernable as paper dolls, just round green blurs against the backdrop of California highway.

That's when Pao remembered something specific enough to help. Both times the green shapes had appeared in real life—in Señora Mata's apartment and at the hospital—they had dispersed when Dante walked through the circle.

But why? And where was he now?

"Dante!" Pao screamed, knowing she didn't have time to test her theory or wonder about its origins. She just needed to stop these things before something even more freaky happened.

But Dante didn't answer.

The spirits did, though, in their own terrifying way. Suddenly, like they'd been given a silent signal, the spinning blobs stopped dead, quivering on their base points like they were waiting for something.

Pao didn't even have time to see if she could pass through them before she realized what they were waiting for.

The circle, tightly formed around Pao until now, began to

widen, the paper-doll arms still reaching out for each other as they created space between them. Space for five shaggy pony-size black dogs to stalk through.

Pao wasn't proud of it, but she screamed then, a high-pitched shrill sound like a girl in the movies. In her defense, she thought, the dogs were almost as tall as she was. They were nothing like the chupacabras she'd fought in the cactus field, or the wolves she'd studied in earth science during their unit on predators and prey.

As she'd so often had to last summer, Pao raced through her mental catalog of folktale beasts, cursing herself (not for the first time, nor probably the last) for not paying closer attention to her mom's stories. As a kid she'd been too busy disdaining their lack of scientific accuracy, and since Pao had returned from the rift, her mom had been too preoccupied to tell her more.

Black dogs, black dogs, Pao thought as she rotated slowly, trying to keep her eyes on all of them at once. Why did there have to be so many stories?

That's when it hit her. The cadejo. It would definitely explain their rotting-meat smell, anyway. She didn't quite remember the story, but she remembered being grudgingly impressed by the idea of a dog big enough to ride.

The real thing was definitely more horrifying than impressive, though.

These cadejos had glowing green eyes, marking them as creatures of the void. Their rumbling growls told her they didn't care that she'd tamed a chupacabra with Starbursts—they were going to eat her for lunch anyway.

Recovered from her initial embarrassing reaction, Pao took

up her combat stance, knowing she was no match for the five slavering hell beasts on her own but determined to go down fighting regardless.

Hadn't she gotten out of worse scrapes than this?

Not without help, came a small voice in her head. And right now she wasn't sure she could count on any.

Finally, after an eternity of sizing her up, the biggest cadejo lunged, its teeth the perfect height to tear out her throat. Despite the limited space within the glowing green circle, Pao jumped sideways, narrowly escaping the monster while thrusting her knife in front of her.

Her strike was too feeble. It glanced off the big dog's hide like it was nothing. But that didn't stop the creature from becoming very, very angry.

With a snarl that chilled Pao's blood, the cadejo lunged again. This time, Pao let the beast's weight do the work for her. She held her knife straight out, level with her chest, and when it connected with the beast, it yelped, backing off to rejoin the circle of its friends.

"Yes!" Pao shouted. "Take that, you gross-smelling jerk! My void dog could eat you and all your buddies for breakfast!"

But her triumph was short-lived. Despite the sound it had made, Pao couldn't see any evidence that she'd seriously wounded that cadejo, let alone the four others waiting for their turn. The next one was ready to lunge—she could see it in its narrowed eyes and tightly coiled muscles.

Pao was surrounded, and alone, and out of options entirely.

But just as the dog crouched, its snarl echoing around her, something in the air above Pao caught her eye.

Still unable to see outside the circle of green ghost things, Pao followed the object's descent toward her, squinting to make it out while trying not to keep her eyes off the cadejos for too long, knowing an attack was coming any second.

Finally, the object got close enough for Pao to identify it, and her heart leaped into her throat.

It was a worn blue corduroy slipper. But even as it turned end over end, nearing the paper-doll ghosts and the cadejos, it was changing shape. The toe became huge and rounded, the heel lengthened into a handle, and the sun glinted off its surface. The luminous magical club made for Pao's outstretched hand as if she were reeling it in.

Without thinking, without hesitating, Pao swung Dante's Arma del Alma at the first dog she could reach.

With a sickening, satisfying crunch, the monster's skull shattered, its body slumping over before disintegrating into what looked like pebbles at the bottom of a fish tank.

One down, Pao thought as three of the remaining four cadejos came for her at once.

Pao needed room to maneuver, and with one of her few precious seconds, she swung the club into the circle of green paper dolls, hoping they'd drift away like wisps of smoke or something. But the force field was impervious to the blow, and it also somehow prevented Pao from exiting.

The cadejos were closer now, wary of the club but murderous after the defeat of their comrade. "Come on," Pao taunted them, holding the club out in front of her.

One of them finally bit—literally. It latched onto the Arma del Alma, its teeth making a horrifying grating sound like a fork in the garbage disposal as the shiny surface of the club refused to yield.

The pressure on Pao's arm was monumental. She almost dropped the weapon in shock, but she managed to keep hold of the handle, using both hands to play the world's most dangerous game of doggy tug-of-war.

The other dogs circled, sensing their opening, ready to strike.

With an almighty wrench, Pao freed the club from the cadejo's jaws at last, and its momentum carried her around in a circle. She accidentally took out the two dogs behind her, their howls rattling her nerves as they joined their companion as fish-tank rocks.

Two more to go. Pao could hear Naomi outside the circle of light now, shouting, though Pao couldn't make out the words. *The barrier must be weakening as I defeat the dogs*, Pao thought. *Once they're all gone, maybe I'll finally be free.*

She hit one dog in the ribs as it tried to slash her with its three-inch claws. But as she was recovering, the final cadejo got its teeth around Pao's upper arm and bit down hard.

Her vision went black with the pain, and she felt the club spin uselessly out of her hand. She was on her knees now, though she didn't remember falling, and she looked up into the beast's glowing eyes, thinking—not for the first time this year—that this was the end.

The police would find her body. She hoped Emma would explain everything to Pao's mom. *Your daughter just wanted to meet her dad. Pao loved you, even though you didn't always see eye to eye. . . .*

Would Dante go on without her? Try to find her father? Get

the answers his abuela needed to survive? Would he always hate her for dragging him into all this?

Taking its time, like it knew she was no longer a threat, the cadejo lowered its head, its slobbering, rotten-smelling mouth now just inches from Pao's throat.

Slobber, Pao thought, almost delirious as something finally surfaced in her memory from the story of El Cadejo. The boy in the story had asked his grandmother how to get rid of one, and she'd told him. . . .

Knowing it was ridiculous, but also realizing that she was totally out of other options, Pao raised her good arm and brought the palm of her shaking hand to her mouth. She licked it all over. Then, closing her eyes, she held it out to the beast just as the boy in the story had done. She prayed the monster would do what he was supposed to and not just bite off her hand as an appetizer and move on to the main course.

A second passed, then two. Pao opened her eyes a crack and met the cadejo's gaze.

It sniffed her hand, then stuck out its massive, snakelike tongue, which was dark red, stained with Pao's blood. Her arm was screaming in pain. But as the cadejo began to lick the spit off Pao's palm, it almost seemed to smile.

Once the beast had gone over her hand twice, like Bruto did when she had bacon grease on her fingers, it sank down on its haunches and regarded her solemnly. Then, with a last mournful howl, its form dissipated, like green vapor rising into the air.

FOURTEEN

Everyone Loves Gas-Station Poultry

When the remains of the dogs were gone, the circle of paper-doll ghosts dissolved, too. Naomi came to her through the remaining greenish haze first, and as glad as Pao was to see a familiar face, she couldn't help being a little disappointed that it wasn't Dante's.

If a life-threatening situation couldn't make him forgive her, what could?

"What the heck was that?" Naomi asked, her expression more worried than Pao had ever seen it. "Those green things—I thought you said they were harmless!"

"I thought they were," Pao said, still shaken, her knees trembling, her arm bleeding badly through her ripped T-shirt. "But this time they weren't alone."

Maybe the green shapes were creating some kind of portal, Pao thought. A way the void could open and let monsters through. But if so, why hadn't Pao seen that happen last summer? And if it was a portal, why did it seem intent on disgorging the most horrific monsters right in front of *her* at the absolute worst moments?

"We were trying to get to you the whole time," Naomi said, grimacing. "But there was no way through. When I told hero boy over there to chuck in the Arma del Alma, he thought I was nuts. But it looks like it worked."

Pao's heart sank further. It hadn't even been Dante's idea to save her?

She spotted him standing a few yards off, his arms folded, looking away with an unfathomable expression on his face.

Guilt? Pao wondered. Or was that just wishful thinking on her part? Maybe it was disappointment. Did Dante hate her enough that he'd wanted the cadejos to finish the job?

Naomi was still talking. Pao had to force her thoughts away from Dante and the pain in her arm to listen.

". . . said something like this might happen. That the magic balance being off could result in unforeseen consequences . . ."

"Yeah," Pao said, not quite understanding and for once barely curious—even though Naomi was discussing the literal intersection of magic and science, which should have been making Pao's brain go haywire.

Instead, she was just tired. And sad. She felt so alone. Even when she and Dante had been distant this fall, she'd never doubted that they'd eventually find their way back to each other.

Now she wasn't so sure.

"Either way, we have to find the Niños as soon as possible," Naomi said. "If this is what Franco was talking about, it's only going to get worse from here. . . ."

At these words, Pao looked up, focusing on Naomi for the first time since the attack. "He knew this would happen? The green things and the fantasmas and monsters popping up everywhere?"

Naomi rolled her eyes. "He says so much stuff, it's not my job to catalog it all, okay?" She hesitated. "But yeah . . . he did say that there would be consequences, and if they didn't get to the source of the buildup in time, things could get ugly. . . ."

"And you're telling me this *right now*?" Pao asked, the spike of annoyance dulling the pain in her arm, giving her the energy to finally push herself up off the ground.

"Listen! I thought he was exaggerating to get Marisa away sooner! I asked her to stay for one more night, just to . . ." Naomi trailed off, shaking her head. "Anyway, that's when he came up with the convenient *we have to leave right now or there will be consequences* line."

Pao glowered at her, but she didn't have time to say anything before Dante finally shuffled over, that strange look still on his face.

"You okay?" he asked.

Naomi put up both hands and backed away to talk to Johnny.

"Yeah," Pao said, though her arm was really hurting now. "Thanks for the club. I'd be a goner without it."

She was watching his face for . . . what? Proof that he hadn't been the one who thought of saving her? Some particular expression that meant he had well and truly given up on their friendship?

Whatever she was looking for, she didn't get it.

"Glad you're good," he said, but he didn't seem at all disappointed when Johnny jogged over, looking even more alarmed than a guy who'd just seen a ghostly portal spit out a bunch of demon dogs should.

"I hate to break this up," Johnny said, not sounding sorry at all, keys already in hand, "but some people just called nine-one-one. Said there were some 'unsupervised Hispanic kids' vandalizing a vending machine, and they had video."

"Vandalizing?" Pao said, disbelieving. "There were weird spinning lights! And creatures from the void! Why are they calling the cops and not, like, the *National Enquirer* or something!"

"White people with RVs see what they want to see," said Johnny, like it was some ancient proverb, and maybe it should have been.

"Whatever," Pao said. "Let's go before the cops show up. Again."

They'd already been described as "unsupervised" and "Hispanic." Considering that, Johnny's vulture vest, and Pao's sock knife—not to mention whatever hidden weapon Naomi was carrying—Pao had a feeling this wouldn't be a *slap on the wrist and take you back to your parents* situation.

Then again, was it ever for kids like them?

Heading back to the car, Pao put on a brave face, even though she had no idea what was going on with Dante and her arm was hurting worse by the second.

As surreptitiously as she could without alerting the whole car to her problem, Pao twisted her arm to take a better look at the bite. So far it was just five tooth-shaped punctures in her skin. A small line of blood trickled down to her elbow, but nothing too bad.

Pao knew, however, that the biggest risk from an animal bite wasn't depth or bleeding—it was the possibility of infection. And that was from a *normal* creature. If the rate of infection for an earthly dog bite was up to 15 percent . . . what was the number for slavering cadejos from the magical void?

The wound needed to be disinfected, that was for sure, but there was no first-aid kit on this impromptu adventure, and there was no time to go back into the bathroom with the cops on their way.

She would just have to watch it, she thought grimly, and wash it as well as she could the next time they stopped.

Back in the car, Johnny pulled out, tires squealing in his haste. In their wake was a crowd of chattering tourists. Pao thought she saw one of them snap a photo of the car's license plate, but she didn't mention it. The last thing she needed to do was spook Johnny and end up with no ride before they even reached the halfway point.

But the road trip—already losing its novelty even *before* she'd been attacked by massive demon dogs—suddenly felt less like a quest toward something and more like they were running for their lives.

The only question was, what exactly were they running from? And what would happen if it ran faster than they did?

When the Niños' camp had been overrun by monsters and ahogados, there had been a clear reason for the attacks. La Llorona had been searching for the matching soul that would allow her to bring her last remaining daughter back to life. But La Llorona was gone now. . . .

Marisa had said the void's magic was neutral . . . unless there was a force inside corrupting it. Pao had learned last summer that the green-eyed beasts and fantasmas weren't able to organize on their own. So someone had to be sending them, but who?

Pao knew that if she sat here thinking in circles forever, she'd never solve the mystery. She needed a brainstorming partner. One who didn't underestimate her like Naomi and Johnny did. One who wasn't hundreds of miles away and only accessible by a device that could reveal Pao's location.

She needed Dante back.

He was right beside her, staring out the window again, his jaw still clenched so tight she could see a muscle twitching in his face.

He'd extended what seemed like an olive branch this morning when he'd said he trusted her, but while that had ended the open hostility from the night before, it hadn't seemed to change anything today. Maybe it was up to Pao to fix things. She was tired of waiting around for him to talk to her, to tell her what was allowed.

She'd never let anyone push her around before. Paola Santiago knew who she was and what she wanted. She'd never even let him win at *video games*, for crying out loud, and now she was going to let him decide the fate of their friendship?

No way.

Pao turned to Dante with her most no-nonsense expression and said, loud enough to be heard over the increasingly loud rattling of the Karmann Ghia's engine, "We're friends, Dante."

"What?" he said, shaking his head irritably like a fly had landed on his ear.

"We're friends, you and me. Always have been, always will be." She could feel herself sitting up straighter as she said it, her voice projecting. "Whatever boy-girl weirdness happened a few months ago? Forget it, okay? If it's ruining what we have, I don't want it. I want my best friend back."

For a second, she could swear his jaw relaxed.

"I know you think I'm responsible for what happened to your abuela," she continued, "and maybe that's true. Weird, bad things follow me around—we know that by now. But I would never do anything to hurt you or your family on purpose, Dante. I'll always be here, right next to you, trying my best to make things better."

Pao took a deep breath, hoping he would turn to her, smile, tell her it was good to have her back. But he didn't. Not yet.

"I get a little obsessive, sure," she went on. "I like to know things, and understand them, and dissect them until they barely exist. Sometimes that probably makes me boring to talk to or not great at guessing the perfect thing to say. But I'll do better, okay? And right now I'm trying so hard to save your abuela, and I have no idea what's going on, and I need you."

Now for the grand finish. The words that would make him finally give in to the irresistible power of her friendship.

"So you have to stop being mad at me," she said. "You have to forgive me, and believe how sorry I am that anything bad happened to anyone. You have to be my friend again, Dante."

This time, he did turn, a half smile on his face.

"Okay," he said.

"Okay?"

"Okay, I'll be your friend again."

It was a little underwhelming, Pao thought. And maybe she'd believed she deserved an apology, too. That this would be a whole back-and-forth thing where they'd lay out all their issues and make a plan of action and by the end of the trip feel closer than ever.

This is a start, she told herself. It was better than nothing.

"Thank you," she said, and she meant it. "Now can you help me understand what's going on with these fantasmas and monsters? I can't for the life of me figure out where they're coming from."

But even as she changed the subject, and he angled *slightly* more toward her and *almost* participated in conversations about dreams, locations, green spirits, and demon dogs, Pao wondered if it would always be like this. Her apologizing to him for being who she was. Him believing he deserved an apology. Was there any amount of work or speeches or gestures that could change that? And, if there was no way to make it better, was this really what she wanted?

When they were an hour past the rest stop of doom, hunger became unavoidable. Johnny, who'd been remarkably (if understandably) quiet since the attack, pointed to a truck stop up ahead with a fried chicken place inside.

"Who's down to see if the headless chickens come back to life and, like, peck out all our eyeballs?"

No one laughed.

"You know, because at the vending machine . . . the dogs, and . . ." He looked to Naomi for help. "So I just figured maybe the chickens . . ."

Silence. Even the car stopped rattling in protest.

"Never mind," Johnny said with a sigh. "Who's hungry?"

"Who doesn't love gas-station poultry?" Pao asked, feeling a little sorry for him—and more than a little hungry.

Johnny laughed too loud, and Naomi joined in, though Pao had the feeling she was laughing more at his flop than her joke. Either way, a little of the tension that had followed them from exit 146 eased, and none too soon.

Pao *was* on high alert for anything spooky-looking as they trudged into the run-down convenience store. Nothing was going to get in the way of her and lunch this time.

But the popcorn chicken and waffle fries, though a little soggy (and possibly made in a kitchen not quite up to health-code standards), were refreshingly of this world.

Pao, Dante, Naomi, and Johnny wolfed them down by the handful in a dingy booth right by the door, in case the bored cashier turned into a Lechuza or something. She didn't, and they all felt slightly better with food in their stomachs. Johnny even picked up the tab, which Pao assumed was a futile attempt to impress Naomi. Pao appreciated it all the same—especially since the haunted vending machine hadn't given her money back, and she only had two dollars left.

While Dante was in the bathroom, Pao turned on her phone under the table, hoping for a message from Emma—even if it was just something to make her laugh—but she didn't get a chance to check before it started ringing.

Incoming call from Mom.

She turned it off immediately and sighed. No Emma, not for a while at least.

Dante returned, meeting her eyes uncertainly before giving another one of his wan smiles. How long would it take for them to get back to normal? she wondered. Would they ever?

"Only an hour away," Johnny said as they piled back into the car. "You guys know where you want to be dropped off?" Pao couldn't help but notice that Johnny didn't sound at all sorry to be getting rid of them.

She didn't blame him. Thinking you were getting a road trip in a shiny stolen car with the girl you liked and instead ending up on some monster-hunting expedition with bickering middle school kids was like one of those expectations-vs.-reality memes come to life.

Either way, they were nearing the end of the line, and Pao had no better idea of where Johnny should drop them than of what kind of toppings an ahogado would order on a pizza.

Pao looked up at Naomi, deliberately avoiding Dante's gaze. There was nothing he hated more than the part of the plan where Pao stopped having all the answers.

"Don't look at me," Naomi said. "I've never been to Fresno before. We're gonna need somewhere to lie low until we can find another ride north. How much money do you guys have?"

Pao felt her cheeks turn red. "Two dollars," she said at the same time as Dante said, "Maybe some change . . ."

Naomi didn't bother to make fun of them, which made Pao feel more pathetic than ever.

"I've got forty-five bucks," she said. "Which isn't even enough for a night in a sleazy motel *if* someone would let us through the door . . ."

No one picked up the thread of the conversation. From tired and worried, the silence in the car grew awkward. If a part of Pao had been hoping Johnny would offer them some help, she was sorely disappointed.

The pressure kept building. Pao was a girl who always had an answer, always had a plan—even if it was one she was making up on the spot. But her past adventures had always taken place only a few miles from home.

Now she was in a state she'd never been to, with people who didn't owe her anything. She was five hundred miles away from one parent, and five hundred miles from the other—who might not even recognize her, and whom she certainly had no business expecting any help from.

Johnny was waiting for an answer.

The pain in Pao's arm was clouding her thoughts. She imagined this must be what it felt like when the teacher called on you and you hadn't done the homework.

Pao had *always* done the homework, though. Maybe that was the problem.

Her hand was starting to go numb below the bite. Was that normal? What were the signs of infection?

Pao started mentally listing the ones she could remember, trying to use the facts to push out the pain.

Pus or fluid from the bite.

Red streaks from the bite.

Swollen lymph nodes.

Loss of sensation around the bite.

Loss of sensation . . .

Loss of sensation . . .

It was no use. The pain was still there, and she was more worried than ever.

They merged back onto the freeway, the car still positively muggy with silence. Beside the I-5 sign, a boy dressed in all red pajamas caught Pao's eye. His long dark hair fell into his eyes, and he held a cardboard sign reading *North*, and nothing more.

Pao looked at him intently as the car passed. How could a boy younger than she was be out here alone, hitching a ride? But underneath that question was the feeling that she'd seen the boy before, though she couldn't remember where.

"We should pick him up," she said, almost without deciding to. Everyone turned to look at her. "That boy—we should go back and pick him up," Pao insisted, louder now. "He's our age—he shouldn't be hitchhiking alone!"

"What boy?" Johnny asked, his voice half-concerned, half-condescending.

"He's right there!" Pao said. "At the exit. He's wearing red paja . . . mas . . ." Pao had turned around to look out the back window, and the boy was gone.

She could still see the sign. The only other thing near it was a trash bag stuck on the pole and blowing in the wind.

"Never mind," she mumbled. "I guess he left."

Dante cleared his throat, like she'd just said something nerdy about chemical reactions at the lunch table with his soccer friends.

What had she done to embarrass him now? Pao wondered. Try as she might, she couldn't remember what they'd just been talking about. . . .

"So, uh," Johnny said. "A destination? My GPS still just says 'Fresno,' and I doubt you guys want to be dumped out in front of city hall . . . which, if I'm not mistaken, is about two blocks from the police station."

"No," Pao said automatically. "Definitely not there."

But she had nothing else to offer. The awkward silence billowed again.

Beside her, Dante had stopped looking embarrassed and instead appeared to be at war with himself. It was enough to pull Pao from her preoccupation.

"Are you—" she began, but he leaned forward before she could finish.

Hanging over the seat, his mouth set in a determined line,

he said: "Take us to Raisin Valley." The grimace grew deeper. "It's just a little ways southwest of Fresno."

"I know it," Johnny said, sounding impressed—which Pao understood 0 percent. "I can take you there."

"What—" Pao started to ask Dante, but he silenced her with a look that said *I don't want to talk about it* as plain as day. He spent the rest of the car ride looking moodily out the window, avoiding Pao's gaze.

But even the mystery of what was in Raisin Valley, and why Dante looked so grim about going there, couldn't hold her interest. Not with the pain *still* increasing in her arm, building steadily to what felt like torture level, making her hairline sweat and her vision blurry.

This is the part of the spy movie when I'd consider selling out everyone I've ever loved, Pao thought grimly. No matter how much she'd sworn in act one that she was tough enough to take the pain, she'd definitely be thinking about it by now.

But even if she confessed to Naomi and Johnny and Dante, what would she say? *Hey, guys, my demon dog bite is getting way worse and I might pass out?* What could they do? She was pretty sure a hospital wouldn't know what to do with a possibly venomous bite from a monster, and even if they did, they'd call her mom immediately. Game over.

Nothing was going to stop her from getting to her dad, Pao told herself, gritting her teeth against the throbbing. Señora Mata's life depended on it. And if Franco's research could be believed, a lot more than just the health of one elderly neighbor could be on the line.

If Franco was right about the anomaly throwing everything

off-balance, it was making the fantasmas and beasts appear in places they shouldn't—places where there were no Niños de la Luz to protect people. This mission was officially about a lot more than it had been when they started.

Trying to ignore her pain, Pao looked out the window. The traffic had thickened, and she understood why when she read the sign coming up.

FRESNO—NEXT THREE EXITS

They had arrived.

FIFTEEN

So *This* Is Where Raisins Come From

Pao had never given much thought to where the country's raisins originated.

Raisin Valley was the aptly named answer to this unasked question, she discovered as they entered it. Evening gathered and dust clouds billowed as they drove down the location's single dirt road.

Well, the *raisin* part was accurate, Pao amended as they passed through. The *valley* part was a bit of a stretch. It was as flat as flat could be around here. A tiny, low-to-the-ground town with a series of ramshackle houses—most of which had at least one broken-down car in the dirt lot outside and a few chickens lazily clucking nearby.

But between the houses, and extending far beyond them, were hundreds upon hundreds of acres of grapevines. Right now they were just stalks, withered and brown and dead-looking, but during growing season there would be enough to get lost in. Enough to fill all the tiny, sticky snack boxes the world would ever need.

"Where to, boss?" Johnny asked when Dante didn't immediately volunteer a destination. Pao got the feeling nothing in Raisin

Valley was particularly far from anything else, but Dante seemed to think hard before answering.

"Another couple minutes this way. House on the right."

No amount of throbbing in her arm could stop Pao's passionate curiosity about Dante's connection to this place. But far from volunteering any information, Dante seemed to disappear further and further into himself the closer they got.

Johnny glanced at the dashboard clock about five times in the three minutes it took to reach the house Dante had described, and Pao knew he was worried about getting the car back before he got in trouble with its hypercritical owner.

Dizzy with pain, and not at all sure what they were walking into, Pao could feel a fear creep into her thoughts and begin to nest there. She had been to more dangerous places than a mysterious house in a small, dusty town, of course, but they were in a different state now, and their only ally who was old enough to have a driver's license was about to leave them behind. They'd be stuck here, Pao thought, until they could find a way to continue. *If* they could find a way.

"Here's fine," Dante said, and Pao tried to meet his eyes, to get even a small idea of what was going on.

He didn't look back, though Pao was sure he felt her stare. His jaw was twitching again, as well as his left eye. He looked deathly pale in the evening light. Like how people always look when they've seen a ghost in movies—people who aren't *used* to seeing ghosts, anyway.

But Dante saw ghosts all the time. He'd seen his (former?) best friend get nearly devoured by ruthless hellhounds and hadn't had any trouble snarfing down chicken and waffle fries right after. And that had been *this afternoon.*

So what could possibly be scaring him so much?

Even though things were complicated between them, Pao couldn't help but feel a pang of sympathy in her chest for whatever it was he was going through.

We'll get through this part, she thought. *For Dante.* Then she'd tell Naomi and him about her arm. About how she feared the bite was infected, or cursed, or something else awful she hadn't even thought of yet.

Johnny stopped the car, and Naomi stepped out into the twilight, folding down the front seat so Pao could climb out, too. Pao managed to get on her feet, but she swayed immediately, bracing herself on the car hood to stop from falling.

"You okay?" Naomi asked, squinting at Pao like the cause of her dizziness might be written on her face. Pao imagined it for a moment: *demon dog bite* spelled out in red paint on her forehead.

She giggled.

Naomi looked alarmed.

"I'm fine," Pao said, managing to keep her voice steady. "Legs fell asleep, that's all."

"Mhm," Naomi said, like she wasn't quite buying it, but now wasn't the time.

Dante, for his part, didn't look any less pale outside the car. Johnny stood awkwardly beside them, his body language saying he couldn't wait to get out of there. As little as she liked the idea of losing the wheels, Pao couldn't blame him. This wasn't a happy place—she could feel it in her aching bones.

But was it a dangerous one?

Another wave of vertigo hit her. This time Pao could see little green sparks at the lower edges of her vision. She thought of the paper dolls. *Not now,* she told them, but even her inner monologue was sluggish and slow.

"Dante?" she said, but he was already moving toward the chain-link fence and jerking his chin for Pao and Naomi to follow. He hadn't heard her. Or he was ignoring her. Either way, there was nothing to do but follow.

"Later, kids," Johnny said, lingering even as Dante walked away without so much as a wave good-bye. "Naomi, safe travels."

"Thanks for your help, Johnny," Pao said, hoping her words weren't slurring. Her tongue felt thick and heavy in her mouth as she turned to join Dante.

Johnny and Naomi's good-bye must have been quick, because Naomi caught up before Dante lifted the latch on the gate. He jiggled it in a particular way to unstick it, like he'd done it before.

When? Pao wondered sleepily. *When had he done it before?*

The green sparks glinted off the fence as Pao walked through it.

She shook her head to get rid of them, but this time they didn't go away. Not completely. There was no sign from either Naomi or Dante that they could see them, too. Did that make it better or worse? Pao wondered.

Like many of the other yards they'd seen on their way into Raisin Valley, the lot around the house Dante knew was packed dirt, pitted with holes. An overflowing garbage can stood a few feet from the door, and discarded furniture and auto parts littered the area.

The house must have been white once, years ago, but now it was so grimy that it had turned a sad beige-ish gray. Even the lingering pink light from the setting sun couldn't improve the aesthetic.

"Dante," Pao said again, but still he didn't turn.

"What is this place?" Naomi asked under her breath. Her hand hovered near her hip, where Pao assumed she had a knife concealed.

Pao wanted to say something to Naomi, but she worried that if she opened her mouth, she would just scream in pain.

It was enough to know that Naomi also sensed the mood here. The desperate sadness verging on something worse. Something sinister. Something that made Pao want to reach for her knife, too.

The only trouble was, her arm wouldn't move.

The green flashes grew brighter at the edges of Pao's vision, following her up the two sunken steps to the cement porch. At the front door, she swayed again, and Naomi caught her elbow.

"Pao," she said, concern edging into her normally annoyed expression, "you don't look so good. Hey, hero boy, maybe we'd better—"

Before Dante could respond, the front door banged open, and a flickering fluorescent light was cast onto the porch.

Black spots were creeping into Pao's vision now, dancing along with the green. She needed to sit down. To get rid of these terrible spots.

And throw up, maybe?

But she didn't have a chance to do any of those things before the woman who had opened the door stepped through it onto the porch. Dante's soccer-star posture collapsed in on itself as her shadow fell over him. Pao's brain was pitching and rolling like the deck of a ship, but she knew she needed to be on her feet for this moment.

"Can I help you?" the woman asked in a voice that was

somehow harsh and hopeless all at once, and Dante folded even further. Pao's skin felt like it was on fire. Sweat was beading up at her hairline, making her shiver a little as the green spots stretched into dancing paper dolls, glowing against the dingy house. Naomi's eyes darted to the spirits, but Dante's didn't move.

His gaze stayed fixed on the woman, who had stringy black hair nearly reaching her waist and a lit cigarette in one hand. She wore stained pink sweatpants and a sleeveless black top.

When she turned, her face caught the light from the window, and she looked familiar somehow. Too familiar to be someone Pao didn't know.

That was Pao's last thought before her knees went all jelly-filled. Naomi caught her again, but this time it was useless. Pao was going down. The green was taking over her vision, the arms of the paper dolls reaching out for one another, closing in.

They were about to take her, when Pao heard it, as faint as if it were coming from another world.

Dante's voice, speaking to the woman in the doorway.

"Hey, Mom," she thought she heard him say. "Can we come in?"

Mom? Pao thought deliriously, and then Dante, and the porch, and all the rest of it were gone. Swallowed whole by the green light.

SIXTEEN

Dreams to Thrill Your Inner Six-Year-Old
at the Least Opportune Time

Pao awoke in the forest and wanted to scream in frustration.

She didn't need to be here, walking down a wide path dappled with green light as eyes watched her from between the leaves and pine needles.

Not when Dante was scared. Not while Señora Mata's clock was ticking. Not when everyone she loved could be in danger.

Her arm was still wounded here, the pain only dimmed, like it was the same song with the volume turned down. Pao held it gingerly as she walked, wondering what was happening to her physical body. If the infection or venom or curse was spreading through her bloodstream. If she was dying.

"Just show me what you need to show me! I have places to be!" Pao shouted, too angry to feel afraid for once, even with all she was facing.

She hadn't expected the forest to react, but a moment later, one pair of eyes detached itself from the wall of trees.

The creature (girl?) they were attached to was tiny—no bigger than a toddler, though her features were much more mature than a child's. She had a round nose, a mouth like a bow, and vivid green hair in a short cut that stuck up at odd angles. Her brown skin was dusted with gold freckles that sparkled in the sunlight coming through the canopy.

Then there were the eyes. Those glowing green eyes that had followed Pao down every forest path she'd walked since this all began, looking at her now like they were waiting for an answer to a question she hadn't asked.

A duendecillo, Pao decided, remembering her favorite pictures from her cuento de hadas book as a kid. She'd never believed in the little gnomes, of course. Still, as a kid, when she'd walked around the cactuses outside the Riverside Palace with a magnifying glass (looking for insects or shiny rocks), a part of her had always wondered what she'd do if she found one.

But this was hardly the time for childhood imaginings, she thought, squashing the hopes of her inner six-year-old.

"What do you want?" Pao asked, trying not to care how cute the creature was. She just needed to get through this dream and return to reality before it was too late. "Listen, I . . ." Pao began when the duendecillo didn't immediately answer.

"Ven conmigo," the duendecillo said in a squeaky voice. Pao had been working hard to make good on last summer's promise to learn Spanish if she got out of the void alive. She knew from her Duolingo app that *ven conmigo* meant that she should follow.

The teeny forest denizen took off with a bouncing gait down the path.

Pao groaned loudly at the sky. "Why can't magical creatures ever just tell me what they want?" she asked. "It's always 'let's go on a mysterious quest through a weird forest' or 'why don't you spend days answering riddles while your friends suffer at the hands of a madwoman?'"

If the duendecillo heard her grumbling, she showed no evidence of it. And Pao, remembering the last plucky dream guide she'd had, counted her blessings. Sure, Ondina had turned out to be all right in the end, but dealing with her sarcastic quips on the banks of the dream river had been nothing short of *pull your hair out* infuriating.

Pao followed the duendecillo until she turned off the beaten path, then she hesitated. Pao had never left the main road of the dream forest before. And just because *this* dream guide was absolutely adorable didn't mean she couldn't also be dangerous.

"I think I'll keep going this way!" Pao said loudly. "Thanks anyway, though!"

Inside her, six-year-old Pao was throwing a fit.

The duendecillo seemed to have heard her this time, because she marched back with a determined look on her freckled face and grabbed the hem of Pao's shirt, shaking her head.

"Ven conmigo," she said, panting as she used all her tiny strength to pull Pao down the narrower path to the left. "¡Quiero ayudarte!"

Quiero was "I want," Pao knew. And *ayudar* was either "help" or . . . "teapot"? That didn't sound right. She guessed the duendecillo wanted her help with something. But wasn't that what monsters always said before they led you to their den to be eaten?

"I'm sorry," Pao said, shaking her head. "I don't have time right now. I'm just gonna . . ."

But before she could finish, pain shot through her arm, so sharp and abrupt that Pao sank to her knees.

"Quiero ayudarte," the duendecillo repeated, a note of finality in her squeaky little tone. This time, when she tugged on Pao's sweatshirt, Pao followed as best she could.

The path was twisted and narrow, trees pressing in ominously from every direction. Pao, used to the wide open sky of Arizona, found her breath coming shorter, like there wasn't enough space for her lungs to expand in this dripping green tunnel.

They walked for about a half mile more than Pao could stand, her pain worse than ever, causing the ground to tilt and shift beneath her feet. Several times, she fell. Always the duendecillo tugged on her sweatshirt, saying "Ven conmigo" in that tiny voice until Pao was following again.

At last, just when Pao thought she would pass out again (was that even possible in a dream?), the path opened up to a small clearing where a waterfall trickled into a pool surrounded by moss. Sunlight sparkled invitingly on its surface.

Even as the searing pain sent her stumbling again, Pao could appreciate the beauty of the place. But what were they doing here?

Her head pounded. What happened when you died in a dream?

Seeming to grasp that Pao wasn't the best at translating, the duendecillo didn't try to speak again. She just bounced over to the edge of the pool and pointed into it.

"I see it," Pao said thickly. "Very pretty. But my arm . . ."

Again, the tiny creature pointed at the water, this time with her eyes wide open, like Pao was missing an obvious point. When that still didn't do the trick, she pressed her hands together and pantomimed diving in.

"You want me to swim?" Pao asked, absolutely certain she would drown if she tried it. The pool wasn't very large in diameter, but the bottom wasn't even visible. It was like a dark watery tube plunging straight down into the center of the earth.

The duendecillo nodded frantically, her green hair growing disheveled and falling into her eyes.

"I can't," Pao said, shaking her head dejectedly.

But the duendecillo was already beside her again, pulling Pao to the edge of the water, though she could barely stay on her feet.

Pao weighed her options. On the one hand, maybe this dream was important, and getting in the water would reveal something vital. On the other, maybe she was dying, and this was her brain's version of walking into the light.

Either way, wouldn't drowning in a beautiful, sparkling pool be better than lying beside it in agony as some demon poison sapped the last of her strength?

There were no other choices. Pao knew she wasn't even going to make it back to the road in her current state, and the longer she stayed in this place, the sharper everything became. The more real it seemed.

She wasn't sure how she knew, but Pao had been leaving her earthly body behind as she walked through this forest. It was time to do something.

Without thinking, without wondering, Pao jumped into the water, leaving the duendecillo and the forest behind as the water closed over her head.

SEVENTEEN
The Last Kid You'd Ever Expect to Babysit during a Monster Attack

Pao had expected the water to be cold, but to her surprise it was pleasant, like in a bath right when it's no longer too hot to submerge yourself.

But the temperature was only one part of the sensation. The sparkling on the surface of the pond hadn't been the sun after all. Winking around Pao were little glowing lights, and the water felt effervescent against her skin, like bubbles.

And then she realized that the pain in her arm was lessening dramatically. Like that volume knob was being turned down, and down, and . . .

Kicking frantically, Pao broke the surface and took a huge breath, hooking her non-wounded arm over the edge of the pool and twisting herself into a pretzel to look at the bite.

There was nothing there. Not even a scar. The pounding in her head, the numbness in her hand, and the shooting pains that had sent her to her knees in agony . . .

Gone. Like a crazed cadejo had never tried to amputate her arm at all.

"How . . . ?" Pao began, looking around for the duendecillo, but she was alone in the clearing. "Hello?" Pao called, trying to climb out to dry land. "Is anyone—"

She was cut short by the sound of suction beneath her. It caused a whirlpool that began to slurp all the glittering, healing water out of the tube.

"Help!" Pao called, not believing she had made it this far, and been healed no less, only to die by going down the drain. Apparently her fear of that as a three-year-old had been justified, she thought deliriously.

Pao was sucked down, down into the mossy tunnel, spinning until she was dizzy and barely knew which way was up.

Just when she'd started to wonder if she'd be stuck here forever, like some kind of purgatory reserved especially for girls who were unfortunate enough to die of demon-dog bites, she reached the end. Of the tunnel, anyway. She was still going downward, but now it was through the sky.

Pao wasn't proud of it, but she screamed as she tumbled through the air like she'd just tried skydiving without an instructor or a parachute, the wind ripping her hysterics from her throat before she ever heard the sound.

Below her was nothing but cracked earth and barren, twisted grapevines.

Grapevines, Pao thought. Was she falling back down to Raisin Valley?

Was she awake now, or still asleep?

The question was enough to make her stop screaming at least, but it made little difference. If she were dreaming, she probably wouldn't die. If she were dying in her dream, smashing into the ground at 120 miles per hour wouldn't change her outcome.

And if she were awake?

Well, okay, if she were awake, this was really bad.

Pao screamed again, for so long that when she opened her

eyes there was a visible dirt patch among the grapevines, growing larger as she plummeted toward it. A rusted red car the size of a pinhead grew to the size of a golf ball as she tried to blink away the streaming tears the sky was pulling from her eyes.

She was hurtling toward the ground now, bracing for impact. . . .

But it never came.

She landed on the hood of the red car without a scratch.

So, a dream, then? Pao asked herself as she slipped down to the dusty ground.

She was in front of the same house Dante had brought them to, but everything was just slightly dissimilar. Like one of those "spot the difference" games from the magazines in the dentist's waiting room.

This car, for instance. She hadn't seen it when they'd first pulled up. And the color of the house was brighter, the grapevines thinner and shorter than she remembered.

So I'm in the past, Pao thought, walking through the lot.

And Dante had called that woman *Mom.* . . .

"Dante?" she called out hesitantly. "Are you here?"

Nothing. Then, suddenly, a ball of dust came hurtling toward her at light speed. Pao leaped out of the way, turning to follow the cloud with her gaze. It looked like Road Runner from the old Looney Tunes cartoons, racing through the desert as the coyote chased it.

But as Pao watched, the dust cleared, and she was looking at a little kid—no older than three. His black hair fell into his face, and his cheeks were smudged with dirt and something red and sticky. He wore blue shorts and nothing else, not even shoes.

She didn't usually have much use for little kids, but this one had eyes that drew her in—brown-black, too wise for his tiny face, and definitely more than a little mischievous.

There was no doubt about it—this was Dante as a toddler. Dante before four-year-old Pao had met him. Dante as a Raisin Valley Road Runner with strawberry jelly on his face.

"Hi, Dante," she said, tears filling her eyes as she stepped toward him, knowing he couldn't see her because it was a dream, but wanting to be close to him anyway.

"Hi!" he said back in his little child's voice, and Pao jumped so suddenly she almost fell down.

"Can you see me?" she asked in disbelief.

Little Dante giggled, putting his hands over his eyes and then flinging them wide.

"Peekaboo?" Pao said tentatively, and he giggled again.

"It's time to go!" he said then, his baby voice all lisps and rasps. He held out his hand for Pao's as a cloud blotted out the sun, sending the lot into an eerie premature twilight.

Pao couldn't help it—she took tiny Dante's hand. "Where are we going?" she asked with a laugh.

He stopped at the edge of the vineyard and looked up at her, his wide dark eyes serious now. "Gotta hide," he said.

"Why do we have to hide?" Pao asked him with a smile, the way you would to a kid playing hide-and-seek if you were babysitting.

Well, *if* you had ever babysat.

"A monster's coming," Dante said, and she would have laughed again, but a little tremor passed through him from head to toe. He was afraid.

"What kind of monster?" Pao asked, matching his serious tone.

"Come on!" He tugged on her hand, not unlike the duende-cillo had done, and pulled her into the grapevines.

They were only a hundred yards away when Pao heard it—a crash so loud it seemed to shake the ground at their feet. Little Dante whimpered beside her, then ran faster, pushing aside the dead vines and pressing deeper into the field.

"What's happening?" she asked him, though she didn't really expect a three-year-old to understand it well enough to explain.

"The monster's coming," he repeated, and then the crash sounded again.

They weren't far enough away to miss it when it happened— the hood of the rusted red car Pao had landed on came flying through the air, falling only a few feet from them.

Dante's little bare feet ran faster.

"What *is* the monster?" Pao asked him, feeling like she should go back to find out, see if anyone else was in danger, but not wanting to leave baby Dante on his own.

He stopped and turned to look at her, crooking his little fin-ger until she was close enough for his liking. When she was, he stood on his tiptoes and whispered in her ear:

"It's a bad man monster."

Pao was afraid now. Tiny Dante seemed to have lost the will to run. He sank onto the ground, hugging his little knees with his chubby baby arms and tucking his head.

For a moment, Pao wanted to hide with him, to make sure they were both safe. But she stood up instead, and what she saw chilled her to the bone.

It was a fantasma, that was for sure. But if it had once been a man, it had mutated beyond recognition. It stretched to the height of the house, its face the size of a metal trash can lid, with at least fifteen pairs of eyes appearing and disappearing across the top half, while the mouth on the bottom half screamed.

The sound was a wordless, terrible howl Pao had begun to associate with impending doom.

Little Dante began to cry into his bare knees.

"I have to go help the other people," Pao said, more to herself than the toddler. "If you can see me, maybe they can, too."

"Don't go!" he cried, clutching at her legs. "Please don't go!"

Pao's heart felt like one of Bruto's tug-of-war ropes. How could she leave little Dante? How could she stay?

In the end, the Bad Man Monster made the decision for her. As Pao watched helplessly, Dante's arms wrapped firmly around her left calf, the horrifying fantasma smashed one of the house's windows and reached one of his pale, too-long arms inside.

"No!" Pao said under her breath, trying to untangle Dante's arms so she could run and help whoever was in this house. But he was crying now, clinging to her desperately. She was stuck there, gaping in horror as the arm slithered out the window like a ghostly snake, a man in its grip.

"¡Papá!" Dante shrieked, and this time Pao had to hold *him* back. "No, Bad Man, no!" he screamed, tears and snot smearing his face.

Pao didn't realize she was crying with him until her tears hit the dirt at their feet. She covered the toddler's eyes as the fantasma shook the man in its grip like a limp rag doll, screeching again when nothing happened, and tossed him aside like a granola-bar wrapper.

The man hit the red car with a sickening crunch and didn't move again.

"¡Papá!" Dante wailed, sobs heaving his little body.

"It's okay," Pao said, sobbing, too, squeezing him tight. "It's going to be okay."

But she knew that was an empty promise.

The Bad Man Ghost was tearing shutters and doors off the house now, uprooting the whole fence at once like the spine of an animal, and throwing it into the street outside.

What does it want? Pao wondered, still shielding baby Dante, afraid to leave him alone. She'd never asked Dante why he lived with his abuela, and he had never volunteered the information. Was she seeing it now? The way he had truly lost his parents?

But his mom . . . His mom had answered the door of this very house what seemed like an hour ago. . . .

The fantasma screamed again, rattling the ground at their feet, and Pao knew she had to do something, anything, to help. That's when she saw the woman, a younger version of the one who had answered the door, bolt out into the dirt patch around the house.

"Dante?" she shouted frantically. "Dante! Come here, baby!" She was sobbing as she called for him, already moving toward the place where the gate had been moments ago. "Dante, please!"

"¡Mamà!"? Dante answered, reaching out for her.

Pao held on to him, knowing he should be with his mom but afraid of what the fantasma might do to him. She tried not to think too much about the fact that she'd met little Dante only a year after this . . . and his mother had been nowhere in sight.

It was this thought, more than anything, that propelled her.

Maybe that's why she was here—to change history for him. To make it better for once, instead of worse.

"Let's go," she told Dante, who was still reaching out. "Let's get Mamà, okay?"

Tearfully, his chin jutting out in a way it still sometimes did when he cried, he nodded. Pao took his hand, and they ran through the dead vines as fast as they could together. Her only hope was that nothing would happen to Dante's mom before they could reach her. That they wouldn't be too late . . .

What happened instead was worse.

They were ten yards from the edge of the vineyard, when Pao realized the calls for Dante had stopped. She looked up, her stomach sinking, expecting the worst. But the fantasma didn't have the boy's mother. It had picked up the red car and was peering inside with its too-many eyes.

Finally Pao spotted her—from the back, her blue dress and long black hair streaming behind as she ran for the road.

"Stop!" Pao called without thinking. The fantasma didn't hear her over the sound of rending metal, and Dante's mother didn't stop running.

"¿Mamà?" Dante asked, pulling on Pao's arm. "I wanna find Mamà."

"I know," Pao said through the lump in her throat, watching from her higher vantage point as the woman—already too far away to call out to even if there hadn't been an enraged, mutated ghost between them—became nothing more than a cloud of dust up the road.

"Mamà," Dante said again, starting to cry. "¡Mamà!"

Pao was frozen, the horror dawning on her as she patted

his head. This was why Dante had been raised by his abuela. Because his father had been killed in front of him and his mom hadn't looked for her son for more than five minutes before she abandoned him.

Pao shook herself mentally. This was no time to freeze or try to process everything that had befallen this small, adorable child currently clinging to her legs. There would be opportunity for that later. Right now she had to get him to safety, and fast.

But how could she keep him safe and slay this horrible monster at the same time? What was going to happen to him after she woke from this dream?

"Come on," she said to baby Dante, pulling him back into the grapes. She would have to hide him. Tell him to stay put while she killed the fantasma and . . . Well, that was enough to get her started, at least.

They were far enough away when Pao found a well, something that would be a good landmark to return to when she was done with the monster. She didn't need to lose him in here on top of everything else.

"I need you to stay here, okay?" Pao said desperately. "I know kids aren't always the best at listening. . . . I know *I* wasn't when I was your age. . . . Well, the age you are now, anyway? Ugh, never mind. No wonder no one ever asks me to babysit."

As she took a deep breath, Dante was still looking at her with curious eyes.

"You know what, Dante?" she asked him, trying her best to sound happy and sweet and full of wonder like she'd always imagined a babysitter would be. "When you grow up, we're gonna be the same age. And you know what else? We're gonna be best friends, okay? The very best of friends. And you're going to be okay, I promise. You'll be with your abuela, and—"

"¡Abuela!" Dante squealed with delight, breaking Pao's heart again.

"Yep!" she said anyway, smiling as big as she could manage, willing the tears to stay behind her eyeballs for once. She wished she knew how Señora Mata had gotten ahold of baby Dante so she could tell him now and he wouldn't be scared. Instead, she told him everything else he thought his little self would want to know.

"Your abuela is the best lady, Dante," she promised. "And she's gonna take amazing care of you. She makes the yummiest enchiladas, and you'll have two best friends, and a PlayStation, and you'll play soccer, and—"

"¡Abuela!" He was pointing now over Pao's shoulder, clapping and grinning, the tears and snot drying on his face.

Pao turned, not daring to believe it, but there she was. Señora Mata as Pao knew her, stooped-shouldered and white-haired and smirking like she knew exactly what was going on.

"¡Señora!" Pao said, her knees weak with relief. "How did you . . . ? Can you . . . ?"

"Yes, I can see you, Maria, and we don't have much time."

Pao's heart, in her throat a second ago, sank a little. Even here, in a shared dream, the señora didn't know her?

Señora Mata picked up baby Dante, tickling his chin and cooing at him in a way Pao never remembered her doing in Silver Springs, even when Dante was small.

Behind them, the fantasma roared again and gave up on the house. Pao could hear him ripping out grapevines by the roots, moving closer to them.

"It's time to get this baby home," Señora Mata said. "You know what you have to do, Maria."

"I have *no idea* what I'm supposed to do," Pao said, panicking. She had thought Señora Mata would help them, but the old woman didn't even know Pao's name. She was going to take baby Dante and leave Pao all alone with the fantasma.

At least they'll *be safe,* she thought.

"He seeks what they all seek," Señora Mata said, her eyes grave behind her big, round glasses. "Su familia."

"His family?" Pao said. "I don't know what you mean. Can you just tell me what to do? Can *someone* just tell me what I'm supposed to do?"

"You have to find his family first," Señora Mata said, like it was the most obvious thing in the world. "They've been gone fifty years. You find them, you purify, and *poof!*"

Pao was about to ask another question, one of at least twenty more fighting to the front of the line in her brain. But the fantasma's next roar was closer, and Señora Mata didn't look any faster than Pao knew her to be in real life.

If she wanted baby Dante to have a chance, Pao would have to let them go.

"I'll figure it out," Pao said with more confidence than she felt.

"Good girl," Señora Mata replied. Then she looked right into Pao's eyes like she was x-raying her soul. "Whatever they say, Paola, whatever you find out, you know who you are, hmm? You're the one who gets to decide."

Pao, as usual, had no idea what she was talking about, but she nodded anyway. "Hurry," she told the old woman. "I'll keep him from following you."

"I know," Señora Mata said with the kind of wink that meant she'd already seen how this all ended, even if she didn't always know Pao's name. Then, clutching squirming baby Dante around the middle, frail old Señora Mata began to walk slowly through the grapevines.

Over her shoulder, little Dante waved a dimpled hand, looking uncertain. "Best friends?" he asked Pao.

She let out a sort of strangled laugh-sob. "Best friends!" she called, just before the fantasma's roar made him bury his face again. "I'll see you soon, Dante!"

When they were out of sight, Pao turned, ready to take on the fantasma. To close this loop in time once and for all.

EIGHTEEN

Find Them, Purify, and *Poof!*

Pao tore through the vineyard, not bothering to be quiet.

In the dream, she didn't even have her sock knife. She had no idea how she was going to fight the fantasma. She just knew she had to keep it from following Señora Mata and Dante. That was the only thing that mattered.

If she could figure out what Señora Mata had meant about the fantasma's family, she thought as she ran, maybe she could stop him for good. She had seen Raisin Valley. None of the other people there deserved the scourge of the Bad Man Ghost any more than Dante's family had.

She reached the edge of the field, repeating the old woman's words like they were more than the sum of their parts. *You find them, you purify, and* poof!

The only question was, how was she supposed to find the Bad Man's family if they'd been gone fifty years?

Were they ghosts, too?

Before she could continue down this line of totally unscientific questioning, Pao heard footsteps in the vines. She looked up to see the fantasma heading for the well.

"HEY!" Pao yelled without giving herself time to come up

with a plan. "OVER HERE, FIFTEEN-EYES!" In terms of insults, it wasn't her most creative, but the fantasma didn't seem to care. It turned toward her with a snarl, half its eyes still restlessly roaming its surroundings, the other half focused on Pao, who had just stepped out of the field.

Pao's first thought was that the fantasma was much more agile than it looked, but Pao knew she was faster. She darted past the car, crossing the open space between it and the front porch like her gym teacher was standing there with a stopwatch deciding her final grade.

She checked behind her to see if the Bad Man Ghost was following, and sure enough it stalked through the dust, clouds billowing around its feet. Up close she could see it was wearing tattered jeans with a massive belt buckle and a flannel shirt. A long piece of hay dangled from its lips. On its feet, dragging through the dust in an awful zombie shuffle, were the most enormous cowboy boots Pao had ever seen.

This man had been a farmer, she thought. And then he was a ghost. A ghost that had mutated into whatever this thing was.

But if Señora Mata was right, if Pao could find his family, maybe she could put him to rest once and for all.

When she was sure he was focused on the house, Pao ducked inside, careful (after what had happened to Dante's father) to stay away from the windows.

His family, Pao thought, racking her brain. *Where would a man who's been dead fifty years go looking for his family?*

Before she could solve the riddle, Pao found herself distracted. This was the house where Dante had lived as a toddler. With his parents. She couldn't help but take it in.

It was small and sparsely furnished, but clean. On the floor were a few blocks stacked into a tower. A shelf in the living room held photos: little Dante blowing out two candles on a birthday cake, Dante and his father with a dog on the porch of this house. A wedding photo—his mom radiant in white with a veil, looking no older than some high school kids Pao had seen around the Riverside Palace, his father in a suit and a cowboy hat, laughing, his head tipped back.

They were happy. And then this fantasma came and ruined it all.

No wonder Dante hadn't ever wanted to talk about what had happened to his parents, Pao thought, her heart aching for her friend. And no wonder he'd freaked out when he thought he might lose his abuela to the void, too. She was the only family he had left.

The fantasma shattered the front window, pulling Pao out of her thoughts and back into the present—or, the current situation at least. She had to put an end to this, for Dante. For his family.

His family, Pao thought suddenly. Where would you find a family that had been gone fifty years?

Pao raced through the house, searching for more photos. Anything that looked older than the ten years since baby Dante had lived in this house.

There was nothing in the kitchen—the drawers contained only normal things like spatulas and potholders and knives. On the windowsill, beside a velita with a picture of La Virgen de Guadalupe on it, was a bottle of Florida Water.

Knowing it was silly, Pao took a match from the matchbook

beside the candle. With trembling fingers she struck it and lit the wick, looking into the face of La Virgen and asking for protection for Dante and Señora Mata—both the past and present versions. Asking for help as she fought to save them.

Pao probably never would have admitted this to her own mother, but she felt better afterward. Like there was a little bubble of light around them all. Even so, she stuck the sharpest knife from the drawer into her waistband for good measure. It wouldn't do much against the fantasma, but it would be better than nothing at all.

Next she checked the hallway closet and the little boy's bedroom.

No old photos.

Out front, the fantasma roared in frustration, and she heard wood splintering, like he was prying the walls apart to fit inside. From the sound of it, it wouldn't be long before he got in.

Pao was running out of time. There was only one room she hadn't checked. The door was closed, and it gave off the same aura her mom's bedroom did back home—forbidden and fascinating all at once.

But there were no adults left to catch her, and Pao was out of options.

She opened the door to find a queen-size bed neatly made up with a white quilt and pillows with pink roses and eyelet lace. The window had been shattered, and there was glass all over the floor. She carefully tiptoed around it to get to the dresser, where there were three photographs standing in heavy silver frames.

The people in the images were obviously related to Dante and Señora Mata. There was his rounded nose and her twinkling, mischievous expression, her white hair and his stubborn chin.

In the front of the house, the walls rattled. There were no more windows left to break. The fantasma was getting in, one way or another. Pao was sure the answer was here, but as she lifted each photo in her hands, she felt nothing. She didn't know what she expected to perceive, but her instincts told her none of these photos was what the fantasma was looking for.

That's when she saw the jewelry box, tarnished silver like the frames, initials etched in the top: *EMMR + RLFA*. Pao opened it, and *there* was the feeling she'd been waiting for. The tingling along her spine, the goose bumps racing up her arms.

Inside the box was a single item—an old-fashioned locket with a clasp. It looked silver at first glance, but as Pao examined it more closely, the color seemed to shimmer and change like an oil slick.

As Pao held it, she remembered what Naomi had said about banishing household ghosts.

They're attached to an object, or bitter about a wrong that was done to them in that location. It's just about tracking down that source, cutting the cord that's tethering them to the world of the living, and setting them free.

Pao lifted the locket, mesmerized, and the ghost-turned-monster's roars went higher in pitch, telling her he felt something, too. The presence of the family he'd been searching for.

With shaking hands, knowing she didn't have time but needing to see, to understand, Pao opened the clasp.

The fantasma screamed, but this time she could hear pain beneath his rage.

In the tiny, circular frame was a photo, the colors all blown out—oranges and blues too pronounced, lighter skin fading into the bright backdrop.

A woman with long, curly hair, laughing, with two little girls on her lap in matching braids and dresses, holding hands.

Find them, purify, and poof!

Now, for the first time since the old woman had disappeared, Pao knew exactly what to do. *Run, Maria,* she imagined Señora Mata saying.

She took off, the locket balled tightly in her fist, the screams of the fantasma nearly unbearable now, filling the house with a sound like she imagined a tortured animal would make.

Just get to the kitchen, she told herself. *Get to the kitchen and he'll be free.*

But when she reached the hallway, she saw him, flat on his stomach like he'd gotten stuck trying to crawl through the hole he'd made in the wall. He took up half the small living room even with his legs outside. His mutated face was twisted in pain, his long arms reaching, *reaching.* . . .

Unbidden, the memory of Dante's father being tossed against the car returned with a vengeance. Pao still didn't know what happened if you were killed in a dream—a dream where you had already been brought back from the brink of death once—but she wasn't eager to find out today.

The fantasma's arm and head extended all the way to the kitchen's threshold. When she entered the hallway, all fifteen of his bloodshot eyes swiveled to her at once. Her skin crawled—the stench of him was awful in the small space. Like manure and rot and decades of misery and sweat all rolled into one terrible cologne.

Pao gagged, but she clutched the locket even tighter. Was it her imagination, or had the necklace started to heat up?

With a running start, Pao leaped over the monster's outstretched arm into the tiny kitchen.

There was no doubt about it now—the locket was hot, burning Pao's palm, though she didn't dare drop it. Tears sprang to her eyes, like when she was three and she'd touched the stove burner because she'd liked its pretty red color.

Pao made for the sink, finally crying out against the pain in her hand, and tried to drop the locket in the basin to stop the burning. The fantasma was still struggling to get through the hole he'd made, like a panicked, angry rat in a trap.

The locket was stuck to her palm, Pao realized with horror. It wouldn't let go—it just burned hotter until she could smell it singeing her skin. She shook her hand. Nothing. She screamed in frustration, her voice lost in the much louder sounds coming from the fantasma.

"Fine!" Pao shouted, reaching for the bottle of Florida Water and uncapping it with her teeth.

She poured the citrusy liquid over her hand, and the hot locket actually sizzled when it made contact. The Florida Water stung viciously, but the locket reacted, its swirling silver color giving way to a bright, brilliant gold.

Behind her, the fantasma's thrashing reached a fever pitch. Frantic squeals, almost piglike, escaped his giant maw, and every one of his eyes was wide with pain and terror.

Pao pressed herself against the sink, praying this wouldn't be like the time she had tried to stop the chupacabra with Florida Water in the haunted cactus field. Back then, the stuff hadn't done anything more than make the monster mad. Naomi would never let her live down a second failure.

But even as Pao had the thought, the locket stopped sizzling. The fantasma's squeals quieted, giving way to moans of pain. His arm retreated out of the doorway, followed by his head, which lost its crazed eyes until it only had two left, blinking at the ceiling of the house before finally closing.

The Bad Man Ghost shrunk to the size of a regular human. He could have been sleeping there, half in and half out of the house. Pao leaned over the counter to watch as he took a final breath, then let it out, finally dissolving into the air just like Ondina had done in the end.

Once he was gone, Pao's knees finally gave way. She sobbed on the floor until the sunlight changed in the window. Then she got to her feet, the now-gold locket back in her hand, pressing against the burn it had left on her palm.

Outside, the quiet was almost eerie. There was no sign that, just hours ago, a family had been destroyed here.

Pao crossed the dirt lot and headed for the vineyard, ready to end this once and for all. Around her, the colors seemed to leach out of the already-barren landscape, the blue sky turning steel gray, the twisted grapevines losing what little brown they held until they looked like stone.

I'm going to wake up soon, Pao thought. This place was loosening its hold on her at last.

She broke into a run, needing to do one last thing before the past spit her out like a cherry stone. She didn't slow down until she reached the well where she had said good-bye to baby Dante and Señora Mata.

The earth around it was hard and dry, but Pao dug into it with her hands anyway, the locket laying harmlessly beside her, still a vivid gold even as all the surrounding colors faded away.

Pao dug until at least one of her nails was cracked and her fingertips were red and raw. She looked down at the hole she'd made—small but deep enough for her purposes.

Picking up the locket, Pao opened it once more to look at the mother and two girls. Hopefully their father would find them now, wherever they were.

"Descansa en paz," Pao whispered to them, remembering the phrase from a funeral she'd attended with her mom. She could have sworn the locket heated up a little in response. Not the destructive burning temperature from before, but a warm glow, like it had been sitting in the sun.

With tears in her eyes—for this family, and for Dante and his parents—Pao dropped the locket into the hole and covered it with the gray earth. As she packed it down and smoothed it over, she waited for the dream to dissolve, eager to wake up in the present.

Instead, something else happened.

Like a seed on one of those time-lapse videos, a plant sprouted from the place where Pao had buried the locket. Pao pushed herself backward, half scooting, half crab-walking away as the strange golden seedling began to grow.

And grow.

And grow.

Within seconds, there was a closed flower bud the size of a basketball sitting at Pao's feet, quivering with life.

She knew this was a dream, and that the plant—or whatever it was—had grown from a potentially corrupted artifact that had caused the death and destruction of people and families just moments earlier.

But Pao was a scientist first and foremost, and there was no way she wasn't going to investigate this phenomenon further.

The colors around her were still fading, the grape fields now looking more like a black-and-white photo than a living place. She stepped forward, ready to pry open the strange pod to see what was inside, but the moment her fingertip touched it, it bloomed into a giant golden flower.

And at its center was an object that made Pao catch her breath.

It was a magnifying glass, and it looked like an antique. The handle was made out of the same gold the locket had been, with identical swirls and embellishments. The lens, surrounded by a gold frame, was thick and sturdy.

Pao stared at it in wonder, this beautiful tool, unlike anything she'd ever seen.

The pistil of the flower raised up a little when she hesitated, as if inviting her to pluck the object. The light coming off it was welcoming and warm against the fading dream landscape.

Pao reached out, wary but entranced, and grabbed the handle, freeing it gently from the flower. When she held it up, it felt perfect in her grip, warm like the locket had been, and buzzing with energy.

"Gracias," Pao whispered. The flower folded up again, shrank, and retreated into the ground like it had never existed. The magnifying glass remained in Pao's hand, but the surprises didn't end there.

Just as the grapevines started to dissolve and the sky turned white, the magnifying glass changed shape like Pao had only seen one other thing do in her life.

As the tool shifted, she pictured herself and Dante in the living room of his apartment, watching with their mouths open as his abuela's old yellow chancla had changed into a man's blue corduroy slipper right before their eyes.

She remembered the first time she'd heard someone say its name with awe, in the camp of Los Niños de la Luz.

She thought of the moment the house shoe had transformed into a fearsome club just in time to save everyone from the Manos Pachonas, and recalled the wonder she'd felt . . . and the jealousy, too.

And now the same kind of magic was happening in her own hand. The magnifying glass that had already been a marvel was stretching out like a piece of taffy, getting longer and longer until it was taller than Pao herself, shimmering in the air until it settled into its true form.

It was a staff. Lightweight and perfectly balanced, a deep-purple color shot through with veins of blue and gold. At the end was a vicious-looking blade no longer than her hand, its surface opalescent like Marisa's water sword.

An Arma del Alma of her very own.

Pao barely had a chance to admire the staff before the landscape dissolved for good. All she could do was cling to it, close her eyes, and let herself be lost.

NINETEEN

The Unlikely Hero

Pao awoke on a strange sofa, gasping for breath, her hairline beaded with sweat. Her head swam like it sometimes did when she'd spent days in bed with the flu.

The first thing she did was yank up the sleeve of her shirt, searching frantically for the infected bite that had landed her in this situation to begin with.

It was gone. The healing in the pool had been real. So did that mean . . . ?

Pao patted the couch all around her, and then her clothes, her heart sinking fast until she felt something in the left front pocket of her jeans. She pulled it out to find a magnifying glass. Not the ornate-handled golden thing she had picked from the flower in her dream—this one sleek, silver, and foldable, with a keychain attached so she wouldn't lose it.

Her Arma del Alma. Pao sighed in relief. It had been real. It *was* real. And it was all hers.

Even though it was more modern now, the metal's shine still swirled like something from another world, and when Pao unfolded it and peered through the lens, everything looked like it was lit from within by golden light.

Pao wanted to examine the object and practice transforming it for hours, but she knew there was no time for that. She needed to find present-day Dante, tell him everything, and show him that, with her staff, she could finally fight by his side instead of waiting for him to come to the rescue.

He'd be happy for her, wouldn't he?

There was only one way to find out.

Gingerly, Pao got to her feet. The wound on her arm was healed, but she still felt like she'd *actually* traversed a magic forest and rescued a child from a fantasma. Her head spun, and she closed her eyes a moment before opening them and looking around properly.

She was in the same living room where she'd seen photos of baby Dante, but there was no comparing this house to how it had looked ten years ago.

It was no longer the cozy, clean home it had once been. The photos were gone, along with the neat furniture and the baby toys on the floor. In the kitchen, clothes lay in piles, dirty dishes were stacked in the sink, and ants crawled away in a trail to the door. There was no more Florida Water on the windowsill. No more smiling Virgen de Guadalupe.

Pao's heart sank as she looked around the unhappy room, cast in bluish light by the harsh fluorescent fixture in the ceiling. She tried to reconcile her pity for the widow with the anger Pao felt at her for leaving Dante alone at three years old.

There was no sign of anyone here—of Naomi or Dante or the woman who had answered the door. Pao checked the bedroom where she'd found the locket. It was empty, the bed rumpled and unmade, a collection of wine bottles and an ashtray on the night table. Pao left quickly. These things were too personal for a stranger to see.

She tried the little boy's room next, but whatever use it was being put to now, it was locked. Pao knocked lightly, and there was no answer.

The empty house made her anxious. Where was everyone? How long had she been unconscious? She stepped out onto the front porch, distracted momentarily by the multitude of stars so unbelievably visible here. There were whole galaxies out there, Pao thought. An infinite number of possibilities. The thought, as paradoxical as it was, grounded her. It gave her courage.

The lot around the house looked as it had in her dream—minus the red car and the white fence, which had been replaced by chain link. Pao remembered the way the fantasma had ripped up the long line of pickets in a single motion. . . .

Dante was nowhere to be seen, but as she stood looking out over the vineyard, she knew where she would find him.

Pao walked toward the well, catching sight of him halfway there. It was surreal to see him looking like his seventh-grade self again, when the last time she'd seen him . . .

Suddenly, Pao felt self-conscious, even a little guilty, about everything she'd witnessed. In the moment it had all been so urgent—there'd been no time to stop and think about what was going on. But here and now, she felt like she had read Dante's diary or something. She knew stuff he had never wanted her to know.

Would it make things between them better, or worse? she wondered.

Pao had thought she was approaching quietly, but Dante—who

was kneeling on the ground with his back to her—stood up when she reached him. He was still wearing his outfit from before: a soccer jersey and tan pants with white sneakers. His hair was the same, too—shaggy, extending past his collar in the back.

But something was different about him.

Pao opened her mouth to say hello, but Dante was quicker.

"You went back, didn't you?" He didn't even turn around to say it.

Pao deflated a little at the tone in his voice. Apparently her knowing what had happened to his parents was not going to bring them closer.

"Yeah," she said, sliding the magnifying glass back into her pocket.

"So you saw everything."

"I don't know *why* I did, though," Pao said earnestly, stepping forward. "I was in this forest, a duendecillo healed my arm, and then . . ." She trailed off, not knowing how to describe the horrors she had witnessed.

"And then you watched my dad get murdered and did nothing to stop it."

Pao stopped in her tracks, leaving a row of grapevines between them.

"There was nothing I could have done," she said. "I didn't even know what was happening until after he . . . Dante, I wasn't even armed."

He couldn't make *this* her fault, too, could he? If he really remembered all this, if he knew what she'd seen ten years ago, that meant she hadn't just been dreaming. She had traveled back in time! She had saved his life!

"There's always some excuse, isn't there?" Dante said. "For the destruction you cause. *I don't MEAN to, I'm never TRYING to hurt anyone,* but everyone around you still gets damaged, don't they, Pao?" His impression of her voice was high and whiny. Cruel. The way the soccer boys talked about the girls they didn't like while hanging at the pizza place after school.

Dante had never joined in those conversations before. It had been one of the ways Pao knew she hadn't fully lost him yet.

Apparently, he'd been saving all his mockery for her.

"If it was all real, why didn't you ever tell me?" she demanded. "You could've warned me! I could've done things differently!"

Dante scoffed. "Our roles in all this were decided way before that day, Pao. There was no stopping what happened." His shoulders tensed visibly, like he was in pain.

"Then why are you blaming me for—"

He ignored her, interrupting. "There's no stopping what happens next, either."

Goose bumps erupted along Pao's arms again. The stars above them seemed to dim a little.

"What are you talking about?" Pao asked warily, trying to calm down. "You don't . . . You don't sound like yourself. Why don't we just—"

Dante interrupted her with a barking laugh. "I'm more myself than I've been in a long time," he said. "Ever since that fantasma killed my father and tore apart my family."

"It was awful," Pao said. "I know. I'm so s—"

"Don't!" Dante snarled. "Don't say you're sorry! You're not. You're not capable of it. You know what my biggest mistake has been this whole time, Pao?"

"What?" she whispered, sensing something awful coming, like smelling a thunderstorm in the air before the first lightning strike.

"Believing you when you played the hero. Because you're *not* a hero."

"I never thought I was," she said in disbelief. She'd known things were bad with Dante, but this? It sounded like some sinister movie character was hiding in the vines beside him, feeding him his lines. This wasn't her best friend talking.

Pao pinched herself, afraid she was still dreaming. But it hurt. Just like his words.

Dante kneeled down again. "My father was killed by a fantasma right in front of me when I was just a kid. My mom ran away, leaving me alone to die."

"But you *didn't* die," Pao said, a tiny seed of hope taking root in her chest. She knew this boy, better than she knew herself sometimes. She could bring him back from whatever this was before it was too late. She had saved him before—why couldn't she do it again? "You didn't die, because I—"

"Yeah, I knew you were gonna try to take credit for that," he said, beginning to dig in the dirt in front of him. "But it wasn't you who saved me, was it? You were going to leave me alone, right here, just like *she* did. It was my abuela who saved me. *My* abuela, a former member of Los Niños de la Luz, who handed down the Arma del Alma to me. That weapon's the *only reason* we got out alive last summer, you know that, right?"

"It's not the only reason," Pao said automatically. Hadn't she been the one who made it through the rift? Fought her way through the ruins outside the glass palace to find him? Forged a connection with Ondina and used it to defeat one of the most feared fantasmas of all time? Gotten them all home safely?

"*I'm* the one with the childhood grudge," Dante continued, like he hadn't heard her. "*I* have the grandma with the mysterious powers and a history with the Niños. *I have the club*." He stood up now, reaching into his pocket for the chancla and turning to face her at last. "And yet *you're* the hero?" He took a step toward her. "Why?"

The slipper transformed immediately this time—he must have been practicing. He held the club at his side and looked at Pao, his eyes bloodshot, his mouth curled into a cruel sneer.

"Why wouldn't it be me?" he asked, swinging his weapon idly back and forth. "I deserve it more—I fit the part. And you have this bad side, don't you, Pao? This selfish, destructive bad side that hurts everyone you love."

"I don't," Pao said, though his words slowed her down. "I don't hurt them."

Suddenly, she was struggling to hold back tears. Sure, what he was saying was awful, but Pao knew who she was. She wasn't about to let someone change what she believed about herself with a few jealous, ill-placed words.

The thing bringing her to tears was the fact that it was *Dante* saying these things. If he really meant them, then it was truly over between them. A lifetime of friendship, gone. And for what?

"What happened to you?" she asked him, stepping closer, making sure her hand was on the magnifying glass in her pocket. Just in case.

Dante would never hurt me, she told herself. *Even if he's hurting, he would never hurt me.*

"I learned the truth," he said, mouth in a grim line now, all humor gone from his expression. "The truth about what happened that day when my father died. The truth about who you are and how little you deserve that hero status you're always lording over us."

"I *never* lorded—" Pao began, but once again Dante cut her off.

"I'm *the only one who can do this!*" Dante said, repeating that cruel impression of her. "I'm *the only one who can find Emma, fight the Manos, end La Llorona for good!*"

"I *did* do all those things!" Pao cried, getting angrier, her fist wrapping around the magnifying glass. "I did them because my dreams happen to tell me what's coming. And no, that doesn't make me a hero, but it does give me the power to help!"

"Yeah," Dante said, his club swinging in a wider arc now. "Your mysterious prophetic dreams. The ones that show you when everyone's in danger way too late to help them without risking a bunch of other people's lives." His eyes bored right into hers. "Haven't you ever wondered *why* you have those dreams, Pao? Why you're connected to the head of every monster in the flipping world?"

"I don't . . . know why I have the dreams," Pao said, though of course she had wondered a thousand times. "All I can do is use them to help the people I love."

"You really don't get it, do you?" he asked. "Big, powerful scientist Pao with the magic dreams and the explosive temper. You really don't see what you are. But I do."

Dante swung the club at her.

He really did it.

Pao's moment of shock was almost too long, but she jumped

back and avoided the first swing, drawing out the magnifying glass just in time. She willed it to become a staff before Dante's club reached her on its second arc.

The lens lengthened in one direction, the handle in the other, and within a second, the staff was solid and balanced in her hand, its knife head glinting dangerously in the starlight.

She parried Dante's blow with the center of the staff, pushing him off her, surprised at how much power the weapon gave her every movement. Pao had never been much for athletics, but this was different. This was *everything*.

Dante's eyes widened in surprise as he was forced back against the stone well. "What is . . . ? Where did you get that?"

"You mean my *Arma del Alma*?" Pao asked. "Guess you don't know everything about me after all." Her satisfaction at interrupting his attempt to define her was the only thing preventing her heart from breaking into splinters.

He readied for another attack.

They were supposed to be fighting side by side, not against each other.

Was this really how their story ended?

"I've seen the real you, Pao," he said, stepping forward, putting his whole weight into another swing. "*He* showed me everything. How weak you are, how much you *don't* deserve to be the face of some ghost-fighting rebellion."

"Who showed you?" Pao asked. "Where is this coming from?"

"A much better friend than you," Dante said. "Or did you think you could isolate me from everyone? Keep me from ever knowing anyone besides you, the way you tried to do with my soccer friends."

"I just didn't want to lose you, Dante!" she said, dancing out of range. "I still don't! Please, think this through. Where are you going to go after this? What are you going to do?"

Dante swung again, and Pao blocked and kept her distance, not willing to strike back. "I'm going somewhere where you can't get into my head anymore," he said. "To join forces with someone who *really* has the power you only pretend to have. Someone who's been hurt as much as I have by people like you."

"Please," Pao said, jumping back when he lunged. He over-extended, and Pao couldn't help thinking it would be the perfect time to attack. But she still couldn't make herself hurt him. "I want to help you. I want to help your abuela. You guys are my family—please don't give up on me!"

"Don't talk about her!" Dante said, swinging again, this time too wide, leaving his left side exposed. He had never learned how to protect himself, only to attack with full power.

Pao let the opportunity pass yet again, keeping her staff still even as the magic in it urged her to fight back. *Not yet,* she told it. *We're not there yet.* She hoped they would never get to that point. She hoped it so hard her heart felt like it was being put through a lemon-squeezer.

"You're not our family, Pao," Dante continued, relentless. "Your *family* is the reason this is all happening. I tried to keep you away from us, tried to protect myself and my abuela, but you just couldn't take a hint."

Hit him, said some combination of the staff's humming magic and Pao's own shifting instincts. Her amygdala, which had always been calmed by Dante's presence as an ally, was rapidly recategorizing him as a threat.

But she didn't obey.

"Do you know what she sacrificed to get me out of here alive?" Dante was asking her now. "To raise me on my own? And then *you* drag the very forces that killed her son back into our lives. You steal her memory and force me to go on this terrible mission when I should be with her! I should *be with her!*"

This time, Pao didn't block fast enough. The club crunched her shoulder, and she cried out. Her whole arm tingled like it had been shocked, and it felt hot and cold all at once.

He'd really hit her. Pao registered the fact almost clinically, like she was a judge sitting on the sidelines, subtracting friendship points, instead of standing here in front of him holding a weapon.

Pao righted herself from the blow and saw that he was standing still, club at the ready, wanting to finish his speech before he struck again.

Dante didn't believe Pao could attack him. But he didn't know her anymore. He was proving that with every misguided word out of his mouth. He didn't know her at all.

Pao lunged forward, her lightweight staff unimaginably quick. She used the handle only, taking care to keep the blade away from Dante. His unwieldy club—great for high-powered shots against clumsy monsters—couldn't keep up with her strikes. Soon she had him against the well, her staff pinning his club arm uselessly to his side.

"It doesn't have to be like this," Pao said, panting, her arm searing where his club had hit it, her knees weak from exhaustion and heartbreak.

"It's always like this," Dante said, a horrible grin lighting up his face. "Heroes fighting villains. Since the dawn of time. Why should we be any different?"

"Because I'm not a villain," Pao said. *And you're not a hero*, she thought.

"Keep telling yourself that," Dante said, still grinning as he spit blood into the grapevines. "You're the one always going on and on about the importance of *critical thinking*. You really should have figured it out by now."

"Figured *what* out?" Pao said, her temper getting the better of her. She angled the staff so that the blade was closer to Dante's arm. "Just tell me already!"

"Why don't you ask your precious papi," Dante said. "Didn't you promise me he had all the answers?"

"I beat you," Pao said, ignoring the dig about her dad. "Fair and square. So if you won't tell me what you mean, then at least tell me where we go from here."

Pao was asking herself that question, too. What was she going to do with Dante now that she had him trapped? What *could* she do? She had only ever fought ghosts and monsters before. They didn't generally stick around after a battle. Pao, as many foes as she'd felled, had never taken a prisoner.

She'd always prided herself on seeing the big picture, being prepared for anything. But how could she ever have prepared herself for this?

"You think you *beat* me?" Dante asked, laughing, his teeth red with the blood he'd spat. "Evil *and* naive. It would be cute if it wasn't so sad."

It was the word *cute* that did it. There was a time not too long ago when Pao would have loved to hear him say it. But he never had then, and now he was using the word as a weapon against her.

She pressed the staff harder, the blade inching closer to his skin. She'd never thought she could hurt him, especially not on purpose, but in this moment it was seeming more and more possible. If he wanted to put them in these roles, if he couldn't *stand* to let her be who she was, then he was right. He was her enemy.

The blade was there, ready to cut into skin. She should have realized Dante wasn't even trying to stop her, but she didn't. Not until he used his other hand to open a golden locket, dirt falling away as the two frames parted.

"No," Pao said, pulling back the staff instinctively, getting ready to knock the trinket out of his hand. "You wouldn't." But it was too late.

Dante spoke a few inaudible words to the locket, then dropped it on the ground between them. Pao knew what would happen a split second before it did, even though she didn't understand *how* it could. The Bad Man Ghost stretched out of the frame like he was toothpaste being squeezed through a giant toxic tube.

In seconds, the fantasma was restored—the same terrifying monster he'd been ten years ago. Two stories tall, cowboy boots and belt buckle on full display.

Only this time, his eyes glowed bright green. All fifteen of them.

"You'll never beat me," Dante said to Pao. "*I'm* the good guy."

And then he ran off, leaving her alone with a roaring monster and a broken heart.

TWENTY

Fighting Monsters Alone Isn't
All It's Cracked Up to Be

The first time she'd faced this monster, Pao had goals in mind.

To keep the fantasma away from baby Dante and Señora Mata as they retreated. To reach the locket and purify it before the fantasma searching for it destroyed more than the family it had already torn apart.

This time, things were different. Pao had no one left to protect. Naomi was nowhere to be found (had she continued her search north for the Niños alone?), and Dante was gone.

Dante was *gone*.

For good.

On the ground at her feet, the locket Pao had risked everything to find ten-years-slash-half-an-hour ago lay motionless, its gold luster faded to an unremarkable brassy tone that told Pao any magic that had once been stored in it had dissipated.

And speaking of dissipating, hadn't the fantasma dissolved when Pao poured Florida Water on the locket? She'd given the specter what it was searching for so it could go in peace. If it had been sent to the void, how had Dante called it back?

But there was no time to puzzle over that mystery. The fantasma roared, and Pao scrambled behind the well for cover. Using her brand-new staff against a kid with a club (Pao refused to even think his name until this was over) was one thing. Using it, alone, against a thirty-foot-tall monster with the power of the void behind him? That was a little different.

With a single swipe of his massive, filthy-nailed hand, the fantasma scattered the stones of the well, sending them crumbling into the depths.

Okay, Pao thought. Maybe it was a *lot* different.

Pao was exhausted. She was miserable. She had been battered and bruised and broken and brought back to life (not exactly in that order), all in the past few hours.

Still, she stepped out from behind the pile of rubble that had once been the well, holding her chin high, her shoulders square, and her Arma del Alma out in front of her.

She wasn't going to let *that boy* be right about her. She was going to prove she *could* be a hero, no matter how little she'd wanted to be one. No matter what *he* or anyone else thought.

It was with that desire to prove the world wrong that Pao struck her first blow against the monster, a swipe to his shin that made him cry out in anguish and confusion. She smiled, imagining how she must look to him from all the way up there. A tiny girl, barely the height of his knee, in skinny jeans and a black hoodie with a long purple stick.

But she had hurt him. And she was going to do it again.

Her next blow got him in the thigh. He was really angry now, swatting at her with his big, slow hands like she would stand still and take the hit the way the pile of stones had.

He would be disappointed, Pao thought grimly. *Can't sit still* was the one criticism all her report cards had in common.

She struck again and again, in the back of his knees mostly, but the ankles, too. She made a couple of stabs straight down into the toes of his gigantic cowboy boots. Each time, he howled in pain and swung a massive fist or a boot at her, but slowly, due to his massive size.

Each time, Pao dodged and struck him again.

The only problem was, her arms were getting tired, and she was out of breath from running and weaving. Soon, she'd be exhausted enough to make a mistake. She had to end this before then, and whacking him again and again from the midthigh down wasn't going to do it.

After her next hit (a long-distance jab right to the patellar tendon), Pao ran toward the house. It was empty now, and she knew from her trip into the past (not to mention, like, the laws of physics) that he couldn't fit through the front door.

He'd have to crouch, Pao realized, picturing the way he'd stuck himself in the hole he'd made in the door during their last tangle. If he was down that low, she'd be able to hit him in one of his eyes.

That should do the trick, she thought, crossing her fingers as she darted through the screen door, leaving it bouncing behind her in a way that would have made her mom scream "*Paola!*" But right now, she wanted to make as much noise as possible. She had to keep him interested long enough to entice him to try widening the gap in the wall again.

Pao thought of the woman who lived here, who'd presumably already had to rebuild the front of her house once, and said a silent apology as she headed for the kitchen.

"You can't get me!" Pao called at the top of her lungs.

Outside, the fantasma screamed in frustration, hammering at the windows in an all-too-familiar way.

Good, she thought. *Keep it up.*

In the kitchen, Pao went straight for that super-loud drawer under the oven, the one her mom was always yelling at her for banging open even though no one could pull it quietly.

As she'd predicted, it was full of greasy cookie sheets and frying pans. It had obviously been a while since anyone had cooked in here (or cleaned, Pao thought, the smell of the sink full of dishes making her a little queasy).

Armed with noise-making devices, Pao headed back to the living room, where the fantasma was already prying at the siding, attempting to widen the too-small doorway. The sound was awful—wood splintering and screaming like it was being tortured.

Anytime the fantasma stopped, or even slowed, Pao banged a frying pan against the biggest cookie sheet she could find, making a cacophony that reignited the monster's fury and sent him tearing at the boards again.

Pao's staff was beside her, propped against the couch, ready and waiting. She knew she could strike a blow through the window or front door, but she remembered what the fantasma had done to *a certain toddler's* father.

She didn't want to be snatched out the window by one of those long-reaching arms. She had to wait until he was stuck again. That's when she'd have him.

The waiting was agony. Several times, in fact, Pao wanted to step into the doorway and critique his dismantling skills. Finally there was a hole big enough for one of his hands to reach through, and half his face, and he was swatting at everything, those ragged, dirty nails desperate to claw Pao into pieces.

Almost there, she thought, dropping the pans and taking her staff in hand again.

Almost.

She heard it at the least opportune moment. Screaming and pounding—faint but definitely there. Coming from inside the house.

Pao didn't think before she turned to look at the boy's bedroom door. The one that she'd found locked earlier.

The split second her focus was elsewhere was enough for the fantasma to get his chance. He seized Pao around the ankle—causing her to drop her staff in surprise—and slammed her into the wall, sending shock waves of pain through her body.

In Pao's brain, there was no plan anymore, just alarm bells, fire truck sirens, and the screams of people on runaway roller coasters. She was going to be smashed to bits by a mutated old farmer ghost that had been resurrected by her ex-best friend. And there was nothing she could do about it.

If only she hadn't dropped her staff, Pao thought, remembering the way it had felt in her hand as the monster got a grip around her waist and squeezed the breath out of her. With a weapon like that, she could have fought back. She could have survived.

When the long, thin purple stick suddenly met her outstretched hand, Pao didn't know what was happening at first. Then she realized that, merely by thinking of her staff, by visualizing it in her hand, Pao had actually summoned it to her.

Any doubt she'd had about deserving an Arma del Alma was

dispelled for good in that moment. This staff was as much a part of Pao as her own arm.

And, luckily, with infinitely more destructive capability.

The fantasma was still stuck in the doorway. He held Pao at arm's length, half his eyes and his mouth squished into the now-wider door frame.

She just had to get to his face, Pao knew. Eventually he would try to slam her against the wall again, or eat her, or something else terrifying. That's when she would strike.

The moment arrived before she was ready. Like *way* before. Pao flailed, knowing she wouldn't be able to get into position in time, but somehow the staff knew what to do (or was it reading her thoughts? Either way, it was really, really cool).

The staff spun in Pao's grip like a compass needle pointing north, and by the time the fantasma had dragged her toward its open mouth, Pao was perfectly situated to jam the Arma del Alma into the closest of the fifteen eyes with all the force she could muster.

Thanks to the wild swings of the giant hand still grasping her, half the staff was buried in his big, ugly head in less than a second. There was no roar. No wail of agony or frustration or rage.

There was only one long sound, like air being let out of a balloon, as the fantasma deflated. His hand became too small to hold on to Pao, leaving her sprawled on the living room floor gasping for breath.

This time, though, when he reached his former size, he didn't float away.

He exploded.

Pao saw the pieces of burning material flutter down like

glowing red rain through the ruined door until, finally, there was nothing left but the scorch marks on the front porch to prove he had ever been there at all.

Dragging herself to her feet, knees shaking, Pao walked onto the porch to retrieve her staff. She wanted nothing more than to lie down on the sofa again, to close her eyes and sleep until her heart stopped hurting and her body stopped aching.

A year or two should do it, she thought. *Three, tops.*

Instead, she dragged herself back into the house, her heart heavy, every limb aching and sore, to investigate yet another mystery.

"Pao?" came a voice from inside the bedroom door. Naomi's. "Pao, are you there? We're locked in!"

"I'm here!" Pao called, trying to sound like her heart hadn't just been through a meat grinder. "I have to figure out how to get you out!"

"There's a key," said another voice. Softer and lightly accented. "He probably took one with him, but there's a spare in the drawer next to the oven."

"Be right back," Pao called.

The drawer was crammed with batteries, a broken remote control, and several random pushpins that stabbed Pao's fingers as she dug through. Lanyards with no keys attached and screws in baggies with folded instructions taped to them.

Finally, at the bottom of the drawer, with what looked to be a handful of sunflower seeds, was a silver key.

Pao walked back to the door slowly, bracing herself for what was going to happen when she opened it. Losing her best friend had been painful enough, but when she told Naomi about it?

When she confronted the mother who had abandoned her son to set all this in motion? That would make it real. And Pao wasn't sure she was ready for real.

Regardless, she pulled open the door, a little nauseated when she saw that the room hadn't been changed at all in ten years. It was still home to the toddler bed painted blue, the toy box, the pile of dusty stuffed animals in the corner.

His mom had kept it all as some kind of shrine. Pao wanted to cry. She wanted to run.

"Are you okay?" Naomi asked, stepping out into the hallway, none of her usual snarkiness in her demeanor. "Where's Dante? What happened? He told us he had something to do. He locked us in here 'for our safety,' and just left. You were out cold. We didn't know if he was helping you, or . . ."

As Naomi spoke, Pao looked behind her at the woman who wasn't even trying to leave the room. She was just sitting on the little boy's bed and staring vacantly at the wall.

It was too much. Pao could feel her stomach doing backflips, the tears building up, the lump in her throat.

"Can you keep an eye on her?" Pao asked Naomi, interrupting her. "I'll be right back. There's one more thing. . . ."

She didn't wait for a response, just ran out the door. She made it as far as the second row of grapevines before she threw up all over the ground, the heaves giving way to sobs that racked her body.

Pao hoped that Naomi couldn't hear her. That she would assume whatever Pao had run out to do was important ghost-hunting business.

Instead, Pao fished her phone out of her pocket, still crying, found Emma's contact by the picture alone, and pressed the button for video. She needed to see a familiar face. To remember that she wasn't utterly alone.

"Pao?" Emma's voice said before her picture loaded onto the screen. "What's going on? Are you okay?"

"N-no," Pao sniffled. "Nothing's okay. He's gone and he hates me and he tried to kill me and I have an Arma del Alma but I have no idea what to do. I'm in way over my head and—"

"Slow down," Emma said, her voice like a cool washcloth across Pao's forehead. "Take a deep breath, okay?"

Pao tried to, dragging air in through her snotty nose and hiccupping halfway through. She opened her eyes enough to see Emma's face, her glittery lip gloss, that little bump in her bangs.

"Good," Emma said, smiling encouragingly at Pao with her perfectly straight teeth. "Now take another one."

Pao did as she was told. Then she blew her nose on her shirt and inhaled again for good measure.

"Are you safe?" Emma asked, not smiling now, but calm enough to make space for Pao to fall apart.

Pao nodded, not trusting her voice yet. "There was a fantasma, but . . . he's gone now. It's quiet."

"Where's Dante?" Emma asked. "You said he was gone—did he get taken? Was it another *ahogada*?" She overpronounced the name in a way that was so cute, Pao almost giggled.

But she couldn't. Not when the next answer was going to make it all real.

"He left," she said, her voice hollow. "For good."

Pao could tell Emma was trying hard not to overreact to this news, and she loved her for it.

"He'll be back," Emma said automatically. "He always comes back. He's just having a hard time with his abuela and everything. It's not your fault, Pao, okay? He'll be back."

Sniffing, Pao shook her head, knowing she must look like a total mess, but not caring. "He said awful things. He's been talking to someone, a new ally. He said . . . He said I didn't deserve to be the hero, and that . . ." She was crying again. She couldn't go on.

"Wow," Emma said. "Listen, Pao that *is* awful, okay? I didn't mean to make excuses for him. Just because he's hurting doesn't mean he deserves to treat you that way. There's no excuse for abusive behavior, even when you're traumatized."

Pao could tell Emma was exerting a herculean effort not to tell her which of the Rainbow Rogues' lunchtime webinars she had learned this from.

"You're right," Pao said. "You're right. It's just . . ."

"He's your best friend," Emma said when Pao trailed off. "He's been with you through everything. You were supposed to be able to trust him no matter what, and he betrayed that trust. But, Pao, it says nothing about you, and *everything* about him, okay? You're not the destructive one. You're not the one who hurts people."

She felt Emma's words move through her like the golden light that had grown her Arma del Alma. They lit her up and made all the empty, cold places easier to bear.

"Thank you," Pao said, knowing they didn't have much more time. Soon she'd be alone again with the weight of the world on her shoulders. So, instead of talking more, instead of explaining, Pao just sat in the silence of the empty vineyard and looked at her best friend and took more deep breaths.

"Your mom will probably call soon, huh?" Emma said after a few minutes.

"Yeah."

"Look," Emma said, "I don't know much about the void or the fantasmas or anything else, but I do know you. And you're not in over your head, Pao. You're the smartest, most capable, most amazing person I know." She took a deep breath. "Your heart is so big, and your instincts are so good, and I know this hurts, okay? But you're gonna find your dad. You're gonna save Señora Mata. And you're gonna do it with or without old what's-his-name, because that's who you are. You *are* a hero. You're my hero."

Emma was blushing a little, and Pao couldn't help it—despite the snot and the tears drying her eyes all crusty, she smiled. A big, genuine smile. "You're my hero, too," she said. "You saved the day just now, that's for sure."

"I know you've known *him* longer," Emma said. "But you're not alone, either. You still have one best friend left, and I'm not ever going anywhere."

The tears were back, but this time they were happy ones. Pao heard the door to the house open, footsteps on the porch.

"I gotta go," she said, though it was kind of the last thing in the world she wanted to do. "Stay safe, okay?"

"You too," Emma said. "Call soon? As soon as you can?"

"I will," Pao promised, not knowing when she said it how impossible the promise would prove to keep.

TWENTY-ONE
You Have Died of Dysentery!

By the time Naomi found her in the vineyard, Pao had collected herself.

"We need to get out of here as soon as possible," Pao said, getting to her feet and brushing the dirt off her pants. She hoped she looked like she'd just been doing something really important and not crying to her best friend.

"What the heck happened?" Naomi asked, real curiosity in her eyes. "How is your arm better? And where's hero boy, anyway? I want him to answer for the three hours I just spent locked in that closet while you were apparently fighting a fantasma alone."

Hero boy, Pao thought, letting it sting for a moment before she moved on. The nickname had a very different ring to it after the speech he'd made.

"He's not a hero," Pao said. "And he's gone. For good. We need to go on without him."

"Gone?" Naomi said, catching up as Pao walked toward the house.

She had a few questions for Dante's mom before they hit the road. Pao had a feeling she wouldn't be seeing her again after this.

"Gone."

"Gone where? Hey, wait up! Aren't you usually, like, busting at the seams to chatter to someone about something?"

"People change," said Pao, and she felt the truth of it in her chest. She had changed today. Forever.

"Listen, if I'm going to help you," said Naomi, "you're gonna have to tell me stuff!"

Pao realized it felt good, being pestered for information by a girl who had once considered herself so superior. Pao planned to keep up this dynamic for as long as she could.

Assuming Naomi didn't up and walk out on her, too.

"Someone has been talking to Dante—in his dreams, most likely. I think it's someone from the void, because this person knew things they couldn't know otherwise. Things about the past. They've been poisoning Dante's mind." Pao left out a lot, of course. Like what Dante had said about her family being the reason this was all happening. Pao was determined to get to the bottom of that on her own.

Naomi whistled, long and low. "So he's turned on us? Joined the other side? I never saw that coming."

"He thinks he's the good guy," Pao told Naomi, not meeting her eyes. It was easier to get this out when they were walking side by side. "He called me the villain. Said I destroy everything I touch. He's made his choice."

"Harsh," Naomi said. "You okay? Didn't you guys have some kind of—"

"I'm fine," Pao said. "I just need to get on the road. I want to make it to the anomaly by tomorrow." She finally turned to face Naomi. "Do you know anything about whatever it is that's influencing Dante?"

If Naomi did, she didn't let on. "No clue," she said. "The only person I've ever known who could talk to void creatures in their dreams was you."

"Señora Mata can access the dreams, too," Pao said. "I saw her in one of them. You sure it's not some kind of Niños de la Luz thing? Or an ancestor of *mine . . . ?*" She was thinking hard about what Dante had said about her origin story, about her not putting together the pieces of who she was.

Like *he'd* been able to do it without his mysterious void ally, Pao thought scathingly.

"Not that I know of," Naomi said, shaking her head. "I've never heard of a Niño with that kind of power. And Dante's grandma? Whoever she is, she was before my time."

"Hmm," Pao said, thinking hard. "Another mystery." *Another question to ask my dad,* she noted privately. She'd never been so motivated to reach him. The list of things she needed him to explain was growing by the minute.

Because, even if Dante had been vague and totally cruel, he had confirmed one thing for Pao before he left—her father *was* somehow connected to all this. The rifts, the void, the magic, all of it. She just needed to know how his puzzle piece fit.

"One more thing," Naomi said, "and I hate to bring it up when this is all so . . . fresh. But didn't we kind of need hero b—I mean what's-his-name—along for the ride? At least for his big, shiny club? Without it, how we gonna deal with the fantasmas that seem to be stalking you? Because you were very nearly roadkill back at that rest stop, and—"

Pao ended this line of questioning by pulling the magnifying glass out of her pocket and envisioning it as a staff, willing it to transform.

Naomi gasped audibly as it did, the butt of it hitting the

ground with a *thud* and the blade stretching toward the night sky. Its gold marbling glowed faintly. Pao filed away that useful fact for later.

"Is that . . . ? How did you . . . ? Where . . . ?"

Pao smirked. Naomi, speechless? Maybe Emma had been right to call Pao amazing after all.

"It's an Arma del Alma," Pao said casually, like she plucked superpowerful soul weapons from dream flowers all the time. "And it's mine."

"Okay, then," Naomi said, trying and failing to match Pao's nonchalant tone. "Hero boy who?"

They had arrived back at the house. The lights were on, but there was no movement inside. It was late, probably past ten p.m., but Pao needed to talk to Dante's mom.

They found her still sitting on the toddler bed, her eyes open but clearly not seeing anything. Pao wondered if something had happened to her, if maybe the fantasma had hurt her. But when Pao cleared her throat, the woman looked up.

"Is he gone?" she asked.

Pao nodded. She knew she shouldn't feel sympathy for this woman who had abandoned her child, but it was hard not to in the moment. "Long gone," Pao said. "Did he tell you where he was going?"

"I don't know anything," the woman said, tears already welling up in her eyes. "I haven't seen him in . . . since . . ."

"Ten years," Pao said as gently as she could. "Since the day the fantasma killed your husband."

The woman gaped at Pao, her eyes wide. "How did you know that?"

"It's a very long story," Pao said, and she felt the weariness in her own voice threatening to take over. "But I was there. I stayed with your son until his abuela got him to safety. Once they were gone, I took the locket and dispatched the fantasma." Pao paused. "Well, at least I thought I did. It came back tonight."

"No!" Dante's mom got to her feet, her eyes darting everywhere.

"Don't worry," Pao said, shaking her head. "It exploded. I don't know how it came back before, but I'm pretty sure it's gone for good this time."

"And my boy? Do you—"

"Why did you leave him?" Pao blurted out. Even though the question was rude, she didn't take it back. She needed to know the answer.

Pao had always tried to make logical sense of the things that scared her. Her obsession with science had begun, in fact, when she'd looked up facts about the Gila River to stop her nightmares about La Llorona. Cold pockets, strong currents, hidden debris—all those commonplace worries were much easier to control than the big, unreasonable fear the ghost elicited in her.

Her research had only branched out from there. Anxiety about climate change had led her to learn about alternate fuel sources. Persistent worries about the earth's ability to support human life had inspired her to check out theories about the habitability of other planets.

Over the past few months, Pao had turned away from science because the world had proven itself too vast and unknowable for any arsenal of facts to protect her.

But this? A mother abandoning her own child in the face of certain doom? Pao had to understand it or else she'd go crazy.

Dante's mom had been silent for so long, Pao didn't know if she'd ever answer the question. But eventually, the frail woman sat back down, tears spilling from her eyes as she looked up at Pao.

"I was afraid," the woman said. "I was a coward. I was so young—only sixteen when Dante was born, still half a child myself on that day. I told myself he'd be okay, that if I couldn't see him, he had gotten far enough away, or he was already . . ." She started crying in earnest then, like she'd been holding back these tears for a decade.

"But after," Pao said, realizing she was being relentless but *needing* to know anyway. To make sense of it all. "When you found out he was alive, that he was with Señora Mata, why didn't you come back for him?"

Why doesn't anyone come back? Pao thought of her father now, knowing, all of a sudden, that it wasn't only Dante's mom she wanted to interrogate.

"I was too ashamed," the woman said. "How could he love me after what I'd done to him? And Rodolfo, my dear Rodolfo, he wasn't around to help. . . . There was no money. . . . I thought . . ." She sobbed once, a heartbreaking sound, then looked Pao straight in the eye. "I thought he'd be better off without a mother who'd left him to die."

"He wasn't," Pao said, speaking for herself and for Dante. "He wasn't better off."

"What do you want from me?" Dante's mom said, looking years older than she had when they'd started this conversation. "He's gone again, he wants nothing to do with me. How does telling this story help anyone? It's over. It's all in the past. I'll never forgive myself as long as I live, but it's too late to fix it now."

"It's never too late to fix it," Pao said, wanting—no, *needing* that to be true.

"Then what do I do?" she asked.

"You help us find out why he's changed," Pao said, meeting her gaze now, asserting "confidence and authority" as she'd been taught in her public-speaking class. "We're on our way to investigate something that could help us find Dante and learn why he betrayed us and whether someone's controlling him. But we need your help."

"Ay, you're too young to say such things!" said Dante's mother, bringing a hand to her forehead. "You're just children!"

Pao took out her staff and transformed it for the second time in the past few minutes, watching with satisfaction as Dante's mother's jaw dropped. "Not normal children," she said.

It was four in the morning when Dante's mom walked Pao and Naomi to the bus stop in the center of town.

She'd insisted they each get an hour or two of sleep, which Pao had protested mightily until she learned the first bus didn't come for five hours anyway.

Pao had been sure she wouldn't be able to sleep—not after everything that had happened. She'd planned to text with Emma until it was time to go.

But Pao had conked out almost immediately. As if a dream had just been waiting to pull her under.

It was a short one this time. Just a single scene in the same dense forest Pao had followed the duendecillo through. Looming large against the pines was a man's silhouette. Her father's? No, this figure seemed different somehow. An ominous cloud of green smoke swirled around his head as a smaller figure knelt on the mossy ground in front of him.

"I did what you asked," said Dante's voice, echoing strangely through the trees. "The ghost has been released."

Pao skulked behind a trunk. The last thing she needed was for Dante and his new "friend" to see her here.

"Good," said another voice in response. It was deep and gravelly—sinister in a way that chilled Pao's blood.

How could Dante think *this* made him a hero? Bowing down to a dude wreathed in extreme sketchiness (at best) who made you give a report? Hadn't he ever seen a movie? Read a single comic book?

This was villain behavior if ever Pao had seen it. Why was Dante so ready to believe in this guy and so reluctant to trust Pao?

"The next phase is being readied as we speak," said the strange, echoey voice. "Can you be sure the fantasma will come?"

"Absolutely," Dante said, and Pao recognized the eager-to-please tone he used with his soccer captain—an eighth-grade boy Pao secretly thought was a complete jerk.

"You'd better be right," said the tall shadow just before Pao's dream began to fade. "The entire operation depends on it. . . ."

These were the words that replayed themselves over and over in Pao's mind on the long predawn walk to the bus stop. Dante had promised the creepy shadow-wreathed guy a fantasma. Was he talking about the Bad Man Ghost? Did he really think that fifteen-eyed freak was any match for Pao? Dante hadn't counted on her having an Arma del Alma.

But Pao had the feeling Dante was talking about something

else. A *new* ghost even worse than the ones they had already faced.

Where was it coming from? What did it have to do with the forest? Or the anomaly, or Pao finding her dad, or Dante's betrayal?

Her head swam with questions, and she was grateful that Dante's mom wasn't asking any of her own. All the woman's curiosity seemed to have been scared out of her by the appearance of Pao's staff last night.

Naomi, too, seemed lost in thought, walking quietly beside Pao down the dirt road.

Pao hated the fact that her go-to reaction was suspicion. Wondering if Naomi was hiding something—if Dante had told the girl more than she was letting on. Pao shook it off, not wanting to give Dante the satisfaction of leaving her paranoid.

"It's just up here," Dante's mom said, pointing to a wooden sign hand-painted with a neat picture of a bus and the word PARADA above it. "The bus is mostly for farmworkers going north to the apples and pears. It won't be too crowded this time of year."

"Will the driver mind that we don't have a parent with us?" Pao asked, glancing at Naomi as if to confirm she still looked as fourteen as she had when they left the house.

Dante's mom shook her head. "Children travel looking for work all the time. No one will think twice as long as you keep your . . . magic stick hidden."

Pao thought of the Niños, of Sal after his parents had been taken, of every orphan child who'd ever had to make their own way. Not all of them ended up part of some mythical story, with a found family of lovable renegades to keep them safe.

Some of them ended up riding a bus alone to another state looking for work.

Some of them were lost, abandoned, and forced to become adults long before they should have.

I should remember to feel lucky more often, Pao thought, despite it all.

"What about money?" Naomi said, snapping Pao out of her thoughts with a harsh reminder of the two dollars balled up in her pocket. The moment in the kitchen when her mom had sent her to the movies with a ten-dollar bill seemed like years, not days, ago.

Either way, Pao was sure she didn't have enough to get to Oregon.

"The bus isn't expensive," Dante's mom said, shaking her head. "Twenty dollars each."

Pao glanced at Naomi again. She knew the other girl had enough to cover the tickets, but would she want to waste half her money on Pao?

Naomi nodded grimly. "We can handle it."

"Let me hand the driver the money just in case, okay?" Dante's mom said. "Tell them you're my nieces and I'm sending you home to your parents."

"Why would you lie for us?" Pao asked, the bus's headlights just visible over the crest of a small hill. "You don't even know us."

"You're friends of my boy," she said, more to herself than them, Pao thought. "You'll find him. You'll keep him safe."

It was more than *she'd* ever done, Pao thought, but she wasn't going to say that to the first adult who'd been willing to help them since they'd left home.

The bus pulled up. It was bright red with green-and-yellow lettering on the side, which Pao couldn't read because it was all in Spanish. There were only three other people on board this early, and they all looked to be asleep.

"¡Todos a bordo!" said the bus driver in a raspy bark. She took a swig from a travel coffee mug and ashed her cigarette out the window.

Naomi slipped Dante's mom the money behind her back, and the three of them stepped forward.

"¿Todas ustedes?" the driver asked. Another glug. Another drag.

"No, solo las niñas," Dante's mom explained while Pao tried to make out the conversation. "Son mis sobrinas. Van a casita en Oregon."

The driver looked like she could have cared less.

"Cuarenta dólares, por favor," she said in her bored drawl. Even Pao understood this part as Dante's mom handed over the two precious twenty-dollar bills.

"Muchísimas gracias," Dante's mom said. "Manténgalas a salvo, por favor."

The driver somehow nodded and shrugged, like whatever Dante's mom was asking her was out of her hands.

Dante's mom pressed herself against the side to let the girls pass. "Be safe," she told them. "And please, help him. Whatever he's done, it's . . . probably because of me. I can't save him myself, so I'm counting on you."

Pao nodded grimly, sensing that Dante's mom wanted to hug them. She stepped away before the woman could act on the impulse. Pao appreciated her help, of course, but she wasn't ready to forgive her for what she had done to Dante.

"Good luck," Pao told her, then walked to an empty seat in the back of the bus.

Naomi followed, settling in beside her, and after the driver's cigarette was flicked unceremoniously out the window, the bus sputtered to a start.

Pao's sole experience with the state of Oregon thus far was from playing *Oregon Trail*—her fourth-grade teacher had been embarrassingly obsessed with all things '90s. The one part of the game Pao actually remembered was the screen that said YOU'VE JUST DIED OF DYSENTERY!

Not the most promising tagline for the next portion of their adventure.

"Oregon, here we come," Pao said quietly.

Her head against the window, Naomi was already snoring.

TWENTY-TWO
Bus Santas Are Even Creepier Than Mall Santas

The first half of the drive went by in strange dollops of time.

Pao dozed off, only to be roused by an old man with what looked like a chicken in a baby carrier. He snapped at Pao for stretching her long legs in the aisle. Next she was awakened by a rough shove. Her head had lolled embarrassingly onto Naomi's shoulder.

"At least I didn't drool on you," Pao said, sitting up.

"Lucky for you," Naomi said with a glower. "You're skinny enough for me to boot out this window."

"Good thing we're only going twenty-five," Pao said, the bus's slow rumble and frequent stops frustrating in her haste to get north.

"Fast enough when the tire crushes your skull."

"Oh, shut up." Pao pulled off her sweatshirt, balled it up, and squished it against Naomi's arm. "Here," she said. "A buffer in case of drool."

Naomi's scoff traveled the length of the bus, but she didn't push Pao away again. Soon her snoring sent Pao back to sleep, her head lolling in the opposite direction.

This time, the dream came in flashes. Single images, like a slideshow.

A forest road, her father curled up on the ground in a fetal position, the green mist covering him. *Come to me, Paola,* said the trees. *Before it's too late . . .*

Next, Dante, dressed in a white outfit trimmed with gold, his hair slicked back, looking like a true hero. His club was at the ready, his eyes closed. But just before the image changed, he opened them, and they glowed green.

Last, a forest clearing with a pool at the center. Three duendecillos huddled at the edge, chattering in their high-pitched voices. It sounded like an argument. In the dirt beside the pool, one of them drew a picture with a stick. The girl with long hair, a tall staff, and a confused facial expression—a remarkably lifelike portrait for such a crude implement—was unmistakably Pao.

The other duendecillos shook their heads and stomped their feet, but the artist kept drawing and speaking to them like she was trying to convince her fellows of something vital.

Just before the forest started to dissolve, marking Pao's return to wakefulness, all three of the duendecillos looked up at something, identical expressions of horror on their faces.

"Wait!" Pao said, but when she reached out her hand, it was only to encounter the back of the bus seat in front of her. She was awake and the forest was gone, but the duendecillos' fear was still palpable.

"Well, it's not like I'm going anywhere," Naomi said, turning away from the window.

"No," Pao said, still shaking off the dream feeling. "It's not you. It's just . . ."

"More dreams?" Naomi asked.

Pao peered around to make sure no one was listening. The

last thing she needed was some superstitious old abuela hearing her talk about dreams and fantasmas and duendecillos and getting her kicked off the bus. Pao wasn't quite sure where they were, but it was definitely still a long walk to Oregon.

Fortunately, no one seemed to be paying them any attention. Everyone was either asleep, wrangling their children, or conversing in Spanish at various volumes.

"More dreams," Pao finally confirmed. "They're always set in this one forest. Sometimes my dad is there, sometimes Señora Mata, but in the last one, it was Dante . . . talking to some clearly evil shadowy guy. They're planning something. I feel like . . ." She trailed off, not wanting to sound melodramatic.

"What?" Naomi asked, no teasing or mockery in her tone.

"Like maybe we're walking into something we're not ready for." And as she said it, Pao felt the weight of her own words. Like confessing it had made her fear real, and now it was threatening to swallow her whole.

Naomi laughed, a kind of severe, barking sound that Pao wasn't sure she'd ever heard before.

Pao looked at her, a little affronted by her reaction. "I think we're in way over our heads here, okay?"

"I'm sorry," Naomi said, still laughing. "But, like, when has that ever *not* been true?" She wiped her eyes with the sleeve of Pao's balled-up sweatshirt. "Like, girl. We're just a handful of teenagers up against a fathomless void of monsters, ghosts, and raw power just waiting to be corrupted by the next maniac. I know you're new to the Niños, but we've spent *decades* being in over our heads, and it's never stopped us before."

Pao wouldn't have admitted it to her, but Naomi's nonchalance about the whole situation made her feel better immediately. Ever since Dante had left, Pao had felt like the entire burden of this mission was falling on her shoulders.

But she wasn't alone. She had an immortal ghost hunter with her, someone who had seen and fought more fantasmas than Pao would probably ever encounter in her lifetime. Just because Naomi wasn't exactly the leadership archetype Marisa embodied, with her rousing pep talks and the *too serious and otherworldly for you* demeanor, didn't mean she wasn't a capable comrade.

"I'll take your silence to mean *Thank you, Naomi. Your perspective on this matter has really helped me manage my anxiety about what's to come!*"

Pao punched her arm lightly. "Giving yourself a lot of credit for basically saying *Yeah, we might die, but we always might die*, aren't you?"

Naomi laughed. "I like you better without moody-what's-his-face around."

"Last summer I thought you liked him," Pao confessed after a beat, readjusting her long legs again, getting a dirty look from the woman in front of her when her knees bumped against the seat. "It made me want to hate you. Who'd have thought he'd be gone, fighting against me, and it'd be you and me on this bus on the way to stop evil."

Naomi snorted loudly. This time, the woman in the seat in front of them audibly clucked. "I'm sorry, *what*?" Naomi said. "You thought I *liked* him? Like in an *I want to hold hands at the movies and practice kissing the back of my hand pretending it's him* kind of way?" She looked utterly offended, which made Pao feel stupid, but also a little lighter.

"Yeah," she said, shaking her head to indicate she knew how ridiculous it sounded.

"You didn't get that, I don't know, maybe he wasn't my type?" Naomi raised her eyebrows significantly, and Pao thought back to the cactus field. The way Naomi had talked about Marisa. "Plus, it was pretty obvious that was your whole thing."

"I don't know," Pao said, not sure why it was important to her to explain this, but finding she needed to anyway. "I wanted it to be me and him so much. Like, in some future version of my life, we'd have this awesome story to tell about how we'd always known each other and . . ." Pao couldn't continue because she didn't really know what she'd wanted anymore. It all seemed so far away now.

"It sounds like you wanted family," Naomi said, not ungently. "And believe me, I get it. But there are better ways to stick someone to you forever than convincing yourself you want to kiss them when you don't."

"Like what?" Pao asked.

Naomi was quiet for a minute, then laughed and said, "I honestly have no idea."

Pao laughed at this, too, quietly, so as not to upset the scowly woman again.

"So what about you?" Pao asked.

Up at the front, the bus driver yelled, "¡Próxima parada, Sacramento!"

"What about me what?" Naomi asked. "You want me to share a personal anecdote to make you feel less weird about spilling your guts to me completely at random?"

"Basically," Pao said, her cheeks heating up.

"Look, there's not much to tell, okay?" She was quiet for a minute. "I kill stuff, I sleep, I eat—"

"You snark," Pao interjected.

Naomi smiled a wide, catlike smile. "I do snark, don't I?"

"With the best."

"I just . . . haven't really left a lot of room for the other stuff. And even when I tried . . ." It was Naomi's turn to trail off, cast her gaze out the window like maybe she'd see Marisa and Franco out there and it would all make sense.

"Sorry," Pao offered. "For bringing Franco back from the void. If I'd known it was gonna salt your game so much, I would have left him down there to be fish food."

"'Salt my game'?" Naomi asked, snapping back from her moody window-gazing to laugh incredulously at Pao. "What does that even mean?"

Pao's face heated up again. "I don't know! My mom says it!"

"Well," Naomi said, "you didn't *salt* my anything. Not anything that wasn't already overseasoned, if I'm following your weird metaphor correctly."

"She's a total dweeb if she picks him over you," Pao said, meaning it.

"It's not even like that," Naomi said, though her cheeks flushed a little. "I just want to be there for her. Help her. Support her without dimming her shine. She deserves that."

"Yeah," said Pao. "But you deserve stuff, too."

Naomi nodded, and for once, she didn't seem to have anything snarky to say.

The next miles crawled by in companionable silence, yet neither of them napped again. Pao was too afraid to dream, and Naomi seemed to be deep in thought as she kept her gaze fixed out the window.

After a while, Pao turned on her phone, hoping to check in with Emma, but there was no cell service on the back roads the bus favored, and she couldn't risk leaving it on long enough for anyone to track the signal.

Instead she watched the landscape grow greener and greener, her anxiety building along with the scenery's beauty. They passed rolling hills that went on for miles. They drove beneath a massive snow-white mountain.

Ten miles from the Oregon border (according to a reflective green sign), the bus slowed and pulled over on the shoulder of the highway. It didn't look like an official stop.

A man climbed aboard, his patchwork coat and pants made entirely of different scraps of bright-red material. He even wore a bright-red Santa Claus hat.

His thumb was still extended as he climbed the stairs, which explained the random highway stop. "Misericordia, por favor," the hitchhiker said to the driver. "No tengo dinero, pero tengo muchos chistes, eh?"

Pao couldn't hear the driver's reply, but a moment later, the man was walking down the aisle, the hems of his red pants soggy from the rain that had begun to fall outside.

Instead of taking a seat, he stopped and talked to the passengers one by one. If they laughed, he stuck out his hat. One or two people dropped in a coin or dollar. Some pointedly ignored him. Okay, most.

Given how peaceful the bus had been before he'd gotten on, and how precious little peace there'd been to go around lately, Pao couldn't help but be irked by the intrusion.

She took in a deep breath to the count of four, held it for four, released it for four, and held it for four, like she'd read on the internet. *When your temper flares, try to humanize the person who's upsetting you,* Pao recalled, and so she tried. This man was alone, out in the rain without protection or resources. . . .

If she were stuck in this same situation as Pao, Emma would say something like *True revolution involves empathy even for people who really freakin' annoy you.*

But the more she tried to humanize and empathize with him, the more Pao realized that the man wasn't just obnoxious—he was *familiar.* Pao couldn't put her finger on what it was at first. His stringy dark hair? Or was it the wide charismatic eyes, just visible under the floppy, dingy white brim of his Santa hat, that made a few people nod and hand over hard-earned cash or food from their lunch containers?

Within half a minute of observing him, Pao was sure she had seen him before—but there was no way that could be. She'd never been this far away from home—how could she have met a traveling, panhandling Spanish-speaking Santa?

Pao watched him closely as they crossed the border into Oregon, her hackles rising more and more as he peddled his *jokes* to a less and less enthusiastic crowd. She didn't understand his words, but his gestures—especially toward the women on board—didn't need translating. She wondered where his stop was and hoped it would be soon.

Then she realized he hadn't approached her and Naomi once.

"Are you getting, like, a seriously weird—"

"Vibe from this guy?" Naomi finished for her. "Yeah. Stay sharp. Keep one hand on that tricky trinket of yours."

"I know I've seen him somewhere before," Pao said, almost to herself as she pulled out the magnifying glass, but Naomi's eyes snapped to her.

"Where?" she asked.

Pao didn't answer right away, because she was distracted. The man had steered close to their seats on his way to do a funny dance in front of some twin toddlers, winking at their mom when they laughed, and Pao could have sworn his eyes locked onto her Arma del Alma as he passed.

"I don't know," Pao said. "The memory is too hazy. I can't put my finger on it."

"Could it have been a dream?" Naomi asked as they passed through a town called Medford.

"I don't think so," Pao said.

"There are fantasmas that mess with your memory," Naomi said, almost offhand. "But I think they're pretty rare. . . ."

Pao was barely listening, because the next sign they passed said, plain as day: PINE GLADE—22 MILES.

"We're getting close," Pao said. "Pine Glade—that's our stop."

"Good thing," Naomi muttered, reaching into her jeans jacket to pat something Pao assumed was her knife. "Because this guy is seriously pissing me off."

"Of course he's not bothering any of the men," Pao said through gritted teeth.

"Right?" Naomi said. "Basura . . ."

Pao tightened her grip on the magnifying glass, willing it not to transform right then and there even though she could feel its hum against her skin, which told her it could. Anytime she wanted.

She didn't know if this guy was a fantasma or just your run-of-the-mill aggressive "nice guy" who seemed to exist to make all spaces less comfortable for women, but either way she was ready to knock the wind out of him at least.

He continued to avoid Pao and Naomi, but his pestering of the other obviously female passengers had increased to full-on heckling now.

"What's he saying?" Pao asked under her breath.

"He's asking why they don't like nice men," Naomi replied, confirming Pao's earlier bias, disgust evident in her tone. "He's telling them though he may not have money, he'll make them laugh if they give him a chance."

"Ugh," Pao said.

"Por favor, querida," the man said to the woman in the seat right in front of them, tipping his hat to her and shaking it so the few coins inside jingled. "Monedas o besos, no me importa."

The bubbling, fizzing, reckless feeling that always got Pao into big trouble had returned with a vengeance. Even she, a level-one Duolingo user, knew what besos meant.

"Lo siento, señor," said the woman, fearful rather than scowling now. "Soy casada." She held up her hands to show him her ring, or the fact that she had nothing to offer, or both.

"¿Quién es su esposo?" the man asked, his chest puffed out. "¿Dónde está?" He looked around exaggeratedly, his fists raised like in a caricature of a fighting leprechaun. The woman shrank into her seat and shook her head, her hands still raised, palms up.

Pao had had enough, and apparently, so had Naomi. They got to their feet as one.

"Why don't you leave her alone?" Pao asked, not sure if he

understood English, not sure of much besides the fact that she wanted to save the scowly woman from one more second of harassment.

The man turned to Pao at last, his eyes flitting (definitely this time) to the magnifying glass in her hand. As they returned to Pao's face, she noticed that his deep brown irises—which she'd noticed specifically when he got on the bus—had changed to a deep forest green.

"Who's going to make me, little girl?" he asked, switching effortlessly to English, his voice now double-layered and menacing.

"He's a fantasma," Pao said under her breath to Naomi, barely believing it. "His eyes . . ."

"I know," Naomi said, "I saw them, too."

"Okay, so . . . ?" Pao was panicking in earnest now. The other ghosts they'd seen on this trip had been more zombie than human, and none of them had been smarter than your typical ahogados or monsters.

But this one was obviously different. He could speak at least two languages, hold a human form, and trick a bus full of people into believing that he was one of them.

This was definitely not the run-of-the-mill kind that had attacked her in the hospital, nor even like the massive, mindless specter that had killed Dante's dad.

The only fantasma Pao had ever encountered with this kind of power was La Llorona herself—and fighting her, even with the help of Ondina and Bruto and the power of the pearl, had almost killed Pao.

"What do we do?" she asked Naomi, knowing panic was evident in her voice, but not caring about looking tough for once.

"What do you mean, what do we do? We're ghost hunters! We kick his freaky butt back to the void, like, now!"

Pao knew Naomi was right. This wasn't the time for a well-thought-out plan. There was a fantasma in front of them, and there was a bus full of innocent people all around. They had a job to do, no matter how superpowerful he seemed to be.

"Cover me. I'm gonna . . ." Pao gestured to the row behind them, indicating that she needed space to transform her magnifying glass into a staff. Santa lunged as she climbed over the seat. His grin was rabid now. He looked less and less human with every second that passed.

Naomi took the full brunt of the attack, swiping at Santa with her knife and forcing him back. Several people screamed. Even more screamed when Pao stepped into the aisle from behind the seat with a six-foot-long bladed staff she definitely hadn't possessed a minute ago.

"¡No se permiten armas!" the bus driver screeched through the intercom.

"Funny," Naomi said to Pao as they switched places. "She doesn't allow weapons, but she doesn't seem to have a problem letting in vengeful spirits of the dead!"

"They never do," Pao said, thinking back to the hospital before she jabbed the butt end of her staff right into Santa's red patchwork gut.

A cold crunching sound rang out through the bus. Two toddlers near the front had started to cry. Everyone had either squished themselves against a window or crouched near the floor.

The man was still doubled over from the blow. At first, Pao thought he was crying—or wheezing, at least, but when he straightened up, he was laughing instead.

With the back of his hand, he lashed at Pao's face, cracking her hard in the cheekbone and sending her flying into Naomi. They both stumbled backward.

Naomi recovered first. "Oh no, you did not just *backhand* my friend. What kind of man hits a kid?"

"But I'm not a man," he said, his head doing a full 360 that made Pao dizzy and nauseous. By the time his face was in front again, Pao was in attack mode, and the old joker was gone. He'd been replaced by a beautiful woman in a long red dress, with dark hair and piercing green eyes.

Eyes that had once been brown.

Eyes that had mesmerized Pao in the mirror of a taquería bathroom all the way back in Rock Creek.

TWENTY-THREE

The Hitchhiker of Doom

"You!" Pao said, realizing at last.

The bus sped up drastically on the narrow highway as the driver gave up hope of enforcing the rules and instead looked for a safe place to pull over as her passengers screamed and crowded toward the front.

But Pao didn't care about the commotion right now. She was too busy recalling the woman and her photo on the altar at the front of the tienda.

Querida Elenita . . .

"Meee," the fantasma replied in a singsong voice.

Pao flipped her staff so the blade was up. She'd been trying to avoid traumatizing the little kids on board, but this situation obviously called for extreme measures.

"I know her," Pao said to Naomi as they braced for another attack. "She tried to get a ride from me in the bathroom in Rock Creek. Before Johnny's."

"When you got all spacey and couldn't answer my question?" Naomi asked with gradually dawning horror. She jabbed her long knife at whichever part of Elenita's body she could reach, but barely scratched the ghost's elbow.

"Yep," Pao said, thrusting her spear past Naomi to catch

Elenita in the neck. She'd expected it to feel like entering flesh, but the blade glanced aside like she'd hit rock instead. "I finally remembered."

"But do you remember . . . me?" Elenita asked, her head starting to swivel just like Santa's had. When she turned back, she had become an older man with long hair in a ponytail. His brown eyes, which had mesmerized Pao before, now had a sinister gleam to them.

"The guy from the side of the road," Pao said, grunting as the man shoved Naomi into her again. But not before Naomi's knife caught his wrist, leaving a gash that bled green ooze.

So we can *hurt it, then,* Pao thought with satisfaction as the green stuff splattered the bus floor. *It just takes a heck of a hit.*

The driver was tearing down the darkening road now, the small lane too curvy for such high speed. The bus tipped, then settled, then tipped the other way. Pao had learned the physics of tipping force in sixth grade from an online video, but there was nothing like the real thing. She barely kept her balance, yet the man stood steady in the middle of the aisle, waiting.

Why isn't he attacking? Pao wondered.

"What guy are you talking about?" Naomi was shouting at Pao as the bus took another hairpin turn.

"He had his thumb out!" Pao said. "Before the rest stop with the cadejos!"

Querido Alán, Pao remembered suddenly, picturing the name on the roadside cross.

"He had his *what?*" Naomi asked. "Oh no . . ."

Whatever Pao had said, it had spooked Naomi. She retreated instead of striking again, and when Pao looked at her closely, her face was ashen.

"What is it?" Pao asked, but Naomi shook her head.

"We need to get everyone off this bus, *now*!"

Luckily, the driver seemed to have had the same thought. On a barely-there strip of grass bordering the densest forest Pao had ever seen, she finally screeched to a halt, throwing the doors open.

"Mission accomplished?" Pao said to Naomi as everyone but them tried to stream out of the bus en masse. The driver seemed content to run all the way to the nearest town, leaving her passengers behind to mill about in confusion.

Alán kept his gaze fixed on Pao.

"¿Qué pasa con las niñas?" shouted the last passenger to disembark, trying to get the attention of the others.

"No se preocupe, señora," Naomi called to her, leaping forward to bury her knife in Alán's thigh. "¡Estaremos bien!"

Whatever Naomi had said, it seemed to satisfy the woman— or maybe she was just looking for an excuse to bolt.

"You planning to tell me what's going on?" Pao asked Naomi when she'd pulled out her knife. Green goop now stained Alán's bright-red slacks, but he didn't seem fazed. He hissed at them threateningly, blocking their exit.

"Haven't you figured it out yet?" Naomi asked Pao impatiently as they pressed forward, gaining ground, their deadly dance moving toward the open door of the bus.

"I wish people would stop asking me that!" Pao growled, swinging her staff a little wildly in her frustration. She sheared off the top of Alán's dark hair, which fluttered to the ground. "I'm a self-taught seventh-grade scientist, not a white lady with a podcast about true crimes!"

But even as she said it, Alán's head began to spin again, and

Pao knew who she would see a split second before he materialized.

The boy in the bright-red pajamas who'd been on I-5, holding the cardboard sign that just said *North*.

Four people, all dressed in red, all interested in the same thing.

A ride.

And then, suddenly, Pao *did* know, and the realization made her feel freezing cold all over—or maybe that was the misty Oregon air coming in through the open door.

"The Hitchhiker?" she asked, incredulous, and Naomi's silence was all the answer she needed.

"That's right," said the little boy, his voice too high-pitched to be natural, his teeth too small and strangely spaced in his mouth when he smiled. "Please, just a ride, that's all I need!"

The two girls pressed forward together, both more hesitant to strike now, though they shouldn't have been. The child in the pajamas was just a costume, and hadn't Pao and Naomi each killed dozens of ahogados who were wearing braces and rubber-band bracelets last summer?

But this felt different somehow.

How had the Hitchhiker been killed in the story? Pao couldn't remember.

She racked her brain as she swung her staff again, frustrated by the minimal damage even its supposedly epic blade could do to this fantasma.

The story hadn't been one of her mother's favorites—Maria usually focused on the ones about the dangers that befell trouble-some children. But Señora Mata had told it to Pao and Dante a few years before, when scary stories were all the rage at school and Dante had wanted one to impress their classmates.

In every version, the Hitchhiker was a beautiful woman who'd been picked up by a lovestruck man. She would ask him to drop her off at her house, and he would drive away. Then, unable to stop thinking of her, the man would invariably go back to the house the next day and ask after her.

He'd be notified that the woman he was inquiring about had died years earlier. Bewildered, he would leave, scratching his head.

But before the day was over, the man would always be found dead.

When she'd heard the story, Pao had, of course, used reason and logic to talk her way out of being scared. But now, with the evidence right in front of her, it was hard to remember what she'd told herself, or even how the story had resolved.

Think, she commanded herself, but the boy's cold stare was scattering her thoughts, and there was no scientific explanation that could make sense of the rotation of the fantasma's head—especially to the person watching it in real time.

"You can't believe everything you hear in the stories," the boy said in that awful high-pitched voice. "We're not always beautiful women. We take the shape of whoever we think has the best chance of being picked up. It's not our fault most people are so easy to manipulate."

"How did you—" Pao began, then shut her mouth and jabbed with her staff, tearing the sleeve of the boy's pajamas as he danced nimbly out of reach. How had the fantasma heard her thoughts?

Haven't you ever wondered why *you have those dreams, Pao? Why you're connected to the head of every monster in the flipping world?* Dante had asked her. Of course she had. But she'd never thought the monsters were in *her* head, too. . . .

"You were a tough customer," the boy said, still not striking back. "We were so thrilled when you got on the bus at last. Much easier to be picked up this way. Of course, the others will have to die now, too. . . . Such a shame." He looked out the window at the confused passengers, who were now walking up the narrow shoulder in a line. The rabid gleam in the fantasma's eye told Pao he didn't think it was a shame at all.

But Pao wasn't going to let all those innocent people die. She would stop this. She just needed to figure out how. . . .

"Why me?" Pao asked, stepping forward again, striking, and missing. Naomi tried again, too, but the boy was too quick, and now he was the one moving toward the door.

If he escapes, Pao thought, *we'll never be able to save the passengers.*

"Orders are orders," the boy said, shrugging. "Though I have no idea what he wants with someone so boring."

"Who's *he*?" Pao asked, matching his steps, keeping the distance between them fixed, trying to shadow without spooking.

The boy yawned, but when he spoke again, his mouth opened too wide and his eyes multiplied like Pao was seeing him through a fly's lenses.

"It doesn't matter, Paola Santiago," he said with the voices of four people layered over one another. "In the end, you'll be dead like all the rest."

And then the Hitchhiker bolted out the door and into the forest.

TWENTY-FOUR

Let's Never Talk About That Fluffy Bunny Ever Again

Pao and Naomi wasted no time, but still, when they had exited the tilted bus to stand on the side of the road, they were alone.

Frustrated, afraid for the bus passengers, Pao scanned the tree line until she spotted a flash of pale skin—the fantasma's bare arm, contrasting sharply with the deep green of the forest around it.

"Wait," Naomi said, holding back Pao before she could charge into the trees with her staff outstretched. "Something doesn't feel right."

Pao felt it, too—a strange vibration in the air, almost like a sound at the wrong frequency for their ears to hear.

"Ignore it," Pao said, shaking off the sensation. "The passengers are still out here. We have to find the Hitchhiker before he hurts someone else."

Naomi didn't seem to be able to fault her logic even though her expression said she was still conflicted.

Pao remembered Dante's meeting with the shadow-wreathed figure in the forest of her nightmares.

I did what you asked, he'd said. *The ghost has been released.*

Was this the ghost he meant? The Hitchhiker? A shape-shifter that could become whatever it thought Pao would respond to? And had been stalking her since Rock Creek?

If she chased the fantasma now, would she be walking right into the trap he had laid for her?

It didn't matter, Pao told herself, shutting down the line of questioning by reminding herself again of the innocent passengers. Whether or not it was part of some grand design, she and Naomi had a responsibility to make sure those people were safe.

"We'll follow him," Pao said. "We'll dispatch him, and then we'll find the Niños and figure out what to do next, okay?"

"It's not that easy," Naomi said, her mouth a grim line. "El Autostopisto is one of las leyendas. The legends, like La Llorona. You don't just dispatch one like any run-of-the-mill ahogado or fantasma. They're different—imbued with the void's power, with a mainline directly to the minds of the ghosts and monsters inside. If you've been seeing him this whole time, I wouldn't be surprised if *he's* the one sending all these fantasmas after you."

"But he said he was taking orders, too . . ." Pao said nervously.

"Exactly. Even together, and armed with an Arma del Alma, it'll be almost impossible for us to stop El Autostopisto on our own. And even if we do . . . anyone who can *send* a leyenda after us?" Naomi shuddered. "I don't even want to know."

Pao understood what Naomi was saying. But she felt urgency pounding inside her like a pulse. All she could think about was the passengers. And the driver, whose only crime had been letting a poor man in a Santa hat ride for free.

"We have to try," Pao said simply. "Maybe we won't succeed, but we have no choice. We owe it to all those people. I jeopardized them just by stepping onto that bus. I can't let them die for it."

Naomi gave Pao an appraising look. "Old what's-his-name sure was wrong about you, pipsqueak," she said, shaking her head.

"What do you mean?" Pao asked, bristling at the thought of Dante.

"You're a hero through and through."

Pao wasn't sure Naomi had meant it as a compliment, but it made her stand up a little straighter anyway.

"All right, hero girl," Naomi said. "Let's go track down a ridiculously overpowered fantasma all by ourselves. Why do you savior types have such bad planning skills?"

"I guess that's what we need you snarky, reluctant adventurer types for," Pao said with a grin. "Now come on—he's already got a huge head start."

Naomi shook her head. "If El Autostopisto has chosen you, *finding* him will be the least of our problems."

They walked together for at least a half mile, any noise from the road muffled by the dense press of trees all around them.

The Hitchhiker was nowhere to be seen, but Pao could feel its presence—a sinister, strange thing lurking just out of sight. She tried to keep their bearings as best she could, knowing they'd have to find their way out of this enormous forest the moment the fantasma had been dealt with.

Pao had been counting on disembarking at a well-lit bus stop somewhere close to town, maybe visiting the post office where her dad had his box and asking for directions.

But when did her plans ever work out like they were supposed to?

From the sound of it, the rain had started to fall again, but they were protected by the canopy of green needles stretching endlessly above them.

Before they had set off into the trees, evening had just started to gather at the edges, yet in here it was nearly as dark as night. Pao knew they were less than five miles from Pine Glade, but that didn't help much when the only landmarks you had were a series of identical trees.

And she didn't even need to check her phone to know there was no cell service in here.

"There!" Naomi called, and Pao saw it. A flash of silver white, like a fish's belly. They followed its occasional flicker, correcting their course, tripping over roots and rocks and fallen branches. There was no path here—neither the wide one that stretched through the forest in Pao's dreams, nor even a skinny one clear of brambles.

The fight to get through the woods was arguably as difficult as the first battle with the Hitchhiker had been. While the desert was always a backdrop, this forest seemed almost sentient, and Pao couldn't decide if it was a friend or an enemy.

Pao's fingers started going numb from the cold after about ten minutes. Apparently, winter in Oregon was a whole different beast than the temperate winters she was used to in Arizona. The cold here had a texture, a smell, and a taste.

Pao wasn't at all sure she liked it.

Still they walked, their feet turning to ice cubes in their sneakers. Once or twice they spotted a flash of hair or limbs, and they redirected, running toward where they'd seen proof that they weren't alone out there. They always arrived too late.

The cold was getting more insidious, reaching its wet way into every exposed crack in their clothing. Their breath became visible in puffs in front of them as the light continued to fade.

But the feeling—goose-bump-causing, prickly-back-of-the-neck feeling that they were being watched—grew stronger the farther in they pressed.

At this point, Pao thought she was moving forward less because she expected to find the Hitchhiker, and more because she didn't know if they could find their way back out.

"So, now that I have you here," Naomi said, as yet another flash of pale skin yielded nothing but a fifty-eighth direction change. "Why don't you tell me what you're not telling me?"

Pao looked away guiltily and was rewarded by tripping over a root and sprawling on the ground. She got up with all the dignity she could muster and said, "I don't know what you mean."

"I've been thinking, and it doesn't add up. What's-his-name's grandma collapses, and you're attacked by fantasmas at the hospital, and because of a dream about some trees you're suddenly knocking down my figurative door ready to head to Oregon?"

"Yeah, and . . . ?" Pao asked, doing her best tough-girl impression.

Naomi huffed. "There's a piece missing," she said. "A big piece. And if I'm gonna follow you in here, a leyenda tracking us, my fate and the fate of a bunch of other innocent people at stake, I think I deserve to be as prepared as I can be, don't you?"

Pao knew she was right. When Pao had started out, she'd had Dante. Naomi had just been a reluctant tagalong. But since then, Naomi had proven herself to be ten times the friend Dante was, and Pao no longer feared being teased by her.

It was time to be honest.

"It's about my dad," Pao said as the temperature somehow dropped even further. "The dreams I've been having about the forest? He's been in them, telling me to come to him before it's too late."

Naomi nodded slowly, digesting this information. "And what do we know about Pops?"

"Not much," Pao admitted, spinning her staff absentmindedly. "He left when I was really little, like three. My mom never talks about him. But he gave me my flashlight. The one that ended up being, you know . . ."

"The key to opening the rift?" Naomi said, eyebrows raised. "And you never thought that maybe he was involved in something supernatural?"

"Señora Mata was the one who gave it to me!" Pao said defensively. "I just figured she'd done something freaky to it beforehand. But I never got the chance to ask her about it, because Dante was always preventing me from—"

"Was that . . . ?" Naomi interrupted, her eyes darting to the left, her knife at the ready.

"What?" Pao swung her staff to attention, blade end pointing forward.

"Careful," Naomi said, taking slow steps toward a bush that rustled before them.

Pao's heart was in her throat. Was this it?

The rustling intensified, and Naomi shifted to the balls of her feet, prepared to attack. Pao, seeing how cool she looked, did the same, overbalanced, and almost fell.

"Really?" Naomi hissed.

"Shut up."

The bush began to part, exposing a dark cavern inside. Pao, her nerves ringing like an alarm clock, stepped forward, all set to stab the business end of her staff into the first living (or dead) thing she saw.

There was a flash of white. Naomi screamed first, and Pao followed suit, telling herself they were battle cries as they both jumped forward, ready for anything. . . .

Well, anything except the fluffy little bunny that hopped out of the bush, looking up at them wide-eyed, frozen save for a little nose twitch.

After a long minute of the three of them staring at one another, the bunny hopped away in alarm, disappearing into the trees.

Naomi sheathed her knife.

Pao loosened her grip on the staff.

"I think we can agree *that* never happened," Naomi said.

"What never happened?"

"Right."

It took them a while to recover from the rabbit incident. Once, they heard a laugh echoing through the trees that sounded eerily like Santa's. Another time, it was a woman's voice, calling out for help.

On each occasion, they changed direction, heading toward the sound. Pao felt like they were following a trail of spooky fantasma-flavored bread crumbs through the magical woods of a European fairy tale.

The only question was, who was laying the trail, and why?

"So, your dad gave you a toy flashlight that ended up being the key to entering the ghost-infested void and defeating La Llorona,"

Naomi prompted. "Then he randomly starts showing up in your dreams. That doesn't really explain the rest."

"Right," Pao said, the quiet of the forest starting to get to her. Earlier, there had been the odd bird and, of course, the demon bunny that could never be spoken of again. But here, it was deadly still.

"So?"

"Right," Pao said again. "So, in one of these dreams I saw Dante's abuela." Pao described Señora Mata's strange behavior, the way she'd called her Maria, and her warnings about Beto.

"Wait, Beto?" Naomi asked. "She specifically said *Beto*?"

"Yeah . . ." Pao said. "Why?"

"I mean, it's nothing," Naomi said, looking away. "There are probably lots of people with that name. It's just . . . Beto was the name of La Llorona's second son."

Beto, Pao thought, with that *aha!* feeling she loved so much. She recalled thinking, back in Señora Mata's kitchen, that the name sounded familiar, but she hadn't remembered where she'd heard it until now.

It was last summer, in the glass palace. In Ondina's final argument with her mother, she had mentioned her two brothers, both of whom had been drowned along with her in real life. Luis, who had died a second time in one of La Llorona's regeneration experiments, and Beto, who hadn't wanted to live if it meant someone else had to die for it. "Ungrateful Beto," as La Llorona had called him, had paved the way for Ondina's sacrifice.

Pao had tried to repress the memories of what she'd seen while under the influence of the pearl—the void's power source, which she'd held in her own two hands for a short time. But now she allowed herself to remember the faces of La Llorona's children. The middle son, almost a man, had looked a little familiar. . . .

Could Beto have survived his mother's twisted test run?

But even if he had, there was no way he could be the same Beto Señora Mata had warned Pao's mother against, could it? The troublesome boy Maria had known before she met Pao's father . . . ?

"Earth to Pao!" Naomi said sharply, like this wasn't the first time she'd tried it. It made Pao think of Dante and their junk food picnics on the banks of the Gila with Emma. Simpler times.

"Sorry," Pao said. "It's just . . . I've heard of Beto. La Llorona mentioned him in the end. But I don't know what he could have to do with my mom. . . . Do you know if he made it out of the void?"

Naomi shrugged. "If he did, we never came across him. Like I said, I'm sure it's not the same guy. Probably just a coincidence, right?"

"Right," Pao said, her mind still a million miles away. Last year, she would have agreed with Naomi. Any good scientist knows that coincidences happen all the time, that there isn't necessarily any meaning between correlations in data.

But Pao had changed since then. She now knew that logic wasn't the only force at play in their world. Sometimes coincidences were simple correlation, but sometimes they were more.

"What are we doing?" Pao asked aloud. "We've been walking for miles. If the Hitchhiker is really going to attack those people, what's he doing leading us on a wild-goose chase through this freezing-cold forest?"

Naomi shook her head like she was coming out of a trance. "It's been over an hour," she said. "We were less than five miles from town. They must be somewhere safe by now."

"He was baiting us," Pao said, shaking her head. "Trying to lure us in here, distract us, and we fell for it. Look, long story short, Señora Mata said some things that make me think my dad has the answers about whatever is going on with her. That, combined with the magic anomaly being in this same area? Too great a coincidence to ignore."

"So we go back? Find your dad?"

"I think so," Pao said. "Are you in?"

"Anything to get out of these cold, wet woods," Naomi said, shivering. "I told you humidity is a silent killer."

Pao laughed, feeling as relieved as Naomi sounded. They would turn back, head for the highway. They would find Pine Glade and the post office, and they'd track down Pao's dad. Once they were reunited with the other Niños, they could come back for the Hitchhiker. An evidence-based, common-sense plan always made Pao feel better.

Seized by momentary inspiration, Pao carved a giant PS in the closest tree trunk.

Naomi, nodding, followed suit with her own initials.

"We were here," Pao said, turning back toward where she thought the highway was, her feet light as air despite the numbness in her toes.

They walked faster than before, eager to escape the oppressive denseness of the trees and return to the road. To a plan not dictated by the words of an evil little boy with a head that spun in a full circle.

Pao looked for the landmarks she'd noted on the way in—a stump that resembled an elephant, a large cluster of mushrooms, the bush where she and Naomi had definitely *not* screamed like preschoolers in the presence of a fluffy little bunny . . .

She saw none of them. Raindrops glistened on every leaf and needle, casting an odd shimmering quality to the area. Was the light different going this direction? Pao wondered. She hadn't remembered the foliage glistening quite so much before.

And then she saw it. The one landmark she hadn't expected. One that made her heart sink in the direction of her left knee.

On the two trees up ahead were four initials.

PS and NC.

The forest had spit them out right back where they'd started.

TWENTY-FIVE

A Tiny Green Ally Can Get You Only
So Far in the Haunted Woods

"No," Pao said, her voice sounding hollow even to her own ears as she sank onto the damp mulch that covered the forest floor. "Not again! This can't be happening again."

Naomi was still on her feet, tracing her own initials in the bark with her knife—but she looked curious, not despondent.

"It's just like our force field," she said with wonder. "But how? Without a rift, what's generating it?"

"Who cares how?" Pao asked, her face in her hands. "We're stuck in here!"

"Really?" Naomi said, raising an eyebrow. "I thought you were supposed to be the hero type. Never known one of you to give up so easily . . ."

"I'm not giving up," Pao said. "But the last time I had to get through one of these things, I had a magic flashlight that was magnetized to the void's entrance—that's just a theory, but I think it's a pretty sound—"

Naomi cleared her throat.

"Sorry," Pao said. "It's just, we tried to get through a force field before, and without the flashlight, it was impossible. How are we going to find my dad if we can't ever get out of these stupid woods?"

"You're asking the wrong question," Naomi said. "We're not just trying to find your dad—we're trying to find an anomaly he may be at the center of. Now, I told you Franco's maps show no entrance between home and Vancouver, BC, so what's creating this force field, science girl?"

"Magic," Pao said automatically, her brain already halfway done with the hypothesis even though she'd never consciously considered any of this. "Enough magic to trick the forest into thinking it's a liminal space."

"Nerdier than I would have phrased it, but bingo."

Pao got to her feet. "Okay," she said, that *on the verge of a discovery* feeling taking over for the first time in ages. "So we must be close to the anomaly. But that doesn't explain how we're going to get through the force field to find it."

She was pacing now, a sure sign that a breakthrough was imminent.

"Did you guys have a special way of getting through the force field?" Pao asked Naomi, feeling really dumb for not asking sooner. "Some way of sensing the way through . . . ?"

"Yeah," Naomi said without hesitation. "We used echolocation. Check it out."

Pao found a stump and perched on its edge, sure she was about to learn an incredible secret, the key to getting them out of this mess.

Eyes locked on Pao's, Naomi made a chirping sound, like a terrible imitation of a bat.

The dense forest didn't produce an echo.

Pao peered around, like maybe the way ahead would illuminate at the sound or something, but nothing was happening.

Was Pao the problem? Could she not see it because she wasn't officially a Niña?

Naomi started laughing. Hard. Like clutch-your-stomach-and-roll-around-on-the-ground laughter. "You should have seen your face!" she howled. "You looked like this was science class and some particle-physics geek was coming to teach you about telekinesis or something." She dissolved into chortles again.

"First of all," Pao said, her face flaming, "telekinesis isn't in *any way* related to particle physics—"

"Echolocation?" Naomi screeched. "You really thought all us Niños were just chirping our way through the cactus field? You are *so* gullible. Give me that staff. You're going back to sarcasm school. I'm the hero now."

"Stop," Pao said suddenly, catching something moving at around knee height in the trees.

"I'll *never* stop," Naomi said, wiping her eyes. "I got you so good, I don't even care if we get out of here. I want to live in this moment forever."

"Stop!" Pao hissed again, and apparently there was something in her voice this time that made Naomi sit up and take notice, because she fell mercifully silent.

"Whoa," Naomi said, standing up as Pao did and moving closer to her while, from between the trees, at least ten pairs of eyes seemed to open all at once.

"They're from my dreams," Pao said in wonder, remembering the wide road lined with trees, these very same eyes watching her as she walked.

"What are they?" Naomi asked, huddling even closer in a way

Pao would have mocked mercilessly if there weren't something magical unfolding before their very eyes.

"Duendecillos," Pao breathed as the closest pair of eyes detached from the trees, their owner stepping forward into the light glowing from Pao's staff.

It looked like the same creature who had led Pao to the pool that healed her arm. The same one—Pao was now sure—who had drawn the picture of her in the sand during the duendecillo argument in her dream. Pao recognized the round nose, the shaggy green hair, the golden freckles across her brown skin.

"Hello," Pao said softly, stepping a little closer. "Do you remember me?"

"¡Sí!" the little one chirped, nodding and beaming, gesturing to her own arm, a quizzical expression on her face.

"Oh, my arm?" Pao asked, patting the place where the bite had been. "It's fine now, thank you. The pool—*your* pool healed it."

The nodding grew even more enthusiastic, the duendecillo's smile wide and bright.

Pao knelt, getting as near as she could while hoping to remain nonintimidating. She had the feeling the other pairs of eyes were the duendecillos who had been on the other side of the argument. This one was breaking ranks by helping Pao.

She wasn't sure how she knew this, except that one rebel could recognize another.

"What's your name?" Pao asked, and the little duendecillo crept toward her. From the bushes, clucks of disapproval sounded immediately, like chattering birds when someone got too close to their nest. Pao ignored them for now, but Naomi drew her knife. "Leave it," Pao said under her breath. "Trust me."

Naomi dropped her arm, though her expression was still wary.

"Estrella," said the little creature in a whisper.

"Estrella," Pao repeated. "*Star.* I love the stars more than anything." She closed her eyes for a moment, calling on the Duolingo lessons again, wishing she'd turned more of those little circles gold.

Behind her, Naomi stood at the ready, just in case.

"Necesitamos . . . uh, your help, Estrella," Pao said, noticing that the duendecillo's glow had grown brighter, her smile even wider. "Estamos . . . lost. Necesitamos . . . to get through the woods?" Pao said, losing the train at the end, hoping her gesture had been understood.

"¡Sí!" the duendecillo said. "¡Conocemos el camino!"

The sounds of disapproval from the foliage grew louder. Pao glanced at Naomi for assistance with translation.

"She says she knows the way," Naomi said, still sounding a little suspicious.

Pao nodded, turning to Estrella. "Will you help us?" she asked, not needing to fake her desperation. She tried to remember every moment she'd spent obsessing about duendecillos as a child. Looking up their pictures in her mom's books, trying to copy them painstakingly in her journals. Dreaming of befriending one. "Por favor," Pao said, looking the creature right in the eye.

Estrella's head turned back toward the bush, conflicted for an eternal second. "Sí," she finally said, causing Pao's heart to leap into her throat. "Te ayudaré."

Pao was about to thank Estrella emphatically, to promise her anything she wanted, but this final act of rebellion seemed to have been the last straw for the other duendecillos.

Led by a larger one, half a head taller than Estrella, the

owners of the rest of the wide eyes stepped out of the trees. There were nearly thirty of them, circling Pao, Estrella, and Naomi in a vaguely ominous way despite their tiny stature.

Like it was time to deliver a long-overdue verdict.

The first thing Pao noticed about the tiny tribunal was how different they all looked from Estrella, and from one another. They all had green hair, skin in varying shades of brown, and clothes made of what appeared to be stitched-together leaves, but that was where the similarities ended.

Some were pixieish like Estrella, but with hair that hung to their knees, or with bald heads or pointed hats. Some looked like brown-and-green versions of those garden gnomes you always see on lawns in retirement communities.

Others were thin and waifish, with long limbs for their height and tiny nimble-looking feet. Pao couldn't stop staring, despite the apparent danger of the situation. She and Naomi were stuck in this place, with no way forward or back, and at the absolute mercy of a group of menacing forest spirits who didn't seem at all inclined to help them. . . .

So why couldn't Pao stop thinking about how *cute* they all were?

Naomi, evidently, was not similarly afflicted with awe. She stepped forward in her brusque way, addressing the leader as Pao stood beside fierce little Estrella and listened.

"¿Qué quieren?" Naomi asked them.

"We want you out of here," the leader said in clear, slow English. He was the garden-gnome type, with a bulbous nose, closely spaced brown eyes, a long green beard, a pointed hat, and a staff made of a thorny twig.

"That's what we want, too," Naomi said. "Help us get to where the magic is. Whatever's causing this. We can help fix it."

"Why would we want your help?" he asked. "You are not of this forest."

"No," said Pao, stepping forward, Estrella at her heels. "But we're from somewhere like this. Somewhere with a magic opening. We can close it—we've done it before. Let us help you. You can trust us."

The leader's eyes crinkled, like he was smiling behind his beard, though Pao couldn't see his mouth. "But that's just it," he said, his voice lower now, more ominous. "We do not trust you. We have seen your kind, and they've brought nothing but ruin to the forest."

From nowhere, the duendecillos suddenly conjured very small but ruthlessly sharp spears. Their circle began to close in.

"I know humans are bad!" Pao said, eyeing the spear points. Sure, the duendecillos wouldn't be able to get her above the belly button, but plenty of damage could be done to her lower extremities. "But we're not here to ruin your forest—we're here to save our friend's abuela! Please, we just need to find my dad."

"It is not the human in you we object to," said the leader, who was not carrying a spear. "It is . . . the *other*."

"What?" Pao asked. "I don't know what you mean, but there's a fantasma in here, okay? It lured us into the forest, and it might be back any minute. If you don't let us help you, it could come back and kill all of you."

The duendecillos didn't answer. Pao looked from Naomi to Estrella, desperate for any idea of what it was the leader was objecting to. Naomi shrugged, her eyes wide, but Estrella jumped forward and began to shout at the others in Spanish, fury present in every line of her little body.

"She's saying the elders are prejudiced," Naomi said in an undertone. "That you're not like the others, and they need to help you or else all could be lost."

"But prejudiced *why*?" Pao asked. She was used to being judged for her skin color, and for the side of town she lived on. . . . Even being a girl sometimes had its pitfalls in the eyes of others. But Pao couldn't imagine the duendecillos caring about any of that.

She could have understood them hating humans in general, given what the human race had done to most places that looked like this, but they'd said it wasn't that, either.

So what could it possibly be?

"They're not saying," Naomi said, fear tinging the edges of her words. "But it doesn't sound like it's going well for Estrella."

Sure enough, the argument ended less than a minute later. The spears were not put away. One of them was used to poke Pao unceremoniously in the back of the knee as the tiny tribunal moved them forward.

Pao walked where they directed her, her mind still going a million miles a minute. Yes, the duendecillos were small, and Pao probably could have kicked a few over and run away, spears or not. But then what? They were in the middle of a forest force field with no way to find the anomaly.

Best-case scenario, the duendecillos were leading them out of the forest, back to the highway where the bus had left them. They could walk into town, find the post office, and figure out where Pao's dad was.

Worst-case scenario . . .

"In here," the leader said, not five minutes after they started their trek. "You will stay. We will decide." Two duendecillos ran ahead, opening what appeared to be a gate in a clump of trees—an entrance Pao never would have seen if she hadn't known to look. It swung open noiselessly, easily twice as tall as Pao, and she, Naomi, and Estrella were ushered inside.

They found themselves in a clearing, much like the one where Pao had climbed into the healing pool in her dream—but there was no water here, just mossy ground, a row of bushes, the occasional rock, and a surrounding circle (about twenty yards in diameter) of trees.

Whether it was magically reinforced or not—and Pao was willing to bet it was—the tree border was too dense to pass through. The only way in or out was the gate, which was, as they watched, disappearing again, the duendecillos along with it.

Pao was ready to collapse on the ground and feel sorry for herself for quite a while, but before she could, she was met with another surprise.

Something rustled in the bushes. Pao and Naomi might have been prisoners in this strange forest cell, but they weren't the only ones.

TWENTY-SIX

Not the Best Time for Pyro 101

"Paola?" The voice was hesitant at first, like its owner couldn't believe she was real, but disbelief gave way to boundless joy as Sal bolted across the clearing and crashed right into Pao, throwing his arms around her.

The young Niño was a little taller now, Pao noted, his hair shorter. But he looked happy. At least, as happy as any nine-year-old could be while locked in a forest cell. She wondered how long he had been in here, and how he had avoided freezing his toes off.

But it wasn't just Sal. There were at least ten other Niños in here with him. Kids Pao recognized from the camp, whose names she didn't know but beside whom she'd fought Manos Pachonas and ahogados last summer.

And once she and Naomi had greeted them all, Pao saw Marisa and Franco waiting against some trees in the back.

"Her, I expected," Marisa said when Pao approached. She was pointing to Naomi, who was avoiding her former leaders by remaining in deep conversation with a pair of white-haired twins a convenient distance away.

"But you?" Marisa continued. "I'll confess this is a surprise."

Pao's former lunchroom bully looked much the same as she

had last summer, with the exception of the way she was wearing her strawberry-blond hair—loose and wavy instead of in the severe braids Pao had gotten used to. It made her look more feminine, Pao thought. More beautiful. But less something, too.

"It's a long story," Pao said, shaking her head. "But I guess we have time." She stepped forward to check the wall of trees that separated them from the rest of the forest. As she'd suspected, there was some kind of magical barrier between the pines. There was no way out save for the gate, which had been closed behind them and was currently invisible.

"Sorry, I'm afraid we don't." Franco hadn't even bothered to say hello, Pao noticed. Which wasn't super polite, considering the last time they'd met, Pao had been rescuing him from certain doom in an underwater palace run by a grieving ghostly maniac.

He was wearing the Niños' traditional black clothing, his dark, curly hair pushed back from his face in a way that looked disheveled yet somehow still absurdly handsome. But his beauty was impersonal, Pao thought. Like a painting. There was no warmth to him.

"Why's that?" Pao asked him, her tone a little short. Wasn't he even a little curious about how she had stumbled upon them?

"We're about to break out of here," Franco said, not meeting her eyes. In his hands was a device that looked a lot like one of those old Game Boys, with buttons and a tiny blinking screen.

"Oh?" Pao said, leaning against the barrier beside Marisa.

"I've been tracking a void-based energy signature through the forest for the last two hours," he said. "It makes passes in a pattern, and if my calculations are correct, it should be passing by again in the next seven minutes."

Two hours? Pao thought. A void-based energy signal . . .

"I know what it is," she said, the connection sparking in her brain like two live wires coming together. "I know what's causing the signal."

"It doesn't *matter* what's causing it," Franco said witheringly, with a look at Marisa that somehow said *Who is this dweeb?* and *Why aren't you getting rid of her for me?* at the same time.

"You might not say that after I tell you what it is," Pao said, waving Naomi over when it became clear she didn't intend to come on her own. Even now, she was dragging her feet.

When Naomi finally joined them, Pao told her, "I was just about to explain why Franco is getting a reading here."

"We don't have time for this," he said, pushing past them without a word to Naomi.

"Marisa," Naomi said after casting a truly poisonous glare at Franco, "it's El Autostopisto. That's why the signal is so strong."

"Nice to see you, too," Marisa said, something a little sad lingering around her eyes. And then, "The Hitchhiker? Are you sure?"

"He's been following us since Silver Springs," Naomi confirmed. "We fought him on a bus, and he lured us into the forest. It's a trap, I'm telling you. Whatever Franco wants to do with that energy signal is going to get us all killed."

"She's right," Pao said. "He's been tracking the signature for two hours? That's just when we first followed the Hitchhiker in."

"If it's really a leyenda . . ." Marisa said, "this is going to be harder than we thought." She looked at Naomi. "At least we're together now."

Naomi stepped toward Pao. "Sure. Let's just figure out how to get out of here, and then you guys can tell us what you've found out about the anomaly."

"And you said you didn't want to come," Marisa said teasingly, but Naomi's expression didn't crack. She just nodded to Pao and walked back over to where Sal and the twins were sparring with knives.

"She's just . . ." Pao began.

"I know," Marisa said.

Pao was going to say more, but just then Franco's voice echoed through the clearing.

"Wait a minute," he said, and Pao turned in time to see him spotting Estrella, who was near where the gate had been, looking utterly lost.

Pao felt awful. Estrella had been ushered in with the rest of them, but Pao had totally forgotten her in the shock of seeing the other Niños. Pao sprinted to reach the opposite edge of the clearing before Franco did, putting herself between the boy and the terrified creature.

"They left a *spy*?" he asked, trying to step around Pao to get to Estrella.

"Estrella isn't a spy," Pao said, narrowing her eyes at Franco. "She's a duendecillo, and she tried to help us. She argued with her own people to try to keep us out of here."

"We need to question it," Franco said impatiently. "Figure out if it knows a way out."

"*She'll* talk when *she's* ready," Pao said, liking Franco less and less the longer they spent with him here.

"What?" he snapped. "You're really going to prevent me from questioning . . . *her*?"

"Estrella," Pao said, kneeling down beside the duendecillo, "do you want to tell Franco what you know about getting out of here?"

Estrella shook her head, green bangs falling into her eyes in her vehemence.

"Do you mind telling *me*?" Pao asked.

Estrella seemed to think for a moment, and then she nodded, holding out a tiny brown hand dusted with gold freckles. She led Pao away from the crowd.

As smug as Pao felt about having a source Franco couldn't get to first, Pao immediately saw the flaw in her plan as Estrella turned to look at Pao expectantly. The duendecillo leader had spoken English, but as far as Pao knew, little Estrella only spoke Spanish.

Unfortunately, Pao's Duolingo owl hadn't graduated her to Secret Information Revealed by Magical Beings yet. And Naomi, who had served as translator before, was too busy sulking in the corner to notice the predicament Pao was in now.

Pao was too proud to tell any of the other Niños she didn't know enough Spanish to help, so she whispered to Estrella, "Speak slowly, okay?"

As it turned out, when Pao quieted her anxiety and told herself she could do it, she understood a lot more than she thought she would. In her memory were the Spanish words her mom had cooed to her as a baby, and on the signs Pao had read, and in the commercials she'd heard on the radio. She also recalled Señora Mata's voice, and the chanting and gleeful shouting of kids at school.

By listening carefully, Pao learned from Estrella that the elders—"los mayores"—wouldn't come back to the cell until they had a new prisoner, or if there was an emergency. Otherwise the door would stay closed, maybe forever. They would most likely die in here.

Pao understood Estrella, and with the understanding came a sense of belonging she hadn't even known she'd been seeking. And also a big dose of dread.

But she had a plan.

"Would a fire—uh, un fuego—count as una emergencia?" Pao asked Estrella under her breath, trying to make sure Franco didn't hear.

Eyes wide, Estrella nodded.

"Gracias," Pao said, pressing her hands together. "Me . . . ayuda"—yes, that was the word—"mucho."

If the grammar was wrong, if Pao's accent wasn't quite perfect, Estrella didn't mind. She beamed at Pao like she had forgotten about the fire question. Like the only important thing was that they'd understood each other.

And for a moment, that was true. But then it was time to burn things down.

The problem with the fire plan, as Franco wasted no time in telling Pao, was that the clearing was so small and so filled with organic matter that they would all burn up before they ever got the attention of the duendecillos.

"You got a better idea?" Pao asked, staring him dead in the eye.

"Yes!" Franco said, waving the Game Boy thing at her. Pao did the best acting of her life when she pretended she wasn't interested in how it worked. "We already missed the last pass of the signature—"

"The Hitchhiker, you mean," Pao interjected.

"But its next pass will be in twenty-four minutes," Franco went on, totally ignoring her. "I can lock onto the signal with this and convert the energy it's producing to send a magical beam straight through the barrier!"

"Where we'll be face-to-face with a leyenda," Pao finished for him. "An extremely dangerous one that we can't hope to defeat, even together."

"With the beam we can!" Franco said, looking ready to stomp his foot in frustration like a five-year-old.

"Let me ask you this, Franco," Pao said as the rest of the Niños watched, some with amusement in their expressions (Naomi, mostly) and some looking fearful or angry. "Have you ever used the beam on anything as powerful as the Hitchhiker?"

Franco didn't say a word.

"Have you ever used it at all?"

"That's irrelevant!" he exploded. "I've done the research—I know it'll work!"

"Well, I actually *have* made a fire before, which increases our odds of success," Pao said, looking around. "Plus, it will warm things up. So, all in favor of fire?"

"Who authorized you to call a vo—" Franco began, but he was drowned out by the sound of at least ten kids yelling, "FIIIIRE!"

Naomi punched Pao on the arm, grinning at her. Marisa shrugged sheepishly at Franco, mouthing *sorry*, though she didn't really look sorry at all.

"Okay!" Pao said. "The Hitchhiker passes every thirty minutes, and it's been six since the last. That gives us ten minutes before the Hitchhiker is at his maximum distance from this place, when it will be easier for us to escape. We'll light the fire a few minutes before then, everyone will huddle near the gate, and as soon as the elders open it . . ." Pao pantomimed busting out dramatically. Sal followed suit, and soon all the smaller kids were doing it, like an audition for the Kool-Aid Man was happening in the world's least likely talent-scouting location.

Pao grabbed Naomi and told her to start hunting for rocks. They decided to start the fire in two locations as far from the door as possible, giving themselves the best chance of getting out before anyone got hurt.

Pao collected a little bundle of dried grass. Too bad she couldn't use her magnifying glass to light it with the sun, she thought. The sky overhead was dark. Instead, she found a nice flat stone at the edge of the clearing and turned it over in her hands, remembering what her mom had always said about using natural materials in rituals—*They work better if you're on good terms.*

With three minutes to go, Pao asked her rock to spark and promised to aim it well. She waved everyone to the door. It was time.

Since her staff's blade was the only one she had, Pao transformed her magnifying glass without thinking and was surprised by the hushed whispers that sprung up from the crowd of Niños near the gate.

The only other Niño with an Arma del Alma, as far as Pao knew, was Franco.

"Let's go, hero girl," Naomi said, already striking her stone with her knife.

Pao followed suit, and soon her little nest of grass was smoking. She placed it gently on a pile of twigs and sticks and stepped back just as the first tiny orange flames began to sprout like wildflowers from the forest floor.

She was almost sad to be destroying even a small part of such a beautiful place.

Almost.

Their work done, Pao and Naomi ran to join the other Niños at the spot where Estrella said the gate would open. Their little fires were already happily kindling, twin columns of smoke reaching for the canopy of trees above.

Any minute now, Pao thought, the duendecillos would sense the damage to their sanctuary and come to investigate.

Any minute . . .

The fires went from cheerful to ravenous, feeding on the easily accessible fuel until they were at least four feet tall and also stretching lengthwise toward each other across the clearing.

The mood of eager anticipation began to change. Feet were tapping, hands were fidgeting in hair, eyes were darting from face to face. Pao looked at Naomi, who was looking at Marisa, who was looking at Franco, who was looking furious.

Beside her, Estrella pressed close.

"¿Pronto?" Pao whispered to the creature, hoping she would know that Pao meant *They'll be coming soon, right?*

"Sí," said Estrella, but Pao couldn't help but notice she didn't sound quite as confident as she had before.

One of the fires reached a tree and raced up its trunk, doubling in size. From a faint scent in the air, the smoke had increased in volume until it was tangible around them.

At least five of their precious minutes before the Hitchhiker supposedly cycled back around were already gone, and there was no sign of the barrier becoming anything resembling a gate.

The fires met in the middle, a shower of sparks celebrating their union. One of the smaller kids, who had just been pretending to be a Kool-Aid Man, coughed into the crook of his arm.

Franco's expression was murderous, and it was fixed right on Pao. *This better work*, it said, *or you've just killed us all.*

Two more minutes passed. The fire was gaining ground quickly, rolling toward them across the clearing, hot enough to burn through the moss, which Pao had hoped would contain enough water to slow its progression.

Forget the Hitchhiker, Pao thought. *This whole cell is about to burn with us inside.* She cursed her own hubris, her insistence on being the one to get information from Estrella, her pride at beating Franco in a vote.

What did any of it matter now?

The smoke was stinging Pao's eyes. Almost the entire ten minutes had passed. The fire couldn't burn through the magic boundary, so it was pushing with all its chaotic energy right toward them.

She tried to get Marisa's attention, to say she was sorry, but Pao's eyes were streaming, and a cough was all she could produce. Was this it? Had she really just crashed in here and ruined everything in under thirty minutes?

The toes of her sneakers began to get hot as the fire reached the cell's two-thirds mark. They only had minutes left. The flames jumped and danced gleefully, ready to embrace them like they were old friends.

Just as Pao was about to throw herself between the fire and the younger Niños to protect them as long as she could, the wall behind them shifted.

At first, Pao thought it was just an illusion, the shimmer from the heat casting some kind of cruel trick on her eyes. But the movement didn't stop. The uniform wall became a gate, and as it opened within an absolute cyclone of ash and smoke and embers, everyone piled into a scandalized group of duendecillo elders.

"Out of the way!" Pao screamed, scattering them with a wide, harmless kick. It did the job. Pao slammed the gate shut the moment she was sure everyone was accounted for, leaving the fire to burn itself out inside.

The prison cell wouldn't be usable again for a long time, Pao thought, and good riddance. The taste of fresh air was reviving her already. She wiped away her tears and drew her staff, pointing it at the elders.

"We're going now," she said. "We're taking Estrella with us, and you won't be following, ¿entienden?"

The little duendecillos looked furious at having been tricked, but even they seemed to realize they were outnumbered (not to mention outsized). They folded their little arms and tucked their chins in defeat.

Pao was secretly glad it hadn't come to a fight. They really were too adorable to stab.

"Can you lead us out of here?" Pao asked Estrella, ignoring the way Marisa was tenderly wiping soot from Franco's face. Naomi was looking elsewhere, but her scowl told Pao that she'd seen it, too.

"¡Sí!" Estrella squeaked, turning one last time to stick out her tongue at the elders.

Pao was elated. Everyone was alive, they were together, and her plan—however poorly it had been executed—had worked!

She was so busy congratulating herself that she forgot all about Franco's clock—and the magic signature that could only belong to one creature.

They were free, yes, but they were also out of time.

TWENTY-SEVEN
The Underdogs Don't Win
the Big Game in This One

This time, it was clear the Hitchhiker didn't plan to pull any punches.

He charged into the outer clearing like he was a raging bull and Pao was one of those guys in a little jacket holding a red cape. The only trouble was, she wasn't the only person in the crossfire.

The Niños, Estrella, and the duendecillos mayores stood there, shocked, as the fantasma barreled into their midst like the Tasmanian Devil. When he straightened up, their shock turned to horror in an instant.

She had been so stupid, Pao realized, to think El Autostopisto had been doing anything but baiting them on the bus. The form he took now made the little boy with the four eyes look like a kitten in the pet store window.

The Hitchhiker was at least twenty feet tall, but that wasn't what made him the most terrifying. On the bus, he had switched forms to unnerve them. Now, unbound by the confines of his own trick, he seemed to have become all of them at once.

On his massive face were four sets of eyes, stacked one on top of the other—a pair from each of the personas he had taken on while following Pao. Closest to his strange, flat nose were the long-lashed eyes of Elenita, fluttering at them as the rest stared menacingly.

His hair cascaded around his face, wild and alive, like snakes.

He was magnificent, Pao thought, with four arms, each wielding a different deadly weapon, and his massive body clothed in a close-fitting bright-red jumpsuit. Then there were his mouths. Elenita's full lips were in the center, and a flat-lipped, more masculine mouth had split in half to bracket them.

When he opened them to speak, a thousand voices came forth, layered like a symphony.

"Who dares to challenge me?"

Franco, Naomi, Marisa, and Pao all stepped forward together, like they'd rehearsed it. "I do," they said as one.

But the Hitchhiker zeroed in on Pao. "Little sister, why do you fight? Your true nature is not to resist, but to succumb. Do you have no idea what power awaits when you join us?"

His words tugged at something deep inside Pao, her feeling that she was bound to this leyenda more tightly than she'd ever believed. She'd carried the same feeling through the haunted cactus field and into the mouth of the void, that there was something bad inside her, and it was a part of her very essence.

"I'll never join you," she spat, and she meant it, no matter who she really was.

I'll find out from my father, she thought desperately. *After we've defeated this monstrosity.*

Pao pointed her staff at the Hitchhiker, her eyes narrowed in fury when she remembered his threat to take the innocent bus passengers to the void.

The blade of Pao's staff glowed in the dark forest, but

El Autostopisto generated his own light as well. It was a malicious luminescence, the kind a poisonous mushroom might give off as a warning of the toxins within.

As if he'd heard her thoughts, the Hitchhiker spoke again, the voices layering horrifically, echoing off the trees. "You'll join us, or you'll die," he said. "That is the way for all of our kind. The world will never accept you, Paola Santiago, no matter how many shiny weapons you force it to give up to you."

"I'm. Never. Going. To. Join. You," Pao said, emphasizing every word. "So I guess that just leaves death."

"No," said the Hitchhiker, bringing one of his hands to his chin like he was pondering. "Not until you are ready to learn the truth."

Pao was dying to ask what he meant. Her craving to know the "truth" tasted like metal in her mouth. But she had learned that there was a time and a place for discovery, and whatever this one was, she didn't want to hear it from a monster.

So, instead of asking, Pao lunged, catching the fantasma by surprise, digging the blade of her spear deep into his red-clothed shin until green blood sprayed from the wound.

When he screamed, it was with every voice at his command. His *victims*, Pao somehow knew, as if she were looking into his very soul. She saw their faces flicker by like photos in a flip book. Elenita, and Alán, and the nameless little boy in the red pajamas.

There were others as well. Many others. With names and stories and families she would never know.

Pao tore her spear out of the fantasma's ghostly flesh, disappointed that he was still on his feet. She'd been rattled by his slideshow of horror, but the moment she severed the connection, her mind was her own again, and the images disappeared.

Looking around at the rest of the Niños, now drawing weapons and preparing to fight, Pao hoped to see signs that they were rattled, too. That they'd seen what she had. But none of them looked haunted. Not the way she was, at least.

And wasn't that always the way?

Once again, Dante's words returned to her. . . . *You're connected to the head of every monster in the flipping world.* . . .

She knew she was. But wondering why had never gotten her anywhere. And now, when it seemed vital to understand, there was no time for wondering. No time for anything but surviving.

The other Niños leaped into battle now, as the duendecillos huddled against the closed door of their burning prison, cowering in fear. All but Estrella, who cloaked herself in a strange green bubble and charged at the ankles of the Hitchhiker with the tiniest battle cry Pao had ever heard.

It was the inspiration Pao needed.

Her heart was full, her spear was warm in her grasp, and her friends were fighting around her. Pao threw herself back into the fray, hoping their efforts would be enough. Praying. Even if they didn't have an Ondina, or a pearl of ultimate power . . . maybe, together, they could take down this horrible scourge once and for all.

Marisa was everywhere, her hair flying behind her like a banner, fearlessly attacking the Hitchhiker with her water knife, her movements as fluid and graceful as a dancer's.

Naomi struck with the stealth of a snake, her white curls bouncing as she jumped, flipped, and slid into whatever opening was available.

The little kids had been strictly instructed to stay behind with the duendecillos, but only one of them had obeyed, and even he stood in front of the tiny elders with a pocketknife drawn, a fierce look on his face like he dared anyone to come close.

Sal, little Sal, was in the thick of the fight, too, shadowing Franco, who hacked powerfully with a glowing short sword Pao recognized at once as an Arma del Alma.

Pao weaved in as needed, offering encouragement, moving the little ones out of the way, and getting in her own hits when she could. Her staff had easily twice the reach of any other weapon in the field, but it took time to position, and when she stretched to jab with it, she left herself wide open.

She used the move sparingly, but each time she reached up to stab the fantasma's ribs, he seemed to anticipate the attack, and no matter what else he was doing, one of his weapons would descend on her.

Twice she took hits to the shoulders, and once to the hip.

Gasping and wheezing from the last blow, she stepped back to catch her breath and survey the scene, and what she saw was far less encouraging than the story she'd been telling herself.

They were losing. Badly. And it had barely been fifteen minutes. More than half the Niños were no longer fighting. Instead, they were at the fringes of the clearing, tending to their wounds or the worse wounds of others.

Marisa was still in the mix, as was Naomi. Sal had been sidelined with a bad cut to the leg, and he sat with the duendecillos mayores.

Pao's vision was going fuzzy—the slash she'd taken on her hip was deep. Blood was seeping into her T-shirt, making the black fabric glisten.

"Not yet . . ." she said to herself, noticing Franco on the attack, the Game Boy device in some kind of Velcro holster on his belt.

They hadn't located the anomaly yet, just a leyenda that seemed hell-bent on making sure they never did. Did the Hitchhiker want to keep Pao from finding her father? Were they going to die in this clearing? Before she'd even gotten the answers she came for?

Green spots began to dance before Pao's eyes, stretching and shrinking like the paper dolls she'd last seen in Raisin Valley just before she plunged into Dante's past and everything changed.

The Hitchhiker took a wild swipe with a long, jagged sword. Three of the remaining five Niños went flying, Marisa included. Tears filled Pao's eyes.

"No . . ." she said, lifting her staff with a heavy arm. She didn't want to go down like this, not standing here crying, letting her friends die. She was going to fight, just like she always did. Just like she always *would* do. No matter what the truth about her was.

And so Pao charged, taking heart from the warmth of the staff in her grasp.

She almost made it to the Hitchhiker, too, but as always, he sensed her coming. Turning away from the last standing Niño, he flipped the sword in his grasp and swung the butt end of it before Pao had time to dodge.

The last thing she saw before she blacked out were whirling green stars.

Don't take me yet, she thought. But, of course, they did.

TWENTY-EIGHT
One Last Trip on the Narcolepsy Express

Pao awoke on the ground, flat on her back, the dream forest's canopy above her as usual.

She groaned as she arose, pain in her hip, though there was no blood. Not here.

Pao began to walk, imagining she was on the same road as always, but this time the scene was different. She was in a perfectly round clearing with a pool in the middle of it, and Pao could sense a magical barrier surrounding her.

Frantic, she looked for a way out and saw nothing but uninterrupted trees.

Pao was back in the duendecillos' prison, while somewhere in her waking life she was unconscious as her friends were fighting—and possibly dying—without her.

"I need to get out of here!" she screamed, but the eerie quiet of the cell absorbed her voice, deadening it.

She wanted to cry, but instead she went to the edge of the pool—the only truly dreamlike thing about this place—and peered inside, expecting to see her own reflection.

What she saw instead almost made her scream again.

It was her face, and it wasn't. Her hair was pure white, her skin even paler than it usually was in the wintertime. But the most troublesome thing was her eyes. They glowed a poisonous green. It was the same version of herself she'd seen in another dream last summer, back at the Niños' camp.

In that dream, she had been a feral creature, had chased Dante and dragged him into the river she didn't yet know held the entrance to the void.

In this dream, she merely stared at herself, curious and a little afraid.

Pao raised her hand. The fantasma in her reflection raised hers, too.

Pao's heart hammered too fast. The answer was within her grasp now, but she didn't want to understand. She needed her mom to explain it to her, or her dad. She needed someone to tell her who she was and why all this was happening.

As her anger and fear took over, the reflection began to change.

Her eyes started multiplying. Then her mouth split into two to make room for a second pair of lips. Her hair went dark and snakelike, and she grew bigger until her face filled the pool.

No! she thought, afraid to make another noise, afraid to feel. Being angry was what had caused this. Did Pao's anger make her a monster? Was that what the dream was trying to tell her?

She stumbled backward, breaking the connection. The forest started to shimmer and fade, a sure sign that she was about to wake up . . . but then she heard a voice calling to her from inside the pool.

"Pao, are you there? Pao, are you okay? It's me, Pao. It's Emma. . . ."

• • •

The first thing Pao saw when she regained consciousness was the green glow of the paper-doll creatures to her left.

The second thing she saw was her phone lying on the ground, Emma's face clearly visible, like Pao had somehow dialed her number while unconscious even though that was impossible. Her phone had been turned off. And it wasn't like the duendecillos had Wi-Fi, right?

"Emma?" Pao said, groggy, her hip still on fire where the Hitchhiker had whacked her. The green things blocked her vision of the battle, but she could hear it raging in the background. She tried to reach her phone, her dream still lingering in her mind.

Her reflection, with white hair and green eyes like a fantasma.

Her face becoming the Hitchhiker's terrifying visage because she'd gotten angry.

The prison cell . . .

Suddenly, Pao had an idea. It was a dangerous one, like all her others, but she understood that there was no other way. She finally managed to grasp her phone, dragging it toward her along with a handful of leaves and twigs. She didn't know how Emma had gotten through, but it was the perfect time for a miracle.

It was time for Pao to say good-bye, just in case.

"Emma!" she said when they could see each other at last. "Look, I only have a second, but—"

"Pao!" Emma was crying. "Pao, something weird is going on at your place. Bruto won't stop barking, and there's this green light and—"

"Green light?" Pao asked. "No, there can't be, not—"

"Look!" Emma said, turning the camera around.

There were identical green paper dolls surrounding Emma, Bruto, and—Pao's heart sank when she realized it—her mom.

"I need you guys to get out of there!" Pao said, trying to sound strong. There was only one thing those green lights could mean. Void creatures were coming.

"We can't!" Emma sobbed. "We've tried, but they won't let us through!"

This is because of you. Pao heard the words in Dante's voice, like he was standing over her now. *You don't mean to cause destruction, but you do, to everyone you love.*

"No," Pao said. "Emma, I'm sorry. I . . ." What else was there to say? Bruto might be able to help, but he was just a puppy, and Emma and her mom . . . they would be helpless against whatever the void coughed up.

Pao wished so profoundly that she could be with them in that moment, staff in hand, to protect them. But she was never able to protect the people she loved. She only hurt them. Dante had been right about that much. Had he been right about everything else, too?

Pao looked through the screen, a thousand emotions tangling in her until she thought she'd fly apart with the strength of them. Emma. Her mom. Her puppy. She might never see them again.

The green light around Pao grew brighter as the dolls encircled her and began to spin.

"Now they're spinning, Pao!" Emma shrieked. "What do we do?"

Pao didn't know. She had no idea what these green things were or what the parallel between her and Emma's experiences meant. She wasn't even sure whether she was dreaming or awake.

Pao closed her eyes. She asked every god and ghost and saint and monster—any person or creature with an ounce of power in this world—to please, please keep her mom, Emma, and Bruto safe.

The green light grew so bright Pao could barely see. A faint whining began in her ears, and there was a vibration in her chest like something inside her was powering the spectacle, draining her like the magic flashlight once had on the banks of the Gila River a thousand miles from here. . . .

And then the last thing she could have possibly expected happened before her eyes.

Emma, Bruto, and Maria disappeared from the screen . . .

. . . and fell in a heap of legs and fur and tangled hair right on top of Pao.

The green light faded. Everyone untangled frantically and sat up. *They're really here,* Pao thought dizzily, *in the flesh.* But *how?* They had been in danger, and she had prayed to the saints and the gods and the ghosts to keep them safe. . . .

But instead, her prayers had brought them *here,* to the least safe place in the known world—and probably some of the unknown ones, too.

Even so, it was impossible for Pao not to feel happiness, and relief, and every other emotion there was. They were really, really here.

Bruto—who was now licking Pao's face with reckless, joyful abandon. Pao's mom, her hair in a bun, wearing her paint-splattered striped pajama pants. And Emma, her eyes still filled with tears, the knees of her light-blue jeans dirty from hitting the forest ground.

All Pao wanted to do was hug them, and tell them it would be okay, and say that she'd never been so happy to see anyone. And let the tears that were prickling the backs of her eyes fall on their shoulders.

Okay, she wanted to do that *and* do a bajillion hours of research into what *exactly* had just happened and how she had managed to bring them through the portal when they'd been only seconds from being devoured by void beasts. But that was beside the point. . . .

Because behind her, with the glaring green light of the spinning portal finally extinguished, Pao could see the devastation that had overtaken this place since she'd fallen unconscious. She knew there was no time to do anything other than what she'd been planning to do before the appearance of Emma and her mom had made everything infinitely more complicated.

All the Hitchhiker's eyes were focused on Franco now, while the rest of the Niños huddled on the ground beside the prison cell gate, still nursing their wounds. Franco was fiddling with the buttons on his Game Boy again, cursing, sweat beading on his brow.

"I love you guys, but you have to get over there!" Pao shouted to her mom and Emma, pointing to where the duendecillos were still crouching, terrified. "And whatever you do, don't watch!"

Pao's mom and Emma did as they were told, shutting their eyes tight, but Bruto stayed with Pao.

"Well, if that's how you want it, let's go, buddy," she said, grabbing her staff from where it had fallen on the ground and sprinting over to where she saw Estrella tending to one of the wounded twins.

"Do you know how to . . . abre la puerta?" Pao asked the duen-decillo, knowing she had minutes to pull off this crazy plan that she'd concocted while half asleep. There would be no time to form hypotheses or do trial runs or anything else. It was time to go now.

Estrella's eyes were very wide. "Sí," she nearly whispered.

"Bueno," Pao said. "Do you trust me?"

Estrella nodded. Pao knew this wasn't really fair, that Estrella had no idea what she was getting herself into, but there was no time to explain.

Unable to remember any more Duolingo Spanish with so much going on around her, Pao spoke as clearly as she could in English, gesturing when she wasn't sure Estrella understood. "We have to get everyone out of the way," she said, pointing to all of them and sweeping her hands to the side. "And then we have to open the door, okay? As fast as we can."

The second Estrella nodded, a determined look on her tiny face, Pao turned and sprinted across the clearing to join Franco. She would have to believe that Estrella had truly understood. She was their only hope.

"Get back," Franco said when she reached him, his voice half a snarl. "I've got this!"

"What are you trying to do?" Pao asked. "Because I have a plan!"

"Is it to barbecue everyone again?" Franco asked, just as a thin red laser dot appeared in the center of the Hitchhiker's face. "Because that was so fun last time!"

He closed his eyes in concentration, turning one dial slowly, the red laser growing larger in diameter as he held it steady.

But he kept his eyes shut for too long. The fantasma lashed out with one of its two functioning arms (the other two hung limply at his sides, green goo oozing from multiple puncture wounds), and before Pao could stab it with her staff's blade, it knocked Franco off his feet and into a nearby tree trunk, where he lay without moving.

Pao swore, her eyes automatically darting to her mom, who would probably have the audacity to ground her even in these dire circumstances. Fortunately, Maria was too far away to hear.

"My plan it is, then!" Pao said to no one as she waved her staff over her head. "Hey, ugly!" she called, and all the Hitchhiker's eyes turned to focus on her. "You want me? Come and get me."

Then Pao flew, running as fast as she had ever run before, her heart leaping when she realized the Niños had moved a few feet and the door to the smoldering, blackened prison cell was wide open. The way ahead was clear. . . .

Clear except for Naomi, who was balancing on her uninjured leg, refusing to step aside.

Behind Pao, the Hitchhiker roared and lurched clumsily, but he would reach her in seconds.

"What the heck are you doing?" Naomi asked.

"No time to explain!" Pao shouted, leaping over a tree stump and skidding to a stop in front of the threshold. "If I don't come back, make sure my mom and Emma get home, and try to save Dante's abuela, okay? They need you."

"Stop!" Naomi said. "You don't have to do this!"

"I do," Pao said sadly. "And I know you're enough of a hero to understand why."

Naomi didn't argue further, which Pao knew was as close to agreement as she was going to get.

From thirty yards away, where they were crouching with the duendecillos, Pao heard her mom scream, "Paola, no!"

But Pao couldn't stop. Not now. Not if she wanted any of them to live.

"Close the door behind us," she told Naomi, patting her leg to command Bruto to stay with her. Then Pao wrenched herself away from everyone else she knew and loved in this world and bolted into the cell.

Despite Naomi's resistance to her plan, the surly girl obeyed, and less than a minute later, Pao was alone in a smoldering prison with a chupacabra puppy, a twenty-foot-tall monster, and no way out.

Well, *probably* no way out, Pao thought. That would all depend on what happened next.

"You think you're so clever," said the thousand voices of the Hitchhiker's victims. "But you and your friends are still going to die. How long do you think this weak forest magic can hold me?"

"Long enough for everyone to get to safety," Pao said. "That's all that matters."

"Silly, naive girl," the layered voices said. "You'll never save them. Not from me, and not from yourself."

Sometimes, when Pao walked away from research that wasn't making sense, or an experiment she couldn't quite get right, she'd distract herself by doing something else—training Bruto, playing video games, seeing how many marshmallows she could fit in her mouth—and find that the problem solved itself a little at a time.

That was the feeling she had now as all the pieces came together. The Hitchhiker's comments, her experiences last summer, Ondina, La Llorona, her father . . .

Dante's hurtful parting words.

Señora Mata's gasped, disjointed warnings.

The fact that Pao had been able to bring her mom and Emma to her despite all odds.

Even Bruto, a beast that should have ripped off her hand the first time she tried to pet him—or at least gummed it to death— was proof of what was starting to take shape inside her.

But just like her third-grade science fair volcano that wouldn't erupt without the final addition of vinegar, there was one more piece of information Pao needed for her truth to expand to its full capacity.

And there was only one person who could give it to her.

Luckily, Pao finally knew how to get to him.

"I don't care what you think," Pao finally said as the Hitchhiker stood eerily still. She could look at him now, right in the multiple eyes. She'd seen the part of herself that was like him, and it scared her, but she also knew there was more to her than monster.

Pao took a knee on the charred ground as the Hitchhiker switched from talking mode to fighting mode, using his two remaining arms to draw his weapons.

"You have nowhere to run," he said. "If you truly won't join us, then you leave me with no choice."

Pao put a hand on the burnt moss, closing her eyes despite the fact that she only had seconds before the Hitchhiker struck his final blow.

I need to see my father, Pao thought, opening the latch of the mental box where she'd stuffed every longing thought of him since she was three years old. Every missed birthday, every Bring Your Daughter to Work Day, every night she'd spent fuming at her mom and wishing, *wishing* there was someone else who would understand . . .

The green paper dolls sprouted around her—comforting instead of menacing now—and she stood up, allowing them to enfold her in their arms of light.

Papá, I'm coming, Pao thought, and she felt herself disappear.

TWENTY-NINE
The Monster Within

The trip through the portal was like when you get nitrous oxide at the dentist. For the first few seconds, you're dreaming all this amazing stuff, like drifting off into space, and everything's getting sparkly around you. And then . . .

You wake up an hour later, with no memory of what happened, dizzy and a little nauseated with half your face numb.

Pao tried to shake off the disorientation, knowing she'd need her wits about her for what was coming next. Bruto leaned heavily against her legs, panting, each exhale a little whine.

As much as Pao wished he was safe at home, there was no denying it was nice not to be alone. "One more adventure before we hang up our fantasma-hunting hats for good, okay, boy?" Pao asked him, and his tongue unrolled in a big, goofy smile.

She patted his head, smiling back, and then at last, as clearheaded as she was likely to get for now, Pao looked around at where she'd landed.

They were in the center of a wide road lined by dense forest. The way ahead was all too familiar, even though Pao had never walked it while awake. This road had always led her to her father, and Pao had to trust it would do the same now.

Patting Bruto's head one more time, Pao jerked her chin forward. "Come on, boy," she said. "It's this way."

If Bruto doubted her, he had the good grace not to say so.

They walked down the road together, Pao stepping gingerly with her wounded leg. The slice on her hip had stopped bleeding, but it was still sore, and it made her infuriatingly slow. She stuck close to Bruto and to the middle of the road, just in case.

The eyes that usually peeked out from the trees along this path were missing. Even though Pao now knew those eyes belonged to a council of duendecillos that thought she was evil, she had to admit the road felt lonelier without them watching her pass.

"Just a little farther," she said to Bruto. This time he called her on the lie, staring up at her with that particular judgy dog-raising-an-eyebrow look that never failed to get the truth out of her. "Fine," she said. "I have no idea where we are—I'm just trying to boost morale. Are you happy now?"

He gave a satisfied—if smug—little sniff, and they continued.

Up ahead, the path grew steeper, and Pao, her leg beginning to burn from the effort, pushed her way to the crest of the hill, where she stopped dead in her tracks.

In the place where Pao had twice seen her father in her dreams, down the hill from where she stood, was one of those shiny Airstream trailers. Parked beside it was a Toyota pickup that looked much older than Pao.

None of that was out of the ordinary. Even the giant satellite-dish-like things on either end of the trailer, humming and whirring with energy, weren't immediate cause for alarm.

What made Pao's jaw drop down to her sneakers was the

seemingly sentient deep-purple cloud that hovered above the scene. When she peered closer, she saw that it was made up of writhing and undulating snakes of energy. It might as well have been wearing a T-shirt that said SOMETHING EVIL MADE ME!

Somehow, she knew that her father was inside that trailer. And that all the answers to her questions were just a small slope and an aluminum door away from being answered.

And so she ran right toward it, her heart pounding, her puppy at her heels.

"Dad?" Pao knocked sharply on the door three times.

No answer.

"Dad, it's me, Pao!"

Nothing.

Bruto whined, then scratched at the door with his massive paw.

It opened outward, just a crack, like the latch hadn't completely caught the last time it was closed, and Pao could hear quiet voices coming from inside. Men's voices.

"Not her," one man said. "Another will come. Please, we'll find a way, just let her go!"

There was a strangling sound, and then: "But we've worked so hard, Beto. This is the last test. Pass this one, and you'll finally be free. That's what you want, isn't it? Your freedom?"

Beto, Pao thought, a thrill going through her. The boy her mother had known before her dad . . . What was he doing here? Was this her chance to find out if he was really La Llorona's son? And if the pleading man was Beto, did that make the other man Pao's father?

"Isn't it?" the second man asked again, and the sound of his voice made the hairs stand up on Pao's arms. It was deep and a little sinister. Dangerous, Pao thought, like the shadowy figure that had ordered Dante around in her vision. That couldn't be her father, could it?

Reluctant to interrupt before she'd overheard more, Pao cautiously drew her staff, willing its glow to dim. A six-foot-long illuminated wand with a bladed end wasn't the stealthiest weapon in the world, but she would have to make do.

Bruto seemed to understand that silence was vital to their survival at this moment, because he stood noiselessly beside Pao, as tense as a taut bow string, waiting. . . .

"Yes," said Beto, his voice flatter now. Defeated. "That's what I want."

"Then let's answer the door, hmm? Let's say hello to the intrepid Paola."

The door flew open before Pao could react, knocking her backward. She almost lost her footing and fell down the little fold-out steps, but she caught herself at the last second.

It was like this, wobbling on one foot, her arms comically thrown out at her sides, that Paola Santiago saw her father in the flesh for the first time in ten years.

He was tall and broad-shouldered, she noticed, taking in the sight of him almost hungrily. His hair was the same color as hers, and just as thick and wavy, but there was some gray at the temples. It was pushed back and disheveled, like he'd been running his hands through it.

But his face . . . His face is what she'd most wanted to see. Her dreams had obscured it every time she got close enough.

First, there were his eyes. Deep brown, like hers, while her mom's were that hazel color everyone always commented on. There were crinkles at the corners like he spent a lot of time squinting into the sun.

His nose was long and straight, nothing like Pao's little rounded one, and his cheekbones were high and sharp. But his cheeks were full, obscuring his jawline in a way that made him seem kind. Soft, like a dad, and not just a guy living in a weird trailer in the middle of nowhere.

"Hi," Pao said after a long minute, finally steady on her feet. "I'm . . . Pao. Sorry—that's stupid. You already know who I am, I guess. I just . . . haven't . . ."

Before she could splutter herself into silence, her dad stepped forward and hugged her. It was one of those long, parent-type hugs that magically makes you feel less sick or sad or lonely than you did before it started.

She thought, standing there, that she could stay just like this for at least a year. Maybe ten of them, just to make up for lost time.

But her father pulled away after a few seconds, almost like he'd received an electric shock. Pao, coming out of the minor trance that seeing him for the first time had caused, remembered the other voice she'd heard through the crack in the door. And the strange, swirling purple cloud above where they were standing. And the million things she had come here to ask this man, and all the people who were counting on her getting the answers they needed.

"Look," Pao said, trying to peer behind him without being obvious about it, "I wish I was just here to . . . you know, catch up, or whatever, but I actually have a lot of questions and not that much time, so—"

He laughed, interrupting her, his demeanor changing subtly as Pao spoke. "Not much time?" he said. "I hope you don't think you're leaving now. Not when we've waited so long for you to get here."

She should have been happy that he wanted to see her, but his words sounded a little like a threat. And what did he mean, *we*? Was it really Beto inside? Her father was still blocking her view of the inside of the trailer.

"I'm here because I have questions," Pao said, sensing it was time to cut to the chase and wanting to give her dad the chance to prove that he was good, that he could help her.

She took a deep breath. "Questions only you can answer," she continued, while he looked on, seeming bemused if anything. "About why my friend's . . . well, my *ex*-friend's abuela is in some kind of coma, and why monsters and fantasmas have been stalking me since I left Silver Springs, and what . . . ?" Pao gestured overhead at the swirling purple mass that seemed to be drawing all the light and color from the forest into itself. "What *that* is, and—"

"She's so like you," her father said to no one, interrupting her. And there was a definite change in his demeanor. His whole expression morphed, like someone was taking over his face, moving in behind it. Someone who held his eyebrows differently and enunciated his words more carefully and—

"Stop," her father said now, cutting off Pao's observations. His face changed back, and his words lost some of their lacquer. "She won't understand. We need to give her time to process."

That's when Pao realized what was going on. She hadn't heard two men conversing inside the trailer. It had only been this *one*. This one man who had clearly lived alone in the woods too long.

"You know what?" Pao said, stepping backward off the steps, Bruto at her heels. "There's something I need to do, just real fast, and then I'll be back, okay?"

The look on her father's face—whichever version of himself he was—told her she wouldn't be leaving no matter what feeble lie she told. She kept moving anyway, the feeling that she'd made an awful, awful mistake crashing over her like a tidal wave.

Bruto's hackles were up now, and he stood between Pao and her dad, growling. Across her dad's face, the two sides of him appeared to be fighting for dominance.

"She's—" he said, nearly choking on the end of the word, struggling to keep speaking even as it was clear he was losing the battle.

"We will not—" Overenunciated this time. Pao backed away farther while he was distracted, even as ownership of her father's face changed again.

"I know I said—"

"Our agreement—"

Pao had made it to the base of the slope, a good thirty feet from where her father stood waging war with himself. She put a knee to the ground and pulled Bruto in with one arm while she envisioned herself back with the Niños, and Emma, and her mom, regrouping, figuring out what to do next together. . . .

"And I'll find—" her father was saying, his voice pleading now, but not for long.

"There's no *TIME*!" The last word hit like a lightning strike.

Please, Pao thought, willing the green paper dolls to sprout up around her, the nitrous oxide feeling to return. . . .

But nothing happened, and it seemed someone had won the argument, because Pao's father was striding toward her, looking like he knew exactly what he was doing.

"Please," Pao said, aloud this time. "Just let me go."

There was the briefest flicker, a warmth behind his eyes, and then they went cold. The voice that spoke next was low and clear, every word precise.

"Go?" her father said. "You haven't even been inside yet."

Pao got to her feet and started running up the hill. She thought she might have a chance of escaping when she didn't hear any footsteps behind her. But what happened next was so much worse than being snatched up by a middle-aged man who had just had an argument with himself right in front of you.

Her father snapped his fingers, and she automatically looked over her shoulder at the sound. She watched with horror as two purple threads separated from the writhing mass and came toward her. She tried to keep going, but they wrapped around her legs and wound up her body, freezing cold to the point of burning her skin.

The energy snakes felt like the touch of fantasma flesh. The purple cloud, like them, like La Llorona's terrible pearl, was from the void—and from the strange way it lit the eyes of the man in front of her, Pao knew exactly how he had summoned it.

"Come on, now, don't struggle," he said when Pao grunted and thrashed against her bonds. "You said you came here for answers, didn't you? What better way to teach than by example?"

Struggling was pointless, Pao quickly found. The more she

strained against her bonds the tighter they twined around her, until she was sure there would be marks on her skin. Like freezer burn on tamales, Pao thought, wishing her mom were here. *Why wasn't I able to summon a portal this time?*

She whipped her head around, panic growing inside her. "Where's Bruto?" she asked through teeth gritted against the pain.

"The beast?" her father replied. "He's waiting for my command. Even the young ones are obedient if you're a worthy leader."

Despite the burn on her arms, Pao wrenched herself around to prove him wrong. Bruto would never follow this man. Bruto had been at her heels, hadn't he? He was probably running back to find the Niños and Emma and her mom now, to protect them. . . .

When she finally caught sight of her puppy on her left, Pao's heart sank. He was sitting up straight and alert, none of the usual floppy puppy in his posture. His shoulders were rigid, his face front like a soldier submitting himself for inspection.

Pao's father snapped his fingers again. "Come," he said in that dark, sinister, overly enunciated voice.

No, Bruto, Pao thought desperately. *Don't do it. Show him you're mine.*

But Bruto ran forward without hesitation. Not with the loopy lope of her puppy running to greet her, but with the laser-like focus of a working dog. Pao wanted to cry.

First her father, and now her dog? She had come here for answers, for family, for proof that she wasn't alone.

Instead, she was more alone than she'd ever been.

This man claimed he had the answers she'd been looking

for, and Pao had been so eager to find them, but what would the truth cost her?

She never asked herself that question enough.

Pao's father reached the trailer steps and reeled Pao in by the energy ropes. As he stepped through the door, she thrashed harder than ever. Pao could sense waves of malevolence coming from the inside. It was the same feeling she'd had at the mouth of the void. Like the place could destroy her, but that part of her belonged there nonetheless.

It pulled at Pao like all her bad thoughts did, activating both her restlessness and recklessness. *Are you ready?* it asked in a persuasive voice. *Ready to know everything? It's time to finally understand who you are. . . .*

THIRTY
It's All in the Eyes

The trailer's interior looked nothing like what Pao had imagined. Her lonely dad, she'd thought, would have, like, a cabin aesthetic. A rough-around-the-edges, too-much-flannel, drink-everything-out-of-a-coffee-mug type of vibe.

This was none of those things. It wasn't even a home.

It was some kind of laboratory.

The small space resembled a weather station more than any-thing, with multiple devices, needles sweeping and jumping as they reacted to various stimuli. She saw several screens—low-tech, like the one Franco had used to zero effect in the fight against the Hitchhiker. There was also a hot plate with various beakers and flasks set around it, bubbling and still liquids in a rainbow of colors.

But the main feature was a metal throne-like chair right in the center of it all, wires sticking out of it in every direction, a round plastic headpiece like one of those archaic (and unsanitary) hair dryers at the weird salon in the basement of the mall.

Somehow Pao knew that chair was intended for her—and it just wasn't because there was no other seating in the room. She could sense her father's thoughts, like they were a neon sign pointing her straight to it.

He'd been waiting a long time to put her in this chair, Pao realized with a sinking feeling. She'd thought she was risking it all coming here. That he'd be surprised to see her. But he'd drawn her here himself, and she'd walked right into his trap.

"Sit," her father said, and the bonds around Pao dragged her with a force of their own, past the instruments and concoctions, until she was deposited unceremoniously on the cold metal chair. Beside her, Bruto dropped to his haunches in a robotic way, obeying her father fully, like he'd never once obeyed her.

The purple threads of the void cloud slithered down Pao's arms and legs to form restraints at her wrists and ankles. There was no way out of the chair. Her heartbeat sped up again in her chest.

"So, Paola, at last." Her father sat down across from her, on a wheeled stool with no back. Pao could see black marks on the floor where he'd rolled from one end of the trailer to the other, checking data, adding an ingredient or two, monitoring his progress on long, sleepless nights working toward a singular goal.

It was a fantasy she'd often had of her dad—assuming his DNA was responsible for her love of science since she and her mom were such polar opposites.

"What are you going to do with me?" Pao asked, a shudder traveling through her. When she'd pictured herself in this moment, it was always as his collaborator, not his prisoner.

"Ah, another question," he said, staring into her eyes like he was x-raying her. "We'll get to them all—especially that one—but let's start with the first, shall we?"

Pao had precious few memories of her father—few enough that she hadn't even been able to conjure his face in a dream— but she knew as surely as she knew her own name that this wasn't the man she remembered. This wasn't the way he had looked at her.

People change, Pao told herself critically. And she'd seen it, hadn't she? Look what had happened to Dante. . . .

"You asked about your friend and his abuela," her father said now, like he was reading her thoughts. "I'll admit they're an interesting family. Señora Mata was so meddlesome when we were young—I wouldn't have minded putting a stop to her. Unfortunately, I didn't have anything to do with her coma. She knew the risks of accessing the void unprotected for that long."

"Liar," Pao said, struggling against the restraints. "She told me you'd found an answer, that I had to get to it first, and it was the only way to help her. I'm sure you know what's happening to her. That's why I'm here, so tell me how to fix her!"

Pao's father examined his fingernails in a bored way. "Carmela only got two out of three right on that one, I'm afraid. Well below her normal average. Must be old age."

"What are you talking about?" Pao asked through gritted teeth.

"I *have* found an answer," he said, his eyes gleaming now in that totally cliché super-villain way, like he was about to announce he'd found a way to euthanize all the world's puppies at once. "And if you *had* discovered the answer first, that would've been the only way to stop it." He surveyed her impassively. "But you didn't. It seems the señora put rather too much faith in you."

Pao's heart sank. It was too late. She hadn't been able to save Señora Mata, and her father wasn't the man she believed he was. She had failed.

But something he'd said before struck her now, and she

zeroed in on it. "You said she was meddlesome when you were young," Pao said. "But the only person she hated when you were young was Beto. The boy my mom loved before you. That's why this is happening, isn't it? Because of him. I know he's La Llorona's son, Dad. If he's doing this to you, we have to stop it."

You must understand, Señora Mata had said. *The two names are one. . . .*

It was the part of the puzzle Pao had never been able to work out. She threw it at him now like a Hail Mary pass. Like when she said one big word to a teacher when she didn't know the full answer, hoping they'd be impressed enough to fill in the rest.

This time, Pao could tell she'd hit a nerve.

"Beto is the reason for the drawbacks," her father hissed. "*Beto* is the reason we didn't get this done last summer, when you were already through the rift. We should have had you then, but you escaped because of his cowardice. . . ."

Pao stayed silent, remembering the lesson she had learned from facing La Llorona last year. Sometimes another person's momentum was the best weapon you had.

"But none of that matters now," her father said, straightening up again, rolling to the end of the trailer and flipping a switch that sparked with green light. "Beto is gone. I am here. And you are in the chair. It's time we finished this once and for all."

Okay, Pao thought. *Maybe silence hadn't been the best choice. . . .*

"Wait," she said, trying to buy herself some time. "You said you'd answer the rest of my questions."

His smile was odd, Pao thought. Like this mouth wasn't used to stretching in that particular way.

My dad always smiled with his mouth closed, Pao remembered, like she was looking at a sepia photograph from a long time ago. This man was smiling with all his teeth.

"The little scientist," he said. "So you did get something from him after all."

"From who?" Pao asked, but he ignored her.

"Your friend's abuela is unconscious because she saw her past self ten years ago, when she brought her grandson home after a fantasma attack. She knew she'd have to cross over, go back in order to save him someday. She just didn't know when that time would come."

"Cross over?" Pao asked. "What do you mean? All that happened in a dream. . . ."

"Surely you understand by now that your dreams *aren't* dreams, Paola." He sounded disappointed, like she'd brought home a subpar math grade. "Yes, you have some of the silly, mundane dreams all mortals do. But when you saw the river at the mouth of the void, and when you walked into this forest, you were not dreaming. You were entering the void, seeing places and times that you could never access in life."

"So when we saved Dante in the past . . ." Pao said, both excited by the discovery and dreading its implications. "We were really *in* the past?"

"The void cares nothing for the construct of time," her father said, though his tone had an edge now. He was growing bored of her questions. "When you crossed over to heal yourself, when you thought of saving your friend, you emerged at the place where he would most need you. That happened to be a time you perceived to be ten years ago."

"But . . . how was Señora Mata there?" Pao asked. "How did she travel into the past?"

"Mortals don't have access to the void without training and instruction, and it costs them dearly to travel into it. She knew the sacrifice she was making. She left her living body. There are no guarantees she'll be able to return to it." His tone said he couldn't care less whether she succeeded, but Pao's blood was running cold.

She thought of the flummoxed doctors at the hospital in Silver Springs trying to get a reading on Señora Mata's vitals. *She left her living body. . . .* But didn't that mean she was . . . ?

"Carmela made good use of her time with Los Niños de la Luz," her father said, a grudging respect in his tone. "She took from the dark side as well as the light. Of course, as a mortal she couldn't access the gateway physically, so she sent her consciousness back through it in a dream to save her grandson. Pity I got to him first."

The gateway, Pao thought. The green paper dolls that had surrounded her before the ambulance came. Señora Mata had created a portal. . . .

"The doctors said it was like her body was there but her consciousness was gone," Pao said, mostly to herself. "They were right."

"They're bound to get something right eventually. Even a monkey could write the Great American Novel if he smashed at the typewriter long enough."

But Pao was barely listening to his probability metaphor. She was too busy thinking about portals. Her father had said they weren't intended for mortal use.

It was the last piece, and Pao was afraid to look at it.

"And the monsters?" she asked, delaying the inevitable. "Why have they been following me?"

An irritated spasm crossed her father's face. "Beto sent them to try to stop you, to scare you into going back home. He almost managed it with the cadejo bite. I had to manipulate that stupid friend of yours to get you back on track after that. . . ."

"Dante?" Pao asked, her train of thought suddenly derailed. "What did you do with him?"

"He's none of your concern anymore," her father said severely, and Pao couldn't help but think that, in another world, this would be his *you're too young to date* talk. "But since these are the last few moments of your mortal life, I suppose there's no harm in letting you see. . . ."

Pao's father reached up and summoned another strand of purple energy from the cloud. Before Pao's eyes, it fashioned itself into a little circular dish, like the scrying mirrors her mom sometimes used.

"Mortals aren't meant to enter the void," he said in his cold, bored tone. "Not until it's time for them to die. If they do somehow manage to travel in and out again, they come back with their minds altered, susceptible. I started speaking to him through his own dreams shortly after you returned, using him to draw you to me. I knew that if you were alone, you'd be too reckless. You'd go looking for connection. . . ."

Pao choked back a sob. La Llorona had abducted Dante as bait, and that had left him vulnerable to this horrible man's ploy. Everything *was* Pao's fault, after all.

"When you've served your purpose, he'll be disposed of," her father said, turning the black mirror so she could see, at last.

Dante, bound and unconscious, dressed in his white-and-gold hero clothes.

"Where is he?" Pao screamed, throwing her full weight against the bonds, tears filling her eyes. When she blinked them away, the mirror had disappeared. "What did you do to him?"

Her previous anger toward Dante began to give way, fear and regret surging in. He hadn't been himself—and she'd sensed it. Her father had been controlling him. Manipulating Dante's jealousy, his fear for his abuela . . .

"He's gone to the same place we all go in the end," her father said. "The same place you're going now. But not to worry—when we open the gates for good, he'll be set free along with all the others. He'll be given the chance we all want—to seek vengeance for our untimely demise."

Pao didn't know what he meant, but she could sense they were reaching the end of this interview.

"Any last questions before we begin the procedure?" he asked, and Pao stopped struggling, slumping back in her chair.

"Just one," she said, sitting up straight. "Why won't you look at me?"

It wasn't the question she'd intended to ask, but it was the one that came out. The whole time he'd been holding her captive, her father had avoided her gaze. He'd surveyed her quickly, he'd glanced her way, but he hadn't looked into her eyes once since they'd embraced briefly on the porch.

"I have more important things to do," he said silkily, but Pao could hear the tension lacing his tone.

"Look at me," she said. "I'm your daughter. Look at me once before you kill me or use me to further your super-villain agenda, or whatever you're planning to do."

She didn't know why she was pushing it, but some instinct told her to keep pressing until he gave in.

"Are you afraid to?" she asked. "If I'm so insignificant, why are you scared?"

"I fear nothing," he said, and stepped toward her.

Pao leaned forward in her seat. "I just want to see my father before I die," she said. "You owe me that much."

He knelt before her, his eyes closed like he was steeling himself for the sight of something horrible. Then he opened them and looked right into hers.

The reaction was immediate. In the timeless depths of his deep brown eyes, a struggle was occurring, like two eels made of pure light wrestling with each other in a dark sea.

Pao saw La Llorona's palace, and a teenage boy with a ghostly cast to his features, pain twisting them as green light grew unbearably bright around him.

She saw Maria's face, young, lit by one of Arizona's spectacular sunsets. Smiling, a flower tucked behind her ear. Before the picture changed, the smile turned to a look of horror, and Maria's screams echoed in the trailer, or in Pao's mind.

Then there was baby Pao, her eyes wide and dark.

She was two, toddling across a parking lot.

She was three, crying as her father walked out the door and closed it for the last time.

Pao was crying now, and her father's chest was heaving, his face twisted in agony. She wanted to stop all this, to let him be evil rather than force them both to experience the pain for another second.

Just as she was about to look away and break the connection, give up the power she had wanted but now couldn't bear, the images stopped flashing. Pao's father's face was still, and his eyes were open, locked onto hers like he never wanted to look away again.

"Paola?" her father said, and this time his voice was raw and scratchy, as if he'd been screaming into a pillow for hours. His expression looked like he was seeing her for the first time since they'd embraced on the porch. "Oh god, I'm sorry, Paola. I'm so sorry."

THIRTY-ONE

The Whole Truth and Nothing but the Truth

"Dad?" Pao said, a lump building in her throat. "César? Is it . . . really you?"

"It's me," he said, getting to his feet, walking slower, his eyes wrinkling at the corners as he took her in. "We have to get you out of here, and we don't have much time. I don't . . . know how long I can hold him off." He pressed his hands together, and the purple bands around her wrists and ankles glowed gold before falling away.

Pao rubbed her wrists and got out of the chair, her knees almost buckling.

Her dad caught her, looking deep into her eyes again, like he was drawing strength from what he found there.

"Is it Beto?" Pao asked, with no time to sugarcoat it. "La Llorona's son. I know Mom knew him before she met you, and I know he was bad news—I mean, how could he not be, considering who his mother was? But seriously, Dad, if he's doing this to you, we have to stop him."

The pride on César Santiago's face as he listened to her was something precious. Something Pao would hold on to forever. It was like she was five years old and had just explained how gravity worked. Before long, though, sadness took over his features again, and he sighed.

"I wish I had time to tell you everything, but . . ." He looked at her again and smiled like he was just taking her in. "It's not Beto," he said. "It's . . . It's so hard to explain. *I'm* Beto, Paola. *I'm* La Llorona's second son. Also known as César, because I—"

But before he could go any further, his face froze, like a video that had caught up to the end of its buffering.

"No!" Pao said. "No, Dad! Stay with me, please!" The tears were falling now, and she stepped forward to grab her father's hands. "Look at me, Dad. Don't let him do this to you. Please stay. Please, please stay!"

"I'm . . . sorry . . ." he said, like he was pulling the words out of the void itself. "I love you."

And then his eyebrows lifted, his wrinkles smoothed, his mouth grew thinner and more cruel, and their hand-holding was no longer a gesture of combined strength. It was a liability.

"Nice visit with daddy dearest?" asked the sneering voice, and he dragged Pao back to the chair himself this time. "I hope you enjoyed it, because that was the last time you'll ever see his worthless, miserable face."

"It's *your* face!" Pao cried, so angry she would have said anything to hurt him.

The man who looked like César Santiago but was not—and wasn't Beto, either—stepped back and slapped her across the cheek. "Don't you ever," he growled. "This is *not* my face. My face—my *life* was stolen from me because of an evil woman's selfish, reckless choice. I have been trapped in this body for far too long. And tonight—tonight I will finally have my revenge!"

With his eyes bugging out, his hair standing on end, the man who was not Pao's father pulled the old-fashioned hair-dryer bubble down over her head. Delirious with fear and confusion, Pao almost laughed at the mental image of herself in the ridiculous helmet. Like some little old lady getting her grays tinted blue.

Pao held back the laugh, as well as the feeling that she was truly losing her mind. She needed to fight, but she was dazed. His words were spreading through her like honey—slow, then faster as they heated. His life had been stolen by a selfish woman? He was wearing the wrong man's face?

And her father, her *real* father, had said *he* was Beto. . . . But how could that—

Suddenly, Pao was back in the throne room of the glass palace, with La Llorona about to perform her horrific experiment to bring back the daughter she had drowned. The experiment that would have required Pao to sacrifice her life so her essence could be combined with Ondina's.

The ghost woman had allegedly performed it successfully once—on her second son, Beto, who had run away afterward.

These facts crystallized in the beaker of Pao's brain until the glass shattered in every direction. The truth she had wanted to know was now painfully, horribly clear, but there was no time to think it through, or to discover what it all meant.

Because the man who was not her father—the man whose soul had been reaped to bring Beto back to life—was strapping the plastic hood to Pao's head now, attaching wires all over it, and breathing heavily, like they were approaching the finish line of a marathon.

"Listen," Pao said in her most persuasive voice. "I know what you're thinking. You're thinking I'm like him. Beto. My father. But I'm not."

The man who was not Pao's father didn't listen, just continued the process of securing her to the chair. His eyes were unfocused now, a vivid intensity humming and crackling within him.

"I don't know my father," Pao said, and had truer words ever been spoken? "I didn't even know who he *was* until four minutes ago."

No answer.

Pao's voice echoed strangely in the bubble. "Look at me," Pao said, trying to form a mental connection with the broken, bitter soul trapped inside her father's body. She projected her own experience onto him. The abject terror she'd felt when she learned she'd been marked as Ondina's soul twin . . . Her horror as the ritual was set up in front of her . . . The hopelessness that had threatened to drag her under . . .

Her father's borrowed hands stilled on the leg restraints as Pao's memories overwhelmed the soul at the controls.

"I'm more like you than him," Pao said softly. "I know how it was for you in the end. The fear. The feeling of being trapped. I barely got out alive."

The man's shoulders shook, and his face was obscured, but Pao thought he might be crying.

"I understand," Pao said as soothingly as she could while every part of her was panicking. "I'm not like them. I never would have done that to you. . . ."

Pao's father's body stood up, the cruel eyes dry as they stared into Pao's. He looked insolent now, like he knew full well that Pao couldn't free his soul, and he was right. Any empathic link she had tried to create with him was nullified by Pao's very existence.

Whether she had known it or not, she was Beto's daughter.

This was why Dante had told her she could never be the hero. *You really don't see what you are*, he had taunted. But now, at last, she saw.

A laugh cut through the static in Pao's head. "You think you understand?" The man's voice was layered with disbelief. "You think the moments *before* the ritual were the difficult part, little girl? You're sorely wrong."

Pao could do nothing but listen in horror as he continued, his voice—so different from her father's—haunted and low.

"Yes, it was frightening when I, an innocent young man, first saw a ghost approaching me by the river. And I was paralyzed with terror when it dragged me under the water to be a prisoner in its palace. But the difficult part? That came later. When that *abomination* separated my soul from my body." He shuddered, but his eyes didn't leave Pao's. "The *difficult* part was the excruciating process of being bound by dark magic to the cold, lifeless husk of her murdered son. The violence of the intertwining as she grew a new human out of us there, in her torture chamber's prism. Bones splintering and regenerating, skin stretching, fingernails and teeth uprooted and replaced. The horror of it."

Pao's stomach churned as she envisioned it against the backdrop of the cave, where prisms had once held Emma, Dante, and Franco. There had been an empty one, too. Waiting for Pao herself.

"And then . . ." he said, his pupils blown wide with madness and memory. "Then we were one. And my consciousness, my *self* was lost, absorbed in another, forever bound to carry out his every whim, desire, and *rebellion*."

Beto's rebellion, Pao thought. She remembered the pain and resentment in La Llorona's disembodied voice when she had mentioned her "ungrateful" son. He hadn't wanted anyone else's life to be stolen for him, but his mother had burdened him with that terrible, unjust reality forever. He'd left her, paving the way for his little sister, Ondina, to set Pao free.

"But eventually I woke up," the man said now, in a chilling voice that indicated he'd been subservient for longer than he could bear. "I began to fight. And in fighting, I discovered myself again."

"What will you do?" Pao asked. "Take the body back? Destroy Beto for good?"

"It's too late for me," he said, shaking the head of the body in question. "I have no body of my own, no life to return to now. But this world—so selfish, everyone too absorbed in their own lives, constantly putting their own needs and desires above others . . ." He trailed off. "I've thought long about how to punish the woman who did this to me, Paola. But you stole that vengeance from me when you freed her."

Pao pictured it now, Ondina and her mother embracing, so human as they let go, forgave, and moved into the great beyond.

"I didn't know," Pao said. "I didn't—"

"It doesn't matter," he said. "Because I have a greater purpose now. That woman was a product of society's sickness. People's entitlement, their greed, a selfishness that has spanned the centuries, poisoning every generation. *That* sickness must be rooted out, the sickness that lives in every mortal on this failed mistake of a planet."

"You're going to open the void," Pao said, her voice hollow in the plastic hood as she put the pieces together at last. "Release the monsters and the fantasmas. Kill everyone."

"A fitting end," he said, his face as triumphant as if he'd already accomplished it.

And who would stop him? Pao asked herself, numb. Who could?

Pao had once believed herself to be a hero, the kind of person who would know exactly what to do in a situation like this one. She'd been so lost in that identity that she'd actually *hoped* to prove herself a hero again.

But everything had changed since then. She'd lost her connection to her father, to Dante, and to everyone else she loved. Her life had been crushed beneath the weight of the truth she had so desperately wanted to know.

Pao was no hero. She was a monster. A product of the woman who had abducted her friends and killed countless people—countless *children*. The father she'd been dreaming of her whole life was the patchwork result of a tragic experiment, and he had surrendered to his other half.

A half whose reckoning had been coming for a long time.

And Pao was powerless to stop it. It had never been her role to play.

"It's been difficult to find a suitable conduit for this energy," the man who was not Pao's father said, bustling around, checking connections, turning dials. "Humans don't have a connection to the void, and the fantasmas are too unstable. You can see I've tried several of them already." He gestured upward toward the purple cloud of raw magical power.

The anomaly, Pao realized. That cloud of corrupted fantasmas was the energy Franco had detected. But she would never get the chance to tell him.

"But you? A human with a connection to the void? The grand-daughter of its most fearsome fantasma? You held the pearl of power in your hands . . . and destroyed it. The void isn't sentient, of course, but if it could *want*, Paola, there's nothing in this world it would want more than you."

Of course, Pao thought. She belonged to the void. So did Beto. They had only been living on borrowed time.

"And now my day has finally come," he said, his voice high and ringing in his excitement. "The day I unleash hell on this terrible, selfish world. They won't know what hit them."

THIRTY-TWO
Don't Feed the Void After Midnight

"Neither will you."

The voice came from behind Pao, accompanied by the sound of the trailer door being kicked in. While Pao was wearing her bubble helmet she couldn't see who it was, but she could hear her captor's shriek of rage in response.

And then, "Beto?"

It was a voice Pao would have known anywhere—her mother's.

"Beto, it's me, Maria. Come back to me, querido."

"He's never coming back!" There was a loud crash as some undoubtedly expensive instrument was destroyed. Bruto started howling. "Never! It's over!"

Someone was unhooking Pao's helmet, disconnecting the wires, and lifting the plastic from her head. Tears began to trickle down Pao's cheeks again. Tears for the person trapped inside Beto's body. Tears for the girl she'd believed she was.

Tears because she wasn't alone, even though she deserved to be.

"Pao?" Emma, her face blurred by Pao's watery eyes, was smiling wide. "Pao, we're here. We found you. It's okay."

"How . . . ?" Pao asked. "Where . . . ?"

"It was your friend," Emma said, loosening the last of the restraints. "Estrella. She led us to you. She's waiting outside. . . ."

Pao got unsteadily to her feet. She had a million more questions, but once again, time was against her. She drew the magnifying glass from her pocket and transformed it into a staff.

There was no need. As Emma clutched Pao's arm, they watched Maria Santiago approaching the shrieking madman, dodging the blows.

"Come back to me," she said, taking his face in her hands.

Pao, on the outside this time, watched the transition. The pain in her father's features, the horror on her mother's. What were they reliving? What memories? What failures?

After what seemed like an eternity, Beto's body went still. His features relaxed. His shoulders slumped forward.

"Maria?" he said, reaching up to touch her face, too. "How . . . ?"

"Later, mi amor," she said. "We have to save our daughter."

"Yes," he said, a little dreamily. "Paola, yes. Yes. It's time."

"Time for what?" Pao asked, walking over the wreckage to join them.

"Let me show you," he said.

Taking a deep breath, Pao nodded.

He nodded back. "We need to hurry," Beto said (it was hard to think of him as her dad, now that she knew his whole sordid history). "But we can do it. I've been developing a machine, and obscuring it from my other . . . from *him* in my mind."

"What do we have to do?" Pao asked, watching him like a hawk for signs of the other soul's reappearance. Pao could handle being in danger herself, but she wouldn't be able stand it if anything happened to Emma or her mom. She'd brought them here; it would be her fault if they got hurt.

"Can I help?" Emma asked, right on time, and Pao was so grateful her tears welled up again.

"Yes," Pao said, clearing her throat. "Can you take Bruto outside? Just for a sec, to get some air?" She tried to communicate with her eyes that she needed a few moments with her parents alone but would tell Emma absolutely everything the moment she could.

"Of course," Emma said, calling to Bruto, who trotted beside her excitedly, a soldier no more. "Just holler if you need anything, okay?"

Pao nodded, knowing Bruto would protect Emma, and turned back to her parents, who had resumed their conversation.

"It's a device," Beto was saying to Maria. "Crude but effective. It will harness the void energy he's been storing here, and I can use it to sever the connection between him and myself. Life from death. Spirit from body. Without a host, he will be a fantasma. Vulnerable. Weak after so long living inside another."

"So we draw him out, separate him, and . . ." Pao's mom began.

"Kill him," Beto said. "Paola, that's an Arma del Alma, is it not?"

"It is," Pao said, her voice sounding far away to her own ears. "I got it before . . . before I knew . . ." She didn't know how to explain that she shouldn't have it. That she didn't deserve it because of who she was.

"You know how to use it?" her mom asked, cutting through her downward thought spiral.

Throat tight, Pao nodded.

"Good," Beto said. "The moment the separation is complete, you must attack. When he's gone, you take this"—Beto handed Pao's mom a can of lighter fluid and a lighter—"and destroy the lab. Then you all run—Paola, use the portal. You can get them out with you."

He was rushing around again, pushing buttons, powering down screens.

"The void is eager to be opened, hungry for this feast he's been promising for months. I don't want anything pursuing you, understand? No surprises."

"He summoned El Autostopisto," Pao said, her voice finally working again. "I trapped him in a duendecillo prison cell in the forest before I came here, but my friends . . ."

"If he was summoned, then destroying the summoner should dispel him."

Pao nodded. "And Dante . . . my . . . well, someone I was traveling with . . . I think . . . uh, *the other* has him captive in the void now. He said Dante would be freed when the opening was made, but . . . can we still . . . ? Is he . . . ?"

Her father looked at her, grief heavy in the lines of his face. "If he's there, it's too late to save him, I'm afraid," he said.

Pao felt the news like a kick to the chest. Dante had been trying to protect the world from her, she realized. From the monster he knew she was. And now he would die for it—if he hadn't already.

It was too much on top of everything else. Pao felt like she was going to be sick.

"Paola, listen to me," her father said, taking her hand. "I know I'm putting a lot on your shoulders, but I need you to do this for me. For your safety. And your mother's. Please, I'm counting on you."

Pao privately thought it wasn't very fair of him to expect this of her when she'd never been able to count on *him*, but she nodded anyway.

A spasm of pain crossed Beto's face, and a spike of anxiety shot through Pao.

"Is he back?" she asked.

Her father nodded. "It's now or never. Querida Maria, watch over the other girl outside, ¿por favor? Paola will tell you when it's safe to return."

"Are you sure?" Pao's mom asked, looking torn. "Do you—"

"I'm sure," he interrupted. "Paola and I have this under control. Trust me, please."

"Be careful," Maria said after a long pause. "Both of you." And she stepped out of the trailer.

"I'm still trying to understand some things," Pao said when she and her father were alone. Now that she finally had the chance to ask him her questions, she dreaded the answers. "When you said 'life from death' before . . . it reminded me of La Llorona's experiment. After you were . . . alive again . . . you met Mom?"

"Yes," he said. "And we fell in love. I thought I could erase my past, start over. I even changed my name to César to leave Beto, my mother, and the void behind. Maria made me want to be human." His smile was soft and bright, and Pao felt the weight of all the years they'd spent apart. All the fear, and the pain . . .

"And then you guys had me?" she prompted when her father didn't continue.

"That's right," Beto said. "The most joyous day of my life." But his face looked anything but joyous.

"And we'll all be together again, right? After we separate you from . . . ? You're coming with us, right?"

A terrible silence filled the trailer. "Oh, Paola," he said. "How I wish that were possible. But . . . I fear he is too much a part of me now. Like I said before, once our life forms are separated, they'll both be weak. I . . . I don't believe I'll survive the process."

Pao felt her face sag, and her father leaned forward to put a hand on her shoulder.

"Don't feel sorry for me, Paola. This is the way it should be. The few years I spent with your mother and getting to see the young woman you've become . . . it's more than I deserved. If this is how I pay for that horrible experiment, so be it. It was worth it. Do you understand?"

Pao had already learned so much, and lost so much, in this trailer, that she barely felt this last, greatest blow hit her. She'd been longing for a father her whole life. And now she had to help sacrifice him. It was the only way to save herself. Emma. Her mom.

The entire world.

"Why couldn't you have done this before?" Pao asked bitterly. "Why did you have to drag me into it?"

"I . . . I was too arrogant," her father said. "I thought I could keep him at bay, prevent him from taking over. I isolated myself from the world, from everyone I loved, for years, to wage my battle with him. And I was successful . . . for a while."

So that was why he hadn't kept in touch, Pao thought. He hadn't done it to avoid her, but to protect her.

Despite the fact that these were her last moments with him, Pao couldn't help but feel angry. He hadn't protected her at all. The greatest threat was already a part of her, had been since the day she was born.

"He upped the ante by reaching out to you," Beto said gently, drawing her out of her thoughts. "That's when I knew I had to stop him." His gaze softened. "But, I confess, I was dying to see you myself, even if just for a little while. See who you turned out to be. Can you understand that?"

Tears streamed down Pao's face. Her anger at her father . . . the limited time they had left . . . none of it was fair. Pao had thought she'd defeated La Llorona in the void last summer, but her curse still lingered in Pao's blood, determined to get revenge in the worst way imaginable.

"What about Mom?" Pao asked, swiping her tears away forcefully. "Aren't you even going to say good-bye?"

"We said good-bye years ago, Paola, when it was obvious I could never be whole. She understands what must be done. You are her first priority, her greatest love. This is what she wants, too."

Another spasm crossed his face.

"Tie me to the chair," he said hurriedly, handing Pao a length of rope and the machine's on-off device. It looked like a TV remote with a tiny antenna and one red button right in the center. "Wait until he takes over again. You'll know?"

"I'll know," she said, wiping her eyes again with the back of her wrists. She secured his hands to the armrests with trembling fingers.

"Push the button the moment he's back. Don't let him speak," Beto said, beginning to sweat along his hairline, as if the effort of keeping his own consciousness within his body was becoming too difficult. "He'll do anything to stop this . . . say anything."

"I understand," Pao said.

"I'm so proud of you, Paola," her father said, his voice full of emotion now. "Please remember, you're not bound by what I am. Or what *she* was. You are your own person—only you get to decide who you're going to be. And you have an incredible guide in your mother. The best there is."

Pao felt his words, his pride, glowing in her chest. She could do what needed to be done. She knew it, because he believed in her. She grabbed his bound hand and squeezed it once, as tightly as she could, not caring if it was dangerous.

Beto was shaking all over, his face twitching as the war raged inside him.

"Wait!" Pao said. "There's so much I want to tell you! I can't say good-bye. Not yet. Please stay."

"Be strong," he told her. "I love you."

And then he was gone.

Pao waited until the eyebrows went up, the laugh lines disappeared, and the eyes opened wide in surprise and fear. "Beto?" she asked in a shaky voice.

In response, the man who was not her father roared in anger and agony.

She closed her eyes, the tears burning behind her eyelids.

"I love you, Dad," she said.

And then she pushed the button.

THIRTY-THREE
Forgiveness, Again

The effect was instantaneous. A purple jet shot out of the remote's antenna like a hose when you press your thumb against the end, blasting the man who was not Pao's father in the face.

The void goo encased the body like a cocoon, and for a moment, all was still. The two—er, *three* of them, alone in the trailer, their fates hanging like a knife above a thread.

Then the goo began to bubble and pulse and stretch, shapes popping out of it only to be sucked back in again. Pao, both fascinated and thoroughly grossed out, waited with her staff drawn, knowing that soon she would need to fight. To protect her family and her friends. To make her father's final sacrifice worth the pain it had caused them all.

In thirty seconds, the ropes around his hands burned away.

In forty, the goo-coated man levitated into the air and hung there, suspended, laid out flat like a body in a coffin at a public viewing.

By the one-minute mark, the goo began to stretch farther and farther, pulling one man's form out of the other like those Russian nesting dolls Pao had played with when she was little (she always lost the tiny one).

Ninety seconds after Pao had pushed the button, there were two human-shaped purple things hanging in the air above her. Then chaos erupted.

The first body fell to the floor with a *thud*. The goo dripped off him, leaving his face exposed. Pao's father, Beto, with a new streak of gray in his hair. His mouth was open, his eyes closed like he might have been sleeping.

But Pao knew better.

She looked at him for a long minute. She hoped he was at peace, finally free of the fight that had dominated his too-short second life. She tried to feel happy for him instead of sad for herself.

Then cold laughter filled the trailer. Pao had been so fixated on her father that she had nearly forgotten his instructions.

She turned just in time to see a fantasma like none she'd ever seen before. Black smoke, entwined with purple, with a man's sharp, clever face and cruel eyes. He laughed again and did a backflip, perhaps testing out his new form and freedom.

Pao knew her orders. She was supposed to kill him quickly. But she remembered what she had said to this man who was not her father. The two of them were alike, and Pao had understood his fear before she understood her father's identity. She had to hold on to that.

"I forgive you," Pao said, shrinking her staff back into a magnifying glass and putting it in her pocket. She stepped forward, wholly at the mercy of the thing in front of her but feeling stronger and more herself than ever.

The fantasma swirled like mist scattered by the wind and then re-formed. "You think you have the power to release me?"

he asked, his voice swelling like the billowing smoke he was made of. "Stupid, arrogant girl. I'll kill you for this."

He lunged at her, and Pao stood perfectly still, knowing she could die, but trusting her instincts. Her father had told her that she got to decide who she wanted to be. And she wasn't a killer—no matter who her grandmother might have been.

"I forgive you," she said again as he reached her, and his smoky arms passed through her like vapor. She didn't feel a thing.

"No!" he shrieked, swirling around, his form shrinking.

"I forgive you for baiting me into coming here," Pao said, advancing on him. "I forgive you for taking over my father's brain. I forgive you for turning my friend against me."

"What is this?" he asked, his voice smaller now.

"What's your name?" Pao asked, peering into his swirling purple eyes.

"What does that have to do with anything?" he screeched, swiping at Pao again.

When the vapor made contact with her skin, she saw snatches of his previous life. Plain as day. A little boy running through his house, a smile on his face. A bedroom door with a nameplate on it.

Joaquín.

He'd been happy. He had loved catching frogs and flash summer rainstorms.

"It wasn't your fault," Pao said, stepping forward again. "You didn't do anything wrong. She was wrong to use you, and he was wrong to let her."

"Stop it! I don't need your forgiveness! I don't need anyone!"

But he was no longer a man. He shrunk until he was just a

little taller than Pao. Until he was the teenager he had been on the day La Llorona's minions had dragged him into the river.

Just a boy at heart, all this time. A boy who hadn't deserved to die.

"It wasn't your fault," Pao said again. "But there's peace out there for you, Joaquín. I've seen it. All you have to do is reach for it."

"I . . . I can't," he said, sounding scared now. "I don't know how."

"It's easy," Pao said, smiling, tears in her eyes as she stepped forward to embrace him. "You just let go."

There was a sigh against her shoulder, the sound of a long-held burden being discarded for good.

"Good-bye, Joaquín," she said. "Be free."

And then the last of his faint purple smoke dissipated into the air, a breeze through the open door blowing it out into the forest air.

Sliding to the floor, her knees weak, her body wearier than she could ever remember it being, Pao wept, silently, for a long time.

When she stopped, the air was clear and cold, and dawn light was beginning to stain the sky outside.

Behind her, her father stirred.

"Mom!" Pao screamed, getting to her feet, backing away. "Mom, help!"

In an instant, her mom and Emma were back inside the trailer.

"What is it?" her mom asked. "Are you okay? Did he hurt you? Did . . . ?"

"Ms. Santiago," Emma said, her eyes wide as she peered over Pao's mom's shoulder. "Look!"

Beto was struggling to sit up, his hair in his eyes, every line of his face radiating pain. Pao was frozen in shock, but her mom rushed to him, kneeling on the ground, her voice thick with tears.

"Beto?" she asked. "Is it really you? How do you feel?"

He coughed, clutching at his chest. "I feel . . . so heavy," he said. "Everything hurts. I . . . I think I pulled something in my back when I fell. What is this?"

Laughing and crying at the sound of his voice, Pao stepped forward and took his hands in hers. "It's called being human, Dad," she said. "Welcome back."

Her mom laughed, too, and Emma stepped up beside her, sliding her hand into Pao's for support.

Still outside, Bruto barked as other voices could be heard approaching.

"What is this, some gross old trailer? Why are you bringing us *here*?"

Pao's heart leaped at the sound of Naomi's snark, and she bolted toward the door, eager to see if the rest of her friends were safe. Before she reached it, though, she stopped and looked back, torn.

"Go," said her dad in a strained voice, his face breaking into a smile that looked much more like the weary mortal father of an almost-teenage girl than a tragic ghost man possessed by a vengeful murder victim.

"You sure?" Pao asked.

Her dad nodded. "We have lots of time now," he said. "Thanks to you."

Pao, still holding Emma's hand, bounded out the door just in time to see Marisa, Naomi, Franco, and all the other Niños tromping down the hill, led by the duendecillos mayores. Bruto bolted halfway up the slope to greet Sal, who ruffled the ridges on the puppy's head. They were safe from the Hitchhiker, Pao thought with relief. It must have been driven out when Joaquín was, just like her father had said.

"Are you okay?" Emma asked her shyly before the group reached them. Pao stopped and turned to look at her best friend.

There was so much she would have to get used to, Pao thought. So much to mourn, but also plenty to celebrate. Her dad was alive, and reunited with her mom! Emma and the Niños were safe, and Dante . . . Well, Pao had been to the void once before, hadn't she? With all these people on her side, maybe there was still hope. . . .

"I'm not sure what I am yet," she said to Emma, and that was the honest truth. She *literally* didn't know *what* she was.

"That's so valid," Emma said. "But I'll be there for you while you figure it out, okay?"

Pao smiled, a real smile. It felt odd, like she was out of practice. "Promise?" she asked.

"Promise."

THIRTY-FOUR

Looks Like Aaron Won't Be Moving in After All

On the drive home—for which Pao's mom had rented a fifteen-passenger van in a place called Grants Pass—Emma got an excited phone call from Drs. Pinky and the Brain.

Apparently, the specialist from Seattle had no more than walked into the room when Señora Mata's brain activity began to register normally again. She was still coming out of sedation and being monitored, but they had high hopes that she would wake up in a few days.

And so, three days after their homecoming, Pao and Emma walked into Silver Springs Community Hospital together, feeling hopeful and scared and everything in between.

Emma grabbed Pao's hand as they entered the makeshift ICU (the old one was still being renovated after the "drug dealers" had ransacked it).

"Listen," Emma said, stopping Pao and looking straight at her. "None of this is your fault. Even if you are part . . . void spirit or fantasma or whatever we're calling it . . . you didn't make Dante betray you. You didn't send him to the void. And even though he said awful things, you still followed through on your plan to save his grandma. I will not allow you to be down on yourself about this. Okay?"

"I'm a paragon of moral virtue," Pao said, deadpan, and Emma stifled a laugh. "Plus, my dad is looking into every possible avenue for getting Dante back. Once we come up with a plan, it's off to the races."

"Do I still get to be your Max Gibson when you go?" Emma asked teasingly.

"As long as you remind me who that is again?" Pao said, grinning sheepishly.

Their giggles faded as they approached Señora Mata's room. The door had been decorated with bonnets—provided by the ladies of Saturday Night Bingo en Español, according to the card taped beside them.

Pao tried not to be offended that Señora Mata had more friends in town than she did, though her own count was increasing. Franco—using an ID he'd gotten from Johnny in Rock Creek—had wasted no time in finding the Niños a warehouse space to rent in town. He said he was ready to turn full-time to his research now that the void was truly no longer a threat.

Since the cactus field near the Gila had lost its force field, the old camp was no longer viable, and the Niños needed a place to set up shop while they figured out what to do next. Pao's dad had donated all his creepy forest-lab equipment to the cause and even cosigned the lease. She wasn't really sure what he saw in Franco, but Pao was so glad to see her dad putting down roots, she didn't even complain.

Naomi was less than thrilled with the arrangement, but Pao had assured her she could escape to Riverside Palace anytime the lovefest between Franco and Marisa got to be too much.

"Ready?" Emma asked, snapping Pao back to the present.

"To tell my elderly neighbor that I got her grandson banished to the void?" Pao grumbled, her stomach roiling with dread.

Señora Mata had awoken that morning. She seemed small and frail and was still hooked up to about a dozen monitors (functioning perfectly since the old woman's return from the portal, thankfully). At the moment, she was sitting up in bed, staring contemplatively out the window.

"Hey, señora," Pao said, trying not to use an *I've got some bad news* tone. Judging from the expression on Emma's face, she had failed miserably.

"Don't give me that look, Maria, I'm not dying yet."

Maria, Pao thought with a heavy heart. So Joaquín had been right. Her memory loss wasn't a result of her field trip to the past, but of something else. Alzheimer's? Dementia? Pao made a note to ask her doctors—who still seemed to believe Pao and Emma were family.

At least she's alive, Pao thought. And she honestly didn't even mind being called Maria anymore. Not since the real Maria had gotten everyone home safely and sent ski-catalog Aaron packing.

"Of course not, señora," Pao said, smiling sadly. "You'll outlive us all."

"How do you know I haven't already?"

Emma giggled, then quieted down as Pao sank into the visitor's chair.

"Don't get too comfortable now, Maria. I have the bingo ladies bringing me lunch."

"Of course you do," Pao said. "Don't worry, this won't take long. We just . . . we wanted to talk about Dante. He . . ."

Señora Mata grabbed at the sheet over her legs like she was on a boat threatening to capsize. Her eyes opened wide, and she looked at Pao as if for the first time.

"He's done it, hasn't he, Paola? He's gone over?"

"How did you know?" Pao asked.

"¡No soy estúpida!" Señora Mata snapped. "I've seen things that would make your toe hairs curl."

"Right," Pao said. "But Dante . . ."

"We all make choices, Paola," Señora Mata said. "I've been ready for my grandson's choice ever since he was a little boy."

"I was there," Pao said. "I know what you did for him. That you saved him. It doesn't matter what choice he made, señora. I'm going to get him back."

Señora Mata sighed, patting Pao's hand. "I know you will try, querida."

"What do you mean?" Pao asked. "I'm going to help him. I'm—"

"Sometimes the die is cast long before we roll it," Señora Mata said, her eyes briefly going dark before brightening again. "But that doesn't stop us from doing what we will, now does it?"

"I have questions, señora," Pao said desperately. "I need to know how it . . ."

"How it ends?" Señora Mata asked, laughing a small laugh. "Of course you do. But it's better if you don't, ¿entiendes?"

"How can you say that?" Pao asked. "You could help us find him. You could . . ."

Emma put her hand on Pao's shoulder. "Pao, maybe we should . . ."

"Now scoot on out of that chair, Maria," Señora Mata said cheerfully. "Did I tell you the bingo ladies are bringing me lunch?"

Pao was caught somewhere between cursing and crying and laughing, but then again, weren't most people on this wild ride called life? "Sí, Señora Mata," she said. "You told us. I hope it's delicious."

"Come back and see me again," she said, shooing them off. "But not too often, Maria. You don't want to be a bother, ¿verdad?"

She closed the door with her cane before they could answer.

In the weak winter sunshine outside the hospital, Emma walked her bike alongside Pao to the end of the street, where they'd have to part. Emma back to her gilded side of town, and Pao to the Riverside Palace.

"Hey, there's a Rainbow Rogues meeting tomorrow," Emma said. "We're protesting biased media coverage of underprivileged people in our community after the story on the drug dealers. There'll probably be baked goods!"

Pao laughed, shaking her head. "I'm supposed to have dinner with my parents."

"How weird does it feel to say that?" Emma asked, reading Pao's mind again. "'My parents'?"

"Less weird than I thought it would?" Pao said. "But we'll see. I don't want to get too attached, just in case. . . ."

"In case your dad turns out to be a ghost brought back to life with another spirit trapped inside his brain that makes him do terrible things in the name of revenge?" Emma asked, one hand against her cheek in an expression of faux shock.

"Fair point," Pao said. "But still, I'm easing into it. It's hard to be happy when . . ." She trailed off, thinking of Dante.

"We'll get him back," Emma said bracingly, stopping at the end of the road. "And your parents? Your . . . unique heritage? We'll figure all that out, too, okay?"

Pao smiled and gave Emma a one-armed hug. "Thanks for always knowing what to say."

"What are best friends for?"

They did their secret handshake for good measure before going their separate ways.

Pao didn't know what the future would bring. There was Dante, and her complicated legacy of hurt and undead children and possessed fathers to sort through.

But she had her parents. Plural. For the first time in ten years. And Bruto, her adorable void baby who almost made being part ghost or whatever worth it all on his own. She had the Niños—no matter how annoying Franco was. Finally, she had Emma, who always knew what to say. Who never gave up on her, no matter how unlovable and prickly Pao was.

Whatever came next, they would do it together. All of them.

It was enough for now, Pao thought as she walked into the setting sun. And wasn't that the best you could really hope for?

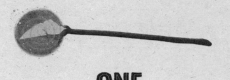

ONE
Poor Patrick

"You got this, Pao!"

"Take him down!"

"On your left!"

Paola Santiago barely heard the noise of the small crowd as she faced down her opponent. He was already missing an arm, his head was tragically lopsided, and he moved in the jerky, unpredictable way Pao had come to associate with drunk people—or toddlers who really needed a nap.

Despite his erratic movements, Pao tightened her grip on her Arma del Alma, a long, shining staff with a viciously bladed end. *Let your opponent come to you*, said her father's voice in her head. *Let them expend their energy circling and crossing the space and striking. Be still water, ready to ripple or wave. Wasting nothing.*

Her opponent had almost reached her, and every part of Pao screamed that she should strike now—leap across the space and finish the job of severing his wobbling head. But instead she waited like still water, until finally, *finally* she was allowed to rush forward and stab through the neck. Then she heard the satisfying *crunch* that meant his head had hit the ground.

Pao felt no remorse, only victory, as she lifted her sweaty

face, pushed her bangs back, and waited for her well-deserved accolades.

"Oh no!"

"Poor Patrick!"

"Someone get some tape, stat!"

Three Niños rushed past Pao in a blur as she groaned, sinking onto the concrete floor. Her magical staff was already shrinking of its own accord into a travel-size magnifying glass she could fit in her pocket.

"Well, *I* thought it was impressive," said a voice from behind her, and Pao turned with a smile to see her best friend Emma Lockwood approaching with a water bottle, her eyes dancing with laughter.

"These milk drinkers wouldn't know impressive if it cut off *their* heads," Pao grumbled, taking the water gratefully and chugging half of it before dumping the rest on her sweaty neck.

"If you wanted the Niños to be on your side, you probably shouldn't have named the sparring dummy," Emma said as they surveyed the scene.

The ragtag group of kids and teenagers who called themselves Los Niños de la Luz were already on her side, Pao knew. And, as her town's protectors against the monstrous creatures of the void, they were important allies to have.

Not just for their warehouse headquarters, either. Though it was pretty awesome. The rafters in its ceiling were nearly thirty feet above their heads. The glossy concrete floor was painted and taped with complicated diagrams of footwork, advances, and retreats, all color-coded according to types of creature. Best of all, it was in a part of town far from any prying eyes. Ideal for monster-hunting practice.

Of course, at the moment, the only creature in sight was an old dummy on a rolling cart. And he was currently missing a head.

"Patrick," Pao said, rolling her eyes at her own folly. "What kind of a name is *Patrick* for a monster anyway?"

"Hey, there are a lot of Patricks in the world," Emma replied. "I'm sure at least *some* of them are monsters."

Pao couldn't argue with that, so she got to her feet and walked over to a section of school gym bleachers that her friend Naomi had "liberated" from Silver Springs High. Then she flopped down, her muscles burning from a long day of training.

"How do you feel?" Emma asked, her eyes x-raying Pao. They looked even bluer than usual against her pumpkin-orange sweatshirt. Despite the fact that it was still over a hundred degrees in Silver Springs, Emma was determined to show her fall spirit.

Pao thought about changing the subject to actual pumpkins, or costumes, or Halloween baking or crafts, all subjects she knew would distract the girl in front of her. But she'd never been able to lie to Emma, or avoid her questions for long, so she told the truth. As much of it as she could bear to say out loud, anyway.

"I'm frustrated," she said, kicking her white sneakers against the bench. "I'm restless. I can take Patrick's head off fifteen times a day, and it's not gonna get us any closer to rescuing Dante."

At the sound of their ex–best friend's name, Emma went quiet for a moment, and Pao knew she was remembering things, too. Things like the trailer laboratory the two of them had found in the middle of the Oregon forest last winter. And the man inside, who'd been Pao's long-lost father and not her father all at once.

Pao had told Emma everything, of course. All the gory

details Emma hadn't seen while she waited outside the trailer. About finding out La Llorona was not only the ghost-deity Pao had defeated in the void, she was also Pao's *grandmother*!

That part had taken a little explaining. See, after drowning her three children in the river, La Llorona had found a way to bring them back to life by merging their souls with those of living victims. Her twisted experiment had only worked on her second son, Beto, which, Pao discovered, was her father's true identity.

Only, the experiment (like most things La Llorona did) had gone pretty horribly wrong. Beto had run away in horror from his mother, changed his name, and tried to bury his past. But over time the soul his was bound to—a boy victim of La Llorona's named Joaquin—started to become more dominant . . . and resentful.

Eventually, Joaquin had hatched a plan to use Pao's connection to the void to tear open its fabric and let out every loathsome creature inside to feed on the living. Luring her to the forest by using Dante as bait . . .

Working with Beto, Pao had managed to free Joaquin's soul, put an end to his awful plot, and get her friends back to safety. All except Dante, who, fed by his own jealousy and anger, had gone willingly into the void and remained there.

Even with the Niños' centuries of knowledge about the void and its inhabitants, her father's memories of Joaquin's machinations, and Pao's own growing desperation to smash her way into that terrible place by whatever means necessary, they still hadn't managed to rescue him. It had already been eight months.

"We're going to find him," Emma said at last, putting a hand on Pao's shoulder. "You said yourself that whoever is keeping Dante wouldn't want to give up the leverage they have over you by killing him, so it's just a matter of—"

"Of finding a way in," Pao said, almost to herself. She had fallen asleep repeating that truth to herself over and over every night since January. But the months kept going by, and Pao's faith in her own understanding of the situation was flagging by the day.

Joaquin had told her, while tied to a chair in his trailer lab, that the void wanted her, La Llorona's granddaughter, who had twice defied its soldiers, who had snatched three living souls from its depths and was determined to take a fourth. But if the void wanted her so bad, why hadn't it shown her how to enter it again? Why wasn't it using Dante to lure her back?

She hadn't had a single vision of its ghost-riddled depths since she'd returned from Oregon. Not one. And she couldn't help but wonder why her dreams, the connection that had allowed her to save her friends and family before, had deserted her now, at this crucial juncture.

Though Pao didn't exactly *want* to be the descendent of an evil ghost woman who had drowned countless children, or to belong, in part, to the spooky, monster-ridden place that had given her power, she couldn't help feeling a little abandoned.

Not that she could ever admit that to Emma. Or anyone else.

"It's my dad, mostly," Pao said when the silence had stretched out a beat longer than she could stand. "He wants to act like I'm just this normal kid, like I shouldn't be getting involved with paranormal stuff, even though I *saved his life* by getting involved with it. I wish he would just let me be who I am."

Before Emma could get to one of the fourteen solutions to this problem she had undoubtedly brainstormed in the past ten seconds, Pao's stomach grumbled, and they both laughed.

"Come on," Emma said, getting to her feet, the bleachers groaning under her bright green sneakers with the rainbow laces. "Let's get out of here. Ice cream? Pizza?"

As much as Pao wanted to hold on to her frustration, to sit here and stew, the appeal of a pizza was pretty undeniable. "Okay," she relented. "But first I have to talk to the biggest jerk in Arizona. Wait for me outside?"

"I'll be the one with the sparkly purple bike."

When Pao opened the door to the warehouse's attached office, Franco was sitting in front of what appeared to be a super-old computer, but Pao knew it was an invention of her father's—a machine that could read magical signatures and measure the intensity of the energy they gave off.

Hopefully the computer couldn't measure the waves of irritation coming off Pao, because she thought the strength of them would probably break it.

"Franco," she said when it became clear he wasn't going to acknowledge her presence beyond a wary glance. "Find anything new?"

"I'm sure Beto would have told you if we had," he said curtly.

"I . . . He's not really . . . I'm asking you," Pao stammered, feeling her face heat up. You'd think that living with a man who'd been studying the paranormal for *both* of his lives would have put her at the forefront of the Niños' activities, but Pao had been relegated to perpetual trainee. Which meant fighting dummies and having her questions constantly brushed aside.

Franco didn't answer at first, just stabbed the buttons on the field unit in his hand a little harder than Pao felt was necessary. But she'd learned from months in this grumpy boy's company that he could never resist the urge to talk about his work for long, so she waited, counting down from ten in her head.

When she got to six, he pushed back from the desk with a huff. "The whole map's a blank! I thought the thing in B.C. was an anomaly, but *every* known entrance to the void that we've mapped in the past fifty years is gone. Just disappeared."

Pao stilled at the mention of Canada. It had been their first trip after they returned from saving Beto. An expedition to the only known void entrance on the West Coast—besides the Gila River one Pao and her friends had destroyed the summer before. Based on Pao's dreams, Beto and Franco had been sure the machines were misreading things, that the void entrance would be there even though no evidence of it could be seen.

They'd all been so hopeful, she remembered. So sure they would get through. That they'd bring Dante back, and this whole nightmare would be over. They'd prepared for months, and Pao had brandished her Arma del Alma without a doubt in her mind, the still-chilly March winds cutting through her sad excuse for a winter coat.

Most of the Niños had been forced to stay behind, their status as lost, escaped, forgotten, or otherwise fugitive children making it difficult for them to travel, so Pao, her father, and Franco (who'd been a smug teenager for a hundred years now) had made their way through the snowy woods outside British Columbia to find . . .

Nothing.

No liminal space. No monsters. No evidence—besides a

black scorch mark on the ground—that there'd ever been a portal to the malevolent underworld there.

To cover his disappointment, Franco had tried asking the locals living near the void entrance about what had happened, but everyone they'd approached had, frustratingly, clammed up instantly at the sight of them. They all categorically denied that they'd ever seen, heard, or experienced anything strange.

That was when, Pao remembered, Franco had started looking at her differently.

And maybe it was also when her dad had started his all-training/no-telling-Pao-anything protocol.

Now Pao wanted to growl like a feral animal, or at least hit something that wasn't headless Patrick. Instead she waited as Franco looked at her with that distrustful, suspicious expression. She tried to avoid it by studying the walls covered in maps, notes, and theories that had been crossed out one by one.

"Any chance it's the instruments malfunctioning?" she asked, just to break the horrible silence between them that seemed to be growing fangs by the second.

"It's not the *instruments* that can't be trusted," he said coldly, turning his back in clear dismissal, and Pao left the office feeling like she always did after an interaction with Franco—like she was somehow contaminated. Like she'd failed to live up to even his low expectations of her.

"Pipsqueak?" The voice drifted across the massive parking lot before Pao could turn the corner that would lead her to Emma. The sky beyond the warehouse was almost dark, the days getting shorter now that winter was on its way again.

"Hey, Naomi," Pao said, not bothering to disguise her bad

mood. Naomi, the queen of bad moods, could hardly hold it against her.

"Isn't it past your bedtime? Papi Precioso must be waiting."

Pao rolled her eyes as she approached. Naomi was sitting on the concrete steps out front, smirking down at her.

"What? Trouble behind the white picket fence?" Naomi's tone was teasing, but after the two of them had traveled hundreds of miles together, traversed a haunted forest, and fought more than one warped fantasma together, Pao could tell there was a grudging respect beneath her casual mocking.

"It's fine," Pao said, shaking her head. "Just sick of being treated like a baby all the time."

"I've been saying it since the beginning, tourist," Naomi said, eyeing Pao with that surprisingly adept intuition of hers. "Once you cross over, it's hard to go back to normal life."

Pao was quiet for a long minute, appreciating the fact that Naomi did not insist on filling every moment with chatter. Emma, as much as Pao loved her, had never met a problem she couldn't immediately offer *several* solutions for, and sometimes Pao just needed to stew.

"It's just . . ." Pao said at last. "Dad expects me to be so grateful he's here. He says I don't need to worry anymore, that he and Franco can take care of everything. But where would either of them be if I hadn't taken charge? Why does he want to force me back into a life I don't fit into anymore?"

Naomi got to her feet, offering Pao a high five as she turned toward the warehouse door. "Look, Beto's not a bad guy, from what I've seen. But you know how I feel about Franco, and about men and their *I've got this under control, little girl* crap in general.

If you want to go after hero boy yourself, you know I'm on your right."

"Thanks," Pao said, not trusting herself to say more. The fact that Naomi would be willing to follow her out into the fray again, even after all that had befallen them on their last attempt to join forces, meant more than Pao was willing to admit at the moment.

And Pao would have taken her up on the offer, she realized. In a heartbeat. If only she had any idea where to begin.

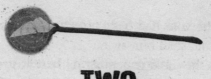

TWO

"Why Don't You Let the Adults Handle This?"

Full of pizza *and* the massive ice-cream sundae Emma had insisted they split, Pao made her way back to the Riverside Palace after dark, feeling marginally more cheerful than she had before the infusion of bread, cheese, and sugar.

Her spirits flagged slightly, however, at the sight of the dark windows of apartment K. Señora Mata—Dante's abuela and Pao's crotchety, erstwhile spiritual guide—had been moved to a care facility for seniors over the summer after a nasty fall had left her with a badly sprained wrist. Her memory hadn't improved, and though Pao visited as frequently as her school and ghost-hunting training allowed, it had been months since the old woman had one of her lucid spells.

And then there was Dante, the boy who had never returned to the apartment they'd shared. He'd been the only constant for so long in Pao's uncertain life. They'd gone through everything together—missing parents, losing teeth, the awkward transition from elementary to middle school. Then had come the strange boy-girl feelings she'd been afraid would ruin their friendship. . . .

But they hadn't. Nothing had, until the green mist. The supernatural quest his abuela had set them on. The final rift.

Joaquin and the void had been able to worm their way into Dante's mind and steal him away.

Sometimes she could remember it like it was yesterday. The hard look in his eyes, and the way he'd swung *his* Arma del Alma (a shining and wildly destructive club he'd inherited from his abuela) at Pao like she was just as much his enemy as any monster they'd fought together.

She knew, in her heart of hearts, that most of Dante's anger toward her was the result of evil outside influences. But were the changes in him *all* due to that? She would never know until she found him.

Pao was turning away when she saw it—just a flicker of movement, a stretching shadow, maybe a flicker of green light from around the corner. Her heart began to pound, her palms to sweat, the pizza to churn in her stomach. Was this the sign she'd been waiting for? Finally? She extended her Arma del Alma automatically, finding that the weight of it in her palm steadied her. Tiptoeing, eyes wide and scanning for anything unusual, Pao crept across the front of the building to the place where she'd seen the disturbance, ready for anything.

A loud *clang* made her jump, but she pressed forward, and for a second, she was sure she saw Joaquin's twisted face, the flashing of the trailer lab's buttons and switches. She closed her eyes and screamed at the top of her lungs, a reaction she couldn't have controlled if she'd wanted to.

"*Paola? Is that you?*" Footsteps. The staff was shaking in her hand. It was all she could do to drag in a breath, hiccup it out, and repeat.

"*What's the racket?*"

"Did you hear that?"

"The neighbors," Pao said, forcing her eyes open only to see her dad running up to her, a look of concern etched on his now-familiar features. The wide brown eyes, the unkempt hair, the lines that barely betrayed what he'd seen and done in his exceptionally long life. But this was no time to wax nostalgic about her father's face. "Dad," she said, still panicked, needing him to understand. "We have to get the neighbors out of here before he . . . before . . ."

Pao trailed off, looking into the alleyway where she was sure she'd seen lights. Shadows. Glowing eyes. Instead she saw a roof rat—a big one, in her defense—staring at her from over the rim of a trash can.

"Are you all right, mijita?" her dad asked, putting a hand on her shoulder and turning her gently to face him.

Confused and embarrassed, Pao saw his gaze move to the staff she'd extended for any neighbor to see. She shrank it at once and shoved it back into her pocket. "I just . . . thought I saw . . ." She trailed off. There was no way to explain the feeling she'd had. That she was somehow back in the woods. Or that Joaquin was here, a fantasma again. The complete lack of control she'd felt . . .

"Let's get you inside," Beto said, unable to mask the pity and worry in his eyes.

Pao scowled at the ground and scuffed the dirt with her sneaker. "I'll be right behind you. I just need a minute."

Beto hesitated, then finally nodded. "Don't be too long."

Alone again, the muttering neighbors having retreated behind their closed doors and blinds to make her their nightly chisme, Pao took deep breaths of the night air and tried to force her heart to slow down, her face to cool, her thoughts to stop racing.

"It was just a rat," she said under her breath. "What's wrong with you?"

The last thing she needed was her mom coming out looking for her next, so Pao blew out her last deep breath noisily, double-checked her pocket for the magnifying glass on its handy key chain, and pushed open the door to apartment C.

She'd clearly interrupted her parents talking about her, because they both looked up quickly from where they were sitting on the couch. The too-wide smiles on their faces told her they'd just agreed not to overwhelm her with questions.

An ugly feeling began to spread through Pao. A feeling that she would have preferred walking into an empty apartment with a fire-hazardy number of candles left burning. A feeling that maybe she hadn't really known what she was wishing for all those nights when she'd drifted off to sleep dreaming of two parents who would notice her.

"Niña!" Beto exclaimed, as if he hadn't just found her brandishing a legendary weapon at a common household pest in a dark alley. "Welcome home!" He motioned for her mother to scoot over and patted the empty cushion between them. "Join us! How was your training? Did you speak to Franco? I haven't been able to get over to the warehouse yet today."

With all the misplaced adrenaline still coursing through her body, Pao wanted to scream or punch something. Instead, she took his lead.

"Training was fine," she said, dropping her bag on the floor and slumping onto the couch. "Franco is a jerk. He says you guys are looking for more magical signatures."

"We've been working on it day and night, mi amor," her father said, reaching out to touch her shoulder in what was obviously supposed to be a consoling way. But Pao didn't want to be consoled.

"Well, what can I do?" Pao asked. "I don't think Patrick needs his head whacked off one more time, so there's gotta be something more useful I can . . ." She trailed off at the dubious expression on his face. An expression that said he didn't think she was ready, and her scene in the parking lot had only proved it.

"Look!" she said, getting back to her feet, too agitated to sit. "I'm not losing it, okay? I know that's what you think. I'm just *frustrated*. My brain has been in mystery-solving, monster-hunting, fantasma-dispatching mode for over a year now, and I'm *good* at it. So why won't you just let me help?"

Beto didn't immediately answer. He just looked at her with that pained, worried expression for several long moments while Pao felt like an insect under a microscope.

"Dante was my friend," she said, trying to sound less heated and more like a normal girl who wouldn't go full warrior woman on a rodent in a parking lot. "And it's my fault he got taken. I can't just sit around and wait for someone else to find him."

At this, Pao's mom leaned forward as if to speak, but after one of those annoying silent adult conversations that only involve eye contact, she stood up and kissed Pao on the forehead. "I'm going to leave this to you and your papá." But, unable to resist, she added, "We just want you to be safe. Especially after . . . all that's happened. We're lucky to be a family again, and we don't want anything to get in the way." Maria walked down the hall to the bedroom she now shared with Beto.

Pao's dad picked up the reins. "Niña, I need you to understand that I don't keep you 'out of the action' so to speak because I do not trust you. I do it because the past year of your life should never have happened. You should not have been left alone to face so much, so young." He paused here, his face full of emotion, and Pao—as much as she wanted to interrupt—found herself waiting for him to continue.

"I left you and your mother when you were small because I wanted to protect you from my past, my identity," Beto said when he had collected himself. "I thought if you could grow up with your mother, and without my demons at your dinner table, you'd have a chance to be the child I never got to be." He dabbed at his eyes before meeting Pao's again. "But fate found you, despite my best intentions, and it changed you. I came back, Paola, because I want to make sure that it never has a chance to do that again. That you have a chance to heal."

"But I *love* it!" Pao said, unable to hold her tongue now. "I love scientific research and solving mysteries, and helping people, and even fighting. I love the Niños, and my Arma del Alma, and—"

"And you love seeing monsters around every corner?" her father asked knowingly. "You love your heart racing and your palms sweating and your mind telling you that you're in grave danger even when you're not?"

Pao was trapped, as he must have known she would be.

"There will be *time*, Paola," he said, reaching forward to take her hands in his. "Time to grow into an adult who can handle these situations. Who has training and knowledge and the wisdom to apply them both. I will help you with that. But these episodes of yours—and don't insult me by pretending this was the first—are simple proof that your mind was not ready for the horrors it has faced, and to expose it to more would be a grave mistake."

"So, you're benching me," Pao said flatly, pulling her hands away. "Until when? Until I graduate from monster-killing school and do an unpaid internship? Come on! Dante is in danger *now*! You need me *now*!"

Beto's expression turned from emotional to businesslike so fast Pao almost checked him for possession by an accountant or a school principal or something.

"I understand your worry for your friend, and your desire to be involved, Paola," he said. "But hear me when I say that Franco and I have spent decades studying these phenomena and fighting their corporeal forms. You are hardly leaving your friend in incapable hands."

The message was clear: Dante was better off with two old dudes chasing after him than with Pao at the helm of the operation.

"Why did you even bring me to Canada, then?" Pao asked, mutinous. "Why not just leave me at home to do my homework or something?"

At this question, an unreadable look crossed her father's face. "I had thought . . ." he began, hedging. "Perhaps the connection with the void that brought you to me would prove useful. But it was wrong of me to rely on a child."

"There will be time, Paola," he said, reaching forward to take her hands in his. "Time to grow into an adult who can handle

MORE MYTHS, MAGIC, AND MAYHEM!

NEW YORK TIMES BEST-SELLING SERIES

ARU SHAH AND THE END OF TIME

ROSHANI CHOKSHI

NEW YORK TIMES BEST-SELLING SERIES

THE STORM RUNNER

J. C. CERVANTES

NEW YORK TIMES BEST SELLER

DRAGON PEARL

YOON HA LEE

PURA BELPRÉ WINNER

SAL AND GABI BREAK THE UNIVERSE

CARLOS HERNANDEZ

NEW YORK TIMES BEST-SELLING SERIES

TRISTAN STRONG PUNCHES A HOLE IN THE SKY

KWAME MBALIA

NEW YORK TIMES BEST SELLER

RACE TO THE SUN

REBECCA ROANHORSE

PAOLA SANTIAGO AND THE RIVER OF TEARS

TEHLOR KAY MEJIA

CITY OF THE PLAGUE GOD

SARWAT CHADDA

THE LAST FALLEN STAR

GRACE KIM

PAHUA AND THE SOUL STEALER

LORI M. LEE

NEW YORK TIMES BEST SELLER

THE CURSED CARNIVAL

EDITED BY RICK RIORDAN

BALLAD & DAGGER

DANIEL JOSE OLDER